ODD
Mum
OUT

Odd Mum Out

Yael Lily

This is a work of fiction. Names, characters, places, and incidents either are the product of the author's imagination or are used fictitiously. Any resemblance to actual persons, living or dead, events, or locales is entirely coincidental.

Copyright © 2023 by Yael Lily

All rights reserved. No part of this book may be reproduced or used in any manner without written permission of the copyright owner except for the use of quotations in a book review.

ISBN: 9798865222545

Imprint: Independently published

For Lady S,
A mum-in-law too good to fictionalise.
We miss you xxx

SEPTEMBER

Tuesday, 4 September. Part 1

It's here. It's actually bloody here.
    Sort of.
    It will be. As soon as I reach the top of this hill.
    But it is *basically* here. The first day of school.
    After six long weeks. Day after endless, thankless day of serving as all-in-one social secretary, housekeeper, HR department, driver, and chef to the two mini despots I created. Of enduring more complaints, arguments, and rage than an easyJet customer service representative and delivering more snacks than a cruise ship kitchen and-
    'Mummeee...'
    This lugubrious foghorn nudges me from my trance. Like a sky-diving instructor might "nudge" an unwitting student from the plane at thirty thousand feet.
    'Mm?' I reply, willing myself on. *One foot then the next. That's right. Keep going.*
    'Mummy?' repeats my five-year-old, Charlie. Because one "mummy" is never enough.
    I answer on autopilot.
    'Yes?' *Translation: Thank you for contacting mummy. Your pointless rambling is very important to us. Please leave a message.*
    'Do you know that children have favourite grownups?'
    'M... hm,' I pant.
    Just get to the top of this hill. Then you will be free.
    This. impossibly. long. hill.

Seriously. Was it always this long? Can hills grow?

'Mummyeee...'

'Mm?'

'Do you want to know who *my* favourite grownup is?'

'That's. Okay,' I pant. 'You don't nee-'

'It's daddy.'

Yep. Of course it is.

'Mhm.'

'I miss daddy.'

Jesus. He sounds like one of the sisters in *Little Women* awaiting papa's return from war. He only saw Jake about fifteen minutes ago.

'Why do you sound like Darth Vader?' he inquires.

He means my breathing. And he's wrong. I don't sound like Darth Vader. I sound like Darth Vader performing the Britney Spears' classic *Slave 4U* on karaoke. This is not because I am unfit. I mean, I *am* unfit. Desperately so. But that's not the reason I'm channelling *Star Wars'* most fashion forward antagonist suffering an asthma attack. No. I would wager that anyone would be out of breath carrying my current load. The book bags and the water bottles. And the bloody PE bags with their useless stringy handles made specifically to dangle at shin height. And especially traipsing it all up North London's answer to sodding Everest.

'Is it because you are carrying Liam?' Charlie adds airily, skipping along beside me.

Yes. Well. There is also that. I am indeed currently encumbered by an entire four-year-old human. Liam took one look at the hill and declared himself "tired."

Of course, a good mummy would have denied Liam this service. Would have told him he was able to walk just fine. *She* would have made the hard choice of enduring any protests and insisted he get on with it. Thus, teaching him an important lesson about endurance and perseverance and other vital life skills. A good mummy would not sacrifice such a valuable teaching opportunity at the altar of finally getting to the top of this effing hill.

I knew all of this. And yet, what did I do? I picked him up. Instantly. Without a word. Of course I did. Because we were already late.

Late. *For school.*

If there is one thing that is drilled into parents, it is that one does not mess with the holy sanctity of school attendance. You get regular charts detailing every absence and late arrival. And woe betide those who fall below a certain percentage. They get a letter. From *The Council.*

I believe the step after that is jail. Or it might be a fine. It all amounts to much the same thing: immediate exile from polite parenting society.

Last year, they even handed out certificates at a special assembly for those children who had "achieved" perfect attendance. Charlie was denied this honour. Because he'd had a week off school.

Why, you might ask, did my then-four-year-old miss *five whole days* of school over the course of an entire year? Was it a cheeky mid-term holiday at a cut price? Or maybe I am the sort of craven mother who keeps him home every time he sniffles?

No. No it was not.

The reason for the absence – the one that meant Charlie did not "achieve" perfect attendance – was an emergency appendectomy. Literal organ removal. Complete with panicked dash to A&E, general anaesthetic, hospital food and a letter from an NHS trust.

This did not suffice as far as The Council was concerned. The child had not been to school for five working days. A disapproving letter was automatically dispatched. All to say, I doubt "couldn't convince my kid to leave the house" would be viewed favourably. Ergo, I had to do it m'laud.

Which is true. All of it. Is it the real reason I am carrying Liam? Maybe. Maybe not. That is something I will take to my grave, thanks very much.

Reasons I Am Carrying My Four-Year-Old That I Will Take to My Grave

1. I have been up since five because Liam has been up since five. He never makes it past six, but this is early even for him. I am so tired I could sleep standing up like a cow.

2. We have already had one "incident" today. By that, I mean Liam taking umbrage with me saying it was time to go. He expressed his displeasure by weaponizing a whistle on a string. I don't know from whence it came. I didn't even know we had one. Wherever he found it, he began swinging it around like a mace and chain. Thus qualifying it as an offensive weapon under section 1(4) of the Prevention of Crime Act 1953. And thereby compelling me to bundle Charlie into his bedroom and shut us both inside with my back against the door. And all while cooing reassuringly to both boys that everything was fine.

3. It is a brazen act of kicking the can down the road. This was not a stand-off I wanted to have in the street at 8:59am. I would not win. In the words of Sun Tzu, "*He will win who knows when to fight and when to fold shamelessly.*" Or something like that.
4. It is Liam's first ever day of school. But only if we get there.

Which is looking increasingly doubtful.

'Keep. Walking,' I pant at Charlie, who is ambling along with the urgency of an octogenarian snail. My words have no effect. Oh, wait, I tell a lie. He has slowed down even more.

Oh, and now he has stopped completely to watch a butterfly.

I stop too. This is a major mistake, allowing as it does for my body to take stock of what I am doing to it. This hurts. So I try putting Liam down, but he is wrapped around me like a limpet.

'Can you walk now, poppet?' I ask, still bent over.

'Mummy,' he remonstrates. Then proceeds to mumble something about counting steps. I take that as a no. Then I note that Charlie is no longer beside me.

Oh shit.

Charlie is now following the effing butterfly.

No. Not down the hill. Not *down* the sodding hill. Up. *Up.* All of this is but a silent scream in my head. I do however vocalise my son's name. Quite loudly as it happens.

'CHARLIE.'

Whoops. Slightly sharper than I'd intended.

And... oh god. I have attracted the attention of a nearby gaggle of mummies. These are actual mummies. Proper ones. Wunder Mummies. Mummies who have already dropped off their children: competent mums who all appear to be wearing... Is that... Yes, it's makeup. They have turned as one judgy organism to inspect the slovenly monster chastising her innocent child. Shit. I smile. It is a self-deprecating smile. One intended to invoke parental camaraderie.

The judgy Wunder Mummy organism glares back. There is a tut.

'Mummy has to put you down,' I croon to Liam. He has his head on my shoulder and looks, to all the world, like an actual angel. The real thing. Big blue eyes, curly blond hair, the whole schtick. What's more, he *is* angelic. Or he can be. For fifty percent of his waking hours. As for the other fifty...

I try lowering him to the ground, but he burrows into me. There's no time to argue. And so I must run down the hill I have just climbed with Liam on my front like I'm Skippy the goddamned kangaroo. Rucksacks and PE bags jangling excitedly around my legs. Somehow I reach Charlie, pivot him bodily and we are back on track.

There is more sweat, more tears and the humiliation of once again passing the Wunder Mummies and then...

Oh. Oh my god. There it is. The gate. The school gate. In my mind a choir sings and the clouds part, bathing it in sunshine.

Haaaa-llelujah.

And now I am chivvying Charlie on, not caring what it looks like and yell-whispering '*Not run- walk. Yes I know the gate is closed. We're late.*'

Until finally – oh thank the gods finally – we are buzzed inside.

'First to sign the late book this year,' mutters Mrs Keen, the school secretary, her smile grim.

I want to grab her by her stupid Peter Pan collar. I want to describe to her, in intricate detail, the morning I have endured. I want to inform her that the fact that both of my children are here at all, not to mention in one piece, is nothing short of a miracle. I would, naturally, be ugly crying through the entire monologue.

Instead, I debate what to write as the reason for our tardiness. I could be honest. But there simply isn't enough space to write "unable to leave home due to younger son re-enacting the film *Gladiator*." So I just scrawl the word "sorry."

And then, Mrs Keen redeems herself. She does so by leading my boys away. Away to their classrooms.

I am free. *Free.*

'Maya?'

What the–

I turn. I stupidly turn at the sound of my stupid name only to hear it again.

'Maya!'

Teeth. Very white, billboard-sized teeth.

'It's Ingrid,' exclaim the teeth.

'Ingrid,' I repeat dazedly.

I knew an Ingrid once. God she'd been annoying. Made school hell for me. She'd been obsessively competitive about everything. Fortunately, this can't possibly be *that* Ingrid.

That Ingrid... What was her surname? Something ridiculous. Clutterbuck, yes, Ingrid Clutterbuck. She was a mousy, jagged thing. Everything about her ended in sharp points, from her nose to her words and even her teeth. This woman – and especially her teeth – are all smooth and silky. And weirdly swelled up in places. It's a bit like meeting a Bratz doll.

No. This is definitely not *that* Ingrid. Were I a cyborg, my facial recognition software would declare a definitive mismatch. Because while it's been two decades since I last saw *that* Ingrid, time could not account for such massive differences. For example, time doesn't change your face shape. It doesn't turn ghostly skin the colour of a rich tea biscuit. Nor does it inflate lips or enlarge teeth or eyes or...

'Maya?' The voice pierces my fog.

'Hm?'

'You okay?' This is not a question. I recognise that instantly. It is an accusation of incompetence couched in concerned pity, complete with sympathetic smile and head tilt.

Ah. Now I see it.

'Ingrid Clutterbuck.'

Like the sun being obscured by clouds, a portion of the teeth recedes as her smile dims. But then they're back.

'It's Danning now,' she gushes. 'So... How *are* you?'

Bloody hell. Another head tilt. Do I look like a bog-dweller or something? Actually, I dare not imagine how I look right now.

'Good,' I pronounce. Then, 'Really, really good. Great. Actually. Just great.' That's quite enough, I tell myself. No good over-egging the bog.

'But what have you been *doing* all this time?' Ingrid demands. 'Gosh, I remember how everyone at school and all the mums always said you'd do something amazing. And what an amazing success you would be. So? What have you done? Are you a writer? You always wanted to be a writer.'

My mouth is dry. Serengeti dry. You'd have more luck squeezing liquid out of a desiccated rock on Mars than you would from between my lips at this moment.

Everyone thought I'd do something amazing. *Ha*. Well. I showed them.

As for being a writer... Am I a writer? I write. For a living. But I'm not a *writer*. Not an author or journalist or academic. I write shitty website copy for companies with names like Reiki of Sunshine and One Nightstand. I am to writing what third-party logistics agents are to the armed forces. A writer once removed. If that.

But Ingrid is tilting her head again. And I cannot take another pity tilt. Not a full one. So I clear my throat and rasp out, 'Oh, you know. Stuff. What about you?'

I attempt my own head tilt.

Something in my neck snaps.

I might be stuck like this.

Ingrid doesn't notice that I am now lopsided however. My inquiry about her wellbeing is what she has been waiting for: A chance to talk about herself. She sucks in air like she's attempting a world freediving record. For a moment I think she might be preparing to swallow me whole. But then she begins talking. At length.

She informs me that she is doing brilliantly. Just brilliantly.

She is a blogger. At least I think that's what she means. She doesn't call herself that. She says she a "lifestyle progenitor", which is word salad my simple brain cannot digest.

'I'm all about real issues about being a working mum and how to balance it all. I don't like to use the word influencer,' she simpers, thereby using it. 'Fergus is always asking me why I do so much, you know? And I tell him that we are so fortunate. That I felt like I had to give back. Share the things that inspire me.'

Fergus is her husband. He is a hedge funder. She and Fergus moved to the area because they fell in love with the idea of their four – *four?* - children attending a *state school*. The last two words are whispered with illicit fervour. Like she's confessing to a sexual attraction to Jacob Rees-Mogg.

'Of course, they'll need to be tutored,' Ingrid is saying. 'And we wouldn't dream of a state secondary, but we wanted them to be exposed to the real world. It's so important they know about social diversity.'

I snort, then quickly attempt to mask it as a cough. But really. Applegate Primary is a one-form entry community school set in rolling fields in North London. It's sweet and charming and probably the prime reason house prices in its catchment area are sky high. Parents mortgage their souls to get their children in. Sure, it's more culturally and socially diverse than, say, Eton, but not by much.

'My eldest, Orwell, started reception this morning. I was just talking to Mr Davies about his needs as a gifted child.' She rolls her enormous eyes, so big they look like two planets orbiting the sun.

Mr Davies is the headmaster. He is said to be great with the kids, but does nothing to hide his utter contempt for their parents. I can only imagine what he made of Ingrid.

A furtive movement in the school office catches my eye and I think I spot the man himself peering out to check if the coast is clear. Then decide it isn't.

'These are my girls.'

My eyes lower to where Ingrid is gesturing. I only just suppress a scream. Three sets of eyes glower up at me blankly from a trio of doll-like faces. Have they been here the whole time? Just silently standing there?

'So sweet,' I croak. They are not. Sweet. Not unless one has fond feelings towards the kids in *Village of the Damned*. God I'm a bitch. They're children.

At least I think they're children. They are so very still. I keep expecting their eyes to glow.

'Zadie and Louisa May are three and Charlotte is two.'

They still haven't moved. They might actually be dolls.

'Hi girls,' I smile.

Nothing.

'Did I just see your two going in?' Ingrid asks.

'Oh, yeah. Liam and Charlie.'

'Just the two?'

'Oh, god, yes.' I say this with far too much enthusiasm.

'Isn't that lovely. You must have so much time for yourself. Good for you.' Before I can even fully comprehend whether I have just been insulted, Ingrid is checking her watch. 'Oh, listen, must dash. Got a photo shoot thing at eleven.' Another enormous eyeroll. 'Fab seeing you. Must catch up.'

As soon as Ingrid is gone, it is like the air rushes back into the room. I am once again aware of ambient noise. I see Mrs Keen, back from escorting my boys, is smirking at me, and Mr Davies takes his chance to bolt out of his office.

By the time I get home, I have had time to digest my conversation with Ingrid. As a result, I am furious. With myself, with the world, with her.

Three things I realised about my conversation with Ingrid on the way home

1. Her son is in reception. That's Liam's class. This is terrible news. I have no doubt my feral child will bite her creepily angelic one. And then I'll have to deal with her passive aggressive superiority.

2. All of Ingrid's children are named after authors. She has given birth to a library. Not only is it incredibly annoying I didn't spot this immediately, but it is also just annoying. I doubt she's ever even read any Zadie Smith. And as for Orwell, I bet the closest she's ever gotten to Big Brother was Channel 4.

3. I have squandered all my apparently enormous potential and have achieved absolutely nothing even remotely exceptional ever.

On the way, I had also managed, with shaking fingers, to send a message to LUNCH. This is the name of the WhatsApp group I share with my two closest friends, Nisha and my older sister, Gabby. Like all WhatsApp groups, it was set up for one conversation about one lunch and that conversation never ended. My message read:

You:
INGRID CLUTTERBUCK SEND KIDS TO OUR SCHOOL!!!

Having imparted this intel to the relevant authorities, I am free to start my work. Which I will. Just as soon as I've googled Ingrid's blog.

Striding into the kitchen, I earn an indignant glare from Sir Francis Drake. Not the 16th century explorer/sea captain/privateer, but our cantankerous tabby. Sir Francis has an impressive array of indignant glares. This one conveys in no uncertain terms that I am being loud and uncouth. I attempt to appease with crunchies and an ear scratch, but it is too little too late.

Once online, I find the blog immediately. Which is incredibly irritating because that means it is popular. But not as irritating as the blog itself.

It's called *Four Is More*. And, according to the homepage, it is all about Ingrid's "crazy, chaotic, fabulous life as a mother, wife, model and entrepreneur."

I tut. I know not why. Then I devour every detail, hoping to find evidence that this is all self-congratulatory bollocks.

Except Ingrid's life does look a teeny bit fabulous.

Bloody hell. She has more than 300,000 followers on Instagram. And almost as many on YouTube.

Ingrid's family has been to Thailand, Dubai, and Japan. And the Maldives. I've always been obsessed with the Maldives. All that white sand and the crystal blue waters. Jake's promised me we'll go one day. And Ingrid's *kids* have been twice. They go skiing every February. The titles of her videos are a laundry list of the places and things I always mean to go and do, but never manage. By which I mean I never even try.

I watch for five entire minutes as Ingrid guides all four of her children through baking a carrot and courgette cake. Somehow, it does not end with everyone crying/screaming/covered in flour. In fact, her kitchen remains pristine throughout, helped by her tiny daughters cleaning up as they go.

And there's more. Like the diary-cam-style videos where she talks about her hopes of adopting a child from abroad. Another child. To add to the four she already has. Why on earth would she want another one? Why?

No. Really. Why? And why is it that I can't even begin to understand it? I love my children. Would walk through fire for them, should the necessity ever arise. But I can barely survive with two. She has four and is still able to be all, *yeah, go on then, let's have another. We'll take it to the Maldives.*

There is only one conclusion to be drawn. Ingrid is a superior human. She is better at humanning than I am. She is better at being a mum, at having a career and especially at going on holiday.

Even her photos are better. My children are like vampires; one cannot capture their image on film. They simply do not stay still for long enough. Ingrid's account is full of sunny shots of her myriad flaxen-haired moppets smiling and laughing. There's one from this morning of the three girls gazing adoringly at their brother in his school uniform. The caption reads:

> Hey fam! Big day in the Danning house. Orwell's first day of primary school. I sent him prepared, belly full of my signature gluten free Pumpkin-quinoa porridge. #blessed #mumoffour #fourismore #mumlife.

The comments underneath are plentiful and effusive.

OMG they're growing up and you're getting younger WTF??

YOUR R MY IDOL!!!

What a perfect start to the school year

And it was. Is. Perfect. Just bloody perfect.
I forward the post to Nish and Gabby, eliciting an immediate response.

> **Nisha**
> Always hated that 🐑. Looks like a balloon.

Nisha is a brilliant friend. My sister on the other hand...

> **Gabby**
> NOOOOOOO. That can't be Ingrid. She looks amazing. OMG she went to that new Dubai hotel. I'm going there Feb. Ask her how it was

I adore my sister. I really do. But she doesn't seem to have grasped her role in this scenario. Had this been a 90s magazine quiz, it would have gone something like this:

> Your friend/sister has just messaged you definitive proof that her school frenemy is now a beautiful, successful, well-rounded human. For the avoidance of doubt, this person is much, much, much more successful than your friend/sister. What do you do? Do you:
>
> a) Baselessly and shamelessly assure your friend/sister that there is no way this vastly superior frenemy is happy and that your friend/sister's life is infinitely better and that she has made perfect choices always.
>
> or
>
> b) ...

That's it. There would be no option b. *There can never be an option b.* And, if there were an option b it would certainly not be to ask said perfect person for travel tips.

So, why has my sister failed in this most basic of duties? Is it because she is a better person than me? Has she risen above all petty concerns and achieved nirvana?

Unlikely. I think it has more to do with the fact that my sister, my supposed flesh and blood, is beautiful. Properly beautiful. Like a real-life Amazon. As in, she's frequently mistaken for Gal Gadot. That's the actress who plays the fictional Amazon, actual sodding Wonder Woman. She has never felt insecure or inferior or experienced so much as a scrap of self-doubt.

And, in a way, it's not her fault. I have had a front row seat to the charmed existence this sort of beauty has afforded my sister. I can see how it might result in a skewed view of reality. People simply *give* her things. I have personally witnessed a traffic warden retract a ticket that Gabby had well and truly earned without her having to say a word. And I'm stone cold certain she thinks Starbucks is a dispensary of free coffees, so infrequently has she been asked to pay.

She might also have a vastly inflated estimation of the frequency of car accidents.

While a teenage me was being reassured that magazine covers don't show real people, I was sharing a bathroom with unequivocal proof to the contrary. And that's not the end of it. Because Gabby is also fun, funny, and just a general bloody delight. Her husband, Hugh, on the other hand, is a pompous nightmare. But they have two amazing daughters and a life and seem to be happy. So who am I to judge?

Oh god. I really need to stop Insta-torturing myself and get to work. I check my emails and find one from Ad at Glowing Ducks Digital.

Tues 04/09 09:01

From: Adamu Mwangi

To: Maya Harris

Subject: RE: Empawrium Pet Supplies

Hey dude, how goes this project? Almost done our end. Can you get it to us next Tues?

Glowing Ducks is a website development agency and pretty much where I get all my work. They design the websites, I write the copy. It's an arrangement that has worked brilliantly in the three years I have known Ad.

We met while trying to escape a local business networking event in which neither of us wanted to network. He told me what he did, and I made him laugh with a joke about the difference between programmers and drug dealers. Then we had a nice little conversation about coding languages.

Impressed by the breadth of my coding knowledge, he'd asked, 'So you're a writer *and* a programmer?'

And I'd had to explain that I couldn't code my way out of a paper bag. And that the only reason that I knew my Python from my JavaScript was by dint of marriage to a software engineer. I had finished with, 'If I'm a coder then HTML is a programming language.'

Oh, how Ad had chuckled mildly.

And I have been his agency's go-to copywriter ever since. It's perfect.

I email back to say I should have it done by then and get a thumbs up in return. This message coincides with another, more shouty one.

WIN A PUBLISHING CONTRACT!

Gosh. All caps and an exclamation mark. Steady on. There again, it *is* eye-catching. In that I'm still looking at it. And now I'm opening the email.

I can't help it. Win a publishing contract. It's my catnip. Because Ingrid was right. I had wanted to be a writer. I'm not sure when I forgot as much.

Of course, this won't be the way to achieve my childhood dream. It's probably all a load of bollocks. You can't *win* a publishing contract. I definitely can't. What sort of idiot would believe an email saying they could–

I read it. Twice.

Enter the Blog2Book Competition!

Can you write? Can you blog? Let the public decide! It's simple:

1. Write a weekly blog on Blog2Book. Any topic!
2. The public votes for their weekly favourites.
3. Last blog standing wins a deal to turn their book into a blog and £10,000!

Yep. Just as I thought. It's rubbish.

Could I do this?

No. There must be a catch. They don't just give out publishing contracts. There's a reason why the £10,000 is barely worth a mention. Much easier to get that than be published.

It'll all be fake, I think, as I google the name of the publisher, Ostrich Books. It'll be one of those publishing houses that make you pay to publish your boo... Huh. No, that is a real publishing house.

Bzzzz

Maybe next year.

Bzzzz

If they run it again.

Bzzzz

Could they rig a public vote? Give it to one of their own authors?

Bzzzz

Of course they can.

Bzzzz

What the actual frack is that buzzing?

Shit. My phone. I scrabble for it, instantly clapping eyes on the caller ID.

Applegate calling.

No.

No, no, no, no, no.

But yes. This is happening.

The call is coming from *inside* the school.

My left eyelid expresses its indignation by way of a violent twitch. My heart sinks. No. No, that's far too serene. The thing plummets. *Woosh.* As though someone installed a trap door from my chest to my gut. Down it goes with a splat.

If there is one thing – one singular happening – guaranteed to spark instant dread into the deepest reaches of a parent's soul, it is this.

Can I ignore it? Maybe it'll just go away.

Bzzzzzzzzzzzzz

I sigh as I resign myself to my fate. Gingerly, I swipe at the screen and lift the device to my ear. I can't help but feel cheated that this moment isn't accompanied by a suitably eerie instrumental. Ideally the *Jaws* soundtrack.

'Hello?'

'Mrs Harris? This is Mrs Keen, the school secretary. Miss Flowers has asked that you come to collect Liam. He's unsettled.'

I blink.

'Unsettled?' My eyelid twitches again.

'Unsettled.'

'What exactly does that... What sort of unsettled?'

But the line is already disconnected.

I gawp at the screen.

For the past two years, Liam had attended nursery. In that time, I was asked/told/begged to collect him early frequently and for a variety of reasons. Biting, kicking, hitting, throwing things, taking things, locking himself in places, locking others out and deliberately hurting himself, to name a few. But whenever this happened, the reason was always named. Spelled out by the nursery manager in excruciating detail. It didn't make for easy listening, but at least I had known what to expect. The ambiguity of the word "unsettled" is... well... unsettling.

Still, no time to dwell. Taking one last longing look at my computer, I run downstairs. Just before I leave, I message Jake. It reads simply:

> **You**
> It happened

Despite the fact that the sky is beating down a determined drizzle, Liam's classmates all appear to be playing outside in the mini playground designated just for the youngest year. All except Liam that is. Or at least I can't see him.

I do spot a child whom I am certain is Ingrid's son, Orwell. I recognise him from the photos. Plus, he's hard to miss, what with his luminous hair and the fact that he's staring at me.

'Are you Liam's mummy?' he asks officiously.

'Um...'

I am saved from answering by the arrival of the reception teacher, Miss Flowers. She encourages probably-Orwell to join in with a game of hop-scotch. He looks unconvinced, but wearily complies.

'Come on,' she murmurs.

I do as I'm bid, pathetically grateful that she smiled at me. I can't help but compare my appearance with hers. Miss Flowers is a head taller than me. She's also fresh faced and rosy cheeked and willowy in her A-line skirt and white blouse. I look like I'm in the first items I found on the floor upon rolling out of bed. Which I am. It's like a Disney princess walking alongside a troll. I shouldn't be here. I should be antagonising billy goats.

We reach the threshold of the open classroom door just in time to witness something chair-like hurtling across the multi-coloured room. I still can't see Liam. I presume he has barricaded himself in the play kitchen as this was the launching point of the aforementioned projectile.

'We decided the safest thing to do was to remove the other children from the classroom,' Miss Flowers explains with improbable calm.

'We had to evacuate,' interjects the vocal equivalent of a parking ticket. It is Mrs Gripp, the class TA. 'He's been at it for forty minutes.'

I smile an apology. She does not smile back. In her late sixties, Mrs Gripp is a grim, squat teapot of a woman with resting clench face. She has a fondness for passive aggressive messages delivered to parents via their children. On more than one occasion last year, Charlie had started a sentence with "Mrs Gripp says..." inevitably ending it with "my hair is messy" or "I need new gym shorts" or some variation on the you're-a-bad-mum theme.

In other words, Mrs Gripp is not known for her cheery demeanour. But nor has she ever appeared quite as malevolent as she does right now. I think I see steam emanating from her ears.

'Why don't we get Liam settled and then have a quick chat,' Miss Flowers suggests, just as a soft-toy Peppa Pig roughly the size of a Labrador follows the chair's trajectory. It lands forlornly beside Mrs Gripp's brown orthopaedic shoes. She surveys it and then me with equal contempt.

Fortunately, it is at this moment that Liam raises his head suspiciously above the parapet. His eyes dart in my direction and widen.

'Mummy!' It is part battle cry, part piteous wail. And just like that, all anger is extinguished.

It's instant. Suspiciously so. Like dumping the entire contents of The Thames on a lit match. It's Hyde transforming into Jekyll. The Hulk reverting to Bruce Banner. Basically magic.

Moments later, my child is colouring in a picture of a happy cow in a manner that can only be described as cherubic. I perch on a tiny plastic chair and listen to a horror story about a different boy. A boy who couldn't possibly be the same one now calmly amusing himself in the book corner.

This other little boy bit a teaching assistant and threw a camera on the floor. He then proceeded to throw more things around the classroom. All the things. And why? Because the teaching assistant had used the camera to take a picture of his art. While he was still painting it. Oh, and he destroyed the painting as well.

By the end of this terrible tale, all of the blood in my entire body has amassed in my head. Like it's having its annual general conference.

Out of the corner of my eye, I see Mrs Gripp twitch. It is then that I notice the large white bandage on the TA's hand. I dare not look directly at her though, lest I catch her eye and turn to stone.

My brain is overwhelmed, so my mouth takes matters into its own lips. It apologises repeatedly and profusely. It assures Miss Flowers that action will be taken. There will be consequences, although my mouth is savvy enough to keep details to a minimum because it's fucked if it knows what those will be. It tells Miss Flowers that we do not condone violence and that we have rules and star charts.

And all I want to do is scream that I don't know how we got here. And I don't know how to get anywhere else. Instead, I am blathering something about parenting guru Gina Ford.

'And I know it's controversial, but we followed all the steps and-'

'Mrs Harris, stop.'

I do. Instantly. Because I am a good girl and I do what teachers tell me.

'I believe that Liam needs more support at school. So, I hope it's okay, but I've made an appointment for you with the SENCO.'

Huh?

'What's the SENCO?'

Tuesday, 4 September. Part 2

There should be at least one upside to having your child sent home early from school for chomping a chunk out of their teacher and wrecking up the joint. At the very least it should signal that your feet have landed firmly at rock bottom. It should guarantee that the day can't possibly get worse. It is therefore disappointing and not a bit galling that mine manages to sink further still.

Not immediately though.

For most of the afternoon, Liam demonstrates unquestioning obedience. It borders on obsequiousness. I am told repeatedly that he loves me and how lucky he is to have such a lovely mummy. He is helpful and polite and I even manage a half hour of uninterrupted work while he plays with some Lego. Not so much as one whine for a snack. This is unheard of.

Then he asks to play Monopoly.

Monopoly - Junior Monopoly to be precise - is the latest in a long line of Liam's fads. Liam has at least two or three such obsessions on the go at any time. Some are games, others TV shows or food or a particular soft toy. Whatever it is, it becomes the one and only thing he wants. At all times.

Some of these have been brilliant. Like his banana phase. For two years, he was never happier than when handed the fruit. Lego had also been good, but short-lived.

As for Monopoly, it is in the running for the hotly contested spot of worst fad ever.

Official Top Three List of Liam's Worst Ever Fads

1. Snails: For six months, Liam was fascinated by the vile, bulbous slime blobs. He spent hours talking to them in the garden, building them shelter and stopping in the street to "save" them. The low point had been when he had insisted on keeping a few as pets. Pet snails. Which meant *I* had pet snails. Snails I had to feed and clean and generally serve. I oscillated between revulsion at the sight of them and guilt at their incarceration.

2. Junior Monopoly: This relative newcomer has achieved an impressively swift climb to the near top of the rankings. I actually used to quite like Monopoly. That was until it became Liam's favourite game. Now I am regularly compelled to play it over and over again ad infinitum like I'm Bill Murray in *Groundhog Day*. I have cultivated a hatred not just for the game, but for its smug, moustachioed mascot, Mr Monopoly.

3. Postman Pat: I still can't talk about it.

Today, we play three successive rounds of Monopoly. This is fine. Annoying but fine. This is what mums do, right? Play with their children. Look at me, being attentive. Next thing you know, I'll be baking.

Except there is a sinister undercurrent to all this jolliness. An iron fist clenched inside this velvety mitten. And it becomes more apparent with each passing moment. As we play, Liam becomes increasingly frenetic and jittery and less coherent. This is bad. This is flashing-red-light, the-ship-will-self-destruct, dolphins-thanking-us-for-the-fish bad. It is, in other words, a sure sign of an impending tantrum. I know this, and yet I am powerless to stop it.

I am faced with three options.

My Options

1. Diversion. Convince Liam to do something else. I suggest this. He doesn't want to do anything else. Only Monopoly.
2. Just say no. This is obviously the one and only correct answer. I am the parent. I think he should stop playing. Ergo, I should say so. I must put my foot down. Every parenting book ever written would agree. If this was Charlie, that is what I would do. I'd say no, he'd whine and maybe get a bit narky, but overall I'd hold firm. I should absolutely do the same here. The danger is that this is seen as confrontational. The danger is that a tantrum goes from being possible, or probable, to inevitable.
3. Keep playing. Keep playing in the vain hope that, despite all signs to the contrary, everything will be okay.

So I am now playing under duress. I'm like Sandra Bullock driving the boobytrapped bus in *Speed*. As long as I keep playing, everything is fine. Or seems fine. But there is always something – something unavoidable – that gets in the way. For Sandra, that was a fifty-foot gap in the road. For me, it's school pickup.

I have to collect Charlie from school. And Liam must come with me.

I explain this to Liam, hoping he will respond to reason. Or, failing that, comedy.

'We can't just leave Charlie there now, can we?' I ask jovially as the clock ticks a minute past the time we need to leave. 'Mr Davies doesn't like children sleeping over at school.'

But no. He does not accept this as a valid excuse for the cessation of play. And the joking only seems to aggravate matters.

He demands "'noth' game."

Danger Will Robinson.

I know instinctively that my reaction to this is critical. Done well, I might be able to forestall any hostile action. But one wrong move and I'm finished.

'Sure,' I mollify. 'We'll play more when we get back.'

Bzzz. Wrong answer.

And that's all it takes. In a flash, Liam becomes John McEnroe circa 1981 in full "you cannot be serious" fury. Except I don't remember McEnroe ever being held by the shoulders from behind, at arm's length as he tried to bludgeon an umpire. Which, to be clear, is how I am holding Liam at this moment; my hands on his shoulders, arms taut in zombie pose.

I try reason again: 'We'll only be fifteen minutes there and back.'

I get a growl.

I try empathy: 'I know it's hard, little man. You want to play now, and you can't. I get it.'

Liam stills. For a moment, I think I've done it. No, no. Empathy no good. Liam emits a rather impressive primal scream.

I try discipline: 'Liam, if we don't go and get Charlie now, you'll lose a star.'

Absolutely not.

The single saving grace is that Liam is unable to land a blow on me in his current position. This gives me time to think. Unfortunately, thinking allows me to realise we're stuck. I'm just here. Holding Liam's shoulders.

A look at the clock tells me there are three minutes to go before pickup. Jack Bauer got 1,440. A look down at my son tells me that there's no way we're leaving this house anytime soon.

Panic. What now? How do I get from here to where I need to be? And what happens if I can't?

Is that even possible? Not picking up your child from school? I have never thought of this as anything but 100% mandatory. I have never given it any thought at all except to do it. School has ended. Child must be collected. End of. And given I don't have a nanny and hadn't made other arrangements and there are three - scratch that, two - minutes before I'm expected at the school gates, I have to do it.

And yet I don't.

I can't.

There is simply no way to compel Liam out of the front door, let alone a quarter of a mile down the road. I watch the big hand pass the 15-minute mark. 3:16. The gates are open.

Part of me can't help but be impressed. Through sheer determination and tunnel-visioned tenacity, my son has achieved something I would hitherto have considered unthinkable.

Fuck.

Although, that's got to be a transferable life skill. In the long run.

Maybe Zuckerberg was like this as a child. Or Steve Jobs. I could be raising the next Elon Musk.

Christ. I hope not.

Then I remember. *After school club. There is after school club.* I let this bathe me in calm for all of one second before I remember. That's only an hour. What then? There's no guarantee that Liam will submit then to what he is refusing to do now.

No. A different solution is needed.

Must get to phone. It's my only hope.

I act fast. I release Liam and bolt for the dining table. He follows in hot pursuit.

You know those police shows where officers under fire hide behind shipping crates as they radio for backup? That's a fair description of the current vibe.

Except I am cooing reassuringly at my son as I scrabble for a solution. Jake's at work. My in-laws won't make it in time. And then I have it.

With some difficulty, I transmit my SOS.

Ten minutes later, I open the door to the sight of Nisha, her two kids, and Charlie.

'Thanks so much.'

'No worries. Any time.'

I'm soops caszh. Nisha is soops caszh. That's us. Just two mums being soooooper dooper casual. Determinedly so. It's a conversation on the doorstep. A chat. A chin wag. Or at least that's what we're aiming for. But there are children present. And thus any attempt at self-delusion is futile.

'Why is Liam hitting you?' inquires Aran conversationally. Aran is in the year above Charlie. His sister, three-year-old Saira, looks on with intrigued horror.

'Oh he always does this,' sighs Charlie just before slipping past me and his brother and into the hall. Now he really *does* sound casual.

There are numerous advantages to being married to a software engineer. But above all, it is a flexible job that allows Jake to leave his office at 5:30 every day in order to be home by 6:15pm. Just in time to perform the nightly ritual of The Nightmare Before Bedtime.

The Nightmare Before Bedtime: A Nightly Ritual

The Nightmare Before Bedtime is a meticulously choreographed dance so carefully and impeccably refined, it would challenge the skills of the Bolshoi Ballet. It takes precisely 45 minutes from bath to sleep, and it requires two trained adults to execute properly. Any deviation results in a disturbingly authentic approximation of *The Purge*.

Tonight, we managed to perform the whole fandango relatively successfully, allowing Jake and I to meet up in the kitchen at 7pm. On the dot. Normally, this would be my favourite part of the day. The few child-free hours where we can sit, catatonic in front of the TV. But not this night. This night, I must tell him what happened at school. And what Miss Flowers said. This night, I must venture into the no-man's land of what I call The Untalkables.

Every marriage has them. Or at least I think they do. Taboos. Those subjects that inextricably divide a couple. The ones guaranteed to set off a chain reaction ending in one of you calling out the other one's mum and the other bringing up "that time that thing happened."

Subjects We Must Never Discuss Ever AKA The Untalkables

1. That time I almost won at chess against him for the very first time, but then he went to the loo and I lost my concentration and the game. It's not just the subject of chess that's off limits. We haven't played it since. We have a similar détente for Scrabble, except I am the undefeated party there.
2. Conspiracy theorists: I truly believe I can argue people round to see reason. He thinks it's pointless. He especially likes to reference the fact that I haven't convinced him of my perspective on this. The last time we had that discussion, it led to a three-day silent treatment. I'm not even sure who was giving whom the treatment. Whatever. It's not worth it.
3. The possibility of Liam having some unspecified underlying nebulous "something." And no, I don't know what. Only that I think it's there and Jake doesn't. Something vaguely medical. Maybe. Ish.

It is taboo number 3 that I now broach. Because today, I learned what a SENCO is. And tomorrow, I have an appointment with one.

'What's the SENCO?' Jake asks.

I attempt nonchalance. 'Oh, um, Special Educational Needs Coordinator.'

'Special Edu... Special needs. He doesn't have special needs.'

The worst part about The Untalkables is the inevitable argument that follows. Not just that its occurrence is unstoppable. But that it's exactly the same argument every single time: nothing changes. Every word and every step has been said and done before.

For example, I know that Jake is about to tell me that he was just as difficult a child at Liam's age. Over to you, Jake.

'I was exactly the same at his age and I grew out of it. You know that. Like that time in the supermarket with my mum. Remember that?'

Not only do I remember it, but I have titled it The Supermarket Standoff and I can recite the bloody thing in my sleep. Because he raises it every single time without fail.

The Story of the Supermarket Standoff

Gather round boys and girls, for the tale of The Supermarket Standoff. The time Jake refused to get up off the floor at Tesco in Watford until his mum bought him Cocoa Pops. Having endured this tactic one too many times, my mother-in-law, Delia, decided to call his bluff. According to her, they had sat there in the cereal aisle for two hours. Or was it four hours? Or six? It becomes ever more outlandish every time it's told. Whatever the case, the climax of the story is that eventually it was Delia and not Jake who surrendered. Jake emerged victorious with his chocolatey cereal, proving he was the most stubborn boy in the land.

If this story actually happened - and I have my doubts - it still doesn't prove anything. And so, I then point out that it is a useless anecdote because:

1. We have ten stories for every one of his mum's.
2. None of Jake's tales include him braining another human.
3. He had been two years-old at the time of the supermarket standoff. Not four.

'Two is not the same as four,' I say in my calmest of boiling tones.

With the Supermarket Standoff dispensed with, Jake plays his trump card. He looks me dead in the eyes and says, 'We agreed.'

Dammit.

He's right.

We *had* agreed. We resolved this the last time we undertook this conversational root canal. We realised that we were rational adults. Adults who believed in facts and science and expert advice. So we'd made a bargain; a solemn pact. We consulted a psychologist and agreed to treat their conclusion as final. In other words, we got a referee.

She was called Dr Swiss. She was in her early fifties and surveyed us with a calm both eerie and weary. This left me in no doubt that she saw us as a pair of middle-class snowflakes who wouldn't know a problem if it inconvenienced them in Waitrose.

As is always the case, I stuttered through a completely inadequate attempt at describing Liam's issues. It didn't help that Liam was in the room. Nor that Liam behaved impeccably for the entire hour in her presence. It was like calling a repairman because your dishwasher had flooded the house on a Biblical scale. Only for said dishwasher to then perform for him without so much as a splutter.

Predictably therefore, Dr Swiss couldn't see a problem. Or rather, she saw the problem as us, declaring that Liam's issues were "behavioural."

'There's nothing wrong. He just needs some discipline.'

It was the modern equivalent of *Monty Python*'s "He's not the Messiah, he's a very naughty boy." It was also a definitive answer. I was wrong. And I was a crap parent. We were bad parents. Somewhere along the road, we had done this. Or not done enough to stop it. Dr Swiss even wrote a report.

Wars have ended with more ambiguity.

And yet here I am, disputing the indisputable.

Wednesday, 5 September

There are many incredible animal migrations in this world. And, thanks to my husband's obsession with the TV show *Our Planet*, I know far too much about too many of them. The most famous of all is called The Great Migration and takes place in the Serengeti. Counted as one of the Seven Wonders of the Natural World, it's a giant ongoing loop of 1.5 million wildebeest, as well as hundreds of thousands of zebras, gazelles, and eland.

On a par with this is the daily walk to school, an anthropological marvel equally worthy of a David Attenborough voiceover. Every weekday during term time, the mummies move with a singular purpose. Sweaty Betty leggings and tops that read "Drop it like a squat" mingle with high waisted trousers and round-framed sunglasses. Suits and jeans stride alongside floaty dresses and pencil skirts. And scattered in all directions are the children. Skipping and walking and chattering. The mummies, usually fearsome, competitive creatures, are united in their pilgrimage to the school gate. To freedom.

I can't help but wonder if the Serengeti's great herd has bad apples. If, among the chaotic order of it all, there is one wildebeest family out of step with the rest. With a mummy smiling that mechanical "oh kids" grimace at everyone walking past as she tries to pull her calf along, but only manages to stand still, calf hanging diagonally from her hands like a water skier from the rope.

We understand each other, that wildebeest mummy and me. We share a bond. Like me, she knows that other calves go home to their mummies with stories about her calf biting and kicking and screaming. She can imagine the conversations taking place in those other homes:

Other Calf: We had an extra playtime today, mummy.

Other Mummy: That's nice. How come?

Other Calf: You know Calf W?

Other Mummy: The one who bit Calf S?

Other Calf: Yes. Well, he got so angry today that the teachers took the rest of us outside.

Other Daddy: What? Who is this terrible calf? Surely their parents must not teach them to behave.

Other Mummy: I know. It's true. You stay away from him, okay poppet?

Is scripting fake animal home time conversations a bit extra? Is it a touch too far? Yes, yes, it is. But spare a thought for Mrs/Ms Wildebeest, who worries that her boys are being unfairly judged. That even though Calf W sometimes acts out, he is actually empathetic and sweet and caring and funny, none of which was mentioned. That he and his brother might be cast out, missing out on play dates and friendships because nobody wants to mix with "*that* family."

Well, fuck that. And especially fuck today. Because even when I eventually drag my calves across the threshold of the school gates, I have not yet won my independence. Today, I will have to wait a bit longer for this. Because first I have a meeting with the SENCO.

I spot Nisha at another gate, waving off Aran. I attempt to reach her. Maybe she'll hang around until my meeting starts. I could use a chat.

'Maya!'

No. Please no. Please let there be another Maya. Or voices in my head. Or-

'Hi!'

'Oh, hi. Ingrid. How's things?'

Ingrid's teeth have a glossy sheen to them today. As though her saliva is shinier than that of others. It's probably the latest thing. I imagine she has it sprinkled with unicorn glitter or something.

'Oh, you know how it is. The uszh. The PTA is planning the Christmas fair. We're recruiting volunteers.'

We? When did she have a chance to join the Parent Teacher Association? Her child joined the school yesterday. But this thought is quickly superseded.

Oh. No. The PTA. I hate PTA events. They always involve being in charge of a stall I don't understand. That and moving furniture.

'Don't look so worried,' she laughs. 'I wouldn't dream of asking you.'

A bazillion tons of stress lift off my shoulders and I join in with her laughter. Then I stop.

'Sorry, why?'

'Why what?'

'Why wouldn't you dream of asking for my help?'

'Oh.' She once again executes a perfect sympathy head tilt. It is a sight to behold. Truly beautiful: Flawless transition, excellent sad eyes, smooth realignment. Ten out of ten from all the judges. 'I got the impression that you were finding things a bit tricky. You just look a bit... overwhelmed.'

She continues, but I am only half listening now. The other half of me is busy concluding that one of my mum's warnings has finally come to pass. The wind has changed and now my face is stuck in one expression. Without a mirror to hand, I can only guess, but I believe it is that of Greek tragedy mask in mid-scream.

'So basically,' Ingrid is pronouncing, 'If you know anyone capable of helping, send them over.'

Hold on. Hold the frack on. Is she saying I'm not capable?

Who am I kidding? That's exactly what she's saying.

'I can help.'

Oh. Oh no. Did I just say that? I did. I just spoke those words. Stop. It's not too late. Take it back. You have nothing to prove.

'Really?' Ingrid coos. And it's not a pleased "really." It's not an oh-that's-great-thanks-so-much "really." It's a dubious one. As in, in *your* condition?

The voice in my head telling me to walk back my offer is now screaming at me to show this bitch just how fine I really am.

'Really.'

Great. I bet I get the hook-a-duck stall again. Or as I think of it, the thankless pool of hell. With this prospect looming over me like a storm cloud following Daffy Duck, I trudge to the school office to await my meeting.

Fenella Gordon-Bley has the air of a woman who loves puppies, but only because they make marvellous coats. Her features are made up entirely of jutting edges and sharp corners. The line of her bob could slice a diamond. Had she been a coffee table, she would have been responsible for multiple child injuries. But she isn't a dalmatian-kidnapping Disney villain or a table. She is the school's Special Educational Needs Coordinator AKA The SENCO.

She leads me to her office, which is nothing of the sort. It is a store cupboard with delusions of grandeur. We are sitting so close to one another I could pluck her eyebrows.

'Does Liam have a diagnosis?' She asks.

This is the first thing she says. Well, other than, "Ah, Mrs Harris. Follow me please."

It is such an unexpected question that I can only "um" a lot. It's the waking version of that dream where I'm sitting a university exam. Except I haven't got the lithe mind of a 20-something. Instead I must parse the intricacies of 16th century philosophy with my useless, shrivelled adult brain. I am simply not equipped nor prepared.

'Well?' She demands. 'ADHD, ADD, PDA, ASD. Any of those will do. Then we can get on with applying for funds.'

Acronyms. So many acronyms. An avalanche of them. Did she say PDA? Isn't that short for public displays of affection? Is that a diagnosis now?

'I, um. No,' I manage. 'Nothing like that.'

'I see.' Her blood red lips purse like a baboon's bum, through which she emits an efficiently short sigh. 'We *can* bid for funds without a diagnosis, but it's risky. The panel doesn't like it. Nothing to hook onto. They'll simply invest in something more secure. I presume you're going to see a doctor? We'll need something Aysap if we're going to make a successful bid this quarter. In the meantime, we'll arrange for emergency funding. Get that ball rolling.'

Invest? Secure? Aysap? Just as I am wondering if I have stumbled into the wrong meeting, the door to the cupboard/office creaks open. Miss Flowers squeezes in. She might have sat down, except there is no third chair and no hope of fitting one in.

'Sorry I'm late,' she breathes. 'Painting incident.'

She is indeed splattered with red paint. She looks more like the witness to a brutal murder than a primary school teacher.

'We were just discussing the acquisition of funds,' Gordon-Bley updates her. 'Mrs Harris is to apply for a diagnosis.'

'For what though?' I blurt. This isn't the question I mean to ask. I am far too frazzled to form one of those.

'*For fun-ding*,' the SENCO replies with deliberate enunciation.

There is a beat of horrified silence. Miss Flowers is the one to end it.

'Right. So basically, we think Liam would benefit from having one-to-one support. That means hiring another teaching assistant. That TA would look after him. Just Liam.'

I am stunned by this. And alarmed. You see, I grew up with the concept of "causing a fuss." One did not cause a fuss. Ever. I would go as far as calling it a central tenet of my childhood. Maybe even my national identity. Causing or allowing said fuss to be caused is, to this day, a social infraction akin to spitting in someone's face.

Unfortunately, in addition to being inviolable, this rule is also unspeakably vague. It's like the British constitution: uncodified. Nobody has ever defined to me what constitutes a fuss. I have only seen it identified on a case-by-case basis:

Specific Examples of Causing a Fuss

1. Me crying, age 7, when my ice cream scoop fell to the floor.
2. Me, aged 29, politely informing a restaurant employee that I ordered a steak and got served a salad.
3. Jake, about a year after we met, breaking his leg in a football match, and calling 999. That's a trick example though. Jake, also a fuss-free child, did not call an ambulance. Instead, he hobbled home on foot, then waited an hour for me to come home before casually asking if I could drive him to the local walk-in clinic.

And now this. They want to hire someone – a whole adult human – just to look after my child. A child who has been deemed medically fine. I would hazard that this very much falls within the fuss-causing range.

'Is that...' I cast around my mind for the right ending to my question only to find there isn't one. I go with, 'Is that necessary?'

'Yes,' they state as one.

'But the council needs to agree to pay,' continues Miss Flowers. 'So, we have to demonstrate that Liam needs it. And a diagnosis of a special need would go a long way to doing that.'

'But he doesn't have a special need. We've been to see people. Medical people.' Why can't I remember what the medical people are called? 'They said it was behavioural.' That word I remember.

'I don't think this is behavioural,' Miss Flowers says. Then seems to regret it. She chooses her next words like she trying to pick which wire to cut on a ticking bomb. 'Obviously, I say this with no medical background. But I think there's something.'

There's *something*.

Those three little syllables send an electric shiver down my spine. She thinks there's something. Someone aside from me thinks there's something. This is so exciting I just sit there smiling dumbly as she continues speaking. But then doubts set in. What if she's wrong? She's a young teacher. And the only person in the world other than me who has ever said anything like this about my son.

'Mrs Harris?'

'I don't want to cause a fuss.'

Dammit. It's like a nervous tic. Fortunately the SENCO ignores my outblurt entirely. Unfortunately, she is spewing yet more acronyms.

'We must apply for an EHCP aysap,' she declares. 'I will send you the forms to apply for an assessment. Please return them by EOW.'

It's like a text message is barking at me. I understand none of it. But I'd like to leave now and so I mumble an assent.

'Good.' Ms Gordon-Bley retorts, the word like the decisive "thunk" of a prison door being closed. Then there is the actual sound of a door closing and Miss Flowers and I find ourselves back in the hallway.

We share an awkward exchange of "thanks for coming in" and "thanks for helping" before Mrs Gripp rounds the corner.

'There you are,' she accuses. 'Flynn has rubber stuck up his nose. Again.'

'Oh, um, right,' Miss Flowers stammers. 'Must dash.' But just as she takes her first step away, she pivots. 'You should film Liam's tantrums.'

I wonder if I misheard her. Did she just tell me to film Liam's tantrums? What for? Posterity? Evidence? YouTube? It takes every facial muscle I own to keep a straight face.

'Er, why?'

'Something a psychologist friend of mine tells all her clients. That way you don't have to rely on your ability to explain any difficulties if you do end up seeing someone. You can also show them.'

Mrs Gripp clears her throat meaningfully.

'Trust me,' Miss Flowers whispers, walking backwards. Then she turns and strides towards the older woman, her skirt billowing behind her like Batwoman's cape.

Friday, 7th September

Each and every day of this school week has heralded new and hitherto unimaginable horrors. Like a bizarro-world version of The Twelve Days of Christmas.

The end count is four chairs a-broken, three children a-kicked, two late book entries a-signed and not a single full day at school. Had there been a partridge, I didn't fancy its chances.

I have also gained a pen pal in the form of Fenella Gordon-Bley. The SENCO keeps emailing me about The EHCP. That's what she calls it: *The EHCP*. I don't even know what *an* EHCP is, so the existence of a very definite one is somewhat alarming. As is the fact that I am supposed to fill out forms about it.

And all this was on top of the standard school-related demands.

THIS WEEK'S STANDARD SCHOOL-RELATED DEMANDS:

1. Being asked to complete a survey about surveys. Some parents have asked to be consulted on more school decisions. Do parents think the school should ask busybody parents how to suck eggs or can the trained professionals get on with doing their sodding jobs? I'm paraphrasing, but only just.

2. Buying Charlie a Tritan (it had to be Tritan and not just any plastic) cup instead of a water bottle because that's what they use in year 1. The water bottle was returned with a post-it note informing me of its unsuitability. It may as well have been a scarlet letter.

3. Delving into the darkest, warmest, dankest depths of the lost property bin. I was searching for Charlie's brand-new coat that he lost after one day. I wish I could say this was a record. I also wish I could say it was labelled with his name. It isn't. I am still waiting for the special stamp I ordered with which to do this. The coat remains missing. Instead, I found four school jumpers, three hats, four odd gloves and one school

shoe. Why only one? Who was the kid going home in one shoe? But no coat. Shit.

4. Daily requests for random items which are apparently vital for my older son's education. Yesterday he had to bring in recycling materials. Today it was £2 for some sort of charity event. And, on both occasions, he remembered this vital information only once we had reached the school gate.

'Why aren't they telling the parents?' I asked him this morning.

'They said it was on the school app.'

But I had checked the app. I had checked it and there was nothing. Nothing except details of year 5's trip to Gateshead last year.

'I'm so sorry,' I said to the mum collecting the donations as I frantically rummaged for change. 'I didn't see anything about this.'

To which she said, with absolutely zero sympathy, 'It was on the app.'

I told her I'd checked the app.

'The other app.'

I blinked. Other app?

'What other app? Do you mean ParentMail?'

A magnificent eyeroll, then, 'We got an email. It told us to download the new app.'

The email was in my junk folder. Gmail is gaslighting me.

And now it is noon and I have been called in to find that Liam has secreted himself inside an enormous chest in the reception class's playground.

Miss Flowers and I gaze contemplatively at the toy chest. The lid is only slightly raised, one stubborn eye peering out of the gap.

'I have someone.'

Miss Flowers utters this in such a low, quiet voice, I think I'm hearing things. Which I am, except not in my imagination. It doesn't help that she keeps her eyes fixed straight ahead. It feels very clandestine. Like she's trying to smuggle me out of East Berlin. I play along. Partly because it's fun. But also because I haven't got a clue what she means.

'Oh?'

'A friend of mine is a child psychologist. She's very good. And she offered to see you on Monday morning. If you want.'

'*This* Monday?'

How good can this person be if they can fit us in at the drop of a hat? But Miss Flowers has the answer.

'Yes. She's had a cancellation.' She tilts her head to one side pensively, gaze still pinned on the toy chest. 'Also, she's met Janice and I told her about the hand thing.'

Janice is Mrs Gripp. Presumably therefore, this person understands the severity of not just biting a teaching assistant, but of biting *that* one.

'Look,' Miss Flowers' shuffles closer, but not before her eyes dart around to check nobody – the Soviet government? - is listening. 'It's totally up to you. He's such a bright, wonderful boy. He just needs a little more support.' As if to punctuate the point, the toy box lid clamps down. 'And you didn't hear this from me, but Mr Davies is going to email you tonight to put Liam on half days for the whole term.'

Monopoly. That's what pops unbidden into my head. So much Monopoly. It'll be half days of Sisyphean levels of the stupid game. Actual Monopoly jail. And how could I work? And what if Nisha can't collect Charlie every time?

'What were her details?'

Instead of just dropping off when she brings Charlie home today, Nisha stays for a coffee. This is exciting. After-school meetups are generally rendered impossible, not by our own schedules, but by our children's. Last year, Charlie did drama, choir and maths club. But this was as nothing compared with Aran and Saira. There are world leaders with fewer obligations than Nisha's kids.

In addition to studying both piano and violin, Aran has tutors for English, Maths and Hindi. He also plays football and cricket. And he has swimming lessons. Actual weekly swimming lessons. Nisha has a regular slot and everything. Swimming lessons are the litmus paper test for the ultimate middle-class mum. And their availability is rarer than gold unicorn poo. They are booked up until the end of time and existing clients get priority. So if your child has not done swimming since before they were born, they cannot get a time slot ever, ever and must make do with holiday crash courses. Like Charlie.

All of this restarts next week. But for now, we take advantage of the lull. Twenty minutes in, my sister joins us, trailing my nieces, Arabella and Mila. The girls arrive in beautiful boho dresses rather than school uniforms, a reminder that their private school is still on their summer holidays.

'Hi Auntie Maya,' they murmur, before running to join the other kids at the dining table.

Nisha and Gabby were in the same year at school, but it was Nish and I who first became friends. At the time, Gabby was doing a convincing *Mean Girls* impersonation and considered herself far too cool for the likes of us. Nisha and I were gaming nerds who spent our time watching *Stargate* and competing at Duck Hunt on my Sega.

Now, having stuffed our offspring full of pizza – with carrot and cucumber sticks in homage to the gods of modern parenting - we sit around my kitchen table.

In a bid for uninterrupted adult conversation, I have settled Liam on the living room sofa with his iPad and a one-hour time allowance on Minecraft. Barring any disasters - zombie horde, village attacks - this will keep him occupied. Getting him off the thing will prove difficult, but that's a problem for future me.

As for the rest of the kids, Zeus knows what they're getting up to while utterly unattended. It's like letting a load of Daleks wander around and just hoping nobody will get exterminated. But it's a risk worth taking.

Within minutes Nisha has us in stitches with an anecdote about one of her clients going to the wrong job interview. She is one of the only people I know who can make a story about banking recruitment funny enough to leave us gasping for air.

'So,' she wheezes, struggling to speak for laughter. 'Fuck knows how, but he's in the entirely wrong bank. He tells them he's there for the interview and... and... they interview him.'

'How?'

'What?'

Nisha nods. Then she says something. But she's laughing so hard it's unintelligible. It takes two tries and one sip of water before she finally rasps, 'He got the job.'

Which completely finishes us off.

Gabby updates us on the goings on at her daughters' school. This is much more interesting than it sounds, given that its exclusivity attracts a number of North London's celebrity parents. The latest gossip involves a TV chef husband whose infidelities have been widely discussed in the media. According to my sister, his wife is unconcerned.

'She doesn't give a shit,' Gabby utters incredulously. 'Says it saves *her* from having to do it.'

'Of course, we have our own famous mummy now,' Nisha says. 'Ingrid.'

I frown. 'She's not famous.'

'OMG, you're like, super jealous of her, aren't you?' Gabby teases, grinning at me.

'Nu-uh.'

Bloody hell. I am 34. Gabby 36. But when we're together we regress to being children. Nisha, who has known us both long enough for this to be perfectly ignorable, doesn't miss a beat.

'Saw her in the playground. The Wunder Mummies were all over her. I thought Jemima B's mummy was going to kiss her hand.'

Jemima B is one of the alpha girls in Aran's class. Every class has a Jemima B. The girl – and it is almost invariably a girl – who runs the joint like it's her own personal fiefdom. In Charlie's class it's Annabelle. I've not a clue who will take the crown in Liam's. But Jemima B has an extra leg-up above them all because her mummy is Alison Bertrand, AKA head of the PTA, AKA parent governor. Or, as I think of her, the Queen B.

'Do you follow Ingrid on Insta?' Gabby asks now, already swiping through the app.

'Yes,' Nish and I reply with varying levels of self-loathing, both reaching for our phones.

Gabby surveys her screen with interest. 'Oh, we've been to that hotel too,' she murmurs. 'Lovely place in the Maldives. Can't remember the name.'

I find the post Gabby's talking about. Images of Ingrid and her family on a beach with waters so clear I can see a clownfish photobombing them.

'Four kids though,' Nisha breathes. 'No thanks.'

'And she's trying to adopt,' I add.

Nisha is instantly and obviously scandalised by this. Her eyes widen and her mouth flaps open and shut. Not unlike a clownfish.

'Bloody hell,' she exclaims eventually. 'That would be five kids. Five kids? Five? Why?'

'Five is the new four,' Gabby deadpans.

We glare at her quizzically.

'You know.' Clearly we don't, but Gabby cannot fathom it. When she finally accepts that she is in the presence of lesser-informed beings, she emits an all-knowing sigh. 'It's all about who can cope with the most. A simple hierarchy really. Time was, super competitive mums had three kids to show that they were the best.'

'The best?' Nisha can't hide her disbelief. 'At what? Pelvic thrusts?'

'The best at coping, at multitasking, at being chill in all the scenarios. At driving bigger cars.' She swipes at the air as if to swat away this inconsequential tangent. 'Anyway, then three became de rigueur. So it went up to four. Now it's five.'

'Like inflation,' I mutter.

'Exactly.'

'But it's not exactly a level playing field, is it?' asks Nisha. 'Like, if someone with loads of money has four kids, but they have nannies and grandparents that help, that's not the same as, like, a single mum with four kids. There should be a scale.'

'A tapering scale,' I suggest. 'Like how your annual allowance is tapered in income tax the more you earn.'

Both women gawp at me like I've grown a second head called Deborah.

'I just did a website for an accountancy firm,' I explain quickly, eager to return to the subject at hand in order to voice one of my long-held fears. 'But what if they just *are* better at coping though? I mean, look at Ingrid. All those kids and she still manages wearing makeup and holidays and... quinoa.' I pronounce it queen-oh-ah.

'I think it's pronounced *keen* -wah,' Nisha offers.

'And she has a job she loves,' I continue. 'Me? I've worn the same jeans three days in a row, I can't deal with the two kids I've got and what am I doing at work? Writing about the best Finchley accounting firms and cat nip. Plus I've never even bought *keen* -wah.'

'Don't tell me you believe Ingrid's hype,' Nisha scoffs. 'I mean, I know you two were always uber competitive at school and stuff-'

'*She* was,' I insist. 'She dragged me into it.'

'Okay. Whatever. But don't compare yourself to her. At least not to the *her* she projects online. It's all bullshit. Fake as fuck. If you're not happy, then change something. But not because of that publicity balloon.'

'And quinoa sucks,' Gabby adds.

The conversation meanders like this, punctuated by requests from various children. The subject turns to Liam's first week at school and I give an abridged version of events.

'They can't just decide he's on half days,' Nisha opines with her usual unflappable certitude. 'They're just trying their luck. School budget is completely shot to shit and they think they can squeeze some money out of the council for an extra teaching assistant. They're using Liam as a cash cow.'

'Cash *calf*,' my sister interjects.

To which I respond with the sardonic *Yes Minister* reference we've used since we were kids. 'Very droll, minister.'

Nisha, evidently on a roll, bypasses this exchange entirely.

'This whole special needs bollocks is just that. Crap.' She seems to reconsider and adds, 'Not special needs as a *thing*. That's real. But as a thing that affects Liam. There's no way he has anything like that. Trust me. They tried to do it with Aran, and I basically told them to piss off.'

I love Nisha. I love that she is trying to assure me that everything is okay. Or at least that it will be. So why doesn't it make me feel any better?

'Here's the thing,' I say, without having fully formed "the thing" in my mind. 'If it's not special needs or whatever.' I note something bobbing around in my peripheral vision and realise it's the pizza crust I'm holding abiding with my hand gestures. 'If it's not medical. Then isn't it our fault? Our bad parenting?'

The "no" that issues from the two of them is instant and vehement. But it is also a stock answer and I'm not having it.

'Then what is it?'

'Liam's just a kid,' Is Nisha's eventual answer. 'No better or worse than the rest of them. They're not fully formed humans. I mean look at my two. They're both effing nuts.'

On cue, Aran lets loose a George-of-the-Jungle-style bellow.

'What exactly *are* special needs?' asks my sister absently, nibbling on her own pizza crust.

'You know,' I say, flapping an arm around vaguely. 'Special needs.'

'Yeah,' my sister returns in a dry "duh." 'Thanks, Captain Obvious, I know the term. And I sort of know what it is. But what actually *is* it?'

'Stuff like dyslexia,' Nisha puts in. 'And...'

'Well, um...'

We share a sheepish silence. Then we resort to Google.

'Particular educational requirements resulting from learning difficulties, physical disability, or emotional and behavioural difficulties,' reads Gabby.

There's a beat as we take it in.

'Oh good,' Nisha deadpans. 'That narrows it down.'

Any further discussion is put on hold just then as a piercing shriek fills the air. A flock of nearby birds takes flight. And I sit up. That was loud. The question is, was it *too* loud? Liam is terrified of loud noises. My mummy senses tingle. Everything else is blocked out as I scan for sound.

My body straightens and my neck cranes as I listen intently. And I hear it. A high-pitched, mournful wheeze.

I don't remember getting up or running to the living room. It's like I transform. One minute I'm Maya Harris and the next I am Supermum: able to hear my children's voices over the sound of a 747 jumbo jet; to leap over Lego towers and dodge Nerf gun bullets; and to know when a loud noise has upset my son one room away.

I find Liam in tears, iPad forgotten.

Something visceral, all-consuming overtakes me when I see one of my kids crying. All I can think of is fixing it. Whatever it is, I must make it better. Fuck letting them manage on their own and learn from their mistakes. Fuck building character. My baby is sad. And I will burn the world down to change that.

I sit beside him and he climbs into my lap, wrapping around me like a koala.

In the next room, three-year-old Saira is informing Nisha that her brother had threatened to kill her.

Aran is summoned and there proceeds a lengthy discussion about the whys and wherefores of why it's not okay to threaten to kill anyone.

For his part, Aran denies everything. He didn't say anything, wasn't there, is unfamiliar with this Saira individual. He may not even be here right now. Then he admits he was there, but not to threatening his sister. Perhaps she misinterpreted something he said. Okay, maybe a mild physical threat was issued, but if a tree is threatened in the woods without a mother present, did it really happen? It is the Boris Johnson approach to discourse. Deny all. If that fails, dither until words have lost all meaning and nobody remembers why, when or how they got there. It is masterful.

And through it all, Liam and I stay on the sofa in our snug embrace. Liam is an excellent cuddler. He has a Play-Doh like ability to mould himself to whatever shape is required and he squeezes with all his might.

'Is he okay?' Gabby whispers, her head poking around the door. I nod. 'Listen, I have to go. Let me know how it goes with the psychologist person. Love you, Liam.' Her expression is pained, hand clasped to her chest as she mouths, 'So sweet.'

Nisha is next to appear.

'I'm so sorry, little man. Was that too loud?'

'Yeh,' Liam sniffs. 'What was that?' Actually he says 'wo wo dat'. Liam has yet to conquer speaking clearly. We did try speech therapy, but he was affronted by the very idea. This means people struggle to understand him. Nisha however is almost as fluent as I am.

'Sorry lovely,' she coos. 'Saira got a bit scared. Loud, isn't she?'

Indignance has crept onto Liam's face and he nods.

'Yu shoo te' ha.'

'I will tell her,' Nisha assures him. 'See you,' she murmurs to me.

That night, Jake and I receive simultaneous notifications of an email from the school. It's the promised missive from Mr Davies, placing Liam on half days.

Jake takes it in his stride. Quite literally. He paces for half an hour muttering darkly to himself and occasionally ranting to the room at large. Sir Francis watches the whole thing with mild interest, head oscillating back and forth like a spectator at Wimbledon.

Then Jake abandons his pointless power walk in favour of scouring Google to find out if Mr Davies is acting within the law. This is followed by more dark mutterings.

Channelling his inner teenager, he slumps into bed and grumbles, 'It's because Liam isn't yet five. Which means he's not yet required to be in full-time school.'

'Maybe it's for the best,' I sigh, scrolling absently through the Next app on my phone. 'He might cope better with half days.'

'But it's insane' Jake persists. 'What? Now you have to give up work and become a professional Monopoly player? I mean, it would be great if that's what you wanted to do, but I know it's not.'

'I can still work.'

A definite pause is followed by, 'Sure.'

'What?'

'Nothing. It just doesn't seem practical. You have, what, two and a half hours between drop off and pickup? You already tell me you don't have enough time to get anything done.'

'I'll manage.'

'Okay. If you feel like you can do it then I'll help as much as I can.' We sit in silence before Jake shuffles into a higher sitting position. 'You know. I just always thought that school was... a given. Everyone goes to school. And that once we had both kids in full-time school everything would start to be...'

'Normal,' I mutter.

'Yeah.' He shifts. 'Like, when do we start having a life?'

'Retirement?'

'Shit. I hope not. I hope we can start before then.'

'We should make a list,' I suggest. 'A list of things we want to do. Like, I want to go to the Maldives. And Japan. And Scotland.'

'You realise one of those is a train ride away, right?'

'And yet I still haven't been.'

'True.'

'What would be on your list?' I ask.

'Mmm. Probably to make *Time Scavenger*.'

Time Scavenger is a video game idea Jake has had for almost as long as I've known him. It's about a guy from a dystopian future who travels back in time to collect a series of items in order to change the course of history. Each level is a different period of time and entails a different item.

'One day,' I say. Although I have no clue if that day will ever come.

'Oh,' he adds. 'And to see The Great Migration.'

Saturday, 8 September

Jake: 'What are we doing today?'

Me: 'Dunno.'

Jake: 'Why didn't we make plans?'

Me: 'Is that an existential question?'

The day never gets off the ground. We do however engage in some quality time as a family. For example, we collectively lose the plot. Liam goes first, apparently because Charlie walked past him. So he starts following Charlie around, thereby setting *him* off. Jake is then sucked into the venomous vortex when attempting to calm them down, which he must do solo because I am form-filling. Or trying to. It is this which eventually sends me over the edge.

It does not in any way help that I don't know why I am form-filling. Except that Fenella Gordon-Bley aka The SENCO, seems insistent that I do so.

The form in question says it's an application to request an education, health and care needs assessment. From what I can tell, it's an application to make an application for an education, health and care plan. Or – because everything must have an acronym – an EHCP. I have yet to discover what that is, but I must really want one because I am completing the world's most impossible document to apply for the mere chance to be assessed for one.

The form is fourteen pages long. And that's without the ten reports it asks to be appended to it.

Each page has four sections, each with impossibly general titles like "communication and interaction" and "cognition and learning." These are then further split into three parts. And each of these parts is a request for information broad enough to accommodate two jumbo jets holding hands. Some of my favourites include:

> What is going well for the child and their family?
>
> What do the child and family find difficult, challenging, or stressful?

And the classic:

> Any additional information that you consider to be relevant.

I'm going to need sugar. All the sugar.

Sunday, 9 September

Sundays mean lunch at my in-laws. Delia and Archibald Fletcher are a 1980's British sitcom brought to life: He the curmudgeonly but lovable patriarch, she the epitome of homemaking ideals.

Attendance is a three-line whip. For us that is. Jake's brother, Matt and his wife, Kelly are exempt from this dictate by virtue of living in the far reaches of the back of beyond. Also known as Clapham.

My mother-in-law is forever informing everyone of this in a scandalised hushed tone. She will then invariably add, "It's south of the river you know" as though she is communicating that it is located atop Mount Olympus.

To be honest, Matt and Kelly may as well live on Mount Olympus or, at the very least, on another planet given the disparity between our lives and theirs. Despite being three years older than Jake, Matt has the carefree lifestyle of a twenty-year-old. Albeit one with a phenomenal budget. He and Kelly are DINKS. That's Double Income No Kids. Only in their case the double is probably more like triple or quadruple, what with both of them earning shedloads in something to do with finance.

When they're not working, I imagine they're out at desperately trendy clubs and bars with ironic names like "The Meat House" or "Stoic." They probably know what a popup is. I don't. I say words like "trendy" and only apply "club" as a suffix to children's activities; drama, football, maths.

We've visited them in Clapham twice. And both times I felt like Kate Middleton trying to play netball while in a skirt suit and court shoes. Old before my time.

Basically, we see them only on high holidays. If that. So it is with some surprise that we arrive to find that they're joining us today. Our first indication is that we have to park our Volvo on the street instead of in the driveway as usual. The latter is occupied by a vehicle James Bond would reject as too flashy.

'Look boys,' I trill like an overexcited *Blue Peter* presenter. 'Uncle Matt and Auntie Kelly are here.'

'Who?' asks Liam. Just as Charlie asks, 'Why?' Which just about covers it.

Once inside, there is a flurry of air kissing, back patting, and greetings. Delia and Archie are inundated with chatter as our boys vie for their attention. It is an uneven playing field, Charlie being taller and speaking with infinitely more volume and clarity than his brother. My heart aches for Liam and glows for Charlie and the rest of me is consumed with guilt at the whole thing. I can't help thinking that it's a neat summation of the motherhood of siblings.

Matt has always treated our children with a wary false jollity. In the same way one might approach an unfamiliar dog. As if he's unsure if they'll bite, lick or mess up his clothes with mucky paws. I'd love to say that this is ridiculous, but my children have form on all fronts. Kelly meanwhile never says more than a communal "hi", attaching to it an expression that is a smile from chin to nose, but empty from there upwards. Like one of the lesser royals. The ones who don't practice enough.

This semi-smile is out in force today, frozen on Kelly's face like she applied it with cement. But Matt. Well...

'Hey Hey! Charlie. Dude.'

A high five hand is proffered and withdrawn just as Charlie attempts to hit it. This is met with giggling guffaws from Charlie, who is a sucker for slapstick.

'Isn't it lovely?' croons Delia, hands clasped to bosom as her face glows with pride.

"Lovely" wouldn't be my chosen description of whatever it is that's happening here. Unsettling, maybe. Jarring. Definitely bewildering.

'Aren't they lucky to have such a fun uncle,' Archie bellows. And I want to point out that for Charlie's last birthday, his "fun uncle" got him a gif sent via text message two days after his actual date of birth.

We watch with fascinated trepidation as Matt and his high five move on to Liam.

'Hey, big man.'

Liam contemplates the hovering hand and then his uncle's face with intense suspicion. He is not one to be taken for a fool, my younger son. Arms folded, brow furrowed, Liam looks so serious and sweet that my cheeks hurt from smiling.

'Say hi to Uncle Matt,' I prompt, my voice the high-pitched faux-cheery one used by all parents desperate for their child to make a good impression.

'Why you here?' asks Liam. And for once I am relieved nobody but me and Jake can understand him. Except this is not quite true. There is one more member of our party who can–

'He wants to know why you're here,' trumpets Charlie. Then adds, 'He didn't know who you were because we never see you.'

At which juncture I interject at great speed and volume and with just a smidge of desperation.

'Isn't it lovely that Uncle Matt and Auntie Kelly are here for lunch.'

Great. Now *I'm* saying "lovely." And it doesn't work anyway because Liam's response is unequivocal.

'No.'

This everyone understands.

To Matt's credit, he smiles even wider, then motions to his still upright hand.

'You're not going to leave me hanging, are you?'

We all look to Liam. Inside, I'm begging him to high-five his uncle. But Liam is now certain he's having his leg pulled. He fixes Matt with an indignant glare.

'You are not hanging.' That said, he stalks off in search of his grandma's iPad.

'Hey mate,' Jake says, embracing his brother.

'Little bro,' Matt returns, as they perform the usual back pats.

'Good to see you. What brings you out to the Stix?'

Matt places an arm around Kelly's shoulders.

'Well, actually, we've got some news.'

Two things occur to me then.

1. Jake hates it when Matt calls him "little bro"
2. No effing way. She's not–

'*We're pregnant!*' Matt and Kelly chorus.

Only they are slightly drowned out by Charlie simultaneously shouting, 'I'm hungry!'

Lunch is a split screen affair. On one side, Delia, Archie, Matt, and Kelly have a civilised conversation about the pregnancy and baby. On the other, Jake and I try to kettle the ones we made earlier.

The excitement of unexpected guests has sent our children into a state of inebriation. Honestly, there's no other way to describe it. They are basically drunk. If they're not laughing hysterically and dancing around, then they're belligerent and reeling for a fight. Right now, we have one of each. Never a good match.

We divide in a vain attempt to conquer. Jake with Charlie and I with Liam, each of us taking turns to utter phrases like, "sit down", "eat your lunch", "do you want to lose a star?" and "careful, you'll break it."

The entire table screeches to a halt at one point when Charlie, realising that he knows something about babies, shares it with the group.

'The Spartans killed lots of babies,' he announces. 'Just left them to die.' His face brightens with the realisation that he has one more nugget of knowledge to impart. 'Killing babies is called infanticide.'

Archie coughs. Then remembers that he is British. And that glossing over uncomfortable silences is a national pastime. Sadly, he jumps straight out of the frying pan and into something significantly hotter.

'How was your first week at school, Liam?'

'My teacher says I'm a chatterbox,' Charlie says, with not a little glee. 'She says I can win in the chatterbox 'lympics.' Without so much as a pause for breath, he adds, 'And Liam bit a teacher's finger off.'

A sterling silver fork clatters to the floor. And that is the only sound because everyone is speechless.

'He didn't bite it *off*,' I hurry to explain. 'It's still… on.'

'Right,' quivers Delia.

'Excellent,' Archie adds.

'Shame you didn't send them to private school,' Matt muses. 'Best thing that ever happened to me. And you,' he says, fork pointed at Jake.

'Oh yes, Jakey was a mischievous one,' Delia chirrups. 'A right handful.'

'Do you remember the time he kicked my boss?' Archie chortles.

'And how he would always scream bloody murder if you tried to make him do something he didn't want.'

All three of them then chorus, 'And the supermarket standoff.'

'And Grosvenor's sorted him out,' Matt says, referring to the private boys' school he and my husband attended. 'Look at him now, almost a respectable member of society.'

Beside me, I feel the heat of my husband's silent fury. This is not how he remembers things. According to Jake, Grosvenor's was a hothouse filled with sociopaths and narcissists and obsessed with academic success at any cost. He despised it so much he refuses to even consider sending the boys to anything like it. And, while he can't recall much from his early years, he's always felt that his family dismissed him as the lesser son.

The boys finish their lunch – or more accurately abandon it – while the adults are still on the soup course.

'Mummy, can I have a treat?' Charlie asks.

Sensing opportunity, Liam drops his spoon in an instant.

'Treat,' he demands.

'I said it first.'

'Just wait until the grownups have finished, boys,' Delia coos.

'No!'

If this was a TV show, the scene would freeze, allowing me to describe the crossroads at which we find ourselves. We have two of what can only laughingly be called options.

Our "Options"

1. The Easy Road: Gloss over Liam's rudeness and fetch him his treat. This is bad. It sets a terrible precedent and guarantees future bad behaviour. But it is also the only sure way to avoid a tantrum right now. In this moment.
2. The Hard Road: Also known as the indisputably right thing to do. To stand our parental ground. To insist that they sit at the table until we have all finished eating and that they apologise for the rudeness. The children learn that they will not be rewarded for bad behaviour. That's the theory. That is what every parenting book worth its Mummyweb recommendation stamp would advise.

I'm sure this advice would work with some kids. I'm sure it would work with Charlie. He'd grumble a bit, maybe even stamp his foot, but would capitulate. It will not work with Liam. Or, it will work, but only in virtually guaranteeing an immediate and spectacular tantrum. There's also something else, something ineffable, that tells me it is the wrong thing to do.

All of this swirls through my head in the one second I have to reach a decision.

'You may only have your treat,' I hear myself declare, in the style of

Rumpelstiltskin setting out his riddles three, 'If you say sorry for being rude and then ask nicely.'

'Sorry!' they shout, before bursting out of the dining room in search of chocolate. Jake and I follow.

'Open it,' Liam demands, holding out a Milky Way.

'What do you say?' I ask, grasping onto the last vestiges of my standards.

'Please.'

And then we are released. The boys have iPad, TV and chocolate. Now we can eat.

Except as we sit down to our roast chicken, it becomes evident that our children had been acting as human shields. Without them, we are forced to endure one of the most insufferable experiences known to parent-kind. That of receiving unsolicited parenting advice from two people who are not yet parents.

'It's all about consistent discipline, isn't it,' laments Matt between contemplative chews of caramelised carrot. 'Having rules and sticking to them.'

Kelly nods vociferously. 'And also listening to your kids. You know? Really hearing them.'

'I think I hear Liam,' Jake says, bottom already divorced from seat.

'No,' I snap desperately. 'You didn't.' I catch his eye and give him my most menacing warning glare. One that communicates with crystal clarity that if he leaves me alone in this room there will be hell to pay.

He slumps back down.

'Do you think you might be giving them too much screen time?' This is what Kelly says next. To my actual face. With her face. Then, because I have no response – not a verbal one anyway – she adds, 'I think so many parents use TV as a babysitter, you know? Rather than spending quality time with their kids.'

I do not kill Kelly. Not even when she opines, upon hearing that I didn't produce enough milk to breastfeed exclusively, that it's a shame I "gave up." Nor when she comments that it's easy to have a career and still be a hands-on mum "if you commit." Not even when she asks why Liam's speech is so unclear and have we considered employing a speech therapist.

At which point I decide to lean into the madness. To tumble head-first down the rabbit hole. Because why the fuck not?

'Oh, we just didn't think talking was that important,' I say innocently. 'Speech... therapist you say?'

Kelly tuts, her opinion of me far too low to doubt the veracity of my ignorance.

'But dear, you did have a speech therapist for Liam,' Delia chimes in. 'I recommended her to you.' Then, for good measure, adds, 'Her name was Lottie.'

'Oh, right,' I say. '*Speech* therapist. I thought you'd said *speed* therapist.'

'I think it's time we got the boys home,' Jake proclaims.

We do not talk in the car on the way home. We can't. Not about Matt and Kelly anyway. Not with two human recording devices in the back seat.

No sooner have we crossed the threshold of our home than Charlie whines that he's hungry. Liam rushes past, desperate to get to the TV remote first.

'We just had lunch,' I remind my first-born. To which he shrugs. Like he's saying, *I don't know what to tell you. Them's the breaks.* Then he too settles in front of a TV.

I watch as both my boys dazedly gaze at screens. And I see it. I see it all.

'We should do something,' I tell Jake. He's at the computer. Yet another screen.

'Yep,' he says absently.

'Jake, Kelly's right.'

I now have his full undivided attention.

'What?'

'She's right. I am a terrible mum. I do use TV as a babysitter. They're down there right now. Glued to the boob tube, the gogglebox, the… the… idiot screen. We are raising goggling idiots. We have to do something.'

'Okay, first of all, Kelly is not right. Kelly is never right. If Kelly were a clock, one of her hands would fall off just to ensure it couldn't happen even once. Secondly, you are a great mum. You do loads with them. You're always playing Monopoly with Liam and Dobble with Charlie.'

'That doesn't count. I don't bake with them. Or take them to art galleries. We haven't even signed them up for Mandarin lessons. They're doomed.'

'You don't bake with them because you are terrible at baking. We took them to the Science Museum last month. And do you know where Charlie picked up all that stuff about the Spartans? From TV. *Disgusting Histories and Mysteries*. Which I watch with him. And, not for nothing, but those two don't have a bloody clue what parenting is like. Matt actually said that having a baby won't change their lives.'

'What? Not at all?'

'He thinks it can all be solved with nannies and night nurses.'

'But Kelly doesn't want nannies. She was very clear.'

'Did you hear the bit about not allowing sugar in the house?'

'Fuck that.'

And soon, we're laughing. Laughing in that uncontrollable way that makes you gasp for air.

'They've booked a holiday in Thailand for a week after Kelly's due date,' Jake gasps. 'With the baby.'

'Stop,' I cry. 'Stop. You'll make me pee.'

Which only sets us off again.

Monday, 10 September

10:45am

It's the anniversary of our first date. A decade ago today, Jake and I went to dinner at Pizza Express in Hampstead after meeting on an online dating website. It is, as love stories go, about as uninspiring as it gets. There was no cinematic meet cute. We didn't lock eyes across a crowded room. We arranged to meet up and that happened.

And yes, there was chemistry between us. There was a spark, an attraction. But far stronger than that was the sense of coming home. It was like parachuting in a month into a relationship. We were instantly comfortable together. We certainly never lacked for conversation. Never struggled for something to say.

But there is a first time for everything. And this is a day of firsts.

We are in our car, sitting side by side, silently staring ahead. It is not a comfortable silence, nor an angry one. This is a new beast. We both want to talk. We keep trying, taking turns to open our mouth with the intention of saying something, only to close it again. No sounds having emerged. Like fish.

Jake is first to relocate the left hemisphere of his brain.

'Fuck.'

Whilst hardly profound, this utterance does at least break the ice.

'Yep.'

'Did you think-'

'No.'

'Neither did I.'

'She seemed very sure.'

'Yep.'

We have just left the office of Dr Ursula Myrtle. Dr Myrtle is Miss Flowers' child psychologist friend. I did not have high hopes for Myrtle. For one thing, she told us not to bring Liam.

'Shouldn't she at least meet him?' I'd asked Jake.

He had only shrugged, saying, 'It'll probably be easier without him there.'

Which was true, but still felt wrong in a data protection-ish way I couldn't name.

Then there was the woman herself. Dr Myrtle was an exotic bird made human. Her features were all delicate dots, her nose rising to a tiny point, her eyes beady and small and never settling in one place. The exotic bit was her hair. Oh my. It was outstanding. Not only was it quite the most vivid shade of orange peel, but it billowed out in three directions in a palm-tree-esque plumage of frizz. I was captivated.

I was also wrong in thinking she wouldn't understand. Myrtle understood. She got what we were describing in a way we had hitherto not experienced. It was a revelation. Even Jake was excited. Where he had started off unenthused and sceptical, he soon leaned in with fascinated focus.

It was after watching the videos of Liam that I'd made on Miss Flowers' recommendation that Myrtle sat upright, blinked several times and gave us what she called her "gut instinct."

'This isn't a formal diagnosis,' she cautioned. 'And Liam will need to undergo tests and observations before that can be attempted. But judging from what you've told me and shown me, there might be a neurological source for his behaviour. Most likely, Asperger's.'

Had Dr Myrtle told us our son was the reincarnation of Genghis Khan's horse, she could not have elicited a more stunned reaction. We had, to say the least, not expected a definitive answer. And certainly not *that* answer.

Asperger's. I'd heard of it. We both had. But that was only from TV and films.

I believe there's a saying about a bit of knowledge being a dangerous thing. Funnily enough, a bit was an exact summation of what we had and so-

'Like *Rain Man*?' Jake asked.

'Not necessarily.'

'Or Sheldon in *The Big Bang Theory*,' I suggested unhelpfully.

'And that other one with the angry Australian,' Jake pitched in, frowning as he tried to recall.

'*Beautiful Mind*,' I called out, thinking that this was fun. Like charades.

'Yes.'

'Guys-'

''I'm pretty sure that was schizophrenia though,' I said.

'Oh, yeah.'

But then I realised something else.

'What about that hacker? The British one who got extradited for hacking into the FBI?'

'Oh yeah. I know what you mean. Can't remember his name though.'

'I'll google it.'

'Hey!' Myrtle squawked.

We stopped abruptly, instantly cowed. Like children told off for talking in class. Myrtle looked like she was regretting meeting us in the first place. But then she reasserted her calm demeanour with a sharp huff.

'Autism is a spectrum,' she enunciated. 'Every person is different. They have different characteristics.'

'Hold on,' Jake said. 'But you said Asperger's. Not autism.'

I was glad he'd pointed this out because I was unsure about whether I'd misheard in the first place.

'Asperger's is part of the autism spectrum. Actually, we're not really supposed to call it that anymore. Some people call it high functioning autism, but others find that offensive. It's a whole thing. But regardless of any label, your son is still your son.'

Which seemed a rather obvious point. Who else would he be?

'How did we not know this?' I ask now. 'I feel like this is something we're supposed to know. I mean, he's almost five. Shouldn't we already have known if he's autistic? Like knowing he has hay fever. And what his blood type is.'

'You know his blood type?'

I do not.

'She could be wrong by the way,' Jake says. 'You need to remember that's a possibility. We won't know until he gets assessed.'

'I know.' But I am about as convincing as Sir Francis swatting a spider. Which isn't very much at all. Because he is a lazy cat who has never caught anything in his entire life. Whenever he does do anything cat-like it's obvious he's phoning it in. An actor doing a haemorrhoid cream advert just to keep his hand in.

'I'm just saying, don't start getting carried away with this.'

'I won't.'

But I do. Almost immediately.

'Mummy, why are you staring at Liam?' Charlie asks me that afternoon. Charlie has always had a loud voice. But it sounds louder now. Possibly because I need it not to be.

'Shhh. I'm not staring,' I murmur furtively. 'I'm just looking.'

A more accurate description is observing. I am observing Liam to see whether he exhibits the signs of autism. Of which I have a list from the National Health Service website. Because the first thing I did after promising Jake not to get carried away was google the living shit out of autism.

Some of the signs I recognised immediately. Like the fact that Liam doesn't answer to his name. Neither of my children do. So much so that Charlie's nursery had insisted we take him for a hearing test. Which he'd passed with flying colours. So when my second child didn't answer to his name, I shrugged it off as a family foible.

Also, Liam definitely gets upset when he doesn't like a certain taste, smell or sound. Like he did when Saira screamed. He's sensitive to clothes labels, which I have to cut out. Labels that never bothered his brother. This is harder than it seems. Because I either cut not enough, leaving a small remnant that's even worse than the label itself or I go too far and make a hole in the bloody clothes.

However, other signs listed aren't as clear cut. Take for example, "Getting very upset if you ask them to do something." On the one hand, this is true. But on the other, I do feel it stretches the meaning of the phrase "very upset" to the point of absurdity. I can't imagine the Hulk's catchphrase being quite as effective if changed to, "You wouldn't like me when I'm very upset."

Then there are the signs that I initially dismissed out of hand. I was able to do so instantly because, as his mum, I know Liam inside and out. I know how he talks and moves and acts. That's my job. But just in case and for the sake of scientific objectivity, I decided to observe him. Just for a bit.

Signs I'd Dismissed Out of Hand

1. Not making eye contact.
2. Not smiling when smiled at.
3. Repetitive movements, such as flapping hands, flicking fingers or rocking of the body.

> Side note: I now have Backstreet Boys' smash hit *Everybody* stuck in my head courtesy of number 3. This is annoying but necessary because I will not live in a world where the phrase "rocking your body" does not instantly bring that song to mind. I just won't. Death would be a sweet release from such an existence.

My conclusions, while preliminary, are less than encouraging, indicating as they do that I am a monster. Cersei Lannister displayed more maternal instinct than I do. I know so little about my child that I failed to notice that he flaps his arms when he's excited. What else haven't I seen? Does Charlie somersault when tired?

On a related note – that of me being wrong – I was also less discreet in my investigation than I had hoped given that Charlie, who never notices anything, has clocked it. And he's not letting it go.

'It is rude to stare,' he tells me.

'That's true.'

'And staring is looking at someone for a really long time and that's what you're doing.'

'Fine, sure. You're absolutely right. I'll stop it.'

'Everything okay?' It's Jake, who has chosen the perfect bloody moment to appear in the doorway.

'Mummy was staring at Liam like this.' Charlie widens his eyes and thrusts his head towards his dad.

'But it's rude to stare,' Jake says, oh so innocently.

'That's what I said,' Charlie answers proudly and, job done, disappears to find a screen to stare at.

'It's good you're not getting carried away,' Jake says when he's gone. 'Cuppa?'

'Yes please.'

7:30pm

Mum calls.

Last year, my parents moved from North London to New Zealand. Why did they move halfway across the sodding world from everyone and everything they know? According to dad, it was my mum's idea. Mum says it was for "the lifestyle."

I think they did it to avoid helping with childcare. Gabby agrees, except she doesn't understand what my problem is. She's just grateful that oceans are providing a minor barrier to mum's ability to sense whenever one of us is hiding something.

But she is mistaken. Time zones and oceans are no match for our mother.

'Hi mum.'

'What's wrong?'

'What? Nothing. How are you?'

'I'm fine. Your father's IBS is acting up. What's wrong?'

I consider lying. Or attempting to lie. Or even just fudging things a bit. I am not ready to lay bare the day's revelations to my mum. My mother will not take this well. Unfortunately, I am a terrible liar. A truly appalling one. My tells are small in number, but gargantuan in impact.

Things I Do When I Try to Lie

1. Hiccup: It's my version of Pinocchio's nose growing.
2. Forget the details of the lies and thus contradict myself.
3. Volunteer far too many details that nobody asked for.

So I tell her. And she reacts with calm, reason, and logic.

'A *psychologist*?' she snaps. 'Are you insane?' She can then be heard yelling the information to my dad somewhere in the background.

'Mum-'

'Why do you look for trouble?' She demands. 'You want everyone to think there's something wrong with him? He'll never get a good job if people think he's crazy.' Then, to truly ring home the "someone's listening" vibe, she hiss-whispers, 'They'll put him on a list.'

'There isn't a list mum. There's no database they put you on when you seek mental health advice. And even if there was, there's nothing wrong with it.'

'I know there's nothing wrong with it. But people judge.'

Ah the considered, contemplative, informed view of my mother.

'So what did she say this… *psychologist*?' She pronounces "psychologist" as an Evangelical preacher might "devil worshipper."

'She thinks he might have Asperger's.'

'What? Ridiculous. Of course she'd say that. She's a psychologist. She's going to diagnose a psychological problem. If you'd gone to a leg doctor, he'd have told you there was something wrong with his leg.'

There is no arguing with this skewed logic.

'Do you even know what Asperger's is?' I ask instead.

'That boy had it. The one they sent to America because he hacked the FBI. So now she's saying you shouldn't have a computer? I'm telling you, it's nonsense. I will buy him a computer.'

I try not to dwell on the fact that my mum and I both had the same cultural touchpoint for Asperger's. I already fear that I'm turning into her. It is the cycle of life. She is turning into her mum and I into mine. Instead, I tell her about the signs I have researched.

'Well,' she sniffs. 'By those standards we're all a bit autistic.'

I decide I can no longer endure this epistemological house of mirrors. There is only one solution.

'Boys, come say hi to grandma,' I trill.

Afterwards, I draft a message on the LUNCH WhatsApp group to update

Nisha and Gabby. This is harder to word than I had expected and I end up sending something that could pass for an Edwardian telegram.

> **You**
>
> Saw Psychologist – STOP – She thinks it might possibly be Asperger's – STOP – Very unusual – STOP – Gabby, mother knows - STOP

My phone rings almost as soon as two blue ticks appear beside the message.

'Asperger's?' Gabby demands. 'Is it genetic?'

Oh. Oh, shitting epic crap. The second she says this, I realise just how much of an insensitive idiot I am. This hadn't even occurred to me. If it's genetic it might impact her girls.

'Oh, god Gabby I'm so sorry. I didn't even think of that. But your girls have never shown any signs, have they?'

'What? No. Not even a trace.'

'That's good.'

'Yeah.'

Something is odd. Her response sounds...

'You sound disappointed,' I laugh.

'No.' This singular syllable is delivered in a tone Shakespeare himself would denote as protesting an approximate fuck-tonne too much.

'What the hell, Gabs?'

'Never mind. You won't understand.'

I can sense her sulking. It's like a heat emanating from her end of the call.

'Gabs. Talk to me.'

'Oh, fine,' she huffs. 'Lots of grammar schools like taking on autistic kids. They think they're good at science and maths and stuff. I just thought...'

No.

'I mean, everybody does it,' she continues.

It is a miracle I recover at all, but I do, if only to tell her, in no uncertain terms, that she is a terrible human being.

'Whatever,' is Gabby's sullen reply.

Nisha doesn't call. Instead she embarks on a rapid fire messaging campaign to express what I assume is every thought she has as they happen. It's a live stream of her mind. It is like reading a haiku as penned by Tigger from *Winnie the Pooh*. Some are sentences. Some are single words. Others qualify as neither. It begins like this:

Nisha

WTF on what basis????

Don't know what to say.

I am SO Sort

*Sorry

U ok???

Who is this world?

*World

ffs autocorrect

*woman

What next?

I can't see why

she thinks tha

t

Looki at nhs site

Makes no senses

    I tell Jake about my conversation with my mum in the hope of venting my frustrations. He does not act as a sympathetic ear. Instead, he says that if my parents know then his parents need to know. Which is exactly what happened when we discovered I was pregnant. My mum guessed at ten weeks because I was - and I quote - "breathing like a pervert." Apparently, she too was a heavy breather in early pregnancy. She had then recalled how my grandmother – her mother-in-law – kept thinking she was a nuisance caller whenever she phoned.

    'Told me off good and proper. They knew how to swear in those days,' she'd murmured dreamily.

    Upon discovering that the baby was out of the bag, Jake had immediately phoned his parents to balance the scales. He does the same now.

    I do not tell him about Nisha and Gabby knowing as well. His head would explode. And in any event, he has his hands full.

    I can hear Jake's mum crying from two rooms away. Sir Francis releases a fart of alarm and bolts through the cat flap. They ask if there's a cure. And if Liam "caught it" from his MMR vaccine.

Which sets my mind whirring. I have only the vaguest notion of the vaccine-autism link. And I should probably have a working knowledge of such things. Given that we might now have a stake in it. And thus I conduct robust research on the matter. By which I mean falling down an internet rabbit hole from which I barely escape with my sanity. But thanks to the good people who "science," I do manage to identify the extent of the known link between autism and the MMR vaccine. This is as follows:

Nothing.

Thank you for coming to my TED talk.

Tuesday, 11 September

I am trapped in a cat box with Ingrid. Ingrid is preening and elaborately cleaning her bottom. And then someone is shaking the cat box and we are being jostled about and she's calling for her mummy.

'Mummy. Mummy, I think you might be dead. Are you dead, Mummy?'

I open one eye. I am not in a cat box. Liam is shaking my shoulder.

'Hi, mummy. Breakfast mummy.' And he runs off screaming, 'Mummy's alive!'

I wipe some drool from my cheek and register pain. Lots of pain. In my neck and back. Why am I at my desk?

Oh yes. Working late. Writing about cat accessories. The Empawrium project. The deadline is today.

Meowtherfucker.

I jostle the mouse to wake my computer and the document appears. Still not done. Argh.

But I can do this. I can finish it after drop off. I have two and a half hours. Plenty of time.

The morning includes the usual fights about getting dressed and whether or not Charlie has brushed his teeth and whether Liam will permit me to brush his. Then I am helping Liam get his shoes on. And I am mid Velcro-fastening when he decides he doesn't want shoes, stands abruptly and drives the top of his skull directly into my eye socket.

My contact lens dislodges immediately and I think my eye may follow, but there's no time for any of that because Liam is crying, inconsolably. And telling me it's all my fault and why did I have to put my face where he planned to move his head?

Just get them to school. Get them to school and there will be peace. These are the thoughts that drive me forwards. I even manage to get the boys to the gate while it's still open.

That's when Charlie asks for "the jam jars." The ones I was supposedly aware I needed to bring.

'There was a letter in my bag,' he says.

'No. There wasn't.'

'Oh. Yeah, maybe I left it in my tray. Will you bring some?'

parenting, that their child was too young, too old. That they didn't qualify for help. Of children not being seen until they had reached crisis point. I think of Janine asking if Liam was a danger to himself or others.

I have not found answers. Only more questions. And some perspective. There are people - mums, dads, grandparents - who have similar challenges to ours. And some who have it about a bajillion times harder than we do.

I drown my sorrow in chocolate digestives. Then, I check the blog. To my surprise, there are ten messages.

'You coming up?'

I jerk guiltily at the sound of Jake's voice from the doorway of our box room office.

'Yes. Yup. In a tick.' I sound like Mary Poppins. I am also fairly certain I am sporting a crazed expression.

'You okay?' Jake's smile is uneasy. 'What are you up to?'

'Tinder,' I reply, surprising myself with this rare moment of quick wit. 'Swiping right and all that.'

'Ah, yes,' he says, faux seriously. 'Did all mine earlier.' And off he goes.

Shit. What did I just do? Was that a lie? Possibly a lie by omission. Huh. Interesting. In one sense, this does not represent a change. Does it? I have already *not* been telling him about it.

But no. No, this is different. An escalation. I am now *actively* not telling. He asked. I didn't tell.

I consider telling him now. I could. I should. It wouldn't even seem like a big deal.

Do it. You'll feel much better.

Why aren't I doing it?

If this was a film, this would be the time to pull out the old angel-versus-devil-on-the-shoulders trope. My angel has had its say. And now my devil wearily informs me that I know exactly why I am sitting frozen in my office chair. It's because I don't want to tell Jake. Because Jake won't like it. He'll think it's a bad idea.

Angel would interject to point out that he'd be right. There is no upside to any of this. Best case scenario, nobody reads it, life goes on. The worst-case scenarios, of which there are many, involve internet trolls, public humiliation, social banishment.

Devil tells Angel to stop being such a fucking drama queen. That I am currently one blog at the tail end of hundreds. Ranked 405 out of 500. I have a grand total of thirty-two votes. Nobody cares about my blog and I'm enjoying it. So why ruin a good thing. Then she tips my angel off the other shoulder.

Bitch.

Still, she has a point. For now, there's no harm. Nobody cares. If that changes, even a bit, I will tell Jake. But it won't. And I'll tell him anyway once it's all done and over.

My angel is back now, looking both dishevelled and truly pissed.

'Fine,' she retorts. 'Do what you want. See if I care.'

Saturday, 29 September

Charlie has a playdate. Her name is Sakura and she is new to the school having recently moved from Japan. I had absolutely nothing to do with the arranging of this meetup. Charlie had merely informed me of it yesterday.

'Mummy, you need to take me to Sakura's house.'

That was the first I'd heard of Sakura. Apparently she was the replacement pupil for Stefan. Him I remember. Hard not to really when a child is twice the height of every other one in his class.

'Stefan left?' I asked Charlie.

'Yes.'

'When?'

'Dunno.'

'Why?'

'Don't remember.'

Flapping crap. Charlie has never been great at remembering things. Unless they're Pokémon statistics or the date of the creation of the Roman Republic. I get nothing after school each day. Zero. Zilch. And believe me I've tried. I even attempted to follow a Pinterest list of alternative questions to "how was your day." To which Charlie found alternative but equally uninformative answers in place of "dunno" and "good." By contrast, I've heard Mila and Allegra go into forensic detail about each and every one of their interactions and those of their peers. They even pick up interesting gossip from the teachers.

Maybe it's a boy-girl thing. Actually, I remember my mum having the same complaint about me. Genetic then.

Whatever the source, it means I don't even have the address of his supposed playdate let alone a time. For all I know, this is all a figment of Charlie's imagination. Charlie is mystified by my frustration.

'Just call her mum,' he says, not looking away from *Inspector Gadget*.

'I don't have her number. I don't even know who she is.'

Eventually I manage to reach Sakura's mummy, Yui, by process of elimination on the class WhatsApp group. I even get him to their house. Which is on our road. Five doors down.

Unfortunately, there is a language barrier, what with Yui speaking very little English and me absolutely no Japanese. Nor any other language come to that. Nevertheless, she seems very nice and I am pretty sure we agreed that I'd collect him in a couple of hours. It's either that or a couple of days.

Jake decides to take Liam out for a walk. Liam refuses. He sees no utilitarian benefit in leaving the house. But Jake is determined and Liam sees an opportunity.

'I will make a deal,' he informs Jake.

There is much involved negotiation. Then an agreement.

Liam agrees to a walk. It must last no longer than thirty-five minutes. It must not include steep inclines. Or in Liam's words, "lots of hurty ups." In return, Liam will receive a Freddo (specified as pre-refrigerated) and thirty minutes extra TV time at a time and device of his choice, even if that impinges on the hour before bedtime, during which he's not usually allowed TV. Jake, realising his mistake, tries to tack on that these thirty minutes must not be on a school night, but he is too late. The deal is done.

International treaties are simpler.

But at least it gives me a chance to do some work. Two days left. I want to say no. That he can cope without it. That when I was at school, I could have forgotten my own lung at home and my mum wouldn't have fetched it. And anyway, we don't even eat jam.

But then a smug voice in my head chimes in. *A good mum would do it. A good mum would have lots of jam jars on hand at all times.*

I tell her to shut up. But I hate the idea of Charlie being the only one without said jam jar and I am already reasoning that a Marmite jar will probably do just as well.

So I do it. I run home and back, eye streaming all the way, and hand Mrs Keen a Marmite jar. She gives me an imperious look that I interpret as "it was supposed to be a jam jar" and so I shoot back one that means, "we eat Marmite, not jam and at least there *is* a jar."

I arrive home to an email from Fenella Gordon-Bley. Our application to be assessed for an EHCP has been successful. Someone is coming to assess Liam. It occurs to me that I really should know a bit more about this. I resolve to do some research and to find out, once and for all, what an EHCP is.

And I will. Today. After I finish the work for Empawrium and Glowing Ducks.

Except my phone rings. It is Mrs Keen. And just as I am wondering what Liam has done, she says that Charlie has a temperature. Can I pick him up?

Nooooo.

But I tell her I'll be there in five and ask if I can take Liam too, given the paltry amount of time before I'm supposed to collect him anyway. I could swear I hear a tut.

At the school I find Charlie in rude health. Never looked better. He is smiling, he is bouncing. If this child has a temperature, I will eat my own hat. I will eat all the hats.

'He has a temperature. We can't keep him if he has a temperature,' intones Mrs Keen. This is payback for the Marmite. Fearing further reprisals, I do not ask why they checked his temperature in the first place.

I do find out however. Because Charlie tells me on the way home that he told his teacher that his head was hurting.

'They sent me to the nurse and she checked and said I was hot.'

'Does your head still hurt?'

'No,' breezes Charlie. 'Can I have beans on toast for lunch?'

Charlie does not have a temperature. I check. I also decide that these are exceptional circumstances and that I can do whatever it takes to allow me to work. That other people manage to work with their kids at home and that therefore so should I. And thus, I let them play on their iPads while watching TV, something we never let them do. I place each boy in a different room with chocolate, crisps and water. It's better than Christmas. They are entertained. They are fed. They are apart.

This works. For about twenty minutes. Until Liam takes exception to Charlie walking past him on the way to the toilet. There is screaming. I run downstairs to find Liam chasing Charlie round the living room. Charlie is scared. Liam is furious.

Must not let Liam catch Charlie. That is my immediate thought.

I try calling to Liam. Then shouting. I do not try to catch him. I know from experience that this would lead nowhere good. But he's gaining on Charlie and I have to stop this. What would Jake do? Jake's always been better at calming Liam. Inspiration and desperation combine and before I know it, I'm running too.

It's a casual run. More of a jog really.

At first, Liam thinks I am chasing him. But when I merrily pass him on the next loop, he stops.

'Wha' you doin'?' he demands.

'Joining in,' I say. 'We're having a run, right? I wanted to have a go. I think I'm winning.'

Make no mistake. This is the tipping point. I might look like I'm pretending to run a race, but I am holding my figurative breath, waiting to see if my gambit has worked. If I fail, we're looking at a tantrum. But if I succeed…

Miracle of miracles, he laughs. Liam laughs. It worked. Comedy worked. All animosity is forgotten as both boys challenge me to races. Then I make lunch. Beans on toast for Charlie, pasta with butter for Liam.

At 1pm I am back at my desk. Until a zombie horde attacks Liam's Minecraft village. Liam is petrified of zombies. He's not supposed to get zombie hordes in creative mode. But he accidentally played survival mode. Carnage - both virtual and actual - ensues. The zombies destroy the village. Liam destroys his room. I get no work done.

At 3pm, I surrender. There's no way I'm getting this job finished today. I call Ad and ask if I can have until the end of day tomorrow to finish the Empawrium job.

'Oh, sure. Everything okay? Usually it's you who finishes the work before us.'

I assure him that, yes, all is well, and then he tells me about a new client.

'Some holistic thing,' he says. 'Can't remember the name. It's one of those where they remove the vowels. Ah. Here it is. Glisten. Spelled without the "e." You heard of it?'

I have not.

'What is it?'

'Fucked if I know,' Ad guffaws. 'They only want it by the end of the month though. That good for you?'

Nope. Absolutely not.

'Yep. Send it over.'

More work. A lot more work. But that's good. Right? It has to be. I can't exactly say no to Ad. I'm his only copywriter. I'd be leaving him in the lurch. Or worse, he'd find another writer. And he might like them better. And then I would never work again.

So I'll be fine with this new project. Because there is no other option.

Plus, I have until the end of the month. That's ages. I'll work at night. And I'm sure I can find time while Liam's at home. Yes. I can do this.

To celebrate, I allow myself a quick check of Instagram. Gabby's husband, Hugh, has posted a selfie of the two of them. Despite being indoors, he's wearing enormous aviator sunglasses and, while Gabby's smile is natural, he's scowling at the lens. I'm sure he thinks he looks like a hard man. I think he looks like Liam when he hasn't pooed in a couple of days. Underneath it reads, "out with bae #partytime #partylife."

I 'like' a picture of a uni friend's latest graphic designs. And a video of an enormous fluffy cat watching someone cooking a steak.

Ingrid has posted a new video called "Priorities" which I refuse to watch. Then watch.

In it, Ingrid is simpering, cross-legged on a cream - *cream* - sofa, bathed in sunshine from what looks like a lantern skylight.

'I wanted to talk about, like, how I prioritise my life? People always ask, like, how I manage that balance between work and family. And I say it's all about choices. And if there's a choice, I put my family first. You know? And it's not just about being on the PTA or taking them rock climbing or crabbing. It's about being present and, like, with them. You know? Really being with them? No phone. No distractions. It's divine. I mean, if I could, I'd just play with them all day, doing tea parties and art and yoga. And the funny thing is... it's supposed to be me teaching them. But I learn so much.'

'Bollocks,' I snap at the screen. Sir Francis, now back and asleep in the corner, twitches an ear in protest. 'It is though,' I insist. 'Total, utter bollocks.'

'And I'm going to tell you how I do it,' she continues, her smile widening.

I want to say that I roll my eyes and switch it off. I really would. Instead, I sit up straight and lean in, like she's about to impart the secrets of the universe. Because, if there is a trick to enjoying playing endless rounds of Monopoly, I want to know what it is. And because I have learned so very, very few things from my little darlings.

Things My Children Have Taught Me:

1. The worst Lego piece to step on is the 4 by 4 brick.
2. People will say it gets easier. It does not get easier.
3. Gaslighting is real. See point 2.
4. A child can and will fit anything up their nose.
5. Some stains cannot be removed. Even with bleach.

'It's all about organisation,' Ingrid purrs, then lifts something A3 sized. 'I use this calendar from Beauti-Cal.com. Their calendars are useful and beautiful.'

A *calendar*? A sodding calendar? How will that help? I mean, it is a nice-looking calendar. And I do like the stickers that come with it. Ooh. It has stamps too.

'Mummy!' Charlie bellows from downstairs. 'I'm hungry!'

'Hold on.'

But no, I remind myself. I'm not a stamps and stickers mummy. I'm not even that other mum Ingrid mentioned. The one who does things like rock climbing and crabbing. I only have a vague notion of what crabbing even is.

I'm not sure what sort of mummy I am. I work, but I'm not one of the Working Mummies; the doctors and office workers and shop assistants. They have proper, actual jobs. But nor am I a Wunder Mummy; the ones with weekly swimming slots who adore playing with their kids.

'Mummy!'

'One second.'

Not to have an existential crisis or anything, but I never set out to be a Wunder Mummy. I suppose I was aiming for Good Mummy. Or, failing that, Good Enough Mum.

THE AMAZING POWERS OF GOOD ENOUGH MUM

1. Has a general clue what she's doing.
2. Can get through an entire day without a major incident.
3. Has something approaching a life.

Right now, even that feels impossible. And I can't fully understand why. Is it just me? Am I incapable of being a mum? Or maybe being an autism mum is different. A specialist sort of mummying. Like I'm an amateur playing in the professional league.

A notification pings onto my screen. An email. It's from that Blog2Book competition.

> LAST CHANCE TO ENTER. WIN A PUBLISHING DEAL
>
> Fulfil your dreams of being a published author and win £10,000. All you have to do is write!

Being a published author. That *is* my dream. Or was my dream. Back when I dreamed. And now I'm humming *I Dreamed a Dream* from *Les Misérables*. Which is the lament sung by Fantine, a destitute character who sacrificed everything just to support her child in 19th century France. So things could be much, much worse. At least I never had to sell my hair or front teeth. Unlike poor old Fantine. Christ her life was shit.

My life is not shit. It's fine. I don't need a dream. What I need to do is become a better mum. I need to learn about autism and how I can make Liam's life better. And, by extension, all of our lives. To put my family first. And what about my job? I'm already working flat out and still struggling to meet deadlines. I have no time to dream or enter competitions.

Right. That's decided then. I'm not doing it.

Phew. That's a relief actually.

I minimise the email only to find Ingrid's frozen face beaming at me from YouTube.

Ingrid gets both. She gets the job *and* the family. And that's fine too. *Tow*-tally fine.

I mean it's not. But that's life. If there was a way that I could enter this competition and still learn more about being a better mum, then I'd do it. But there isn't.

Is there?

It pops unbidden into my mind; the merest hint of an idea.

Maybe I'll just test it out. I'll just open a new document and jot down the idea. Just to see it in print.

> The Special Mum: The diary of a common garden mummy navigating the world of special needs.

There it is. Okay, I've done that. Done.

I could always jot down some thoughts.

Which I do. In between shouting several rounds of "just a minute!" into the air much as Yosemite Sam would shoot cartoon bullets. And then I jot down more. And, before I know it, I'm typing quite a lot more. It's all a bit frenzied. A click clacking, foggy, frantic mess of all my frustrations and fears and doubts. Like emptying out all the disparate fragments of my mind and piecing them together into a form that might make sense.

And now there is a new message on my screen.

> Thank you for entering Blog2Book. Your blog, The Special Mum, is live!

I am then summoned once more with a cry of "Mummy!"

Wednesday, 12 September

Woke up in the office again after another late night working to finish the Empawrium project. This time with Sir Francis looking down at me in bemused disgust. Like he had expected better of me. No idea why or how I ended up in the foetal position on the carpet. Presumably I tried to make it to bed but gave up.

On the plus side, I got the work done and emailed it to Ad just before collecting Liam. He emailed back with two more new projects. They are multiplying. Like how they tell you not to pluck out a grey hair because two more will grow back in its place.

So, counting Glistn, now I have three new projects in total. But it's all completely fine because I have until the end of the month to complete them. That's ages. Loads of time. Easy. I am in no way cacking myself.

Thursday, 13 September

We were about halfway up *that* hill today when Charlie asked me if I'd put "the knitting yarn" in his bag. As though it was something we had discussed and arranged. As in, "you said you had the keys, right?" Except this was the first I was hearing of it.

'It wasn't on either of the apps, in your bag, or in an email.'

'Oh, I know mummy. Mrs Rochester had the idea yesterday and thought it would be fun.'

I'll bet she did. Well, I was not playing ball on this one. And certainly not ball of yarn. I informed Charlie that:

a) I do not own any knitting yarn on account of the fact that I do not knit; and

b) I would not be running home and back to bring any.

'But mummy, all mummies knit.'

I did not allow myself to tabulate just how many myriad stereotypes this assumption invoked. Nor could I imagine where Charlie would have picked up such an old-fashioned idea. Jake and I may not be a paradigm of perfect parenting, but we've always done our best to steer our kids away from bad messaging. We don't even let them watch old Disney movies after I read an article about how badly some of them have aged. These were things that had never occurred to me. Like how Snow White is 14 when a stranger kisses her. And that the creep does so while she's asleep. All of which to say, I have no idea where the all-mummies-knit thing came from.

'When have you ever seen me knit?' I asked. 'Or Nisha? Or auntie Gabby?'

He really had to think about that one. His eyebrows even knitted together in an adorable little frown.

Now I am home and perusing my emails. Ad's sent over the information about the new projects. One of the projects is fine. A local law firm needing copy for a revamped website. The next is fairly straightforward. If only in so far as I can vaguely comprehend what it is that the client actually does. His name is Guru Chi and he is a life coach and pet healer. I certainly have questions. For example, whose life gets coached? But there's nothing insurmountable there.

As for the third project, I know that the client is called Glistn and that... I think they sell... Or provide...

Nope. Nope that's it. That's all I know. Everything else is comprehensively incomprehensible. It all sounds like the random rantings of a senile great aunt. Take this sentence in their company description:

> Glistn is a revolutionary redirection of emotional inflation, harnessing of the power of being and externalising the inner goddess.

After half an hour of guessing, I narrow it down to:
1. a mood enhancer
2. tampons - I wouldn't put anything past the industry that thought we'd want to rollerblade in white shorts while on our period
3. fish oil. I'm always hearing extraordinary things about fish oil

Friday, 14 September

9:25am

A spot of unplanned paperwork to get done this morning before I can do my work. It's another form. *The* EHCP form. The real one this time. Apparently the first one was a drill.

It's a bit annoying what with the bazillion projects I have on the go, but it's fine. I'll have this done in thirty minutes tops.

11:45am

What the actual flapping crap. Two hours I've been at this. Two hours and twenty-two minutes to be exact. And have I finished this form? No.

Have I even started the form?

I don't know. I thought I had. Offered up pretty much everything short of my immortal soul. Then scrolled down the page to discover I'd reached Section A.

Which made no sense. Surely, I reasoned, I had just completed section A.

There is no letter before A. And there had been a section. It was pre-labour all over again.

Pre-Labour: The First One

I endured two weeks of pre-labour with Charlie. Although I don't call it that. That's far too civilised. As though it was an amuse bouche. Oh, no. I prefer to say 336 hours straight of haha-fooled-you-I-can't-believe-it's-not-labour followed by fifteen hours of the real sodding thing.

And now I was experiencing pre-sectioning. Unacceptable. Nevertheless, I rallied and reminded myself that it was merely a few more pages. That writing words was my job. And that Fenella Gordon Bley was too scary to ignore. And so, on I faced Section A.

SECTION A: KEY BACKGROUND INFORMATION

That was it. The entire wordage of Section A. The form itself offered zero guidance as to what I was supposed to write. Just a massive blank space in which I was to write it. I decided I'd go back to that one and moved onto section B.

SECTION B: THE CHILD'S VIEWS, INTERESTS AND ASPIRATIONS

Then another yawning blank space.
I'd snorted. Couldn't help it. It was the word "views." All I could imagine was a *Newsnight* situation with Liam opining on the latest movement of the pound sterling and the recent foreign policy shift. It was ridiculous.
I'm not saying that Liam doesn't have views, interests and aspirations. It's just that they broadly resemble those of a Bond villain. He wants living robots and all the money in the world and a snail army.
That's when I had the dazzling idea of checking the rest of the form. Just to prepare. Only to see that it was twenty-five pages long.
Twenty-five pages.
I had goggled at this, unable to imagine how I was supposed to provide that volume of content. Did it even exist? Liam was four years old. There simply wasn't that much to say.
Over the next hour, I came to a conclusion about The EHCP Form: *It is not a form.* Much in the way the Tardis is not a police box. Oh, it looks like a form. It's a document with words and spaces for answers. But – and I cannot stress this enough – it is *not* a form. For starters, there are no questions.

No obvious requests for specific information. Only headings with words like "sensory" and "cognitive." Then wormhole-sized spaces underneath which I am presumably supposed to fill with words. Oh, and an invitation to "Please feel free to append extra sheets if you run out of space."

I had then given some consideration to, if not a form, what is it? A thought experiment? An MK Ultra exercise? A Kafka novel?

And that's when I realised another thing: I had no idea what I was doing this for. Other than because Fenella Gordon-Bley had told me to. What exactly was an EHCP?

The council's answer was of little assistance, defining it as:

> A document that identifies the extra needs of a child and sets out the additional support to meet those needs.

This means absolutely nothing. Broken down to its constituent parts and then reassembled, the best interpretation I came up with was that an EHCP is a plan. Or, more precisely still, a plan to plan.

I may have primal screamed. Then I zoned out for a bit and came up with the following:

WOULD YOU LIKE TO DESCEND INTO MADNESS?

SHORT ON TIME?

FILL IN AN EHCP FORM!

EHCP FORMS: BECAUSE THE RED TAPE WASN'T RED ENOUGH

After that, I discovered that EHCP fits perfectly into the Aretha Franklin song *R-E-S-P-E-C-T*. And by perfectly, I mean you must mangle one of the world's most iconic songs to shoehorn it in. Which I am sorry to say I did. At considerable volume.

'*R-E-S-P-E-H-C-P, find out what it means to me...*'

This little detour eventually led to where I am now. And where I believe I was always destined to arrive: Mummyweb.

In theory, Mummyweb is an online parenting forum; a place where parents can share problems, questions and answers. Their tag line? *The village it takes to raise a child.*

I search the site for posts about EHCPs. The good news is, I am not alone in my confusion. There are many, many – oh so very many - piles of threads about EHCPs.

As for the bad news, it is that I have no time to read them. It's time to collect Liam.

8:09pm

Jake can't understand what all the fuss is about.

'It's a form,' he states when I show it to him. As though it's obvious.

'It is not a form.' The words boil out of my mouth like I'm an overfilled pot.

He suggests I let him take a look and that we can work on it together. Which I do. Gladly. The questions begin ten minutes later.

'What sort of background information do they want?'

'Does Liam have "views"?'

'Are you sure this is all of it? There aren't any questions.'

'What do they actually want?'

'What is this for, exactly?'

I have no answers. But I do have a song.

Sunday, 16 September

'Remember when partying meant something totally different?' Nisha asks absently, shovelling a handful of salt and vinegar crisps into her mouth.

'You mean downing a bottle of supermarket pinot then going to a crap club where we danced on any elevated surface we weren't too drunk to reach and ending up barefoot at a chippy?'

'Yeah.'

'Nope. No recollection of that at all. This is all there is now.'

We gaze pensively at the thirty children throwing themselves around a church hall to the sounds of SClub7. Charlie is dancing with Lexi. A minute ago, he was dancing with Ava. Ten minutes ago it was Sorcha. Now Lexi is trying to lift him and spin him around while Charlie spreads his arms out like he's Kate Winslet on the Titanic. Charlie has the enviable ability to derive endless joy from any situation and draw others in with him. Like a puppy.

Children's parties are a staple feature of my weekends. And, given that there is at least one a week, there is little time for much else. I am always the one who goes to the parties. Never Jake. I do the parties and anything else that involves "people." Jake does sports and being "the fun one." Today, he's taken Liam to Sunday lunch at his parents.

It's worth saying that this is my second party in as many days. At the same venue. With the same entertainer: Captain Wiggles. Yesterday I was here with Liam. Today is Charlie's turn.

The thing about doing both in such quick succession is that I can't help but compare and contrast the experiences. It's like comparing the organising of a picnic with planning a coup. There is simply more that divides than unites the two.

How I attend a party with Charlie

1. I attend.
2. I bring Charlie.
3. Half the time, I remember the gift.

That's it.

Parties with Liam: Rules of Engagement

1. Perform Recon: Upon arrival at any given venue, I become Brad Pitt in *Spy Game*. I note exits, layouts, and potential threats. Which kids may wind him up? Is the entertainer versed in crowd control?
2. Employ advance countermeasures: Choosing and adopting optimal position to stand (never sit) for maximum visibility.
3. Maintain alertness: I am at Defcon One at all times. Or is it five that's the high one? No. One. I think. Basically whichever one best describes a constant state of readiness and preparedness to pounce into action at the merest hint of trouble. This means no socialising, no snacking, and no checking of my phone.

Yesterday, I got sloppy. I allowed myself to get distracted.

It had started off okay. I had done the recon and identified the ideal observation post: against one wall, equidistant between two possible escape routes (internal doors) on either side of the hall and within sight of the extraction point aka the exit. My eyes were laser focused on The Principal aka Liam as his eyes were laser focused on Captain Wiggles aka the entertainer.

It was immediately apparent that Captain Wiggles was the primary threat.

Liam loves entertainers. Especially the slapstick ones. And I was worried he might try to "get involved." There was precedent for this. The Mr Bubbles incident. It hadn't been pretty. It ended with me dragging him away like I was his best mate holding him back from a fight with the biggest bloke in the bar.

So I was focused. I was in the zone.

I was ambushed.

'Maya, hi. How are you?' Ingrid sidled up to me.

Keep it light, I told myself. *Light, light, light.* But maintain visual of The Principal.

'Very fine thank you.' I had said, eyes not leaving my son. 'And how are you today?'

'Really? I heard Liam's been having some issues. All okay?'

'What?'

'So nice of Mel to invite Liam after what happened.'

It was a lot to take in. My brain froze like an overtasked laptop. What was she talking about? And who was Mel?

Then it got worse.

'Ingrid, hi.' It was one of the Wunder Mummies. Swiftly joined by another. And another. And then I was in the middle of a goddamned gaggle. It was like the Alfred Hitchcock film *The Birds*. Where one minute there was one solitary crow and the next they covered an entire fence. I just stood there, air kisses flying around me like deadly pecks along with exclamations of "so good to see you." As if they hadn't seen each other within the past 24 hours.

By the time I extricated myself and looked around, the kids were no longer sitting. They were in the obligatory lunch conga line. The lunch conga line is an inextricable facet of the children's birthday party. I believe it is enshrined in the party entertainer constitution:

> *Thou shalt shepherd the children to dine via the traditional dance of the conga lest they stray.*

As the line meandered towards the brightly decorated tables, I scanned every child in turn. Where was Liam?

We have lost sight of The Principal.

Shit. Oh fuck.

I think it was then that Ingrid asked me something about baby teeth. Then I heard another mummy gush, 'James has lost all his baby teeth and it's well ahead of when he's supposed to. The dentist said it's a sign of advanced oral development.'

Even as I scoured the room for any sign of my son, I remember thinking that surely losing teeth wasn't an accomplishment. As I visually confirmed that all three doors were closed and the world around me faded away, I contemplated that there was no achievement too random for parents to compete over.

I don't remember asking if anyone could see Liam. I don't remember who helped me. I do remember Captain Wiggles, puppet still on hand, asking if everything was okay. And panic. I remember cold, sweaty panic.

Liam knew nothing of this drama. He was ensconced behind the curtains of the stage, where we eventually found him.

And now I am back at the scene of my most recent trauma for the birthday party of Charlie's classmate, Maceo. Nisha's son, Aran was invited because the two play football together. Which is great because it means I don't have to socialise with the other mummies.

Not that I have anything against these mummies. Well, not all of them. Most of them are perfectly nice. Last year, when Liam was still at nursery, I was around for pickup and drop-off. So I chatted with them at the school gates and at parties. But I haven't seen them all for so long. I feel like an outsider. And I worry they will have heard about Liam's issues at school. And that if they haven't yet, they will.

Ooh. Cupcakes.

'Here's what I don't get,' Nisha is saying. 'I read that page you sent me on the NHS site with the symptoms of autism. And I went through the signs and... they're so... vague. Like the one about kids being upset when told no? What kid isn't? Last week, Saira screamed so loudly when I told her she couldn't watch TV, I thought the neighbours would call social services. I sort of judge them for not doing it. Not sure what more it would take. She sounded like she was being stabbed repeatedly in a shower. What was I saying?'

'That all kids get upset when told no,' I provide, settling on a cake with pink icing.

'Right. I'm saying it's a question of where you draw the line. I mean, sometimes it's obvious. Like my neighbour's five-year-old. Have you met Annie?'

I have not met Annie.

'Anyway, her son is completely non-speaking, never smiles, never makes eye contact. He's obviously autistic. Liam though? He's always smiling and laughing and he makes eye contact.'

'I don't know.' I say through a mouthful of cupcake. Though it comes out as "ay-oh-oh." Because cupcake.

Someone else might have asked me to repeat myself. But not Nisha. As my best friend, she can understand me even at my most incoherent, whether through sobs or drunken slurring or baked goods. It is a skill we do not question. Like how Lassie's owners could interpret that a bark meant that Timmy was down a well again and not that Lassie was, say, hungry.

'I've thought all of that,' I admit, cupcake now internalised. 'I don't even know which outcome I prefer.'

'Surely it's better if he hasn't got it.'

'Not really. At least if we have a label or a condition there's stuff we can do. They'll have research and techniques and things. Otherwise we're back to square none.'

'Oh. Heads up.' Nisha murmurs as she dusts herself off. 'They're doing that bloody lunch conga line.'

That they are. And unlike yesterday, I spot my child immediately. Charlie is at the front, smiling ecstatically as he congas his way to the tables. The birthday boy, right behind him, doesn't seem to mind that his position has been usurped. In fact, he offers Charlie his place at the head of the table.

Charlie has this effect on people. He's always being given things. I can only hope that he uses his powers for good. It's not that he would ever do anything intentionally bad. But I do worry about him accidentally starting a cult.

Tuesday, 18 September

Oh, dear god. I can't. I cannot. After school clubs are back. They've been back for two days and I am already planning my escape to live with the turtles in the Galapagos Islands.

I google "Can I live in the Galapagos Islands."

No. Apparently, they're very picky about who gets to live there. Because it's so nice. Ooh, they have penguins too. I love penguins.

Charlie wants to do all the clubs. Liam wants none. Which means they'll be on totally different afternoon schedules. And so this entails remembering different pickup times for each day of the week. And gasping at the cost. How much for tech club? Why? They don't even have to pay for a venue. It's run at the school. Are they including the cost of buying him a computer?

Then there is the practicality of coordinating the days Nisha can collect Charlie because Aran also has clubs. Some of these clubs are at school, but not on the same days as Charlie's clubs. Others are elsewhere. And remembering to bring things. And for Charlie to remember to bring them back.

Yesterday was drama class, today is guitar. At 10am, Mrs Keen, the school secretary phones to tell me that Charlie had forgotten his guitar. Which was just as well because I need to bring in Liam's show and tell.

For the record, I had not forgotten about show and tell. That would require being told about it in the first place. There had been nothing on the apps, no emails. For Galapagos' sake, isn't it enough that I get him to school for the five minutes a day he spends there? Now there are accessories?

I rummage furiously through the house for something worthy of both showing and telling. Everything is fraught with danger. Danger of forgetting it at school or it being damaged or, as in the case of the now empty snail house, reminding him of something that must never again darken our doorstep.

I choose a book. *Don't Let the Pigeon Drive the Bus*. It is, quite simply, a masterpiece of satirical absurdity. The best book ever illustrated. It has become our family bible. And Liam, quite rightly, thinks it is hilarious.

When I get to the school, I mention to Mrs Keen about not knowing about show and tell.

'I asked the class rep to put it on the WhatsApp group.'

Of course there's a class WhatsApp group. Every class has one. I'm on Charlie's one, although they never post anything.

So now there are three apps, emails, bag notes and two WhatsApp groups.

I cannot. Forget the Galapagos. I'll settle for the Shetlands.

Wednesday, 19 September

Big news. Big, important news. We have a date for Liam's NHS appointment. His autism assessment. This is completely unexpected. Dr Myrtle had warned us that these are often months, even years down the line. Ours is next week.

I got the call today. In the middle of mine and Liam's fifth round of Monopoly. They had a cancellation and would I like an appointment next Thursday?

And I said yes. Well, actually, I said, 'Hold on Liam, mummy's on the phone. Take my turn for me. Sorry, yes. Next Thursday is great.' Then, 'Yes, that time I meant you.'

Of course I said yes. Why wouldn't I? Getting an answer in a few days rather than a few months? It's a no brainer.

Because I have realised something. I don't care what they tell me. I just want an answer. Whatever it is, I want to know. Because then we can get on with helping our child.

Thus I spend all afternoon in the best mood. Until Jake gets home. And is all "practical."

'Can we get everything ready by then?' he asks. His tone, by the way, is the same one he uses when the boys ask for a foodstuff we know for a fact they don't like. As in, "Are you sure you want Marzipan? I know it looks like a frog, but you spat it into daddy's eye last time."

Well, I am not a child and I know exactly what I'm doing.

'I'll get it done.'

He's not giving up that easily though.

'And you know what it is we have to do? All the documents and evidence we'll need? Because we still haven't finished that EHCP form for school.'

'You agreed that that thing isn't really a form.'

'And what about your work?'

'I have until the end of the month. Loads of time.'

'Fine, but it still seems like a lot.'

Our eyes are locked. This is a challenge. Like Phileas Fogg wagering he can travel the world in eighty days. Only without The Reform Club. And not fictional. He won that bet, right? I've never actually read any Jules Verne. I should. I should read *Around the World in Eighty Days*. And *Journey to the Center of the Earth*.

Where was I? Oh. Yes.

'I'll get it done,' I enunciate. Then wish I had a mic to drop.

Reception Class Chat
Today

Maya Harris Has Been Added.

Emily
Hey! Pls welcome Liam's mummy Mata. Not sure how bt she was missed off class list.

Thursday, 20 September

The bastarding NHS form is trying to outdo the sodding EHCP one in the category of "Form that is not really a form." For example, is it a form if it's just a request for you to recount everything that has ever happened to your child, any other children in your family, other people's children, you, and your extended family? No. No it is bloody not. That's a family history book.

> Please feel free to append extra sheets if you run out of space.

Argh.

Oh, and then there are the requests for copies of every document ever produced about my son. I dig through old folders and files like a dog looking for a bone. I search for Liam's birth certificate, his drawings from nursery, and his Red Book.

Thoughts on The Red Book

Like all new parents, I got a Red Book for each of my boys. It's a complete record of your child's development and health, from birth weight to vaccinations. Basically, at the point in your life where you're at your most discombobulated, forgetful and sleep deprived, you are asked to become custodian to a physical document your child will need forever. It would be like giving Frodo the One Ring when he was blind drunk. It was inevitable I'd lose it eventually.

And I think eventually has arrived. I cannot find it. I do find *my* birth certificate. And Charlie's Red Book.

Oh god. There's no way I can finish this by tomorrow. And I can't ask Jake for help. Then he'd know he'd been right about this. I'd never hear the end of it.

As a soundtrack to my misery, my phone hasn't stopped buzzing since I was added to that bloody reception class WhatsApp group. I don't remember Charlie's class group ever being this active. There are questions about reading books and the standard of maths being taught and whether the grass in the field is dangerously high.

Bzzzz

My phone. Again.

Oh, that is it, I fume as I retract my head from the back of a cupboard and reach for my mobile. You lot are being muted.

But the notification is not for yet another question about whether anyone's cleaner has extra hours to spare. It's an email. An email I almost delete. Partly because it looks like spam.

NEW VOTES FOR YOUR BLOG

They do like their ALL CAPS at Blog2Book. Is there anything sufficiently exciting or urgent to warrant type-shouting it? I have the same issue with the boys' headmaster.

Mr Davies writes almost exclusively in capital letters. Sometimes, it almost makes sense. Like, "NO after-school club TODAY" or "DO NOT PARK on yellow lines." Other instances, like "WELCOME our NEW pe TEACHER" or "Buy Cakes TODAY", do raise more questions than they answer.

It's as though he thinks we are all feckless idiots who don't read school messages and that's the only way to break through the fog. Which is probably true. As such, my own internal filter has adapted to take note of such hyperbolic missives.

Then when I realise what it is, I consider deleting it anyway. I'd forgotten all about the blog. Hadn't wanted to think about it. I had grasped almost immediately after posting it that I had overshared. Despite changing all the names and writing anonymously, the whole thing felt wrong. And Jake would hate it. He detests and deeply distrusts putting anything online unless absolutely necessary. Believes that it's just an invitation for trolls and scammers. He doesn't even have a single social media account.

Then I think, what's the harm? I'll look. I need to close the account anyway.

YOU HAVE 10 VOTES

Would you look at that? Ten whole people had read my words. Not just that, but they had then clicked the vote button. They tapped their mice. Or their screen. For me.

It's rather thrilling.

Maybe I have a chance of winning, says a little voice. Maybe there weren't that many entries. Or they were all rubbish. Or accidentally deleted by some bug in the system.

Except then I check the list of entries.

Fuaaaarrrgghck.

The Special Mum is at number 456. Out of a total of 505 entries. It is sandwiched between Wokerati Warrior and The Power of Glove. I am slightly more popular than a blog that reviews gloves, but less so than a 50-year-old bloke lamenting that all millennials are snowflakes.

The top 3 entries are as follows:

Blog2Book Entries: Top 3

Blog Name: The12

About: A gang of students tell all about life in the dorms. Geordie Shore at university.

1324 votes

Blog Name: Ol' McConnells

About: The chronicles of the funny parts of farm life with what appear to be some very charismatic chickens. Their latest post is entitled, "Who Run the World?" alongside a photo of a line-up of "the girls" a-laying.

1105 votes

Blog Name: F*ck Picnics

About: The diary of a teddy bear. A teddy bear with seemingly deep pockets who reviews the world's top hotels.

1045 votes.

I browse through other entries. Many are travel blogs with stunning photos of beautiful, exotic places. Or aspirational parenting blogs like, Peas in Pod, about the life of six-year-old triplets and child models, Molly, Melody and Maddy. There are quite a few book blogs. Which is rather meta if you think about it. The idea of turning a book blog into a book.

I don't stand a chance. Of course not. It's not like I had expected to. Plus I don't have time for this. It requires me to post at least once a week. Which would mean posting today or tomorrow. Impossible. I've got the three projects for Ad. One of them for a product I cannot even identify. Plus, I still have to recount every second of the life of my second born for the NHS.

I guide my mouse to the top of the screen, intending to close my account and leave the blogging to those rich in time and eggs.

Ooh. Look. A little red envelope. Messages. I'll just take a little look...

Six messages. For me?

Nope. No. Five are for me. I'm fairly certain the one asking about chicken feed was sent to me in error. I forward it to the chicken blog people.

But still. Five real messages.

A mum in Exeter said I had saved her sanity. That just knowing she wasn't the only one going through something like this had brought her to tears. Happy ones.

A dad in Croydon said his son had recently been diagnosed at ten and that he wished he'd read my blog years ago.

Another wrote:

Dear Special Mum. I love your blog. Made me laugh.

All three asked that I keep going and said they couldn't wait to read my next entry. For about five minutes, I channel Sally Fields at the 2011 Oscars in a "They like me! They really like me!" sort of way.

Then anxiety kicks in. Because there's no way I can keep doing the blog.

Is there? And what if I do? What if my next entries are crap? What if I can't think of anything else to write? What if these people are counting on me and I let them down?

Fortunately, the final two messages disabuse me of any notion of a job well done. Both writers have gone to great lengths to inform me that I am wrong. About everything. And that I am a terrible, ungrateful, uninformed, careless mother.

God, the relief.

If my blog does become crap, at least it might turn these two into my greatest fans. Although maybe not. They don't seem to agree on much other than my wrongness.

One took issue with my stance on the MMR vaccine. She said it was poison and part of a globalist plot to control the population. She then directed me to a website that promised to cure autism.

The other did not believe in autism. Nor in what they called "LBBBQ." Or that the Earth was round. They were not however incurable in their scepticism. They did believe the lizard people were "behind it all." And had I tried Glistn?

FFS.

So there. I shouldn't keep blogging. I have no business doing so. I should stick to writing about high-end cat trees and my son's nursery experience.

Oh shit. Speaking of my son, it's pickup time.

Liam and I have developed a new routine this week. Or maybe it's a cycle. Whatever its label, it is intolerable. It has unfolded identically for each one of the last three days after school. Every day, about a third of the way through our walk home, Liam has an epic tantrum. It is masterful. A work of art. A review would commend it for its complete coverage of the genre, reprising as it does, all the classic moves.

Tantrums: The Greatest Hits

1. Demanding the Impossible: On Monday, he asked for a robot that could talk and think. On Tuesday it was all of Charlie's toys. Wednesday was never having to go to sleep ever again.

2. Outrage at Impossibility of the Impossible: When informed that he cannot have the world's first functioning AI/everything Charlie owns/the sleep schedule of Maggie effing Thatcher, he does his best approximation of The Hulk. Which I find all the more impressive as he's never watched or even read The Hulk. There's no shirt ripping – not yet anyway – and the only colour alteration leans towards red rather than green, but the rest is all there: The roar, the grimace and, of course, the destruction. Except instead of... Actually I have no idea what The Hulk does. Destroy cities? Save people? Is he good or evil? Whatever. The point is, Liam becomes focused on destroying his own version of an immortal enemy: Me.

And because we are on a street with a road and cars and maybe the occasional person, I cannot move away. I must in fact stay as close as I can, especially given the likelihood of number 3.

3. Putting himself in as much danger as possible: Liam has been known to try to scale third floor balconies and jump into rivers, but a quiet residential street does somewhat limit his environmental opportunities. He mostly attempts to make a dash for the road. Thankfully, again, this is on a peaceful street with minimal traffic. But it's still nonetheless terrifying.

On each day, these tantrums have lasted around an hour and a half. Residents have peered out, then shuffled out to politely inquire if everything is okay. Which it patently isn't.

'Fine thanks,' I responded on each such occasion, as I deflected blows and swipes.

After standing awkwardly for a minute, possibly pondering the prescribed etiquette, no doubt considering and discarding the possibility that I was kidnapping this child, they asked if there was anything they could do.

'Lovely of you to offer,' I said, while preventing my child from launching in front of a bicycle or a pigeon. 'Nothing comes to mind.' I have yet to think of something they might have done by way of assistance.

Still, it's not all bad. We have provided entertainment for dogs and cats and, on one occasion, a fox. When Liam does eventually stop, we are both exhausted. But not too tired to play Monopoly.

But not today. I have determined that today will be different. Today, I will drive. As long as I can get him in the car, we can at least get home and provide entertainment for our own cat and neighbours rather than random ones.

Except Liam, sensing the ruse, refuses to get into the car. I try putting him in. Not possible. He is too strong. And anyway, he knows how to undo a seatbelt.

Something is different though. Nobody emerges from their homes. This is both a relief and an indictment of my existence. Liam must notice, because instead of trying for the road, he runs to the front door of one of the houses. And knocks.

I am stunned by this course alteration. So stunned, I do nothing. I just watch.

The nice old lady who answers the door is delighted, if surprised, to find a small boy there.

'Hello, good to meet you,' he says. And it's like he's Eliza Doolittle at the end of *My Fair Lady*. Or George VI in *The King's Speech*. He speaks as clearly as he has ever spoken before. Instantly, all the hitting and pinching and kicks are forgotten. I beam with pride at my adorable little man. Then he says, 'Can I live with you?'

The nice old lady is taken aback. I am mortified, but still frozen in place. Both Liam and I watch the lady with morbid curiosity.

'Oh how lovely,' she chuckles nervously. 'But you should live with your lovely mummy.'

To which he explains that he no longer wishes to reside with me and that I am a terrible mummy and he would rather live with her. When she demurs again, he lists the qualities that make him an excellent housemate, including being good at building Lego and not needing much space. Both of which are true.

Having failed to convince her, he demonstrates quite the can-do spirit and moves onto the next house. And the next. And I follow and say nothing because this is better than the alternative. With each house, his patter becomes increasingly slick. Until, at the last house, he assures the old couple that not only is he willing to share a room with others, but that he is confident he could finish their extension for free if they're willing to consider Lego as a building material.

I swear I see the husband contemplating it. Which I can't help but think speaks volumes for Liam's persuasiveness. Even if it did involve him telling them that I said he couldn't call Childline. Which I hadn't. I had merely suggested that his problem – not liking his dinner – was not sufficiently serious to merit such a call. I explain this with a nervous, we'll-look-back-and-laugh-about-this-someday laugh. They do not join in.

If there is one positive to dredge from the gooey cesspit that was today, it is that I write about it for the blog. The words trip from my fingers onto the keyboard with ease. I even feel better afterwards. This is like therapy. Free therapy.

I shouldn't feel guilty about free therapy, should I? It can only be a good thing. Which is how I justify not telling Jake about it when he asks about my day. I shouldn't neglect my mental health just because he doesn't like the Internet.

The cat isn't convinced though. Sir Francis sees right through my lies and remonstrates by pointing his bottom in my exact direction and farting.

Friday, 21 September

It is bake sale day at school. I know this because I receive a text at 7:05am – we get texts now on top of everything else – telling me to "BRING CAKES." I wonder whether I could get away with sending such a message to everyone I know on a regular basis. A moment later, another one pings through. "BRING CASH."

I have neither cakes nor cash. Which could be the title of my autobiography: *No Cakes, No Cash: The Maya Harris Story.*

I do eventually find a twenty-pound note in the pocket of a coat I haven't worn for a year. I'm hardly going to give Charlie twenty quid though. He'll come back with the entire stall. Actually, that sounds good. I bloody love homemade cake. And some of the mums are amazing bakers. I cannot bake. It is a source of great distress. Plus it's for charity. I'd give twenty quid to charity. So I hand it to him with strict instructions to bring back change.

An email informs me that today is also hearing test day. Which is fine. Good even. Until I go to collect Liam at midday.

'The hearing tests are this afternoon,' Mrs Keen tells me. 'You can either bring him back at two or take him to your GP.'

At least Liam doesn't go selling himself door-to-door today on the way home. He reverts back to a standard tantrum.

And to top it all off, my first-born child does not know how to pick cake. When Nisha drops him off after school, he is holding a multipack of mini rolls and a fiver. I glare at the purple packaging.

'Had they run out of all the proper cakes?' I ask him.
'No.'
'And you went for mini rolls?' How is this possible?
'It was tidy,' he explains. 'All the other stuff had icing everywhere.'

I sigh dreamily. Icing, icing everywhere. That's the dream. And instead, I have just paid fifteen pounds for a pack of glorified sponges.

Saturday, 22 September

We go to Gabby and Hugh's house for lunch. Not that it is a house. I mean, if it's a house then it shares a category with our 1950's semi. And that's only possible in the same way the word "cat" encompasses both Sir Francis and a Siberian tiger.

It might be a mansion. Maybe an estate. Possibly a palace. Whatever it is, it's perfect. It doesn't matter how many times I've been here; I never cease to be astounded by the perfection. They have one of those carriage driveways the size of an airport runway encircled by a redbrick wall and dotted with perfectly coiffed topiary. Because one does not trim topiary. It is, invariably, coiffed. Same goes for poodles.

Their entrance hall could accommodate our entire first floor and they have a sweeping staircase that splits in two directions. My favourite room however is the kitchen. Dear god, the kitchen. It is a masterpiece. Fuck museums, I say. I'll take the showrooms of Poggenpohl and Schiffini any day.

The boys love it here too. Not for the quality of workmanship or storage capabilities, but for the cinema room and general running space. They always spend the first few minutes at Gabby's bolting around the place. As though I usually keep them caged.

Mila and Allegra watch them do this now with a sort of bemused detachment. Whenever I see Gabby's girls alongside my boys, I am struck by the vast differences. At all of nine years of age, Mila and Allegra are basically little women. And not in the sweet, Louisa May Alcott way. These two would eat Jo March for breakfast. They are beautiful, intelligent, wealthy, and unshakably secure in the knowledge of all three.

Jake and I join Gabby and Hugh on the vast corner sofa that occupies just a fraction of the kitchen space.

'How've you been?' asks my brother-in-law, his arms slung wide on the back of the sofa either side of him. Confident and relaxed, he looks every inch the king of his castle. He is one of the only men I know handsome enough to pull off an entirely bald head. Some men would probably trade in their whole head of hair for a modicum of his chiselled jaw and piercing eyes.

He is, in short, the very model of modern success. Except that his success is anything but modern. Hugh is Hugh Courtenay. He is heir to the Courtenay empire, a major player in the international pig farming industry established in 1066. Hugh was parachuted into senior management in the family biz straight out of university. He has since taken on the role of CEO, his father having retired a few years ago. But from talking to him, you would think he'd founded the effing company. In fact, he frequently lectures us – and especially Jake – on business matters.

'Oh, you know. Nothing new,' Jake glimmers. 'Boar-ing really.'

I shoot him a glare. It has begun.

Jake and I have a little bit too much fun with the source of Hugh's wealth. We compete to drop into the conversation as many piggy puns as possible. Jake usually wins in terms of quantity, but that's because he shamelessly shoehorns in any old gag. I prefer to maintain a level of quality in my word play. My greatest achievement was over dinner with the in-laws when I mentioned how much I loved Hamlet. Jake almost choked on his roast chicken.

Hugh, who can never be said to be the sharpest boar in the pen, has never clocked on. Gabby has. And frequently tells us off for it.

Today, Hugh is in top form. We all listen as he talks about his excellent tennis technique and reminds us how he once almost became a seeded player.

'Remember when we played, Jakey boy? Gave you quite a thrashing.'

'Yes, you *shoat* me,' sayeth my husband.

Dammit. That was a good one.

Over lunch, Hugh waxes lyrical about his macrobiotic diet and how we should give up processed food.

'Wouldn't that be bad for business?' Jake asks.

Hugh is nonplussed at being interrupted.

'What? Oh. Yes. Quite right.'

'Don't hog the sauce, babe,' I murmur, congratulating myself on the rare two in one.

Jake coughs.

'Auntie Maya,' says Mila. 'Why don't you ever wear makeup?'

'Mils,' Gabby chides.

'What? She needs it.'

'Her pores *are* huge mummy,' Allegra confirms. 'You should let Mils do your makeup, Auntie Maya. She's a pro.'

'She is really good,' admits Gabby.

Which is how I end up in a chair, my niece examining my face like she's a builder sucking his teeth about some previous shoddy work.

'You haven't been moisturising properly,' she tells me as runs a large brush along my jawline. 'And do you even use toner?'

'Um...'

There is a tug on my arm and a disembodied, 'Want home mummy.'

It's Liam.

My instinct is to shoot up from my seat and leave. When Liam says he wants to go home, he means instantly. Failure to adhere to this in the past has led to many a tantrum. And so far today has been so uneventful and he's managed so well, there's a part of me screaming "get out! Get out while you still can!" But I can see that Mila's putting in so much effort and I can't bring myself to disappoint her.

'Five minutes,' I say to my son. 'Okay?'

'*Five?*' he yells. Like the workhouse master in *Oliver Twist* bellowing. "*Moooooore? You want more?*"

'Liam,' I utter, not a bit desperately. 'This is really important to Mila. She's just doing something for mummy and then we'll go home.'

There is silence. I cannot see my son's face, what with my face being indisposed, but I can sense him considering my proposal.

'Five?'

'Five.'

'Okay.'

Wow. Sometimes, just sometimes, everything falls into place.

Sunday, 23 September

Matt and Kelly are at Sunday lunch. Again. She is fourteen weeks along. Her baby – and it is hers, with Matt not mentioned at any point - is currently the size of a lemon. Last week it was the size of a peach. She turns the colour of a tomato when Jake questions if a peach is smaller than a lemon and then a shade of beetroot when he googles it.

She wants to know if I did yoga when I was pregnant. She is. Three times a week. And swimming. And jogging.

'Because mum's health is vital for the baby's health,' she ministers, before asking me about my experiences of labour. I give her the sanitised version. Pure facts: number of hours laboured, methods of extraction, birth weights. This is both because I do not make a habit of telling expectant mothers birth horror stories, and because I know anything I say will be used against me in a court of mummyhood. And that is a legal system about as consistent as Henry VIII's Tinder profile.

For example, you never know where people stand on issues relating to childbirth. Matters like pain relief method, birthing venue, and type of birth are divisive to an extent that usually requires international peacekeepers.

My own experiences taught me that what works for one person might not work for another. It might not even work for the same person more than once.

For example, when giving birth to Charlie, I got so high on gas and air that I was convinced I was in an episode of *The Simpsons*. And the epidural meant I barely felt a thing.

Liam's birth was a different story altogether. The gas and air only made me feel a bit queasy and the epidural failed on one side. Why only on one side? Who knows? Maybe it was so I could compare and contrast the relatively painless left with the excruciating right. Like those split screen absorbency tests on old nappy adverts. The ones where they poured blue liquid onto two different nappies, one of which must have been coated in sticky back plastic so the liquid just slid right off and the other being the advertised product. *On this side, we've given the mother an epidural. But on this side, we haven't. Can you see the difference?*

Somewhere along the way, Liam's heart rate dropped and then there was a lot of panic and urgent muttering. Eventually a doctor had extracted him by ventouse. Which is the medical equivalent of using barbeque tongs.

That had been my first experience of second child guilt. Nobody tells you of this. It is the agonising self-doubt that plagues every mother with more than one child. A constant sense of imbalance in your mothering. So that even your greatest achievement with one only makes you question your efforts with the other.

From the moment Liam was born, I felt I had let him down. That it was my fault Charlie's birth had been so uneventful while his was so traumatic. Simultaneously I felt inordinate guilt at what I saw as my abandonment of Charlie. Would he be forever scarred by this first night ever away from his mummy?

He wasn't. Charlie slept through the whole thing and hadn't even known I was gone.

Nevertheless, I do not feel the need to relive it all now. With Kelly.

Delia and Archie spend the whole meal looking pained and uncomfortable. And that's before Kelly's asked me if I ate my placenta. The source of their unease? Liam's possible diagnosis. Having missed last week's lunch due to other engagements (birthday parties), this is the first I've seen them since they found out about it.

Delia keeps asking if I'm okay. And then if I'm really sure. Archie greets me with a bear hug and then avoids me entirely. They look at Liam with such deep sorrow, I worry they think autism is terminal. I almost miss their usual mix of guilt and fear towards my second born.

Over Kelly's chatter, I hear Archie ask Jake how "the autism" is going.

'Dad, it's not a work project,' Jake huffs. Because we are all teenagers in the presence of our parents.

'He doesn't even look autistic,' Delia contributes. 'Julia – you remember Julia. Her mother died last month?' We do not. 'Well, her friend's grandson is autistic and all he can say is no and cheese.'

It is just as well that this is utterly unanswerable because Jake doesn't get the chance to offer one before his dad adds, 'Asperger was a Nazi, you know.'

'What...' Jake is evidently flummoxed. 'Dad what do Nazis have to do with anything?'

'I'm just saying,' Archie chunters through a mouthful of roast chicken. 'It's a bit odd, don't you think? That his condition is named after a Nazi. With us being Jewish.'

'Dad-'

'Mummy. Are we Jewish?' Charlie asks.

'He doesn't know he's *Jewish*?' Delia looks fit to faint.

'What is ooh-ish?' Liam asks.

'It hasn't come up,' Jake mutters.

This at least diverts the conversation. Even if it is towards Delia revealing to Charlie that he is one of the Chosen People. Then Charlie asking if we believe in Jesus. To which Archie grumbles something about Jesus also being a good Jewish boy.

In a rare show of unity, Matt and Jake then burst out with, 'He's not the Messiah. He's a very naughty boy.'

Four days until the initial NHS appointment.

Monday, 24 September

9:30am

Oh-ho, these NHS forms think they are *soooo* clever. They think they have me fooled with their multiple-choice questions. Well I have your number you bastards.

Take the questions about family medical history:

> Does any close family member have the following conditions? Tick as appropriate. If yes, please specify:

Neurological disease

Learning problems

ADHD

Autistic spectrum disorder

Mental health issues for which they have been formally diagnosed

So far so good. Tick or don't tick. And then they hit you with:

Any other significant problem. Please specify.

So basically everything ever. I scream. But only on the inside.

What counts as a significant problem? How far does "close family" extend? Should I include aunts and uncles? Cousins? I decide it's a sliding scale of closeness and severity of the condition. So I would include the fact that my mum always thought I was "dyslexic or something, but didn't think it worth checking", but only mention a great aunt with a minimum of seven disparate personalities.

Which is all fine except I know barely anything of my family's medical history. I think my grandad had angina. Or was it a stroke?

I call Gabby. She knows less than I do.

'Call Mum,' she says. Which is exactly what I was hoping to avoid. Just before hanging up, she adds, 'Oh and tell her that face cream she wanted is discontinued.'

And thus it is Gabby who is spared a call with mum.

Mum is thrilled to be asked to catalogue our family's ailments. Just thrilled. She is like Cassandra of Troy in her knowledge of terrible fates befalling others. Only while Cassandra was cursed by Apollo to make true prophecies but never to be believed, mum takes a perverse thrill in listing the ailments and deaths of everyone she has ever known.

'Your father has his IBS. Uncle Stephen is coeliac.' There's a pause. 'Well. He says he's coeliac. But he's always been a bit off and I saw him eat a pretzel. Your grandfather died young. But that was a car accident. Your father's mother was a compulsive liar.'

'Was that medically diagnosed?'

'Write it down.'

And now it's the NHS I feel sorry for. They've bitten off more than they can diagnose.

'Anyone in our family ever been diagnosed with autism?'

'Of course not, darling. We didn't have it in our day. We just got on with things.'

'You mean you swept stuff under the carpet.'

'Don't be difficult.'

'What about Uncle Graham?'

'What about him?' Her tone indicates that I must tread carefully. The carpet is bulbous beneath my feet.

'Well. He's not exactly a people person.'

'He's just very forthright.'

'He told me I had a fat head.'

'It did take time for your proportions to even out.'

By the end I have an A4 sheet filled with what can only be termed accusations so vague they'd have been thrown out of court in 17th century Salem.

'Oh, by the way,' she adds. 'Gina Eisman died.'

'Who?'

'Gina,' she insists. 'Gina Eisman. You know. The one with the hair.' I don't know. 'Terrible business,' she continues. 'Huge row over the estate.'

I remember to pass on Gabby's message about the face cream.

'Rubbish,' my mother barks. 'Of course it's not discontinued. I've been using it for twenty years.'

I try explaining that one does not follow from the other, but mum is undeterred. So now I am tasked with finding a moisturiser that no longer exists. But we're living in a post-factual world, so all is not lost.

11:30am

Huh. My blog has twenty new votes. I cannot decide if this is a good or bad thing. It might not be a thing at all. I have risen to the lofty rank of 451. Five places. Although that is now out of a total of 500 instead of 505, so it might be solely due to dropouts. Maybe not though. Wokerati Warrior has catapulted to spot 105.

Good for him.

Utterly dismal for society. But good for him.

More exciting are the five new messages I've received, all definitely addressed to me. My favourite is signed Tepid Mess. Tepid - I feel we're on first username terms - says that I could be writing about her life. But, she tells me, we are not alone. There are many of us out there, cast into the fringes of polite parenting society. And we have Facebook groups.

Intrigued, I log onto Facebook. And am amazed to discover that people still post there. Oh, look. Uncle Graham says he's running for a local councillor position.

The Wunder Mummies are evidently prolific here. Just today they exchanged a flurry of messages. The catalyst for this appears to have been their leader, Alison B AKA Queen B, sharing a pic of herself, hair newly dyed a shade of honey blond. It is remarkably similar to Ingrid's hair colour. By which I mean that it is identical. The caption?

> New Hair, Don't Care!

Best I can tell, the Wunder Mummies' preferred mode of communication is via motivational quotes. Things like:

> You did not create your children. They created you.

To which my episiotomy begs to differ. And:

> The future is like a cloud. You can decipher what shape it takes.

Clouds are masses of floating water or ice. Maybe a statement about climate change?
Then there's:

> Every day is a chance to live your second chance life.

Proof positive that putting words in a line doth not a sentence make.

When I finally look at the groups Tepid has suggested, I see they're for parents and caregivers of children with special needs. They are also all closed groups that require you to join before you can see the posts.

Am I qualified to join? The current members all probably have a proper diagnosis. Something to say that they belong there. I have a hunch. Albeit a professional hunch. Still, what if I get rejected? I couldn't take being refused entry to a Facebook group. I decide to wait until after we know for sure.

Tuesday, 25 September

Jake: 'We have that NHS assessment thingy in a couple of days, right?'
   Me: 'It's an initial appointment thingy. And yes.'
   Jake: 'So, what, it's like a meet and greet? Do I need to be there?'
   Me:
   Jake: 'No, it's just. No, yeah. Yeah, of course I'll be there.'

Wednesday, 26 September

Ha. I have done it. I have bloody gone and done it. All the forms.

EHCP form to school - *check*

NHS forms to NHS - *check*

Now just to finish my actual work. Three massive projects. Which is fine. Because I have until the end of the month. Which is in...

Fuck.

That can't be right. I have ages. Loads of time.

I have four days.

My eyelid twitches.

But that is still okay. I have always met deadlines. More than that, I hand things in early. Except that last job. But aside from that, I have a perfect record. So this will be the same. And I will not examine that logic.

Thursday, 27 September

We have a diagnosis. For Liam. Liam has been diagnosed. With autism. They just went ahead and did it right then and there. One diagnosis. No waiting.

Okay, it wasn't quite that simple. And they didn't say autism. They said Asperger's. Which I am now almost sure is the same thing, but I wish I'd double checked at the time. It was just all so much and I was gripped by a sudden fear they'd take it back.

God I'm tired. We all are. It has been the sort of long day that bled in from the night before. So it's more like two days in one and it's only midday. None of us got any sleep last night. Well. Except Charlie. Charlie has a knack for strolling carefree through the chaos of life utterly unscathed. He came to breakfast bright eyed, bushy tailed and oblivious to the rest of us looking like extras from a George A. Romero set.

I didn't sleep because I needed to work. Then I didn't work because Liam wouldn't sleep. And Jake got involved somehow.

As for this morning, the plan had been to drop Charlie at school and then for me and Jake to go on with Liam. But just as we were leaving, I got a text.

Pipe BURST. School CLOSED.

So it was a family outing. Which was fine. It was only supposed to be an initial appointment. Except when we arrived, we were not greeted by a nurse or a single junior doctor as I had expected. Oh no. We were met by a psychiatrist, a paediatrician, a psychologist and a therapist. A medical battalion.

Oh, and Belle.

'Do you mind if Belle sits in on this?' asked Dr Willis, the psychiatrist, as the door to the room opened again and a smiley face appeared around its edge. 'She's in her final year.'

Dr Willis was indecently handsome. As if that wasn't distracting enough, he also had an American accent. Which felt strange. I'd never come across an American working in the NHS.

Then there was Belle. Belle. You don't often meet a Belle, do you? Not surprising I suppose. I mean, it takes some exceptional confidence in your child's future appearance to force her to introduce herself forevermore as beautiful, doesn't it? After all, I can't be the only one who instinctively judged whether she suited the name. With the benefit of hindsight, I wonder if they might have gone for something more forgiving. Like Anne.

All of which shouldn't have made a difference, but meant I was entirely too preoccupied to answer him. Fortunately, Jake, with his ability to act like an adult in all situations, nodded and replied that it was 'no problem.'

'Hey Liam,' Dr Willis had said, crouching down to his level. 'How are you doing today?'

Liam, who has a politician's knack for never letting the question being asked be a barrier to the answer he wishes to give, replied, 'My daddy is here.'

'Yes he is.'

'My leg is fine now,' added Charlie, before I hurriedly handed him my phone, already open to Candy Crush.

'So today we're going to assess Liam for autism.'

I think I speak for both me and Jake when I say our eyes popped out of our sockets like we were old-timey cartoon characters.

'Today?'

'Now?'

Yes. Today and now, Dr Willis confirmed. Then asked if that was okay because they happened to have all the staff on site and we had completed our forms so thoroughly they felt they had enough to go ahead.

We stammered that "yes, yes of course it was fine." I may also have glowed quite excitedly at the praise for the thorough forms. Then shot Jake a smug, look-who's-practical-now look. Because once a teacher's pet, always a teacher's pet.

What happened next was like a cross between *The Krypton Factor* and Orwell's *1984*. Jake was whisked away by the psychologist to "answer questions" while I stayed with Liam and watched as he was put through his paces in various tasks. These ranged from Play Doh construction to standing on one foot with his finger on his nose. The latter of which I'd always thought was reserved for testing sobriety.

Charlie played Candy Crush, only stopping occasionally to alert me to messages and alarms on my phone. Dr Willis would be talking only for Charlie to announce, "Grandma wants to know about the face cream" or "Auntie Gabby sent a bad word." Then, "Mummy, where is Shit's Creek? That's where she is."

I spent the entire time with my shoulders hunched up to my ears in terror. What if today of all days, Liam didn't show them what they needed to see? Or what if he showed them the wrong thing? And not knowing what the right and wrong things would even look like, I was left to speculate. It reminded me of when I spent a month pretending to love jazz music to impress a boyfriend. It all sounded the same to me. Just noise. As though several musicians of completely diverging genres were simultaneously playing different songs.

Jake was returned to us an indeterminate amount of time later. Just as Liam attempted to sing a verse of "Old Macdonald" and I had given him up for dead. He didn't look far from it.

We must have been there for around two hours when Dr Willis said it.

'We're confident we can diagnose Asperger's.'

At which point, Charlie looked up from my phone, cheerfully announced, 'Grandpa says Asperger's was a nasty,' and then went back to crushing candy.

Thank God he can't pronounce Nazi.

'So, what happens next?' Jake asked.

'How do you mean?' asked Dr Willis.

'Oh, um, I'm not exactly sure,' Jake murmured laughing nervously. 'I suppose I'm asking what the next steps are. Is there a therapy we're supposed to start? Will someone contact us?'

Psychiatrist, paediatrician, psychologist, and therapist all looked back at us in dumb confusion. Belle was beaming.

'We have a leaflet,' she announced, thrusting forth a folded sheet of glossy A4. As Jake reached out for it, the medical team seemed to be holding their collective breath. As though awaiting approval.

'So, Your Child Is on The Spectrum,' Jake read aloud.

'Well, there you go,' said Dr Willis, slapping the palms of his hands on his lap and thus drawing a line under things.

By then, both boys were showing signs of unrest. Charlie was bug-eyed from too much Candy Crush and Liam was pulling on Jake's arm. And so, we left.

The first thing I did when I got home was to request to join all the Facebook groups for special needs carers. Because I am a special needs carer. It's official. I have the password, the secret code. I can say Shibboleth. It was a bit anticlimactic though given I still had to be accepted by moderators. I sat and stared at the screen for a bit, but nothing happened.

So, I wrote a blog post. It was somewhere between a diatribe and an Oscars acceptance speech. I described the mess in my head. How I was happy. And worried. And confused. And relieved. Then I asked anyone who might be reading my post what they did after their kids were diagnosed.

After which I checked Facebook again. Nothing. My requests were still pending.

One of the Wunder Mummies had posted another quote though:

> A goal without a plan is just a wish.

Said every serial killer.

Mum phoned. She tutted and huffed and said things like, "well, it's done now I suppose." Then she told me the world is going to hell in a handbasket anyway and had I heard that Uncle Graham was a local councillor now.

Jake read the "So, Your Child Is on The Spectrum" leaflet and concluded that it told us nothing that we didn't know already. Which is nothing.

'We need a plan,' he tells me that evening.

'A goal without a plan is just a wish.'

'What?'

'Never mind.'

'The question is, what does this mean for Liam? What can we do to help? What therapy or treatment is out there that will make things better? I'd imagine there's some sort of pathway. Some standard therapies that are recommended for kids on the spectrum.'

Making things better? This possibility had never occurred to me. No. That's not true. Of course I have wanted things to get better. I also want to win the lottery, but I've never considered it a feasible option.

Jake is right though. There will be a standard plan that everyone follows.

'The leaflet is written by an NHS department called CAMHS,' he says. 'Maybe we should see if they can help.'

The idea of help fills me with something like hope. Maybe this is what we needed all along. Maybe, after countless dead ends, we've finally found the right route through the maze.

'You coming to bed?' Jake asks, already there.

'I just need to finish off some pages.'

I try to sound nonchalant. No big deal.

I haven't confided in Jake as to quite how massive my workload is.

This is highly unusual. Until recently, I would have described mine and Jake's level of honesty as complete. More than that. In text speak, it would be TMI. We overshare.

We've always been like this. It is our custom. In our house, the question "how was your day?" can be roughly translated to mean "Please recap every moment of your day and how you felt about it. Please go into extra detail on all items of food."

Surprises are non-existent.

We are, in short, nauseating. It's just our way.

Or it was. But now I am hiding not one but two things from him: my work mess and the blog. Does this mark a turning point? Have I just knocked us off course? Are we now on the path that leads to separate bedrooms and eating silently across a long table?

No. No, surely not. That is patently ridiculous. For one thing, our table is round.

Also, it's not like I'm lying. It's just that I can't stand the thought of him worrying that I'm overdoing things. And anyway I'm not. After all, everyone has phases where they have to put in a little extra time at work. And sometimes a little extra means working until 1am every night. And who among us doesn't regularly fall asleep at their desk or office floor?

Yep. I have this totally under control.

Friday, 28 September

CAMHS stands for Child and Adolescent Mental Health Services. And according to their colourful, happy website, they are the part of the NHS that helps young people with all things emotional or behavioural as well as mental health generally.

The national CAMHS website directs me to my local council's CAMHS website. This sends me to a specific hospital's website, which refers me right back to my local council's CAMHS website.

I decide that if I am going to be passed around from one department to another, I may as well do it the way God intended.

'Thank you for calling Child and Adolescent Mental Health Services.'

After thirty minutes of this robotic message being repeated in between bouts of at-least-it's-not-music ringing, I get through to Janine. How to describe Janine... Janine has seen and heard it all before. She is Ellen Ripley from *Alien* and Sarah Connor from *Terminator* and Aria Stark and *Buffy the Vampire Slayer*. She has no time for anyone's shit and she conveys as much in her tone.

Janine asks, with the hard-bitten weariness of a war reporter, if Liam is a danger to himself or others. I um and er about that for a bit. She asks what sort of help we're seeking. I tell her I was hoping she'd tell me. Then I mention the diagnosis.

Janine sighs. It is a resentful, vexed exhalation that tells me I know nothing. That I am a mere babe in arms. She tells me they don't deal with autism. She asks me Liam's age.

'He's too young for CAMHS. You should talk to paediatrics.'

I am a deflated balloon. A deflated balloon at another dead end.

But there's no time to dwell. I have work to do. Three projects. Three days.

After collecting Liam, I check Facebook and – yes – one of the groups has approved me. I'm in. This is better than getting a place at university.

The group is called *SEN For Help*. It has over 5,000 members and describes itself as a place for parents and carers of kids with special needs as well as professionals in the field.

It is a revelation. A curtain lifted. Look at all these people. They all seem like normal humans. Tired and out of their depth, but just people. Some have very young children, some teens and young adults. There are mums, dads and grandparents as well as teachers and psychologists. Most have diagnoses, but a significant minority don't. And best of all, some of them seem just as lost and clueless as I am.

I drink in the posts. I am entranced by one in particular. It could easily have been written about Liam, so similar are the characteristics and behaviour described. This little boy is five rather than four and was recently diagnosed with autism after years of uncertainty.

The mum talks about the relief of finally having an answer to a question she didn't know she was supposed to ask. She describes the desperation of not knowing what she was doing wrong and how she has felt trapped within a life she didn't recognise as her own. She says that, as happy as she is to have a diagnosis, she doesn't know what to do now. That she thought there would be a pathway for her to follow and advice and professionals, but that none of that has materialised. Then she asks one simple question: What next?

I'm hypnotised. That's *my* question. And there are over 200 replies underneath. Some are messages of support. Others of commiseration. Many rave about different therapy types. And of course, they are all bloody acronyms. Every last one. Things like OT, DBT and CBT.

WTAF?

One of the therapies suggested - something called ABA - has a massive sub-string under it. It looks quite interesting actually. And by that, I mean it's kicking off. People calling each other all sorts of names. Ooh, someone got booted off the group.

I make myself focus. *Stop looking at the funny arguments. Look for the helpful advice.*

What I find are horror stories. Parents not believed, told it was bad parenting, that their child was too young, too old. That they didn't qualify for help. Of children not being seen until they had reached crisis point. I think of Janine asking if Liam was a danger to himself or others.

I have not found answers. Only more questions. And some perspective. There are people - mums, dads, grandparents - who have similar challenges to ours. And some who have it about a bajillion times harder than we do.

I drown my sorrow in chocolate digestives. Then, I check the blog. To my surprise, there are ten messages.

'You coming up?'

I jerk guiltily at the sound of Jake's voice from the doorway of our box room office.

'Yes. Yup. In a tick.' I sound like Mary Poppins. I am also fairly certain I am sporting a crazed expression.

'You okay?' Jake's smile is uneasy. 'What are you up to?'

'Tinder,' I reply, surprising myself with this rare moment of quick wit. 'Swiping right and all that.'

'Ah, yes,' he says, faux seriously. 'Did all mine earlier.' And off he goes.

Shit. What did I just do? Was that a lie? Possibly a lie by omission. Huh. Interesting. In one sense, this does not represent a change. Does it? I have already *not* been telling him about it.

But no. No, this is different. An escalation. I am now *actively* not telling. He asked. I didn't tell.

I consider telling him now. I could. I should. It wouldn't even seem like a big deal.

Do it. You'll feel much better.

Why aren't I doing it?

If this was a film, this would be the time to pull out the old angel-versus-devil-on-the-shoulders trope. My angel has had its say. And now my devil wearily informs me that I know exactly why I am sitting frozen in my office chair. It's because I don't want to tell Jake. Because Jake won't like it. He'll think it's a bad idea.

Angel would interject to point out that he'd be right. There is no upside to any of this. Best case scenario, nobody reads it, life goes on. The worst-case scenarios, of which there are many, involve internet trolls, public humiliation, social banishment.

Devil tells Angel to stop being such a fucking drama queen. That I am currently one blog at the tail end of hundreds. Ranked 405 out of 500. I have a grand total of thirty-two votes. Nobody cares about my blog and I'm enjoying it. So why ruin a good thing. Then she tips my angel off the other shoulder.

Bitch.

Still, she has a point. For now, there's no harm. Nobody cares. If that changes, even a bit, I will tell Jake. But it won't. And I'll tell him anyway once it's all done and over.

My angel is back now, looking both dishevelled and truly pissed.

'Fine,' she retorts. 'Do what you want. See if I care.'

Saturday, 29 September

Charlie has a playdate. Her name is Sakura and she is new to the school having recently moved from Japan. I had absolutely nothing to do with the arranging of this meetup. Charlie had merely informed me of it yesterday.

'Mummy, you need to take me to Sakura's house.'

That was the first I'd heard of Sakura. Apparently she was the replacement pupil for Stefan. Him I remember. Hard not to really when a child is twice the height of every other one in his class.

'Stefan left?' I asked Charlie.

'Yes.'

'When?'

'Dunno.'

'Why?'

'Don't remember.'

Flapping crap. Charlie has never been great at remembering things. Unless they're Pokémon statistics or the date of the creation of the Roman Republic. I get nothing after school each day. Zero. Zilch. And believe me I've tried. I even attempted to follow a Pinterest list of alternative questions to "how was your day." To which Charlie found alternative but equally uninformative answers in place of "dunno" and "good." By contrast, I've heard Mila and Allegra go into forensic detail about each and every one of their interactions and those of their peers. They even pick up interesting gossip from the teachers.

Maybe it's a boy-girl thing. Actually, I remember my mum having the same complaint about me. Genetic then.

Whatever the source, it means I don't even have the address of his supposed playdate let alone a time. For all I know, this is all a figment of Charlie's imagination. Charlie is mystified by my frustration.

'Just call her mum,' he says, not looking away from *Inspector Gadget*.

'I don't have her number. I don't even know who she is.'

Eventually I manage to reach Sakura's mummy, Yui, by process of elimination on the class WhatsApp group. I even get him to their house. Which is on our road. Five doors down.

Unfortunately, there is a language barrier, what with Yui speaking very little English and me absolutely no Japanese. Nor any other language come to that. Nevertheless, she seems very nice and I am pretty sure we agreed that I'd collect him in a couple of hours. It's either that or a couple of days.

Jake decides to take Liam out for a walk. Liam refuses. He sees no utilitarian benefit in leaving the house. But Jake is determined and Liam sees an opportunity.

'I will make a deal,' he informs Jake.

There is much involved negotiation. Then an agreement.

Liam agrees to a walk. It must last no longer than thirty-five minutes. It must not include steep inclines. Or in Liam's words, "lots of hurty ups." In return, Liam will receive a Freddo (specified as pre-refrigerated) and thirty minutes extra TV time at a time and device of his choice, even if that impinges on the hour before bedtime, during which he's not usually allowed TV. Jake, realising his mistake, tries to tack on that these thirty minutes must not be on a school night, but he is too late. The deal is done.

International treaties are simpler.

But at least it gives me a chance to do some work. Two days left.

YAEL LILY

OCTOBER

Monday, 1 October

If you had told me this morning that I would end this day by quitting work for the foreseeable future, I would have laughed. Not aloud though. I was in no fit state to express audible mirth. There's an outside chance I might have raised a dubious eyebrow in your general direction. But more likely, I would have stared straight ahead in a mute, dead-eyed stupor until you got bored and walked away.

But the point is, I had no plans to stop working. I thought everything was fine. Better than that. I was killing it at my job. I had just finished all three projects for Glowing Ducks and delivered them on time. And all it had taken was staying awake for the major part of three days. No. Big. Deal.

To put it into context, the longest known time a human has gone without sleep is 11 days and 25 minutes, a record achieved by a 17-year-old American in 1965. Soldiers in battle have been known to stay awake for up to four days at a time. Which makes three sleepless rotations around the sun seem paltry by comparison. And totally worth the dizziness, headaches and mild hallucinations.

So what changed in the past twelve hours? Well, for one thing, I've had a nap. For another... I'd best start from the beginning.

8:55am

'Mummy, why are we walking to school?'

We were walking because I couldn't trust myself to drive. Did I tell Charlie that though?

'It's nice to walk.'

'It's raining very hard.'

'My socks are soggy.'

The morning was a series of discombobulated flashes. I remember walking to school, being convinced I would collapse mere feet from the gate and arriving back home. I do not recall dropping off the kids, nor how I came to be in possession of an invitation to a Halloween party at Ingrid's house. And, crucially, I cannot remember falling asleep on the sofa.

1pm

'Hi mummy.'

This is how I woke up. On the sofa. In my house. With Liam, who I had just delivered to school and definitely hadn't collected, casually strolling past.

'Hey.' This was Jake. Jake was there.

I think I grunted in response. Then realised I was holding something. A piece of card.

YOU ARE INVITED TO THE DANNING FAMILY ALL-HALLOWS' EVE SPOOKTACULAR!

At some point Jake brought in a cup of tea. And then he informed me that the school phoned to tell him I hadn't picked up Liam.

'So I came to get him and found you here.'

I had fallen asleep and left Liam at school. And that is why I did it. Why I will stop working for the foreseeable future. Even though it is the one adult thing that is truly mine. Even though I worry it might mean Ad finding another writer and that I never work again. And although, as Jake pointed out repeatedly over the coming hours, Liam had been safe and no harm was done.

All this was true. But there is a limit. There is a limit to the depth and breadth of parental ineptitude which I would tolerate in myself. And this, I was determined, would be my nadir. No lower would I sink.

Not if I could help it anyway.

Saturday, 6 October

Oh wow. Holy fricking shit. This is it. A turning point. An actual effing turning point. I have discovered something truly magnificent. And all the more so because it is so simple.

Ear defenders.

I tried them on the suggestion of Tepid Mess, the same blog reader who'd pointed me in the direction of the Facebook groups. She raved that they had changed her life, adding:

If your son is anything like my girl (& it sounds like it), these will make a BIG diff.

I'm thinking of erecting a shrine in her honour. How does one erect a shrine nowadays? Is there a kit? I'm sure Pinterest will have answers.

Anyway, I'd been intrigued. But a tentative googling of "ear defenders" shifted that feeling to flummoxed. Then dubious. The results were images of burly workmen wielding jackhammers and wearing large, cumbersome – for lack of a better term - headphones. Except these weren't for listening, but to protect professionals from hearing loss caused by excessive noises.

And so I kept searching. This time I took a more targeted approach. I tacked the word "kids" at the end. This proved more fruitful. Now I was shown children wearing multi-coloured, mini versions of the adult ones. There were even photos of the offspring of celebrities wearing them at festivals and F1 races.

Nevertheless, I remained confused. I'm ashamed to say it now, but in that moment, I questioned the wisdom of Tepid Mess. How would protecting Liam's hearing change anything? We didn't find ourselves in many especially loud places. No Wembley tickets or building projects in our near future. How could these possibly have changed Tepid's whole family's life?

Fortunately, I never say no to Amazon one-clicking my way out of a problem. And so, by 7pm the next working day, Liam became the proud owner of a pair of Lego themed ear defenders.

'Absolutely not,' Jake announced when I revealed them. 'He'll look like a weirdo.'

His arms weren't so much crossed as hermetically sealed together across his chest. We went back and forth, with him arguing that Liam had to learn to live in the real world and not be pandered to and me pointing out that that hadn't worked out brilliantly so far now, had it?

'And how will these help?' He'd demanded.

I was ready for this. I had done my homework. Since my introduction to the subject, I had conducted intensive and extensive research. Which basically meant adding the word "autism" to the end of my search term.

'He might be suffering from sensory overload,' I proclaimed with sanguine certitude. I may or may not have been pretending to be Canadian TV psychologist Linda Papadopoulos. The stunning one with the hair and big brown eyes any doe would kill for. 'Kids with autism often have heightened senses which make it harder for them to cope in what others see as a normal situation.'

'Are you doing an accent?'

'No.'

Yes.

Next, I cued up a YouTube video which emulated how sensory overload felt. I had watched this video. For about two seconds. Before quickly switching it off because it was, in a word, unbearable. I would happily sit through an entire concert of cats scraping claws on chalk boards than ever be subjected to those sounds ever again.

Still channelling Dr Linda, I murmured, 'Now, I want you to imagine that Liam experiences this every day.'

I hit play and ran away. Ran like I have never run before. It was a hero-jumping-out-of-explosion-range departure.

I was barely out of eardrum bursting range when I heard a bang and then, 'Ow! Okay, okay. We'll try the ear things.' Then there was a grumbling that sounded like, 'Where's the fucking pause button?'

That was Monday. On Tuesday, Jake and I introduced the ear defenders to Liam just before school.

'Why does he need those?' Charlie asked.

'We think...' Jake crouched down and beckoned both boys over to him. He made a show of looking around to check nobody was listening, then whispered, 'You know how Superman has super hearing and it can get really loud? We think Liam might have super hearing syndrome. These are Super Sound Blockers. When Liam wears them, he hears like a mortal.'

If Jake has a superpower, it is branding. He is convinced that children will accept anything as long as it is presented correctly. Thus, Jake doesn't make toast. He makes Super Daddy Toast™. The same goes for Daddy Dinner, Daddy Drink and Daddy Walks. ™, ™, ™.

I hate to say it, but it does work. None of these are nearly as exciting as they sound and yet if I suggest a walk/bolognese/bloody Marmite toast, my boys turn into intellectual property lawyers demanding proof of authenticity.

Having espoused his latest campaign on behalf of Orwell's Ministry of Truth, Jake looked like he was done. He should have been done. But he couldn't resist adding. 'Remember boys, with great power comes great responsibility.'

Liam was thrilled, his chest puffed out so far, I half considered he might burst with sheer joy. Charlie frowned his most serious and thoughtful frown. It was like the physical manifestation of watching the cogs of his mind turning.

'Daddy,' he said finally.

'Hm?'

'That's Spiderman. Not Superman. With great power comes great responsibility. But that's okay.' He patted Jake's shoulder with weary consolation. 'You're old so you forget things.'

Jake looked disgustingly smug as he stood up.

'Job done,' he murmured.

To which I muttered, 'You really missed your calling making Soviet propaganda.'

And with the ear defenders – sorry, Super Sound Blockers ™ - significantly oversold, we left. What happened next was unexpected and magnificent.

Or maybe I should say what didn't happen.

There was nothing. No things. None of the jittering or jumping or bolting usually such an incontrovertible part of the short trip from home to school. Liam got into the car. Then we travelled in said car. And finally, Liam calmly got out of the car and walked – *walked* – alongside me.

I walked straight into a lamppost. Because rather than look at where I was going, I was staring at him.

And there was more. At the school gate, Charlie ran to his friends, but Liam paused and looked up at me.

'Mummy I am so happy I cannot hear the cars.'

Everything went a bit blurry then what with me going misty eyed. As I tried not to burst into happy tears next to a little girl who was already crying, I vowed to search Pinterest for shrine making tips. Because dammit I was making a bloody massive one for the goddess that is Tepid Mess.

Fortunately, the harsh reality of primary school mores slammed me conveniently back down to earth.

'Mummy,' Charlie called, running back from the playground. 'Do you have my show and tell?'

Twatety fucksticks.

Incredibly, the calm has continued thus far. Four entire days without incident. This is great. Phenomenal. A miracle worthy of papal recognition. But rather than enjoy or celebrate, I have spent this period on a perpetual knife edge, constantly anticipating the worst. I hardly dare draw breath and will not speak of it for fear that doing so will make it float away.

I am, in short, becoming my mother. Mum is a superstitious conspiracist to her very core. Her beliefs are not codified or organised in any particular way. She simply harbours a general, all-consuming fear of tempting fate by saying anything positive or making any assumptions. This could be a goodbye that includes a "see you soon" or a bland comment about the "lovely weather we're having". It is also the reason why she never told Gabby or me we were clever or talented or looked nice. At least that's what I tell myself.

And why? Because apparently some evil force is standing by, ready to snatch it away. This becomes all the more confounding when presented with the prescribed antidote should such an utterance be expelled. Spitting. Spitting three times in quick succession, ideally with sound effects. Apparently evil has the power to rob you of good fortune, but not to withstand mild dampness.

It was like being raised by an anxious alpaca.

But I do not plan to follow in my alpaca's hoofsteps. I am a logical person. I know that nothing I do will alter the efficacy of the ear defenders. And I will acknowledge that. I am seizing the day. I'm taking these puppies out to see what they can do. Maybe ear defenders will allow us to do things we'd never thought possible.

THINGS WE HAVE HITHERTO CONSIDERED IMPOSSIBLE:

1. Hiring a babysitter. There is no nanny super enough.
2. Taking my boys to a playground, park, soft play, trampoline park or any other public setting alone.
3. Travelling on an aeroplane.
4. Going to the dentist, hairdresser or any appointment with both boys without Jake.

I choose number 4 as my testing ground. Primarily because my children need haircuts. They could presently elevate a prince up a tower using only their long locks. As for me, I am ridiculously proud of myself.

Look at us being normal. Just like everyone else. I bet that mum over there with her two boys thinks I'm just like her. Ha. Fooled you, lady. This is a charade.

There is one problem. I hadn't accounted for the fact that it is a Saturday morning and therefore the place is rammed. It's also very noisy. But Liam and Charlie are happily waiting, playing on my phone and an iPad. And Liam has his ear defenders. It will be fine.

Liam goes first.

'What's he having?' Asks the barber. He is a large man with mounds of hair everywhere except his head.

I hate this question. Despite having been the mother of boys for some six years, I have yet to master the language of male hairdressing. I try for what Jake always tells me to say.

'A short back and sides, please. Slightly longer on top.'

The man stares at me. I stare back.

I have not provided sufficient information. He asks about grades and bandies around various numbers. Eventually we agree to try a length and widdle down if needed.

'Take the headphones off young man,' he instructs Liam. Liam does so, but immediately recoils at the noise. I convince the man to just cut around the headphones. He is unimpressed.

Then Liam gets hair in his eyes. And down his back. And begins to squirm in the seat. And no, he won't agree to clippers. It will have to be done with scissors.

'But look.' The man turns on the clippers. 'It's nothing.'

No.

'It'll be much neater. And it's so gentle.' The man runs the clippers along his hand.

Nope.

'It doesn't hurt.'

By now, Liam looks both panicked and frustrated. The man looks frustrated and panicked. And thus I declare that it all looks fantastic. Couldn't possibly be better.

'But I haven't done the neck.'

'That would ruin it,' I insist.

Charlie is next. And the man and I repeat our dance of the seven grades. Except with Liam pulling my arm and demanding to leave.

Assuring him that we'll go just as soon as Charlie's hair is done is futile. Pure folly. Liam has had his haircut and cannot understand why on earth we are still here. And before I know it I am outside on the pavement having after-school flashbacks while gripping onto him as he attempts to launch himself into the path of a passing Renault Clio.

'Excuse me.'

Liam and I freeze frame to note who it is disturbing this precious mother-son moment. Shite. The other mum with two boys looks down at me, pointedly indicating that she needs to get past. I have been unmasked as the fraud I am.

At home, Jake cannot understand why only one child has had some of his hair cut. And I cannot explain to him that it was either this or only having one child because I'd have had to leave Charlie behind.

So there you have it. The fates were tempted. I was punished. I'm off to buy some healing crystals.

Logged onto Instagram to see Kelly's posted a photo of an obscenely large bump with the quote "You Never Understand Life Until It Grows Inside You."

This somehow manages to simultaneously mean nothing and make no sense. An impressive feat. It's also unspeakably creepy. But we're seeing them at the in-laws tomorrow and I need the goodwill. So I "like" it.

Sunday, 7 October

We're back from lunch at Delia and Arthur's. Kelly informed us all that her baby is now the size of an avocado. Delia, who had been in the kitchen during this announcement, re-entered with a tricolour salad. Then wondered why nobody was eating it.

Now Jake is playing Snakes and Ladders with Liam.

Not Monopoly. Liam had said no to Monopoly and thrust the other game into Jake's hands.

We had both stared in amazement at the box. Then at our son.

'This?' Jake had asked.

'This. Like Kai.'

'Not Monopoly?' Jake checked.

'Kai like this,' insisted Liam.

I love Kai. Kai is my favourite person ever. For Kai hath rid us of Monopoly.

'Who's Kai?' I mouth at my husband. I get a shrug.

With Jake looking after the boys, I go upstairs to the office. It's that time of the week. The time I spend doing the online food shop. I have one of those weekly slots, which means the app automatically fills my basket every week with what it calls my "usuals". These are supposed to be the things I tend to buy every week, gleaned from my regular shopping basket, my favourites and my preferences. Does this mean I live in a perfectly automated world where I need do nothing but await the nice purple delivery van? Fuck no. That is because it is all a con. In reality, my usuals are divided into three categories.

THE TRIFECTA OF SO-CALLED USUALS IN MY ONLINE SHOP

1. My usuals: things I actually need and want every week. Milk, eggs, chicken, etc.

2. My unusuals: Stuff I need every few weeks. Washing up liquid, Calpol, toilet paper.
3. Anything else that I have ever bought even once and has therefore made it onto my "favourites" list and is thus fair game for the app to decide I want to buy every week forever and ever. Birthday candles, highball glasses, that super expensive organic chicken breast pack I only bought because they were out of the usual stuff.

All of these things are on the shopping list. Every week. I have tried to remove them from my "usuals". I have removed them from my favourites. I have tried doing this plus editing all the pre-filled baskets for the coming weeks. I have tried emailing the shopping app people. I have performed sacred dances to the gods of ecommerce. Nothing works. The same products boomerang back into my basket. Like in a horror movie where the murderous doll won't die. And thus I must spend time every week scouring my shopping list just to make sure there isn't yet another bottle of clothes bleach or bag of salty and sweet seaweed that I tried once and made me gag.

It is as I am doing this that a new horror catches my attention. Wheaty Wheatums are out of stock. My blood does not simply run cold. It freezes over. Wheaty Wheatums are Liam's favourite cereal. It is the only cereal he will eat. And he eats a lot of it. Three bowls a day, minimum. He calls them Weezows. They are an integral part of our lives. They were out of stock last week, but that had been fine. We still had several boxes left. Even now, we have enough to get us through the next week. But that's it.

What if they've stopped making them? No, I can't think like that. It's just some weird fluke. They are a popular cereal. It's fine. It'll be some weird supply issue. I'll go to the supermarket and get some. Yes, Yes, that's what I'll do.

Monday, 8 October

'Excuse me,' I say to the shop assistant at my local Waitrose. 'Do you have any Weez, um, Wheat Wheatums, in stock?'

They do not. Another mum overhears and joins us.

'When will they be back in stock?' She asks. Her eyes are as wide as mine feel.

The shop assistant doesn't know. And she looks a bit scared now.

'Excuse me,' says a dad with a baby in a shopping trolley. 'Do you have any Wheat Wheatums?'

At home I google "Wheat Wheatums stock problems". Mummyweb has a thread on it. A user called Finleysmummy says she emailed the company and they're in the middle of updating the recipe and that the stock issue will be resolved in the next few days.

Jake thinks it'll be fine.

'You said yourself we have enough to get us through the whole week.'

'Yes,' I breathe, like a dragon might exhale fire. 'But they are changing the recipe. The recipe will be different.'

'No they're not. Companies do this all the time. It's just so they can put new and improved on the box.'

Oh how I hope he is right. The idea of having to explain to Liam that he will never again eat his precious Weezows is one that I relish about as much as having electrolysis on my entire head.

Tuesday, 9 October

I should have known it would come to this. To me, sitting across from a six-foot tall, yellow member of the avian species, telling me my son is being suspended from school. I can see now that it was inevitable; the only logical next step in the Magritte-esque surrealscape that is my life.

'I have spoken to Liam about the gravity of his actions,' Mr Davies intones sombrely. There is an agitated rustle of feathers as he adjusts his beak. 'And that is why we have decided that he is excluded from school for half a day.'

I have to hand it to the headmaster. It should be impossible to exude pompous gravity while dressed as Big Bird, but he's almost pulling it off. Behind him, a large poster declares that today is Mental Health Awareness Day.

As such, the kids had "the option" to wear something yellow. The email about the day jauntily suggested a hairband, socks or a hat. Because of course all parents have an entire rainbow of clothes available just for events such as this.

There is, naturally, nothing optional about any of it. You cannot be the mum who sends in a child without the requested item. Just like you can't opt out of World Book Day or Dress as A Space Hamster for No Sodding Reason Day. Doing so is tantamount to insurrection. You may as well surrender your Ring doorbell and announce your withdrawal from the middle class right there in the playground.

My boys don't own anything even remotely yellow. I'd considered Amazon one-clicking the problem, but that way lies bankruptcy. And anyway I'd thought of it too late. That's why Liam is currently sporting a "headband" made of white card which I'd hastily coloured-in and glued into a loop. Somewhere, Charlie is wearing his. I was quite proud when I'd produced them. I thought it was resourceful of me in a Pinterest sort of way and looked quite jolly. Most importantly, the boys liked them.

It looks rather less jolly now, lying dejectedly askew on Liam's head and pulling apart at the joins. It is the least subtle metaphor possible for the trajectory of this day.

'You're suspending him?' I ask. Although my tone is so flat, it's more a statement of fact.

'We call it a temporary exclusion nowadays.'

I am trying – I truly am – but I cannot process the information.

'But he's four.'

'He is a member of the school community. And, as such, it is vital that he understands that actions have consequences.'

'I agree there should be consequences,' I say, my tempo glacial. 'But…' I scrabble for an alternative way to communicate the point. Nope. I've got nothing. So I just repeat the same point, only in a slower whisper. 'He's four.'

By way of illustrating my point, I gesture to my left, where Liam is transfixed by a fish bowl. He is tiny, which makes the whole thing even more ridiculous.

Mr Davies crosses his wings noisily. 'He bit Miss Vine.'

I had never heard of Miss Vine before this morning. I am informed she is a teaching assistant and was assigned to look after Liam for the day. Apparently, the school plans to get a permanent TA solely for Liam. But while they search, they are rotating different members of staff into the role. Miss Vine had incurred Liam's wrath for informing him break time was over and insisting he put away a bike.

If Liam wasn't in the room right now, I'd point out to Mr Big Bird that this is ludicrous. That only last week I had to explain to my second born that cats and dogs are not the same thing. That he still muddles up he and she pronouns. And that he thinks he's going to marry *me* when he grows up. I might also be tempted to shake out the feathers that have evidently lodged in his brain.

But Liam is here. Because Mr Davies insisted on it for some unfathomable reason. So I say and do none of these things.

I attempt a final subtle nudge in the direction of logic.

'There's no point. He won't understand what it means. Wouldn't it be better to talk it through with him and take away some privileges or something?'

'We can do that as well. But I have a duty to my staff and to the other children to show that we take such behaviour seriously. They must see that something has been done.'

It's midday when I take Liam home. Exactly the time he always leaves. And he'll be back tomorrow morning. As usual.

At home, I inform Liam that he has lost five stars for biting Miss Vine and that me and daddy will decide what else he is to lose. Because there is no way I'm bearing the brunt of that bad news solo. I even get him to make an "I'm Sorry" card for Mrs Vine.

As he absently scrawls something on a piece of card. I test Mr Davies' theory by asking my son if he understands why he's home from school. Liam stops, looks at me like I'm an idiot and replies that he lives here.

'But do you understand that you got sent home early because you bit Miss Vine? That children who hurt others aren't allowed to go to nice schools?'

'Do they get sent to jail?'

'No, but–'

'Do they get killed?'

'No.'

'So I will not be dead?'

'No.'

Satisfied that death is not on the table of possible sanctions, he ceases his card making, hands me the result and goes in search of Lego.

'But they don't get to go to nice schools,' I try. 'Like your nice school.' Nothing. Then, inspiration hits. 'With Kai.'

His hands cease building. His eyes swivel suspiciously sidewards.

'Okay.'

Then he is back to his construction.

Translation: he will take it under advisement.

Jake is furious when he learns of Liam's exclusion. This is a first. I am usually the angry one. Jake does not "do" fury. Passive aggressive, irritable, indignant, yes. Maybe the odd bout of boiling resentment, sure. But never proper fury. The kind where I worry the smoke coming out of his ears might set off our fire alarm.

He rants and raves, using phrases like "how dare they" and "not on my watch" and other idioms Victor Meldrew usually has all to himself. And solemnly vows to avenge his son.

Then he goes to his computer and types a sternly worded email.

Wednesday, 10 October

Liam shows zero signs of remembering yesterday's events when I bid him farewell at the school gate this morning.

'Remember to say sorry when you give Miss Vine the card you made,' I tell him.

To which he replies, 'Who?'

'Oh, Mrs Harris?' Miss Flowers is trotting towards me, cheeks pink with the exertion.

'Yes?'

'Would you mind accompanying Liam on the class trip tomorrow?' She pants. 'I'm so sorry to ask, only we don't have enough staff to cover and I'm worried Liam might get overwhelmed.'

The reception class WhatsApp group has been abuzz with talk of tomorrow's trip to Bekonscot, the miniature village. I was looking forward to it because they wouldn't be back until 2. That meant two whole extra hours. I was gaming the system. I was sticking it to the man. I was beating them at their own game.

Goddammit.

As we're all sitting down to dinner, I hear the bleep of the electronic cat flap, followed by actual flaps. Then screaming. Then more frantic flapping. After ten years of languor and torpor, Sir Francis has chosen this as his moment. He chose today as the first time to drag in a bird. And not just any bird. A live fricking magpie.

We watch in astonished horror, both boys screaming, as cat hurries bird into the next room.

Jake and I lock eyes in a mutual show of being truly fucked. Then we launch into action. We mount an FBI-raid-style takedown. Jake really does think he's re-enacting every takedown from *Law & Order*, *The Wire* and *24*, instructing me to 'Close off all exits,' while he edges towards cat and bird, back against the wall.

The effect is somewhat ruined by the backdrop of shrieking children requiring us to constantly shout back that "everything's okay!" And to "hold on a minute!" And "nobody's dead!"

The biggest challenge proves to be separating cat from bird and ejecting cat from the equation. The magpie doesn't cover itself in glory. In fact, it becomes clear how it had allowed itself to be captured by the world's least convincing cat. It keeps flying towards Sir Francis and basically landing in his mouth.

I do manage to finally remove Sir Francis from the room, leaving only Jake versus bird. I wait on the other side of the door with two hysterical boys and one hysterical cat. There is an inordinate amount of flapping – bird

– and screeching – Jake - culminating in a cry of, 'Open the door!' And a dramatic dash and release.

I spend the rest of that afternoon scrubbing down the playroom like I'm TV psychopath Dexter. The whole house reeks of bleach.

Thursday, 11 October

Today will go down in history as one of the worst of my life. Not that I keep a tally of such things. But if I did, prior to today's events it would go something like this:

Top Three Worst Days Before Today:

1. My 21st birthday. My parents threw me a surprise party. Except the surprise was on them. I'd contracted a nasty case of food poisoning, so that as soon as my aunts, uncles, grandma, friends and assorted plus-ones had yelled "Surprise!", I had obliged by empting the contents of my stomach onto the floor. Incidentally, nobody believed it was food poisoning. They thought it was a hangover. Pity was withheld, I was forced to party on, my mum periodically sniping at me to "make an effort."
2. A wasp stung me in the nostril when I was eight, only for it to become infected and make half my face expand into a flat surface from nose to ear. I'd looked like a hairless Persian cat.
3. Day trip on a holiday to Italy while pregnant with Charlie. Decided to join a group bus tour of some of the local sites, unaware that we had been allocated drunk-racist guy as our tour guide. It was supposed to be a half-day, but the bus broke down at the junction of nowhere and beyond. It took three hours for a replacement bus to arrive. It was 38 degrees, there was one toilet and twenty pensioners I had to fight for it. And all while avoiding eye contact with our guide, Massimo, while he ranted about which races were to blame for what.

But these are, each and every one, cherished memories as compared to my ordeal over the past ten hours. Today was Liam's class trip to Bekonscot Model Village. Or, as I will forever remember it, THAT class trip.

Highlights of THAT Class Trip

Let's start with the coach, shall we? Google Maps said – nay promised - it was a 45-minute journey to Bekonscot. It took us two hours. Then three on the way back because some bastard in a Jag broke down in the single open lane on a stretch of the M25. Five whole hours in a tin can with thirty children and six adults, with only pin-sized window openings for air. It was an overwhelming, thick fug of stench and sound. I felt sick the entire way there and back, not helped by the coach driver's deeply held religious opposition to driving in a straight line. The temperature was the only thing that vacillated more violently than the vehicle itself, veering between Arctic and hellfire with gay abandon.

Aside from me, Miss Flowers and Mrs Grip, there were two other mummies on the trip, in charge of six children apiece. Both of them mistook me for a member of staff because I only had two kids under my charge: Liam and his assigned partner. Even though that made no sense. Because the staff had more not fewer children in their groups.

I don't remember the mummies' names, only their children's. And thus I mentally labelled them according to the *Handmaid's Tale* law of nomenclature. I know the one with the blond bob was of-Felicity and that the one who's superhero jaw didn't deter her getting a pixie cut was of-Harry. Both had the same reaction to discovering my identity as of-Liam.

Them: 'Oh. Yes. Right. I've never seen you at pickup. Do you work?'

Me: Having to explain about Liam's half days.

Them, with raised eyebrows: 'Oh. Why?'

Me: Explaining about diagnosis and awaiting a dedicated teaching assistant while silently wondering why I couldn't just tell them to mind their own sodding business.

Them: 'Does he really need that? Probably just trying his luck. Where will the school find the money? If he really can't cope, maybe he needs a special school.'

Liam's partner was Orwell. As in of-Ingrid. Orwell also had questions. So many fucking questions. He wanted to know why I only had to look after the two of them and was it because I wasn't as good as the other mummies. He asked why Liam always got angry and why Liam "talks that way" and he did so right in front of Liam. I asked him why his mummy wasn't on the trip. And yes, I know it was wrong and I should be ashamed of myself.

'She's making plans for the arrival of my new Chinese brother,' Orwell replied, unblinking. Then he asked why I didn't have more than two children and was it because we didn't have enough money?

At which point I tried to distract him with the old look-over-there trick.

'Look at the small Big Ben,' I exclaimed, mildly hysterically.

He didn't even look. Or blink. Instead he told me he'd been there loads of times before and anyway it was for babies.

The one thing that made it all just about bearable was Liam. Liam loved every moment of it. He was entranced by the little world just as I had been at his age. He gripped my hand the entire time, telling every school friend we passed that I was his mummy. What's more, I noticed that children constantly sought him out. That they laughed at his antics and joined in with their own.

'He and Kai get on especially well.' Miss Flowers said to me as I watched Liam and a little girl chattering and climbing in the playground.

Ah. So this was the legendary Kai. I'd have to tell Jake I had seen him in the flesh. And that he was a she.

'He's very popular,' Miss Flowers added.

'Really? I thought with the... behaviour things...' I tailed off, unsure how to finish.

'At this age, kids are incredibly accepting. That'll change, but so will he.' Something caught her eye, making her face fall. 'Oh, God. Orwell, leave that pigeon alone.'

My heart soared unexpectedly, released of a weight I hadn't even realised was there. Liam had friends. He was liked. In that moment, as Orwell was separated from pigeon, I felt so much love and optimism, I thought it could power me for a year.

But then came the interminable journey home. And Liam demanding an exact time of arrival every nanosecond. And why weren't the cars moving? And why was that lane faster than ours? And we were going to be late. Or run out of petrol. Or die. And me trying to dampen his increasing ire with soothing words proving about as effective as hiring a wolf for the position of sheepdog.

I was so engrossed in mollifying Liam, I didn't even notice when Orwell vomited on my shoes.

We arrived, dehydrated and demoralised, an hour after school pickup. Charlie was delighted by our tardiness. I had signed him up for after-school club for that day, not knowing that it is the nearest thing to a real life recreation of *Lord of the Flies* aside from soft play.

'They had biscuits! And iPads.' Then, on the way home, he'd asked, 'You'll come on my school trip too, right mummy?'

Shite. I couldn't exactly say no. Still, at least there won't be a coach. We're travelling there on London Underground. So maybe it won't be that bad.

All that alone would have been enough to get this day a solid space on the top worst days list. What really propels it to a top spot though is waiting for me at home. On my computer.

Three identical subject lines glower at me from my inbox on Blog2Book. They read "YOU'RE BLG".

I am BLG? I wrack my increasingly expansive suite of acronyms, but no. There is no BLG. According to Urban Dictionary it refers to the band, Boys Like Girls. Either that or "Bitches Love Granola". I like granola. I cannot claim to love it though.

Whatever it means, it's at the top of three very angry emails about my blog.

Extract: Angry Email No. 1

NOT TANTRUMS MELTDOUNS

Mama Bear

Extract: Angry Email No. 2

DO URE RESEARCH

Tiger Mom

Extract: Angry Email No. 3

MELTDOUWNS NOT SAM AS TANTRMS

Mommy Mouse

I feel sick. And tired. My heart is pounding and my head is throbbing and I've lost all feeling in my feet. I imagine this was how Goldilocks felt when confronted by three furious bears.

The situation is not improved when I, on the advice of Tiger Mom, google the words tantrum and meltdown. In fact, all it does is plunge me into a vortex of dread and doubt.

Tantrums v Autistic Meltdowns: A Brief Summary

1. Tantrums are goal oriented. A child wants something, is told no, loses their proverbial shit. Autistic meltdowns are caused by being overwhelmed. They are a totally involuntary reaction to a sensory overload

or unexpected factor. This makes sense. Often times, Liam's anger erupts from utterly inexplicable demands. Like the time he destroyed his room because I wasn't able to drive him to Mars after an afternoon spent in soft play. He wasn't upset about my inability to Elon Musk him 317.59 million kilometres across the galaxy. He was over-stimulated.

2. Meltdowns and tantrums can look the same. Screaming, crying, stamping, the whole megillah. On the other hand, some meltdowns result in a complete shutdown with the person unable to speak or move. I am ashamed to say that I had a little moment upon reading this. A little moment where I fantasised about Liam switching to that type of meltdown.

3. Tantrums require a witness. Meltdowns happen with or without others present. I can attest to this. On more than one occasion I had been completely unaware that Liam was even angry about something until I heard a door slamming in the distance. It was like that philosophical thought experiment about a tree falling in the woods. If a meltdown happens when nobody's around, does the bedroom get destroyed? The answer was a resounding yes.

Thus, tantrums are not meltdowns. And I wrote the word tantrum about a bajillion times to describe what were clearly meltdowns. I really do know nothing. And that is now on the internet for all to troll.

Reason inserts itself into my thought process. "So what?" It asks. "So you made a mistake. It's not a big deal. You didn't mean to offend anyone and anyway, it's just a blog. It'll go unnoticed."

Reason is joined by Logic. "Just explain. People will understand."

It is then that Panic, Paranoia, Anxiety and Anecdotal Evidence rock up to beat the living shit out of Reason and Logic. And throughout, they yell incomprehensibly about nobody caring what you mean and being cancelled and publicly shamed and turned into a meme.

"All the memes!" Shrieks anxiety.

Anecdotal Evidence is in its element. "Ever heard of that girl who posted that thing and got off a flight and her life was ruined? Cat bin lady? Couch guy? Ed Balls?"

Everyone stops.

"Ed Balls?"

"You know what I mean. He did the... Never mind."

I do know what anecdotal evidence means. I know what happens when someone makes a mistake on the internet. Oh fuck. What have I done? Why didn't I tell Jake? Why did I ever start this blog?

And this is how my conflicting thoughts cause me to freeze, overwhelming me like a crashing computer in an eternal loop.

Oh. Hold on. I just got it. BLG. Blog. She meant to write blog. Your blog. My phone buzzes with a notification.

You Have Been Added to the WhatsApp Group PTA Christmas Event.

Thursday, 11 October

The new Wheat Wheatums have arrived. The box says "New and Improved Recipe!" I decant the cereal into one of my plastic IKEA cereal dispensers and stare at it. It looks the same. Right? Is it a slightly darker shade of brown? Is it a lighter shade of brown? Oh god.

Jake and I embark on a hushed-whisper argument along the lines of:
'He'll notice.'
'No he won't. I tasted it. It's exactly the same.'
'I should say something.'
'Don't you dare.'
'You're sure I shouldn't warn him?'
'Absolutely not. Are you mad? Just pretend everything's normal.'
'You do it.'
'But you usually give him it.'
Liam takes one look at the contents of his bowl and declares it a fraud.
'Just try it,' I wheedle. It's Weezows.'
Jake leans in close to my ear.
'Mm, maybe not.'
I turn away from the table, my tone that of an unexploded bomb.
'What?'
'It tastes different.'
'You said it was the same.'
'It's almost the same.'
'That's not the same. It is different. That is the fricking opposite of the same.'

Over the coming two hours, it is evident that Liam has decided that we are responsible for this injustice. That we have conspired to deprive him of his beloved Weezows because we want his life to be miserable and bad. He tips the bowl off the table. Then he starts the door banging. Followed by telling us he's leaving forever. Then struggling with the front door. Jake is smug at this point. He has installed an extra lock.

'He won't be able to budge it,' he murmurs to me. 'It's unbreakable. Locks.com ranked it first for durability.'

And so, we let Liam pull and push and generally abuse the front door, safe in the reassurance offered by locks.com.

For the record, the lock stays put. The door remains locked. Hermetically sealed. So locked that we are then unable to open it later that night.

'I'll have to remove it,' Jake marvels. But it won't come off. 'He must have budged something in the mechanism,' Jake grumbles, peering closely at it.

He refuses to call a locksmith. Which is why the boys and I must leave the house from the back door the next morning. And I call the locksmith myself when I get back from drop-off.

Friday, 12 October

'I did something online.' I tell Nisha this over the phone in the style of Liam Neeson in Taken, informing the kidnapper of his "very special set of skills". Then I add. 'And I haven't told Jake.'

'Porn?'

'What the- What is wrong with you? What about my extreme social awkwardness makes you think I'd do porn?'

'You don't dance or do parkour. And Sir Francis would never let you film him. That's the only one left. Unless you're gambling.'

'No.' And I hurry to explain before she can conjure up any other possibilities. I am interrupted when I notice Liam hovering over Charlie, a glazed smile warning of an incoming attack.

'Liam, no. Don't touch your brother. I don't care if he looked at you.'

When I return to Nisha, she's found the blog and read a couple of entries.

'These are great,' she says. 'And you really don't have to worry about those emails. I actually think they've done you a favour.'

'How's that?' I ask, not convinced.

There's an exasperated sigh and I imagine Nisha rolling her eyes.

'Your whole schtick is being new to this autism thing. So, it makes sense you don't know the lingo. Put out the blog tonight with a note saying there will be a follow up and tomorrow write another thing about these emails and correcting it all. There's probably loads of mums who also don't know.'

Is she right? She might be. No. It cannot possibly be that simple. I must drift into silence for a while, because now it's Nisha's turn to ask if I'm still there.

'Maya?'

'Yeah.'

'You know you have to tell Jake, right?'

'Yeah, fine,' I grumble.

Then she regales me with a story about Aran swearing in school. Mr Davies had called her in to complain that he had taken to yelling "cock-a-fucking-doo" at random times.

'Where did he hear that?' I ask. 'It's genius.'

'Fuck knows. But he's got me saying it now.'

When remonstrated, Aran had denied doing any such thing, despite the overwhelming evidence of over thirty witnesses to the contrary. Apparently he'd blamed the Mandela effect.

'They don't even know yet that he's behind the spate of thefts in his class,' she guffaws. 'Every time I open his bag it's like a fucking lucky dip. Rulers, pens, a hair clip. I suppose I should be grateful he's good enough at it not to get caught. Little shit.'

'Are you worried? What are you going to do?' I ask.

'No fucking clue. So far, I've just been sneaking the stuff back in. I've been in that classroom so much lately Mrs Dixon asked me if I'm suffering separation anxiety.'

We laugh at this and, by the time we disconnect I'm smiling at Nisha's deliberation of whether she is a modern day Robin Hood.

Bzzz

Shit. Another effing notification. I know without looking that it is from the PTA Christmas Event group. I know this because it has been nonstop ever since I was added to it.

This is due, in large part, to the fact that of the thirty group members, not one is capable of writing a concise, complete message. Instead, they split their thoughts over three or four missives. Then they overlap with others doing the same. And then everyone is messaging at cross purposes. And everyone is confused. So there are clarifications. And so on.

Which would be fine (ish) if they were relaying important information. From what I can tell, most of it isn't even related to the PTA, let alone the Christmas Fair. It is people asking if they're supposed to bring a PE kit in. And there was one very long discussion about the marital status of various members of staff.

I look down as there is another buzz.

Ingrid
Check it out

Also Ingrid
My latest FIM post!

Ingrid Again
It's on Insta guys!

Ingrid... Once more for the cheap seats
BIG NEWS COMING.

Then she sends a series of Memojis. These are emojis made to look like the sender. I think they look like those police sketches of suspects. Specifically the ones from the 1970's that made everyone looked like a scuffed peanut.

For some reason, presumably a deep psychological flaw I'm better off not acknowledging, I do check her "Insta". It's a photo of her and her husband, both looking into the camera with wide eyed enigmatic expressions, an Austen Powers finger to each of their lips and a caption that says, "Watch This Space!"

I frown at my screen. I have to hand it to Ingrid. It takes whale-proportion-sized balls to tell thirty busy school mums to check out a post that said nothing except that there would be more posts.

I'm all ready to tell Jake as much when he gets home, but he also has something to say.

'I have the answer.'

I hadn't been aware there was a question.

'I've been thinking about Liam. About his future,' Jake babbles, lifting his laptop out of his work bag and flipping it open. 'I don't want him disadvantaged just because he's autistic. So I did some research.'

I too had been researching things in relation to The Special Mum. Especially autism terminology.

'Did you know that some people are offended by saying that someone is autistic?' I ask. 'You're supposed to say he has autism. Because it's only one part of their identity.'

'Okay, I don't want him disadvantaged just because he has autism.'

'Ah, but others are offended by that because they see it as a fundamental part of who they are.'

Jake frowns without looking away from his laptop. 'Which are you offended by?'

'I don't know. That's the thing. I think I'm supposed to have an opinion, but I don't.' I don't mention that this makes me worry I'm a bad special needs mum. I have visions of being voted off the special needs mum island.

'Don't worry about it,' Jake says. The screen of his laptop displays a spreadsheet. I should say, Jake loves spreadsheets. They combine his favourite things, namely data, sorting and filtering. If it can be confined into columns and rows, Jake has forever immortalised it into one of his complex, multi-formula creations. And this one is a behemoth. A beast. It is the spreadsheet that has eaten all the other ones.

'It's called ABA,' he begins excitedly. 'Applied Behavioural Analysis. It's the gold standard of autism therapy. Totally based in science.'

My mind drifts for a moment to the faint bell tolling in the distance. I've heard of ABA. I can't remember where from…

'I mean, it's a tad pricey and reasonably intensive,' Jake is saying. 'But they really get results.'

'Gosh,' I breathe. 'Quite the sales pitch.'

'Sales?' He scoffs. 'They don't need sales. This sells itself.' His eyes gleam with a convert's zeal. And he is in no way finished. Not even close. 'Seriously. Their trained experts use tried and tested techniques combined with data to address all types of behaviour in children with autism.'

'Not *data*,' I gasp. Normally, such blatant sarcasm would incur return fire. An equally snarky retort. At the very least an eyeroll. But to my horror, Jake takes my words at face value.

'Yes,' he gushes right back. 'And Caroline said they even have ways of dealing with tantrums.'

I look into my darling husband's unblinking gaze and resign myself to the obvious. Jake has been lobotomised. Somewhere between our house and his office, his sense of sarcasm had been surgically removed.

I may have drifted off into my own head for a time because when I zone back in, Jake is saying, 'She's a leading expert in the UK's ABA community. We're really lucky she had a spot open up so soon.'

'Sorry, what's that now?'

'Caroline,' Jake repeats. 'She's going to help us put together our ABA team.'

Caroline. Caroline, of course. Caroline will solve everything.

'Who?' I croak.

'The ABA consultant. Have you even been listening?'

No.

'Yes, yes, of course. Caroline. ABA. Next week.'

'And you're on board?'

For some reason, all I can think is, who says "on board"?

Saturday, 13 October

'I think Jake has joined a cult.'

Nisha and Gabby both freeze like contestants in musical statues. As well they might. I have hissed this at them apropos of absolutely nothing. I had no choice. We had, just seconds earlier, furnished our children with snacks. Even by the most generous of calculations that gave us five minutes of uninterrupted conversation, tops. There is no room for preamble.

Gabby is the first to break formation. She always was crap at musical statues.

'Explain,' she intones gravely.

I tell them about the ABA. And about Caroline and Jake asking if I'm on board.

'On board?' Nisha interrupts. 'Who says on board?'

'I know.'

'So what did you say?' She asks.

My exact words had been "Right there with you. On the board. Ship. On board." Because what else could I say? Who are you and what have you done with my husband?

Having relayed all of this, I pin my sister and friend with a "well?" glare, awaiting their dispensation of wisdom.

'It might not be a cult,' Nisha offers. 'He might be cheating on you.'

'I think Hugh's cheating on me,' says Gabby contemplatively.

Nisha and I both lose control of our lower jaws at the exact moment that the imaginary timer runs out on the children's eating clock.

'I don't want to,' Charlie yells.

Liam is crying. He pushes Charlie and now Charlie is crying.

'Mummy I need weewee,' Saira whines.

'I don't need this shit,' opines Aran.

We never quite manage to bring things back under control after that. We try hypnotising the children with TV, but none of them can agree on a film or show. And so we are left on a ridiculous cliff hanger and unable to help Gabs.

'Can we meet for drinks later?' Gabby asks.

Nisha and I look at her askance.

'At night?' I ask, just as Nisha says, 'Somewhere out?'

'Yes, at night somewhere out. You're talking like you never go anywhere after dark.'

Nisha and I share a look. It is one that says, I won't tell her if you don't.

'I go out after dark,' I inform her. After all, I took the bins out last night and it was pitch black.

'Okay,' Nisha says reluctantly. 'Rishi's on call, but I think my mum can babysit.'

'I'm not sure,' I say, unable to imagine leaving Jake alone with both children. What if he did it to me?

'Please?'

I look at my sister. Gabby needs me. Right now. And there's no way to have this conversation in daylight, child-waking hours.

'Okay.'

'You're not drinking?' Gabby asks, eyeing my orange juice.

'God no.'

'Preggers?' She parries.

I fix her with my best one-is-not-amused scowl.

'Wash your mouth out.'

I am in a bar. I can't believe I'm in a bar. I haven't done this since… Well, in a long time. Oh, and it's 8:30pm. As in, at night. It's dark outside and everything. Gabby, who has a nanny and thus a proper social life, said I looked like a dog with its head out the window as Nisha drove us here. I couldn't help it. I was marvelling at how many people were out. At night. *Look at them*, I'd thought. *Driving and walking. Ooh, those ones are in a restaurant.* My tongue may have lolled in the excitement of it all.

As for alcohol, I am not equipped to drink and parent. Doubly so as Liam wakes at least once a night. Even sober as a judge, I do not cope well on first waking. I become a hybrid of Frankenstein's Monster and Mr Bean, all lurching movements and clumsy antics. The one time I came home sloshed from a cousin's wedding, Liam awoke from a nightmare and asked why mummy was acting like SpongeBob. In truth, Jake usually does the nights, but that leaves me in charge of mornings and if there is one creature more fearsome than Drunk Night Mummy, it is Hungover Morning Mummy.

I used to drink. And go out. All the time. I was once the sort of carefree party animal who felt at home in places far rowdier, not to mention trendier, than a North London branch of All Bar One.

Things calmed down significantly by the time Jake and I got married. We went to bars and restaurants, but it was all much more civilised. We had long ceased seeing the attraction of cramming into loud basement clubs for the privilege of queueing for both the bar and loos. We frequented rather than crawled pubs. And we definitely didn't select a venue on the basis that they were doing two for one on vodka and Redbull.

Obviously, it all came to a screeching halt when we had Charlie. Up all night was no longer an optional extra, but an inescapable reality. Bottles were filled with formula rather than sambuca. And weekends lost all meaning.

I think I'd always assumed that there would be a time when we'd start going out again. When we would reclaim a portion of our pre-parent lives. That seems to have been the case for most people. They'd dip their toes in the water three or four months after the birth, then within a year or two, they'd have some sort of regular rhythm.

Our toes remained bone dry. I was pregnant within six months of Charlie's birth. Then Liam arrived and it started all over again. Except it seemed infinitely harder. Because it *was* infinitely harder. Because having two kids is not like double of one kid. It is not twice a known quantity. It is an escalation. Like adding the detonator to the bomb. We never had the energy or will to attempt leaving the house. It was all we could do to have dinner and collapse on the sofa.

And it wasn't like we could merrily hire a babysitter. We couldn't ask someone else to do what we couldn't even do ourselves.

In short, it was like we never graduated from the newborn phase. And now I am the "lady" at the bar clutching her handbag and juice, suspiciously eyeing the young folk.

As soon as we've all been served, Nisha prompts Gabby to tell us what's been going on.

'Oh, you know, the usual clichés,' my sister sighs.

'What? Like you found a text?' Nisha guesses.

'He told me he was working late.'

'Oh,' I gasp, understanding immediately. Nisha does not. Her husband, Rishi is a senior neurological consultant at one of London's busiest hospitals. He always works late. And early. And all the time. Hugh on the other hand...

'Hugh doesn't work,' Gabby explains, morosely slugging her wine like it's vodka. Only once she has slammed it down does she belatedly make bunny ear speech marks with her fingers, presumably for the word "work". 'He says he does, but it's all busy work. Pretend.'

I know this. We all do. Hugh is a mere caretaker of the family business. A business with enough staff and senior managers to ensure it ticks along nicely. But none of us dare to say so in Gabby's presence. And I've never heard *her* actually say as much. Up until this moment, we have all played along with the pretence that Hugh "works" to earn money.

'Plus, he's an idiot,' Gabby mutters. 'Constantly texting and hanging up the phone when I walk in. Last time I asked him who he'd been talking to. You know what he said?' She laughs mirthlessly. 'Nobody. He couldn't even think up a decent lie.'

'But you've never actually seen anything from or to another woman?' Nisha checks.

'Don't have to.'

'Actually, you sort of do,' I put in, surprised that I'm suggesting giving Hugh the benefit of the doubt.

I've never liked Hugh. He is a smarmy poser. On a fictional character traits scale, he's somewhere in the region of *Mad Men*'s Don Draper, only without the talent or occupation. It's fair to say I've given this some thought. For example, I wouldn't compare him to *Wall Street*'s Gordon Gecko. If only because Hugh has never had cause to chase money. It just drops into his lap like an obedient pup. I haven't the psychological expertise to determine if he is a psychopathic nightmare a la Patrick Bateman of *Psycho*. And in any event I just don't believe his waters run that deep.

All of which to say that I wouldn't put it past him to be a lying, cheating bastard. Nevertheless, Hugh and Gabby have a life, children. And the evidence stacked thus far isn't exactly a glaring indictment of infidelity. It takes some coaxing and her imbibing three more large glasses of Malbec, but Gabby seems to take this in.

'Fine,' She declares. 'I'll holoff on dudment.' She turns glazed eyes on me. 'Waddabout you, sis? Wass going on with Dakey?'

'Dakey?' I deadpan. But Gabby is beyond the reach of snark.

'Dakey,' she confirms, unrepentant.

'It's nothing,' I sigh, uncomfortable for my minor niggles to follow on from Gabby's major one. 'He's just a bit off, you know?'

'How's he coping with the whole diagnosis thing?' Nisha asks.

'Fine.'

'Srsly?' Gabby garbles.

'Dear god. How are you still such a lightweight?' Nisha laughs, then calls to the bartender. 'Can we get a strong coffee here please?' I'm unprepared when she turns her undivided attention my way. 'Are you sure he's fine?'

My friends' line of questioning catches me off guard. Of course Jake has been fine. Why would they think otherwise?

'I mean, he struggled before the diagnosis,' I venture. 'But as soon as a doctor said it, he accepted it. And he hasn't said anything. He's just surprised me with this sudden devotion to a therapy I've never heard him mention before. It's weird, but all of this is.'

'I'm not sure he's fine,' Nisha hedges.

The bartender arrives with the coffee and she pointedly shoves it Gabbywards.

'Drink.'

'Yes mother,' grumbles Gabby, executing an eyeroll of which her sixteen-year-old self would have been proud.

Nisha watches to ensure that my sister puts cup to mouth then swivels back to me.

'Look, I think it's amazing how brilliantly you're coping with this. I don't think many people could do the same. I know I wouldn't.'

Gabby nods in emphatic agreement, but after receiving a stern eyebrow raise from Nisha, sullenly returns to drinking her coffee. 'Maybe this is like one of the five stages of grief or something. Like denial or bargaining. I'm just putting it out there. You don't have to deal with it right now if you don't want to.'

'Maybe,' I mumble.

'Right.' Nisha clears her throat and shuffles about on her stool. 'Next up, tell your sister about the blog. Then we'll sort world peace.'

'I don't think you need us for that.'

'Yeah, seems like it's well within your...' Gabby waves a manicured hand elaborately before dropping it. 'You know.'

My sister shows an appropriate amount of interest in The Special Mum. Exactly the amount I show whenever she sends me a clip of the horse-riding competitions in which she occasionally competes. It is more than that shown to a school mum telling you she's running a marathon, less than when watching your kids perform in the school nativity.

Gabby, who seems to be sobering up, eagerly finds the Blog2Book website and scours the contents. She skims one of my posts, but is more interested in the competition.

'Oh my god,' Gabby's eyes widen at her phone screen. 'This one is nuts.'

'Quite literally,' Nisha smirks when Gabby shows her.

I don't need them to specify which blog.

'The student one?' I guess. 'Yeah, they're really gunning for gold, but I think the chickens are still in the running. So to speak.'

'There's still ages to go though. Nothing stopping you from winning.'

'Yeah, Nish,' I guffaw. 'Only four hundred or so blogs in my way.'

'Three hundred,' she corrects.

'No, I'm number four hundred and something.'

'Not according to this.'

And she's right. I smile as I see I am now the proud resident of number 312 on the chart.

'Speaking of blogs,' Gabby purrs. 'Did you see that Ingrid's announced she's going to announce something?'

'How is that a thing?' I demand. 'Announcing an announcement. When did we start doing that?'

They both ignore me in favour of speculating wildly as to what the announcement might be. Suggestions include climbing Mount Everest en famille, a new house/car/pet and another pregnancy.

'I'll bet it's just where they're going for half term.'

I choke on my orange juice.

'Half,' splutter, cough. 'Term?' Cough, splutter, splutter. 'When?'

'Next week,' Nisha replies, looking at me like I should know that. Which I should. And might have done if I didn't exercise a strict head-in-the-sand code of pretending school breaks won't happen.

'The girls are already on half term,' says Gabby. 'They've gone to a camp in Switzerland with their friends, but next week we're all in Mauritius.'

I have never understood how it is that private schools charge so much and yet have what seems like twice the amount of holidays. There again, I can't imagine a world where I could say that my boys are at camp in North London let alone Scandinavia so there's that. And Mauritius.

'You got plans?' Gabby wisely directs this at Nisha. She knows what my answer would be. Zero. Zilch. Nada. Nisha's answer is not much better.

'I'll be in Brum for a mandatory inspection.' "Mandatory inspection" is Nisha's name for her visits to Rishi's family in Birmingham. This is delivered with a sulky pout. Because apparently we must all have a turn at being Vicky from *Little Britain* tonight.

'Glum in Brum,' Gabby scoffs, earning a death stare and a warning.

'I will end you.'

'It won't be that bad,' I intercede, adopting the feverishly cheerfully BBC presenter voice I use trying to convince the kids going to the dentist will be a blast. It works just as well on Nisha as it does them. Which is to say not at all.

'Do you not remember last time?' She asks, a touch of hysteria in her voice. Ah yes, last time. When Rishi's mother got a bee in her bonnet about them moving nearer to Birmingham. She even phoned the hospital director to see about a transfer. The hospital director, himself the son of some very pushy parents, had at least understood why a consultant's mummy was calling. 'And now his parents are obsessed with the kids knowing Hindi. Apparently his brother's kids speak it so much better.'

'But you send them to classes for that, right?'

'Ha. Not the right classes and not enough. And why do I not speak to them in Hindi all the time? And have we considered moving to Birmingham? And why don't I just stop all this work silliness and cook proper meals?' She sighs. 'How did you get your parents to run away?'

'Just luck I guess.'

Sunday, 14 October

LUNCH
(You, Gabby, Nisha)

You

[Photo]

Gabby, would you care to explain yourself?

        Gabby

        Whered u get that?

You

I'll ask the questions thanks yo very much.#
Insta. Someone tagged you

ODD MUM OUT

Gabby

Oh yeh! My yoga instructr Clara. Nice pic

Whats wring with it?

*wrong

You

You woz SLOSHD last nite. How dare you do YOGI at 8am with this supermodel??? And make me look at it?

*yoga

Nisha

Unaccep

table

Blood hell she is hot 🌶

Gabby

Clara?

Nisha

No the tree 😶

behind the Ruby Rose lookalike

Gabby

SHIT. You seen Ingid latest vid???

You

What? No

🙈

ADOPTION UPDATE - BIG NEWS!!!
FOURISMORE ✓ • 1 HOUR AGO

Ingrid: 'I am just so excited to share this with you all. So, our adoption agency just showed us a picture of a little boy. And he is perfect. I don't know how to explain this. I just know he's ours. It's not official yet. They want to talk to us about some of his needs. Um, long-time followers will know that, like, to adopt from the country in question when you already have kids, they only allow adoption of kids with special needs. But we are so okay with that. I have a lot of experience working with kids with special needs as part of my charitable work and we have been doing so much research and we are just so prepared. I know we can give him an amazing home.'

Sunday, 21 October

Lunch at the in-laws. Kelly wanted to know how we possibly hadn't realised earlier about Liam's autism and do we think we might have missed anything else.

At which point Charlie came into the room and told me my face looked like a tomato.

And tomorrow it's half term.

Monday, 22 October

'What can I have?'
'Stop singing!'
'Don't want an apple. I want a Freddo.'
'Paw Patrol is on a roll!'
'FREDDO!'
Summer holiday flashbacks.
Fuck this. I wish I was a penguin.

Friday, 26 October

Oh, the joy. The peace. Jake has taken a day off and is playing football with the boys in the garden. For the first time in days, my head bobs above the flash flood waters of half term.

It's been eventful. There was a day out at a National Trust property with Archie and Delia, a couple of days at a kids' multi-activity camp, play dates and lots of rest and relaxation. For Charlie. Only for Charlie.

Liam, on the other hand, refused to leave the house. At all. Under any circumstances. Thus, this football game in the garden is the first time my son has seen daylight in seven days. Likewise, I have not ventured into the great outdoors since last Friday.

'But there's a maze,' Delia had crooned to my second-born on the morning we were supposed to go to Cliveden.

'And sandwiches,' Archie had added. Archie loves sandwiches. Lives for them. I can relate. There is little I will not endure for a bit of Leerdamer between two slices of Hovis. Or any carb for that matter. It's how he and I bonded when we first met. Over a lively discussion about fillings. So it is understandable that Archie would deem bready goodness a powerful draw. It is also wrong.

It is wrong because Liam has made up his mind. That done, there is nothing that will change it. Nothing. I know this from experience. No, sod that. I know it because Jake and I have conclusively proved as much through rigorous scientific methods. Ish.

Scientific(ish) Evidence That Liam Cannot Be Swayed

1. The time I tried convincing him to leave a birthday party bouncy castle by offering him an entire chocolate cake at home. The birthday boy left before we did.
2. In Liam's clingy-to-daddy phase, Jake promising him a new toy if he would just let go of his leg. Then all the toys. Jake fell asleep with Liam still attached.
3. The time I refused to give him another 50p for a sodding mechanical fire engine outside Sainsbury's that he'd already ridden twice. I stood my ground. I was determined. It helped that I didn't even have any coins left. When I showed him my empty purse, he frowned for a moment. Then flagged down a passing old lady to donate to his cause. Which she did.

Margaret Thatcher famously said, "the lady is not for turning". Well, she was a bloody carousel compared to my son.

Put in a positive light – because why the fuck not – this is an invaluable trait that will take him far. He could grow up to be a formidable negotiator. Or CEO of a tech company. Or President of the United States. Who cares that he wasn't born there and so should be disqualified from running? He can make it so.

He's not stubborn. He's headstrong. He's not mulish. He's unshakable. Whichever way you spin it, we have to live with him in the meantime.

Can we change him? Should we change him? In a world that prizes certitude over sense, a society where the strong-willed triumph over the cerebral, should I be trying to soften his edges? Because Jake and I are the only ones who can. We're the ones responsible for socialising him.

Fuck knows. The point is, Delia and Archie attempted to reason with him and to bribe him and finally, they did what I'd suggested at the beginning and just took Charlie.

I wouldn't have minded Liam's desire to shut himself away for a week. Would even have welcomed it. I am not above a bit of home hibernation. And it might have been quite nice. Had Liam's mood not been darker than a Norwegian Christmas. Which is what it was. In fact, were it to have a colour, it would be that shade of the blackest black developed by MIT scientists, only without the need for vertically aligned carbon nanotubes.

He spent every waking moment in a gargantuan grump. We've had all the greatest hits – sometimes quite literally – this week. We averaged one major meltdown per day, signposted each time by a series of preceding mini ones. It's like living on the surface of a tectonic plate that's having a sneezing fit while suffering from the hiccups. I even thought about devising my own version of the Richter scale for meltdowns. But then decided that that was too depressing.

Facebook assures me that all this is perfectly normal. The mums of SEN For Help have been posting up a storm with anecdotes of a similar nature; of kids who regress or whose behaviour intensifies in the holidays. According to one member, it's the transition from school to home, the change from structured to unstructured days, which causes instability and emotional dysregulation.

I had to look up that phrase. Emotional dysregulation. Put far too simply, for I am a humble creature, Liam's reactions to emotions are supersized. It's like the saying about how everything is bigger in Texas. Liam's response to a feeling is louder, more pronounced, more exaggerated. Generally, just "more".

This makes it sound benign. Good, even. Like the parents of children who struggle to cope with their emotions might have to contend with nothing more than excessive skipping or extreme smiling. In severe cases, a child might jump atop the sofa while on a well-known chat show in a hyperbolic declaration of love.

But no. The list of examples of emotional dysregulation reads less like a recount of Woodstock and more like the progressively incoherent night of a drunk lout after their team loses on penalties.

Signs of emotional dysregulation include:

1. A tendency towards angry outbursts.
2. An argumentative and/or defiant disposition.
3. Holding grudges.
4. Problems complying with rules.

All of which nicely summarises my week. Now, however, I have my first taste of freedom. An hour, maybe even two, when I am not in sole charge of my delightful offspring. So, how am I spending it? Am I running in a field breathing fresh air? Watching TV that isn't about cartoon dogs with dubious problem-solving skills? Going to the Post Office?

No. And actually, I do really need to go to the Post Office to return something. But instead, I am at my computer. Like the cave dwelling hermit I long to be, writing my latest blog post for The Special Mum.

This has become my version of "me time". Some women do self care. Others jog or garden or do courses on interior design. I rant and rave online about the ridiculousness of my life. And it's bloody amazing. Seriously. It's like tidying my brain. I am Marie Kondo-ing my mind, putting everything into neat little paragraphs and bullet points. Except instead of discarding anything that fails to "bring me joy" or whatever it is that Marie says, I yell about it virtually.

OMG. I think I have a hobby. Me. A hobby.

The best part is, I'm developing a little following. Very little. Tiny, actually. There's about twenty of them. But they are lovely. There's Moody Mummy, Dad of Dan, Ginny Fizzy, FMLauren and Not Tiger Mum, among others. All of them have at least one child with special needs. Moody Mummy has three: a 7 year old boy and twin 4 year-olds. Her eldest is diagnosed with autism and ADHD, while her younger two are awaiting diagnosis.

However it is Tepid Mess with whom I chat most frequently. She was the one who introduced me to all the Facebook groups and has proved a font of knowledge in all things SEN. Tepid is a single mum of a ten-year-old daughter with autism whom she refers to as D. Apparently when D goes into meltdown, she completely shuts down. She stops talking, curls up in a ball and rocks. I told Jake about this, omitting, of course, how I had heard of it.

"Wait. So, is this after the kicking and hitting?" Jake had asked.

'No,' I'd revealed reverently. 'Instead.'

At which a look of confusion and awe had spread across my husband's face.

'So,' he'd hesitantly ventured. 'There's no physical stuff? The kid just...' Here, he had shaped his hands into a ball roughly the size of a hedgehog.

'Yep.'

Jake had blinked slowly. 'Wow.'

'I know. Imagine it.'

Jake had sighed, a faraway look in his eyes. 'That's the dream.'

This sort of thinking obviously makes us monsters. Horrible, despicable monsters. It also made us wrong. That's quite important. Because, as it turns out, the greener grass on the other side of the fence is actually artificial turf.

In other words, shutdowns are every bit as shit for all involved as outbursts. D's shutdowns can last for weeks. That's meant missed holidays, missed school and Tepid missing so much work, she lost her job. Tepid has even been threatened with actual jail for D's supposed truancy, so it turns out that's true.

Oh, and if all that wasn't enough, the fact that D shut down instead of acting up made it virtually impossible for Tepid to get her help.

Okay. So, I'd been baffled by that one at first. I believe I responded at the time with a bajillion question marks and no fewer than three confused emojis. How could anyone doubt that D needed help? She had a diagnosis. Actual medical reports. What the actual flap?

Tepid's answer had been about as cheering as joining the line in the Post Office.

Tepid Mess: Kid doesn't set the classroom on fire? Doesn't send the TA to A&E? Well then, they're fine.

It took me a while to get my head around what she meant by this.

Special Mum: You're saying they ignore her cos they can?

Tepid Mess: BINGO.

Having been told her daughter didn't qualify for any sort of financial or medical assistance, Tepid took what I think of as the persistent approach, but which others might equate with Captain Ahab's obsessive desire for vengeance against the whale that took his leg. Which is to say she phoned and wrote and badgered until someone listened. At the same time, she also got a new job and managed to spend her evenings learning educational law. The point is, she is a legend and who I want to be when I grow up.

Writing the posts has become second nature. It's a letter to friends. Admittedly, not everyone is a friend. I have plenty of negative responses. But I hardly get any death threats. Or at least any that imply commitment to the cause. I'd say I have found the perfect online balance. Just popular enough to exist. Not well-known enough to troll with conviction.

Today's blog is about the terrors of half-term and, as soon as I finish, I totally plan to go outside and join my family. Just after a quick check of Instagram.

The first post in my feed is by Irina, a mum I knew from the boys' nursery. I have never before experienced envy of Irina. She does not, by any standards, lead a carefree life, what with being a single mum to two sets of twins born within a year of each other. Having moved from Italy and thus having zero by way of support system, she had only just pushed out the third and fourth babies when her husband left her to pursue his dream of becoming a professional unicyclist. And yet, the two sets of identical boys and girls rock pooling on a beach in Norwich look like an Enid Blyton novel made flesh. It is, at minimum, a metric fuck-tonne more than I've done this week.

Gabby's posted some photos of her and the twins on a beach. Oh look. A pic of Hugh on the phone.

Ingrid has shared a photo of her family on a plane to a "surprise destination".

Seriously. Who the fuck turns their half-term holiday into a cliff-hanger? Like anyone cares where they go on holiday. Except people do care. The pic has been up for less than a day and already has thousands of likes.

'Mummy!'

Oh. Shit. My family. I should be outside with them.

'Maya,' Jake calls up. 'Bit of a situation here.'

The "situation" is both of my children falling in fox poo. One after the other. First was Liam. Then, Charlie, curious to see what the fuss was, followed suit. Judging from their clothes, they then proceeded to roll around in it just to really get it everywhere.

What follows reminds me of the laser scene in *Ocean's Twelve*. The one where French thief and Ocean's rival François Toulour weaves magnificently through a maze of constantly shifting laser beams. That's us trying to get the poo-clothing off the boys, only instead of trying to avoid the lasers/poo, they seem to actively seek it while screaming out helpful things like "It smells!" and "You're a poo face!".

The doorbell rings at 3pm.

Jake rushes to answer it. He never does this.

'That'll be Caroline,' he calls.

He says this like I should know who that is. Do I? Should I? A panicked search of my memory returns only an answering roll of tumbleweed. Fortunately, the tumbleweed tumbles away, replaced by the memory of Jake telling me about her. She's the therapist person. ABA. Yes. Shit. I had meant to look it up.

My husband enters the room accompanied by the living embodiment of an iStock image captioned "casual businesswoman". Her heels are high. Her trousers are floaty. Her cowl neck top tight. She has red lips, an Anna Wintour bob and a ballerina's poise. Oh, and she's tall. Neck-craningly so. It makes me feel like a toddler.

'Hi, I'm Caroline.'

Her voice is deep. Elizabeth Holmes deep. As in the woman who was the subject of that podcast, *The Dropout*. She famously faked having a low voice. Of course, that's quite far down the list of her offences. They do not make true crime podcast series about people being pretentious. Still, there's no reason to think that Caroline's voice is anything but genuine, I remind myself.

I make drinks while Jake attempts to kettle the children into anywhere but with us. It is a game of whack-a-mole. Every time one sits down the other gets up.

Sir Francis then makes an appearance. As a rule, our cat ignores guests. He sees them as beneath him. But he takes one look at Caroline and... well, that's it. He doesn't stop looking. He just sits there staring at her.

'He likes you,' I marvel. This is complete guesswork. I have no idea how Sir Francis would behave if he liked Caroline. It's never happened before.

Finally, we are settled and Caroline asks us about Liam. Jake does almost all the talking. I've never seen him like this before. He's like that kid in the class whose hand is permanently strained in the air, propped up by their other hand. The one the teacher never calls on because they're so bloody annoying. He is me.

'Right,' says Caroline. She relinquishes the pen she's been using to write notes and looks us in the eyes. Both of us. At the same time. I don't know how, but she manages it. 'Let me tell you about what I do.'

She explains that ABA is Applied Behavioural Analysis, a therapy that uses reinforcement strategies to improve social, communication, and learning skills.

As she talks, it becomes ever more evident that Caroline is something I can never be: A proper grownup. She probably emerged into the world fully formed with a pension plan and an ISA. Everything about her exudes inherent capability and certitude. I can say with confidence that Caroline has never offered a seat to a pregnant woman who wasn't pregnant. Or knocked over a jar of Dolmio in the Sainsbury's world foods aisle and turned at the sound only for her handbag to topple two more. She would certainly not be so preoccupied with nodding along in an important conversation that she has no idea what's been said.

Bugger. I really have to focus.

'ABA works,' Caroline is saying. 'It has more scientific evidence behind it than any other intervention. And I have seen it work to improve communication skills, attention, and academics while decreasing problem behaviours. I would expect to see noticeable improvement within two months.'

'So how often would he see you?' I ask this to appear engaged and like I belong in this adult conversation. But Jake and Caroline look awkward. Like I have just offered to show them my episiotomy scar.

'Remember, he won't usually see Caroline,' Jake says.

'I'm a consultant,' Caroline adds. 'I lead the ABA team. I'm going to spearhead your search for a tutor and supervisor. That's who will attend the sessions with Liam. Around twenty hours. Then we'll all meet at regular intervals to discuss progress and plan ahead.'

I blink.

'Twenty hours? A month?'

'A week,' Caroline says. 'I really would recommend forty, but I understand that's not tenable with school.'

I am still stunned when Caroline leaves. Sir Francis follows, disappearing through his cat flap. The boys, having been quiet for thirty whole minutes, make up for it now. Charlie chats at us in a series of non-sequiturs.

'Mummy did you live in the olden days?'

'Will you come to my wedding? Will you cancel all your other plans and make sure you can make it?'

'Cats are better than dogs. But not better than penguins.'

'Not naming any names but some of the girls in my class are very annoying. Like Sienna.'

Jake is corralled into a Snakes and Ladders marathon. A tetchy one. That ends with Liam refusing to go down a snake because "it shouldn't be there". If it was me, I'd let it go. Jake insists that Liam follow the rules.

Liam insists that Jake is the worst daddy ever. He wishes he could change family and that anywhere is better than this.

Ultimately, it is the snake who suffers, with Liam shoving it and the board it slithered in on into the kitchen bin. Then he kicks the bin, bursts into tears and tells Jake it is all his fault.

'Mummy,' Charlie drawls, sidling up to me as I hold closed a door Liam is trying to slam. Charlie doesn't appear bothered by this.

'Yes?'

'I love you.'

'Love you too.'

'If everyone in the world followed the rule to respect your elders then I think grandpa would be the king.'

Saturday, 27 October

WhatsApp has exploded. I have 213 messages across four groups. The first I check is LUNCH.

> **Nisha**
> Have you seen?????

> **Gabby**
> YES WTF

> **Nisha**
> I Know!

> **Gabby**
> It's really something.

> **Nisha**
> I'm crying! 😭

> **Gabby**
> Me too!!! 😭

This is unhelpful. As are the messages they sent asking me where I am and why aren't I watching? Then speculating that maybe I *am* watching and that's why I'm too busy to respond. Watching what?

I get my answer from the reception class group.

There is a video; a YouTube clip entitled "Dante's Gotcha Day! Part 1" It was posted by Ingrid and is a fifteen-minute-long montage set to Take That's song *The Greatest Day of Our Lives*. It chronicles her family travelling abroad to adopt a child.

As the song reaches its crescendo. Ingrid and co are shown waiting. The kids wave homemade flags saying things like "Welcome to the family" and "We love you little bro". One of the twins is eating their flag. Orwell looks like he might vomit. I say this from experience.

The little one arrives in the ample arms of a blurred-out person surrounded by other blurs. He looks to be around 18 months-old. Hard to tell though, what with his head plunged into a blurry bosom.

Ingrid's smiley face fills my computer screen. Her cheeks are wet. Her mascara is flawless.

'I can't believe it's happening,' she sniffs. 'We are so blessed. We have our son.'

And now I'm crying. Because it really is beautiful and it would take a monster not to be moved by it. This is reassuring. It never hurts to confirm that one is not a monster.

'As my long-time followers know,' Ingrid continues. `We chose to adopt a child with special needs. Because no child should be denied a loving home and we know we can provide that in spades. And now that Dante is with us, I can't imagine having any other child. He was always meant to be with us.'

Then she thanks her sponsor, Gym Sparks, and everyone who donated to their GoFundMe, finishing with, 'Don't forget to hit subscribe.'

Sunday, 28 October

Instagram Posts of @fourismore
Today

07:04: Dante waking up in his new bed!
07:15: Family breakfast! Chia seed porridge
07:30: Dante exploring the house!
07:34: Dante's ADORBS new outfit from @chickenbabies. Thanks guys! We love it xxxx
07:39: My latest Gym Spark threads. You like?
07:45: Going to the park! Wellies on!!!
08:30: At the park! Loving the leaves.

#adoption #proudmummy #newbaby #partofthefam #4ismore #gymsparks #cbapparel #gotcha #qualitytime

Monday, 29 October

Inset day. Bloody inset day. Which our school insists on tagging onto the end of every school holiday, just to make them extra shit.

INSTAGRAM POSTS OF @FOURISMORE

TODAY

07:08: Dante looking SUPER CUTE in @gagaforgoogoo outfit. Thanks guys! We love it xxxx
08:15: Bonding with grandma. My 🤍!!!!
09:50: Already a pro at TV studio!! Watch us on @riseandshine
09:55: Peekaboo! I see you.
10:30: Outfit by @mamamamabanana. Addicted to their clothes!!!

#adoption #proudmummy #newbaby #partofthefam #4ismore #gymsparks #cbapparel #gotcha #qualitytime #mamabanana

Tuesday, 30 October

Best. Day. Ever.

It doesn't even matter that the school sent a text about a spotty dress up day I'd never heard about but which is happening tomorrow including the obligatory "BRING CASH". It doesn't matter that Sir Francis is in a feud with a squirrel who stands outside the bifolds staring maniacally into the house. I don't even care that Charlie brought home three school jumpers – none of them his - that I then had to wash. Or that it's Halloween on Wednesday and I only realised after overhearing two mums talk about it this morning.

None of that can bring me down. Because this is the best day ever.

THE BEST DAY EVER: A SUMMARY

1. The boys are back at school.
2. Another inset day has been and gone.
3. I am in love with a woman called Cheryl.

Ah, Cheryl. What to say about Cheryl... Well, she's in her fifties, about five feet tall and, judging by the accent, hails from Scotland. Her spiky hair is bright pink and she has the warm yet no nonsense demeanour of Ron Weasley's mum, Molly. She is, in effect, Molly Weasley without the witchcraft. Although I wouldn't put that past her.

I met her this morning when dropping off Liam. It went something like this:

Miss Flowers: 'Mrs Harris, Liam, this is Cheryl. Cheryl is going to be helping out.'

Me: 'Hi, lovely to meet you.'

Cheryl (halo a-glowing, choir a-singing all around): 'Hello. I'm Cheryl.'

She then knelt down to Liam. 'Are you Liam?' There was some profuse nodding. 'I hear you know where everything is. I don't know where anything is. Could you show me round?'

I had to resist the urge to follow her. But I managed. And off they went. I watched as Liam led her away, chest puffed out with pride at being given the task of imparting vital knowledge.

Then Miss Flowers dragged me off into another room where we proceeded to fangirl.

'Oh my god she's amazing,' Miss Flowers gushed. 'She's got a level 4 Certificate SEN support.'

'Level *four*?' I gasped. I had no idea what this meant, but Miss Flower's excitement was infectious. Plus, it sounded impressive. I mean, it's more than one, two and even three.

'I know,' Miss Flowers squealed. 'We got so lucky. She's from a special needs charity and she came with all these visual aids and ideas. She even brought staff room biscuits.'

Oh, Cheryl is good people. She does however now sound like something produced by Mattel. Like how Valentine Barbie came accessorised with a framed photo of Ken.

The Cheryl Doll Advert – 90s Style

Introducing Cheryl! She's level 4! Comes with her very own visual aids and biscuits! Can pose a choking hazard. Batteries not included.

God, the 90s were weird.

But Cheryl is not weird. She is amazing. I know this because Liam ran out of school with a massive smile on his face and told me as much.

'My new teacher is amazing.'

He didn't remember her name or what they did or why she is amazing, but he was happy. So happy. He even agreed to collect Charlie. Nay, he suggested it.

And so I joined the other parents for pickup for the first time that term. A few of the mums in Charlie's class did a double take on spotting me. One said she thought we'd left the school. Another was surprised to discover I had another kid.

The big news however was Ingrid and her adoption.

'Isn't she wonderful?'

'I couldn't do it.'

'I wonder if she'll take mine too.'

'When will Charlie come?' Liam asked for the fiftieth time that minute.

'Hi Liam,' a passing girl called.

'Say hi,' I prompted.

'Where Charlie?' He whined instead.

'Liam! Hi.' This from a boy probably in the year above Charlie.

'You should say hello,' I said desperately. Nothing.

And then it happened. Not the arrival of Charlie's class. Fuck knew where they were. No. This was much more significant. A sight to behold.

It began with a distant kerfuffle. A rustle in the trees. And then, gasps as they came into view. Part-swarm, part battle-formation, a gaggle of mummies marching towards us. In the midst of it all was Ingrid, glorious in her - presumably Gym Sparks brand - activewear, a double buggy ploughing the way before her.

The battle swarm arrived just as Charlie's class did, subsuming several children into its ominous cloud and departing. No sight of Charlie though, much to Liam's agitation.

'Everyone else is here,' he growled, like an adorable human time bomb.

Sensing we were on the verge of explosion, my panic rose commensurately to the level best known as which-sodding-wire-do-I-cut. Where the hell was Charlie?

But, like I said, this was no ordinary day. It was the Best Day Ever. Therefore, Charlie sauntered out just in time and meltdown was averted.

Huzzah.

In other good news, The Special Mum is up to number 204 in the Blog-2Book rankings.

'Mummy, I want Weetabix.'

'What's the missing word?' I ask automatically, my eyes skimming the comments to the post.

'Please Weetabix, please.'

I provide Weetabix. And Cheerios. And melon, mango, strawberries and carrot. All before Jake arrives and my best day ever continues because he suggests a takeaway.

Maybe, I think, just maybe, this good day is the start of an upswing. Maybe I'll have a good week. Or fortnight. Or month.

Wednesday, 31 October

'This is a bad idea,' I murmur.

I am staring up at a Georgian facade so grand it would embarrass Louis XVI. Louis might have been confused though, what with the gravestones in the driveway, the ghoulish figures in every window and the miles upon miles of cobwebs hanging from any and all inanimate objects.

'Are you kidding?' Nisha exclaims beside me, her small witch hat rakishly angled on her head. 'This is awesome. I paid 50 quid last year to take the kids to a Halloween thing and that was crap compared to this. Plus, I want to see the house.'

This isn't just any Halloween house of horrors. It's Ingrid's. And we are here as invited guests for her All Hallows' Eve Spooktacular. By the looks of things, the entire school has been invited.

'Me too,' Gabby enthuses.

'I'm worried about sensory overload,' I explain. 'I've been reading up and–'

But Charlie rings the doorbell before I can fully air my concern.

'Greetings.'

'Jesus,' Nisha barks, as Gabby shrieks and I jump back.

A ghoulish butler has stepped through the still closed front door, his severed head held in the crook of his arm.

'Do come in,' says the butler's head.

'Mummy look a ghost.'

'It's not real,' I promise Liam. 'It's a hologram.'

'So realistic,' Gabby marvels.

The front door opens with an elaborate creak.

'Cooool,' Aran breathes.

All the kids are transfixed. More so as we step inside.

'Bloody hell.' Nish might be exclaiming about the grandeur of the double staircase and triple height ceilings or she might be accurately describing how this place has been decorated for the party. If the outside was over the top, the inside has found a whole new level and leapfrogged that one too.

Ghost holograms mill about amidst very alive and lively children. There is an enormous 3D full moon on one wall emitting spooky hues that shift from yellow to white to red. The music is, in a word, loud.

Had I had time to explain sensory overload before we had entered, Nisha and Gabby would be able to appreciate just how bloody terrified I am right now.

Sensory Overload: A Real Horror Story

1. People with autism have trouble processing everyday sensory information.
2. Too much sensory stimulation can overwhelm the person's brain.
3. This is called sensory overload.
4. In extreme cases, it can lead to meltdowns.
5. This house is the mothership of sensory overload.

Even without the Starship Sensory Overload to contend with, Halloween was always going to pose a challenge. Liam has been jittery and jumpy since breakfast. This only intensified after school when he demanded to put on his costume before we had even reached the front door. I managed to hold him off until after lunch, but that was it. Since 12:45, Liam has been Spiderman.

'Maya, Nisha, so good you're here. And Gabby! It's been years.'

It's Ingrid. Or rather, it's Marie Antoinette. And she's holding a pumpkin.

There are airkisses and exclamations and then Ingrid introduces her pumpkin to us.

'This is Dante,' she beams. 'Dante is so excited for Halloween.'

I cannot see Dante's face as it's buried in Marie Antoinette's neck and obscured by orange material. He might be excited. Or he might be asleep. Ingrid is definitely excited. Her eyes are the size of the fake moon. 'Now, go inside and get some lovely treats.'

The children all rush ahead into the kitchen, where there are tables piled with food, all of it suitably spookily styled. My personal favourite is a watermelon that's been cut to look like a monster.

The kids throw themselves upon the buffet then almost immediately recoil with wails of "yuck" and "what is that?"

'It's healthy,' shouts a small girl dressed as Greta Thunberg, accusingly.

'I ate a carrot,' cries a ghostbuster. 'I thought it was a Wotsit.'

'It's a trick,' howls a werewolf.

Gingerly, Nisha, Gabby, and I approach the table.

'They're right,' Nisha breathes. 'Look.' She points to what I had assumed was a bowl of sweets. But now realise are lychees.

'And that,' Gabby gasps, standing over what looks like blocks of chocolate. 'It's carob,' she whispers.

The children, bruised from their brush with vitamins, begin to get restless. One child asks their mummy if they can go trick or treating. And it becomes like a cry of fire in a theatre. Soon, they are all at it. Until Greta Thunberg yells 'Let's go!'

It's not pretty, what happens next. We are a mob. A large one. Some of the children even have pitchforks, albeit plastic ones, to complete the picture. So, while Ingrid's neighbours open their doors with broad smiles and bowls filled with colourful treats, they instantly pale on seeing our horde. Even though it is a very polite horde, abiding by the one-item-per-visit rule and thanking their victims.

We proceed, locust-like, through the affluent neighbourhood, parents yelling reminders to "say thank you" and warnings of "don't step on the flower beds", until bags are filled.

Later, I will not be able to pinpoint the exact moment Liam spiralled out of control. It might have been during the trick or treating, where he became increasingly hyper with each house we visited. It might have been when we got home and he became obsessed with the idea of handing out sweets to anyone who came to the door. By this point, we were getting the older kids. I say kids. I swear some of them were in their thirties.

Of course, all the children are maniacs by the time they get into their Halloween bags.

'How is this different from a pub crawl?' Nisha asks contemplatively as we surveyed our pile of children, each in different forms of drunken stupors on my living room floor.

'They only had a couple of chocolates each,' muses Gabby.

'They ferment the sugar to alcohol just by looking at it,' say I.

'Lucky bastards,' Nisha sighs.

Charlie, a lightweight to his core, conks out at 9pm. Liam does not. Instead he swings between fits of maniacal giggling and bouts of yelling things like "What? It's Halloween!" every time we try to get him to bed.

There is a stage where his eyes begin drooping. I think it's around 11pm. But then the house across the road starts setting off fireworks. Literal fireworks.

Are they serious? FFS. It's not even November yet.

Liam is ecstatic. Watches the whole thing. Then when it's over, insists on waiting to see if there will be more.

I am furious. I want to go and tell them. Tell them that it is bad enough that we must expect unexpected explosions for the entire month of November as though we are living in a reenactment of The Blitz. I want to point out, at high pitch and volume, just how annoying it is that what was once fireworks "night" has spiderwebbed out like a crack in a windscreen to encompass a whole fecking season. And that at the very least we should not expect them before Halloween has sodding ended. Because while they have teenagers and have probably slept sometime in the past month, we have small children. We never sleep. Ever. So if they could hold fire for just one more night we would be ever so fucking grateful. But for some reason Jake doesn't think I should.

NOVEMBER

Thursday, 1 November

7:05am

Ha. The kids are hungover. It's like watching baby zombies.

And hey, we're past Halloween. This could be a good day. Maybe even another Best Day Ever.

6pm

Fuck this. Fuck absolutely everything. Abso-fucking-lutely everything. But especially fuck Ingrid.

Fuck Ingrid and her fucking Insta-life and stupid fucking face.

'It's not about you,' Nisha assures me.

'Oh, it's definitely about you,' Gabby confirms.

'Yeah, alright, maybe,' Nisha admits.

Ingrid has posted a video called "No Stress Special Parenting".

In it, with perfectly manicured hand to heart, she talks about what an honour it is to be the parent of a child with additional needs. She calls the mothers of children with special needs "special sisters". And declares that she will be sharing her No Stress Special Parenting Method™ on her blog for the benefit of all her special sisters. Or at least those who are top tier Patreon subscribers to her channel.

'There is one particular special sister I'd like to thank,' she smarms. 'Someone who inspired me to develop this technique. Who made me see that not everyone is as fortunate as I am. Not everyone naturally finds the tools and strength and intrinsic internal power of their essential motherhood. I won't give her real name. I'll call her... Naya. I see you, Naya. I see you call for help. I know that some days, maybe every day, it's too hard to put on makeup or nice clothes. You're too tired to notice a fray in your child's school jumper. Or bring cakes to the bake sale. I see you and I am here for you. Thank you for being my inspiration.'

I then called Nisha and embarked on something approximating a rant. I may have pointed out, at a pitch that made next door's mini bulldog howl, that Ingrid has been the mother of a special needs child for five minutes. I've been doing this for years.

'And what jumper?' I screeched. 'His jumpers are fine.'

'I'll be there in five,' Nisha had said. And, just before hanging up, 'Don't read the comments.'

It was good advice. What a shame that I had already contravened it. The frayed school jumper had truly captured the comment makers' imaginations. The word "negligent" was littered liberally throughout, as was praise for Ingrid's generosity of spirit.

Now Nisha and I are sitting at my kitchen table.

'Whatever you do, don't confront her,' Gabby warns from my phone's speaker.

'But she's telling everyone I'm a shit mum.'

'She's telling everyone that *Naya* is a shit mum. It's a perfect cover. If you confront her, you're basically calling yourself out.'

'Yeah,' adds Nisha. 'Then she can be all "Like, *god Maya*. Why would you think it was about you? The world doesn't revolve around Maya Harris."'

'Or,' Gabby suggests helpfully, 'Have you asked yourself why it is that you identified yourself in that description?'

'Oh, hers is better,' enthuses Nisha. 'That. That's what she'd say.'

Dammit. They're right.

Friday, 2 November

Today, I became embroiled in what I can only describe as gang warfare. There I was, having returned from drop off, minding my own business, when I was confronted by an intruder.

It was the squirrel. The one who'd been staring at Sir Francis through the back door. Now staring at me from the sofa. It was like one of those thriller tropes where the hero turns on a light to find someone waiting in their home.

How had it got in? I looked at the cat flap, it being the only conceivable entry point, even though it was programmed to only allow entrance to Sir Francis. Who, incidentally, was sitting by his flap. On the outside of it, staring in.

I just stood there. Looking at the squirrel. The squirrel looked at me. Ditto Sir Francis. It was a standoff.

'This is awkward.'

I said this before I could remember that I was talking to a squirrel. Then I did remember and added, 'Excuse me,' before backing out of the room slowly.

Googling "squirrel in my house" – because I was too embarrassed to ask Siri - returned articles advising against feeding the creatures lest they try to get inside. This was of bugger all use. So I phoned several pest control companies. Only one place answered.

'Can't be a squirrel,' said the man.

'It is.'

'Can't be. Not the season.'

'I don't know what to tell you. I'm looking at it. It's a squirrel.'

'On the sofa?'

'Yes.'

'Nah. Can't be.'

I sent him a photo.

'That's a squirrel.'

'Yes. Can you help?'

'How's Wednesday after next?'

'What do I do until then? Charge it rent?'

He hung up.

That avenue exhausted, I returned to Google with my big bushy tail between my legs.

One article told me to wait and see if it found its own way out. If this was unlikely, I could try and catch it in a blanket and release it outside. Helpfully, it added that, while squirrels can carry rabies, they might not. But that it was best to wear gloves and protective clothing.

I won't go into what happened next. Sufficed to say that the squirrel did not like the look of the blanket, that the blanket became soiled and that Sir Francis was no help whatsoever. I still have no idea how the squirrel got inside.

'Can't have been a squirrel,' said Jake when I told him. Then, presented with the pictorial evidence, 'Bloody hell that's a squirrel. How did it get in?'

At least The Special Mum is still doing well. Up to number 203.

There has been one other undimmable bright spark this week. It is that Liam has had a brilliant time at school. He has not threatened, thrown, hit, bitten or kicked a single living thing. And that my love for Cheryl reaches new heights every day.

'How are you doing this?' I asked her, when she was telling me about Liam taking part in activities and helping put the bikes away. I was not expecting an answer. I had come to believe that Cheryl's powers were of a mystical nature and not for mere mortals such as myself to decipher. I was fully prepared for her to just smile and vanish in a haze of fairy dust.

Instead, she taught me about PECS. It stands for Picture Exchange Communication System and is exactly what it sounds like. Using pictures to communicate instead of words.

'Liam finds it easier to take in information visually,' she explained. 'It's just another way to reduce his stress.'

It is also, I cannot help noticing, yet another dubious acronym. That can't be a coincidence. Like there has to come a point where we all acknowledge it's being done intentionally. Like the acronym creators of this world are two twelve-year-old boys sniggering as they unleash PDA, ODD and PECS onto the rest of us. Next there'll be a therapy called Liminal Mindset Facilitation And Optimisation. Or Formative Mindful Linking.

Sunday, 4 November

Kelly, while rubbing her non-existent bump: 'Oh, there's this blogger you have to follow on Insta. She's like, an expert on special needs. Oh, what's her name?'

Me:

Kelly: 'The one with loads of kids. Gorgeous hair.'

Me:

Kelly (consulting her phone): 'Oh, here it is. She's called Ingrid Danning. Her blog is Four Is More. Are you writing this down? Never mind. I'll send it to you. Oh. Looks like you already follow it.'

Me: 'Do I?'

Kelly: 'She is a complete angel. Adopted a child with special needs from the Third World. Can you believe that? You should watch her latest video. She told this story about this one mum...'

Me (with Melissa Manchester's song *Don't Cry Out Loud* playing in my head as I smile and nod):

Kelly: 'I mean, what kind of mum lets her kids go to school looking like trash? At least you're better than *that*.'

Me: 'Thank you.'

Kelly: 'Oh, you're welcome.'

Monday, 5 November

I am today years old when I learn what a social story is. It happens while I am browsing the SEN For Help page. The longest thread is a post by a mum asking for advice on making Guy Fawkes Night bearable for her autistic twins.

This mum is obviously a superhero. Not only does she think to plan ahead for the occasion - something which never occurred to me – but she has already come up with loads of practical plans that she has generously shared. And did I mention she has autistic twins? Twins. That means there's two. At the same time.

It being Guy Fawkes Night tonight, I am too late to implement most of her excellent ideas. Like having a countdown calendar. Hers is all colourful and laminated and on the fridge. But I do download a social story to read to Liam.

This is basically a comic strip. It uses simple images (which I now know are PECS, thank you Cheryl) to provide a step-by-step account of what Liam can expect to happen. It's editable so I can tailor it to our situation. Which is that we are going to a local fireworks display. The story starts with putting on coats and gloves and finishes with going home and to bed.

Will it work? I'm a bit sceptical. It is just a story. How much of a difference can it make? Also, mine doesn't look as nice as the photo of the superhero mum's shiny copy. Apparently she has a laminator. I want a laminator.

Liam, however, seems unbothered by the tattiness of my efforts. He is entranced when I show him the story and makes me read it three times, grasping my arm as he gazes down at the printed A4 paper. Then he asks if he can have it.

That evening, Jake and I take the boys to a fireworks display at the local cricket club. Liam has taken to the social story with the fervour of a biblical literalist. This is good in that it means he remembers to take his ear defenders because the stick child in the pictures is wearing them. I would definitely have forgotten. Plus, he seems to find security in knowing what to expect. The story includes things I would never have thought to tell him about. Things that seem obvious, but weren't to him. For example, that we will drive, and that it will be dark and cold.

So that's the one hand. The good. *Yay.* As for the other hand... Well, that hand is clutching the social story with an iron grip. Literally. He hasn't put it down since I gave it to him except when he went to the loo and even then, not without me promising to hold it in his stead and him sharing a look with Sir Francis that I read as "watch her".

What's more, Liam is not only following the story. He is holding us all to it like it hath been sealed in our very blood. It starts thirty minutes before we're due to leave.

'We will be late,' he frets, while performing a staccato version of star jumps.

I promise we won't be. Yes, I'm sure. I show him the Google Maps travel time estimate. I assure him that I have petrol. And yes, I am qualified to drive. And park. And tell time.

It is all as nothing. At the age of four, my child has taken on micromanaging. This includes supervising us all donning our shoes and coats and constantly checking his sodding watch.

I remind myself that Charles Dickens was notoriously obsessed with time and punctuality. Maybe Liam will write the next *Tale of Two Cities*. Although I rather fear he's more likely to instigate a bloody revolution than fictionalise it.

'Really great this new social story thing,' Jake grumbles, in a rare moment when Liam has stepped away.

I am about to retort that it was worth a try and tell him about Dickens, but Liam is back.

'Faster daddy.'

Smug, I flash Jake an insufferable ha-ha-you're-in-trouble smile which he pretends not to see.

At the park, we meet up with Gabby and Nisha and their respective kids. Jake's eyes light up upon noting that only one of the husbands is there. And it's not Hugh.

As we converge, there are back pats, hugs and air kisses.

'Rishi, mate, you look like shi-' Jake stops just in time to note that Saira is right there. The three-year-old is attached to Rishi's leg like an adorable limpet. 'Ship,' he finishes lamely.

Rishi laughs and the two men exchange back pats.

'Some of us work for a living,' he retorts. As he smiles, I realise Jake is correct. Rishi does look like ship. Like a handsome, boyish ship left to rust. Can ships be gaunt?

'You're giving your daddy a lovely cuddle, Saira,' I smile down at her. Nisha's daughter, already a master of resting-unimpressed-face at the tender age of three, glares up at me, enormous brown eyes filled with naked suspicion. She tightens her grip on Rishi's leg.

'She hasn't let go since he got home,' Nisha deadpans. 'Which at least means she still recognises him.'

We laugh and Nisha visibly glows as Rishi squeezes an arm around her shoulders.

'It's been insane,' he admits.

There is a cry of 'Auntie Maya!' I only just have time to register two honey-haired human missiles barrelling my way when they reach their target. I am encased in a fierce double hug.

Huh. This is new, I think, gazing down at Allegra and Mila. Now, I adore my nieces to my very core. They are kind and fun and clever and any number of other brilliant qualities. What they are not – and have never been – is demonstrably affectionate. This PDA – the classic type – is unprecedented.

I thus approach the situation with the caution it merits: as though negotiating a minefield blindfolded.

'We missed you,' Allegra gushes somewhere around my armpit.

What. Is. Happening.

'Hi girls,' I manage, shooting Gabby an emergency WTAF look. Her responding eyeroll is magnificent.

'Nice try,' my sister mutters. 'Leave her alone.'

'Auntie Maya,' Mila wheedles. 'Can you tell mum that we're old enough to go around on our own?'

'She cannot help you,' Gabby insists.

The words reach their marks. The embrace ceases with stark immediacy and my nieces' sullen faces come into view.

'Mo-ther,' Allegra whines, stretching the word well beyond its syllabic capabilities. 'This is lame.'

'Yeah, we're not babies,' Mila huffs. 'Lucinda and Juno's mums let them.'

Then there are eyerolls. Dear lord, the eyerolls. They are epic.

'Yeah, well, Lucinda and Juno's mums can do what they want. You're staying where I can see you. Unless you want me to make you watch the True Crime Channel again.'

Yet more eyerolls. But the threat works and the girls trudge away just far enough for their mutters to be uninterpretable. This conveniently also means they cannot hear our mutters. And, with Jake and Rishi supervising the remaining children with the unenviable required sparklers, Gabby takes the opportunity to update us on her suspicions about Hugh.

'Clara, from my tennis club, says I should confront him. But I don't have any proof. I was sure he was having it off with his secretary, Lila, but that wasn't it.'

'How do you know?'

'I sniffed her.'

'Excuse you?' I inquire.

'I asked first,' she insists, as if that explains everything. 'Oh, come on. I told you this.'

Nisha and I erupt into a chorus of "no you didn't" and "why are you sniffing other women?" amongst other things.

'Oh, I must have told Clara. Right. Whoever he's shagging, she wears the fragrance Arianna Grande 2.0. He stinks of it.'

Nisha and I inhale audibly. This is surely the most shocking thing Gabby could have said.

'I know,' says Gabby, an eyeroll not far behind.

'You're sure it's not from your girls?' Nisha checks.

To which I add, 'Yeah, I can't imagine anyone over the age of 12 wearing that.'

'My girls wear Coco Mademoiselle, thank you very much. Actually so does Lila. I've quite taken to her. Was very understanding about the whole sniffing thing.' Then, she does something even stranger than a scratch and sniff approximation of Nancy Drew. She giggles. 'Clara says I should be on the lookout for a twenty-year-old with a high ponytail and daddy issues.'

'You seem remarkably okay with this,' Nisha hedges. She is evidently as bewildered as me.

Gabby shrugs. She actually shrugs. Like she missed out on the last slice of cake. Not at all like her husband of ten years is having it off with someone who smells like teen spirit.

'I was upset. At first. But Clara made me see that I can't change it so I should get past it. Oh, look. Fireworks.'

The fireworks silence us all with their hypnotic buzzing, popping, and sparkling. The children are mesmerised. Even Allegra and Mila look skywards with wonder. And, for the twenty minutes they light up the sky, we are all preserved in a frozen tableau of quiet awe.

Which makes it all the more jarring when, as soon as they stop, Liam insists that we must leave immediately.

'It is finished,' he declares. 'We go home.'

Tuesday, 6 November

I am on top mummy form this morning. Not only do I remember to provide Charlie with a black top for his class assembly, but I attend said assembly. This involves resisting my natural instinct of running away from the school gate as soon as the kids are dropped off lest they boomerang back for any reason.

Instead, I enter the school hall to find that every one of the seats allocated for parents are taken. Every last one. I check my watch. 9:01. The kids only went in a minute ago. How? How did these people get here so fast? This is witchcraft. Sorcery.

I stand at the back with the nannies and dads and others not informed enough – or bothered enough – to bag a chair. I am therefore at eye-level with Mr Davies when he comes out to introduce the production. He has the look of a pheasant awkwardly surveying the hunting convention upon which they have accidentally stumbled.

'Gosh. Lots of parents here.' He wrings his hands nervously as he takes us in. 'Lots and lots.' He clears his throat. 'So. This class assembly is part of anti bullying week. Because we are. Anti. Bullying. Year one has worked very hard on this. Well done year one.'

He is about to step off the stage, but remembers something.

'Oh, and we will be collecting donations on the way out. There'll be a box.' He mimes holding a box. 'Please give generously. We need things. Books. Light. Teachers.' Then, 'Not that that has anything to do with anti-bullying week. The donations. It's not a shakedown. Ha. We're not taking your lunch money.'

Silence. A good beat of the stuff. During which my gaze and Mr Davies' lock. I am gripped by the same impulse I get when my children spot me in an audience. Which is to provide my undying support. This manifests on an inverse scale. The worse the performance, the more undying the support. Mr Davies gets a smile that could power Coventry for a day and two thumbs up. I only just manage to restrain myself from mouthing "love you". Although judging from the headmaster's traumatised expression, I might have done it without realising.

The children file onto the stage, in their black tops with yellow ribbons wrapped around them. They are bees. It all starts fairly normally. There's a song and a dance, allowing the four children with musical talent to make themselves known. The rest look lost.

That's all par for the course. Standard stuff. But then it takes a turn. Some of the bees accuse some of the other bees of being wasps. As things progress, I realise that this is a sort of interpretation of *The Crucible*. Yes, that's right, the highly controversial play by Arthur Miller that was an allegory for McCarthyism in 1950s America. It's the Salem Witch Trials. With bees.

Quite frankly, it all gets a bit *Lord of the Flies*.

The children embrace the concept of wild accusations with escalating enthusiasm. Lots of shouting of "wasp!" and pointing at the kids playing the wasps. It is impossible to look away. The audience is so stunned that not one mobile phone is raised to film it. This may be the first time since the creation of the iPhone that a child has performed to something other than a sea of Apple logos.

Charlie is one of the accused wasps. Yet he is blissfully unaware of the fictional persecution being laid upon him. He is chatting happily to a girl, also wasp, beside him. Then he sees me and waves.

'Mummy! I'm a wasp!'

Christ his voice is loud. And super clear. I can barely hear the little girl reciting the line "I saw buzzy sting a human and live". And yes, everyone has turned to look at the mum of the loudest wasp in the beehive. And yes, I am making it worse by smiling like a lunatic and waving with both hands.

Maybe he'll be a great orator. Or actor. Or town crier.

When I get home at half ten, I am confronted by mounds. Literal mounds. The kind that require a sherpa and yak to scale them. The filing, the shredding, the washing, the dishes, all loom in precarious piles. I consider whether they have reached the point of unignorable. Then the washing pile meows.

I bet Ingrid's washing pile doesn't meow, I think darkly as I dig to locate Sir Francis.

'There you are.'

He does not, as I had expected, embrace his freedom. Instead, he sniffs incredulously in a "no shit Sherlock" and promptly falls asleep.

As I dance my dance of the thousand laundry loads, I realise that I am completely off-base about Ingrid. She wouldn't have a washing pile. She'd have a system. The No Stress Laundry Management System ™.

I reduce the mounds to what I determine to be a respectable level before I return to my computer.

Wednesday, 7 November

Ingrid is on morning TV. I learn as much from a message on the reception class WhatsApp group.

INGRID IS ON TV!!

No matter that this contravenes the strict rule about only posting school-related messages. Earlier today, I posted a question on there about spellings and was rewarded only with the deafening sound of crickets. Not a single answer. But the replies to this message can't arrive fast enough.

> OMG you look AMAZING
>
> SRSLY where that dress from?
>
> Well done Ingrid! They love you.
>
> Our own celeb!

Dictators receive less flattery.

As for Ingrid, she does indeed look amazing on the big sofa with the two smiley presenters.

'My trademark No Stress Special Parenting Method teaches my special sisters to tune into their child,' she simpers. 'Because having a child with extra needs is different, but it shouldn't be more difficult. That's a myth perpetuated to make mums think they can't succeed. But they can. It's all about understanding and meeting your child's needs.'

I do not understand a word of this, but the presenters are hanging onto every word. The female one - Georgina something - is nodding like a bobble head doll throughout. Her male counterpart is squinting with the thoughtful concentration of one in the presence of true genius.

'So Ingrid,' preens the male presenter. 'I have to know about the mum who inspired you to do this. The one you call Naya.'

Ingrid beams. I boil.

'Yes,' she sighs. 'Naya is a classic example of a mum who believes she cannot be a good mum. All the signs are there; the tatty clothes, the lack of effort. She's basically given up.'

'And to let her child wear a jumper with a hole in it,' gasps Georgina Something, her head now shaking side to side as opposed to up and down.

'*What jumper?*' I beseech the screen. Sir Francis raises his head at this, surveying me with disapproving hooded eyes. 'What?' I implore. 'They're all fine. No holes. I checked.'

Friday 9 November

Sad news from the blogosphere. Hetty, one of the McConnell chickens, has died. She will be remembered for her fearless, uncompromising leadership of the coop. Rumours of foul play are said to be unfounded, although her absence has created a power vacuum.

Felt guilty making roast chicken for dinner.

Also, Jake reminds me we're having our first ABA session tomorrow. Caroline has found us a tutor. Apparently, I had known about this because we'd talked about it last week. I'd even put it in the calendar.

I think I had blocked it out. Of my head that is. Not the calendar. It's still in the sodding calendar. Just before a birthday party in Charlie's class that I also forgot. Shit. I haven't got a present.

Saturday, 10 November

As Jake shuts our front door, I hover in sombre anticipation. I sense his disappointment. I know he feels lost, frustrated. I do too. But we can deal with this together.

We've just had our first ABA session. The one Jake's been so excited about. The fact that it's so clearly unsuitable for us is going to be a big blow.

It was just too regimented, I decide. It's premised on the idea of following a sort of script. If Liam wanted something, he had to ask in exactly the right words. This worked the other way too. If he was asked something, there was a very specific correctly worded answer. This might be exactly what another child needs, but we both know it isn't right for Liam.

I watch as Jake, leaning against the recently closed front door, tips his head back to touch it.

'Wow,' he breathes.

'Yep.'

'That was brilliant.'

Oh-*Kay*. Unexpected item in the baggage area.

'Don't you think?' he asks. This is rhetorical, being as he doesn't wait for me to answer. Instead, he proceeds to babble like a Disney princess who just met her prince. It's all there; the flushed cheeks, shiny eyes and dreamy expression. He has not burst into song, but that statement necessitates the appendage of the word "yet" on the end to render it accurate. What he does do is chatter, using ineffectual adjectives, sending words like "great" and "good" and "nice" bouncing off the walls. As in, "It was great. Wasn't it great?" This conversational black hole offers me no clue as to what about anything that has just transpired Jake thought was great/nice/good.

'Wasn't she nice?' he asks now.

She, by the way, is Roisin, our ABA tutor. The person our great leader – Caroline – has assigned to do the sessions, the first of which just took place.

I suppose she was nice. If only in the sense that she wasn't not nice. For example, at no point did she insult our mothers. Or imply that we were as thick as two planks of wood. I cannot point to something she did which would demonstrate conclusively that she was anything but "nice".

There again, Roisin doesn't strike me as "nurturing" or "fun" nor any other characteristic that suggests a calling to work with children. If anything, she should be fronting in a Swedish rock band in the 90s. She has the spiky pixie haircut – ash blond, natch –, teeny tiny frame and severe facial features to pull it off. And even though she was smiley to maniacal proportions, nobody had told her eyes.

'Maya?'

Oh Christ, that last question required an actual answer.

'Nice,' is all I manage.

'And I know what you're thinking,' he hurries on. 'It's early days. We don't know how we'll get on moving forwards.'

I have no idea what I'm thinking but it is definitely not that. How? How are we so far apart on this?

'What did you like about it?' I blurt out. I need to know.

'Everything. It was so clear and structured. And there was a proper plan. And there was data.' He is actually glowing now. 'Let's have a takeaway,' he declares, departing the room with a Zorro-like flourish.

Monday, 12 November

Tis officially The Season. Not even halfway through bloody November and we are already jingling all the bloody way. I received formal confirmation of this yesterday, i.e. I heard Mariah Carey's *All I Want for Christmas* playing in Marks & Sparks. Jake disagrees. He thinks you have to hear both that and WHAM!'s *Last Christmas* before declaring merriment underway. He is wrong. And even if he isn't, I have a stocking full of other evidence, your honour:

SUBSTANTIVE PROOF THAT IT IS CHRISTMAS: A NAUGHTY LIST

1. The school Christmas post box is up. Both children desperate to send cards but harbour no intention of producing them.
2. Collections have begun for staff gifts. Cash Only. Deliver to class rep in the playground. It's a test to see if you can pick said class rep out of a line up. I'm screwed.

3. The roles for the nativity have been announced. Charlie is Joseph. Liam is a diplodocus. We are not taking questions at this time.
4. There is a theatre trip to a pantomime. It is for all the infants. There will be a coach. Charlie has already volunteered me.
5. Prep for the Christmas fair is in full swing. Stalls were allocated on the PTA WhatsApp group. And, because I was playing snakes and ladders when this took place, I got the sodding hook-a-duck. Ducking marvellous.

'Please, please, please. Don't make me do it alone,' I beg Nisha. 'I'll be your best friend forever and ever.'

'As opposed to what?' she deadpans, one eyebrow arched just enough to communicate her apathy.

'I'll sort Aran's nativity costume,' I blurt. This is an act of abject desperation and Nisha knows it. I am in no way equipped for the task. I have yet to come to terms with the fact that ASDA doesn't do a nativity dinosaur costume. What's more, Aran's role, whilst more pertinent to the Jesus story, is a significantly trickier proposition.

'You'll do Aran's costume?'

'Yes.'

'You know how to make a costume for myrrh.'

That's Aran's role. Myrrh. As in gold, frankincense and.

'I'll figure it out.' By which I mean I will Pinterest it. 'You said it was something from a tree?'

'A sap-like resin that comes out of certain tree bark,' she recites.

'Yeah, yeah. I'll sort it.' Even I can hear that I am in no way convincing.

'Bloody hell. You really are desperate.'

I nod.

Nisha rolls her eyes. 'It's fine,' she huffs. 'I'll do the stall with you. And don't worry about the costume. I'm just going to write "myrrh" on an orange t-shirt.'

'You're the best.'

'I know. It's a privilege and a burden.' We both laugh before she asks, 'So how was the first ABA sesh? Is there hope out there for our wayward sons?'

'God no.' I tell her about the session and mine and Jake's opposite reactions to it. 'It was so weird,' I breathe. 'Having such a different view about something so important. But according to everyone online, that's normal. They made it sound like ABA is the Marmite of therapies. Like people either love it or hate it.'

'I thought you were going to say dark and sticky,' Nisha quips. I snort and watch as she frowns thoughtfully. 'I don't love or hate Marmite. I think it's okay.'

'Me too. Jake loves the stuff.'

'Huh.' Nisha leans forward, her face alive with the promise of an idea. 'Okay. How's this? Say we're the weirdo exceptions to the rules of Marmite. And say ABA equals Marmite. So, if you give ABA a chance you might end up thinking it's also okay.'

I consider Nisha's theory. On the one hand, it could be utter crap. Total bollocks. A logical fallacy not worth spreading on toast. But on the other...

'Better than anything I've got,' I shrug, and we both relax into our seats with the satisfaction of a matter settled.

Wednesday, 14 November

ABA take two. I'm starting to get it. Yes. I can see the benefit of this. I can see how the structure and data all works together. Maybe Jake is right. Maybe I will be one of the effusively positive mums telling other parents about how ABA changed our lives. We'll be able to get a babysitter. And go on days out. And travel abroad. I spend an hour on Tui fantasising about all-inclusive breaks.

Saturday, 17 November

Third ABA session today. Back to thinking it's not for us.

The blog readers are split on the matter. Some, among them Tepid Mess, tell me to abandon ship now.

> **Tepid Mess:** When you know, you know. Trust your instincts!

The rest say it hasn't been long enough to decide.

Wednesday, 21 November

Me, through gritted teeth: 'Just write your name. I'm not asking you to do anything else.'
Charlie: 'But I did that.'
Me: 'You did that on one card. There are twenty-eight more.'
Charlie: 'But I don't even like Felix. He eats his bogeys.'
Me: 'Well Felix gave you a card. Stop slumping. And whining.'
Charlie: 'Can't you do this?'

Me: 'You're the one who wanted to send these things.'

I can neither confirm nor deny whether I did in fact go on to forge a child-like scrawl on almost sixty cards. In unrelated news, I may have carpal tunnel syndrome.

Friday, 23 November

Schoolbags are a font of knowledge. There is much to learn from the contents of a child's bag that cannot be extracted through questioning. In order to get to this valuable intel however, one must negotiate the bag's natural defence mechanism of general disgustingness, i.e., crumbs, broken stationery, other children's artwork (never your own child's), sludge, primordial ooze, etc. It's hazardous work, but it pays off.

For example, it is only from checking Charlie's bag that I locate the accident form that explains the enormous bruise on his knee. I also discover that he's been awarded star of the week. I find the certificate amid the broken pencils and unidentifiable mush. Fortunately, it is laminated and thus largely unharmed.

'Charlie, you didn't tell me you were star of the week. Well done.'

I do not add that he had insisted, under questioning, that nothing at all of interest had happened at school today. Even now all I get is, 'Oh, yeah. I forgot.'

The sight of the certificate makes me glow with pride. Pride that is totally unfounded. Because everyone gets to be star of the week at least once a term. This puts the teachers in the awkward position of having to invent achievements where there might be none. Last year a kid got it for not untying his shoelaces.

Ah, but, I think, that doesn't mean that my genius cherub hasn't done something wondrous to merit *his* award. Maybe he wrote a great poem. Or was kind to someone in need. Or...

What the crap.

> For demonstrating excellent road safety skills.

That's what it says. Right to my actual face.

Charlie doesn't have road safety skills. I know for a fact that the sum total of Charlie's road safety skills amount to exactly zero. No. Actually, I would go as far as saying that he is road skills impaired. His lack of awareness is so complete, so all-encompassing that it has necessitated my jumping in front of two cars, one cyclist and a horse. The only way I keep him alive is through military grade vigilance and a total disregard for my own wellbeing. I'd still lead him around on one of those toddler leashes if any of them fit him.

There are two possible explanations for this laughable accolade. The first is that Charlie's teacher is an absurdist comic genius and future author of the next *Catch 22*. The other is that it was Charlie's turn and they had to write something.

Liam's bag is heavy. Extremely heavy. And, before I can ask if he's got rocks in there or something, I find my answer.

Yes. Yes, he does have rocks in his bag. Pebbles according to Liam. Piles of the things. And a note from Cheryl saying that Liam has developed "a fascination" with them. Apparently they were learning about fossils and he became convinced he could find one.

Maybe he'll become an archaeologist, I think, as I perform my own dig through the mess. However, even the scantest sift through his finds casts a mammoth-sized shadow of doubt on this hope. There appears to have been a startling lack of quality control in Liam's pebble selection process. It looks more like he just took a handful of whatever lay on the ground. Amid the actual pebbles, I find a one penny piece, a paper clip and clumps of mud. I try to sneak the organic elements out to the garden, but am caught brown handed. The next thing I know, one of my Lakeland Tupperware boxes is serving as a rock sorting tray.

Saturday, 24 November

Bubbles burst. It happens. Like in the 90's with dotcoms. Or the Dutch tulip crash of 1637. Or my childhood dream of joining All Saints. And today, the Harris house is undergoing its very own bubble pop.

The ABA bubble.

This morning was our fifth ABA session with Roisin. Caroline had come to witness our "team" in action.

It was never going to go smoothly. Mainly because Liam has cottoned onto the fact that these are not fun play sessions, but mandatory demands on his time. And Liam does not brook demands. Especially if they get in the way of him watching TV on a Saturday.

'Is the lady coming tomorrow?' he asked me last night. It was part question, part threat.

I have to commend my son here. He may not remember names or faces, but he knows his routine back to front. This question was, therefore, not so much an inquiry as it was a shot across the boughs. We both knew it. As soon as I answered that yes, "the lady" aka Roisin would be coming tomorrow, Liam's mind was set on one thing and one thing alone: making it not happen.

From then on, I was under siege. Taking part in a wildly unbalanced battle of attrition. Liam would not stop in his campaign to prevent the session going ahead. It started with badgering and whingeing. Then escalated to throwing things. And finally, to all out war.

Sleep was a temporary reprieve. Like the German and British soldiers playing football on Christmas Eve during World War I. Hostilities reasserted themselves this morning.

Had it been up to me, I would have cancelled. But Jake was determined.

'This is the whole point of ABA,' he'd argued excitedly. 'To stop exactly this kind of behaviour. You'll see.'

And we did.

'As soon as he calms down, he'll get his reward,' Roisin said confidently over the sound of Liam's screams.

'What happens if he doesn't? Calm down,' I'd asked.

'He will,' Caroline had assured me.

To be fair, he did. But only because he managed to find the TV remote.

'No TV until you finish the game,' Roisin told Liam, as he watched TV.

We all watched Liam watching TV.

'So what's the end game?' Jake asked. 'What happens now?'

'We just keep going,' Caroline had said.

'And next time we hide the remote,' Roisin piped in, like a contestant on *The Apprentice* who's just thought of going from shop to shop to sell remaining stock. Ten minutes after the task is over.

'And then what?' Jake asked.

'He will eventually comply.'

It was Jake and my turn to exchange a look.

'So this is a battle of wills?'

'Exactly,' said Caroline, in the manner of Henry Higgins proclaiming "I think she's got it."

'We've been fighting that battle,' Jake said. 'He wins. What we want to know is how to stop the meltdowns. Not how to prevent them or wait them out. Once a meltdown has started, how do we stop it? You said you had the answer to that.'

Not long after that, there was a conscious decision to un-team, expressed by Jake leading Caroline and Roisin to the front door. That was about five minutes ago.

'Jake?'

'Yeah?' He emits the single syllable with the pith of a pin prick, his eyes glassy.

'The door will stay there if you let go,' I promise.

He blinks.

'Huh?' He looks at his hand. The one that's been welded to the front door ever since he shut it. 'Oh, yeah, right.' The appendage drops and his face unfreezes, although his eyes are still unfocused. 'Were they always that mad?' he asks vaguely.

'Yes.'

This seems to shake him out of his stupor. His alarmed eyes flit to mine. 'Why didn't you say something?'

I consider this. Apparently for too long, because Jake asks, 'What?'

'Oh, you know,' I say. 'We were testing it out. And you seemed…'

'What?'

'A teeny bit… Obsessed?'

He looks like he's about to say something, his mouth open in readiness. But he clamps it shut and stalks to the kitchen, with me in his wake.

'Is Liam okay?' he asks.

Together we establish that Liam is just fine. Better than that. He is still watching his beloved TV, only now Charlie is there too, as is Sir Francis. It is a picture of domestic bliss. One that fails to mollify Jake, who proceeds to make us coffee in a manner that would best be expressed in Batman-comic style exclamations.

BANG!

He docks the kettle.

CLANG! PING! BING!

He stirs.

CLACK!

He places a mug in front of me.

'It's not a big deal,' I say, hoping to save our mugs from further indignity. 'So, it didn't suit us. We tried it. We'll try other stuff.'

'There is no other stuff,' Jake exclaims, then repeats more quietly, his tone furtive. 'There is no other stuff. This was it. The stuff. It's not like he can lie on a psychiatrist's sofa and blame it all on you.'

'He will eventually,' I offer.

'In how long? And what do we do in the meantime? Because for now we're screwed, aren't we? Stuck in this sodding cycle. No holidays, no life of our own. And it's not *his* fault, I know it's not. And I love him. But when he's hitting you or me, I struggle to even *like* him. And I saw a kid his age today who was well ahead of him in talking.'

He swigs his Nescafe like he's downing a vodka shot before continuing.

'And Charlie? What sort of life does he have? And this. This was supposed to be the answer. And then there's work. I want to do more, to be more, but I can't, can I? Not when I...' He pauses. Then takes another, more contemplative sip of his drink.

I hadn't realised I'd been holding my breath until I let it out now, sensing a break in Jake's frustration. When he next speaks, he sounds more sullen than furious.

'And I did something to my wrist and it fucking kills, but I don't have time to go to a doctor because if I'm not at work I have to be here.'

SPLAT. Bubble remnants everywhere.

I stand there, trying to unpack the entire cargo hold my husband has just dumped before me. This is not how things usually go. I am normally the ranter to his rantee. This reversal is so unexpected I am caught on the hop. I want to reassure him. I want to give him a new answer to replace the old one. But I have nothing of the sort. And I know from experience that a rant is not a cry for help. It's not a request for a solution or a fix. It's a release.

'That is all quite shit,' I agree.

Jake reaches out to put an arm around me. And together, we sip our coffees in front of the kitchen sink.

'You should go and see a doctor by the way,' I say. 'If you need to.'

'I know,' he mumbles.

Sunday, 25 November

Kelly has a bump. Not really. Sort of. It looks like she has a lemon shoved up her top, but it is definitely there. Her baby is apparently not the size of a lemon, however. At 23 weeks, it is a grapefruit. So sayeth the pregnancy app.

Delia is less than impressed when Liam comes in from the garden with what basically amounts to a pile of rocks, complete with the things crawling under them. She is horrified when she discovers that my children have no idea that tonight is the start of Hanukkah. A fact that she learns when Liam asks why there is a "stick thing" on the table. Jake and I share an "oh shit" glance.

'It's a menorah,' she beams. 'For Hanukkah.' When this is met with blank indifference, the beam dims. 'The Jewish festival of lights?'

'Some of the kids in my class are Jewish,' Charlie offers.

'*You're* Jewish,' Delia wails. Then tries to tell them the story of Hanukkah. Although she doesn't know it completely. So Archie joins in. As do the rest of us. We get there in the end, at which point both children remain unimpressed and Charlie wants to know why the Maccabees didn't call the power company. It is Matt, of all people, who saves the day.

'There are presents,' he says. 'One for every night.'

That does it. Instantly, my little sceptics transform into rabbinical scholars. Even though Liam refuses to let any candles be lit as he fears it will cause a house fire.

'Then we will all die,' he adds helpfully. Then, to his grandparents, 'You are old. You can die. I cannot.'

The car ride home is a divided affair. Half the car is excitedly speculating about possible presents. The other half is wondering where the fuck they can find one present, let alone sixteen. And Liam is clutching a menorah that Delia gave him. Presumably so we can *not* light candles for the next week.

Monday, 26 November

Breaking News: A washing machine was destroyed today in a pocket-full-of-pebbles incident. Witnesses say it was caused when an idiot, believed to be one Maya Harris, mum of two, shovelled all the clothes in as though stoking a furnace and did not check the pockets. When approached for comment, Harris said only:

'I usually check. I swear.'

Sir Francis Drake, a close personal friend of Mrs Harris, looked unconvinced.

The technician who called time of death was baffled. After sucking his teeth, shaking his head and tutting excessively, he stated that he had never before witnessed such reckless stupidity.

'Who doesn't check?'

DECEMBER

Sunday, 9 December

'I. Kill. You,' Nisha mutters. Or I think that's what she said. The chattering teeth make it sound like "Ah Ki Oo.'

'Not.' Chatter, chatter. 'Me.' Chatter, chatter. 'Them.'

As one, Nish and I flit our eyes over to the school hall, which is aglow with Christmas lights and just close enough for us to hear the music and laughter. At one point, the wind changed and we could even smell mince pies.

'Fuck this,' Nisha manages to utter. It is the umpteenth such utterance. On the other occasions - before the cold had saved us both the cost and bother of being cryogenically frozen - she had followed this up with the suggestion of packing up and leaving.

'Can't. Leave. They will. Know.'

'What do I do?' A group of children has appeared. The boy who asks the question is looking at the stall as though it has personally wronged him.

'Hook a duck,' I chant. 'Two tries. One pound.'

'In the summer fair it was three tries for 50p.'

'This isn't the summer fair,' Nisha says.

A girl with the warmest looking puffer coat I have ever seen sneers in our direction, 'Why is this the only stall outside?'

We had asked the same thing that morning.

'Health and safety,' explained the PTA mum, eyes on her clipboard.

'The water would be a slipping hazard inside.' Seeing something behind us, her bored expression morphed into a wide smile. 'Oh, Ingrid's here.' And, without another word, she had gone to find her queen.

Now, Nisha and I share a glance before I turn back to the children of the corn.

'Two tries. One pound. Take it or leave it.'

I want them to leave it. I want them to take their body warmth and woolly hats and go. Leave us to endure our banishment in peace.

But the boy reaches into his pocket with a dexterity I no longer possess and hands over a pound. A moment later he dips the hook into the paddling pool. Hook finds duck and he pulls. Nothing.

'It's stuck. The water's frozen,' he complains.

'So?'

'The duck won't come out.'

I consider telling him it's a metaphor for the unfairness of life, but knowing my luck his mum is on the PTA. So instead, I hand him a packet of sweets.

As we watch the group disappear back into the hall, Nisha once again mutters, 'I. Kill. You.'

Tuesday, 11 December

The school always does two showings of the nativity. This is a fine example of supply rising to meet demand, the school lacking sufficient space to house all the parents, grandparents, nannies and other miscellaneous people just dying to see an adorable if badly mangled version of the story of Christ. Yesterday, Archie and Delia went. Today Jake and I are boiling in our coats in the school hall, it being too cramped to attempt their removal.

As a child dressed as an enormous bird delivers a monologue about the stars, Jake leans towards me.

'I thought the pigeon had died in the last scene,' he whispers, apparently under the delusion that logic has any sort of application here.

'It's like *Pet Sematary*,' I shoot back. 'Nothing stays dead.'

To which he nods in acceptance.

A moment later, there's a tap on my shoulder. 'Was the dragon in or out of the deal?' Nisha asks urgently.

'In, but only if the other dragon would do it too.'

I hear Rishi snort a 'told you so' before he is sternly shushed.

Bing, bing bong.

It is the inimitable sound of a Ring doorbell. And one of the main reasons why I always keep my phone on silent. Except for today. Because I am expecting a package.

I freeze. Jake freezes. Everyone does. It is a momentary torpor followed by frenzied shuffling and relief from everyone except the culprit. Which is me.

'Leave it on the doorstep,' I whisper into the receiver. The courier is bewildered. Jake is scandalised.

'Put it away,' he hisses.

'Wait. It's important,' I hiss back. Then, to the courier, 'Yes. That's right. Just there. Thank you.'

And with as much dignity as I can muster, I put my phone back where it belongs. Which is with the camera lens pointed at the stage.

By the time we get home, I am buzzing with anticipation.

'It's here,' I squeal. I am tearing into the Amazon box that had been waiting on our doorstep, ignoring Jake's weary suggestion that scissors would be far more efficient. He doesn't understand. The scissors are in the next room. There simply isn't time.

As my bounty is revealed, I raise it aloft, gasping at its majesty.

'What is that?' Jake asks.

'The iX400.'

'A laminator.'

I close my eyes at this abject ignorance.

'This is not just a laminator,' I inform him haughtily. "This is the iX400. It was rated four and a half out of six staplers in *Office Monthly*.' When this fails to impress, I pull out the big guns. '*Administrative Ease* called the iX400 the hottest laminator in its price bracket.'

'That just sounds dangerous.'

Upstairs, I snap a photo of my treasure and post it to The Special Mum, tagging Tepid Mess with the caption, "Look what arrived! Xmas Prep is underway #iX400, #SENDXmas #SpecialMums".

That's right. I have become a hashtagger. Although that sounds more like a paraphilia than a social media practice. Maybe a potato fetish.

Almost as soon as the post goes live, likes and comments materialise beneath it:

YOU SUCK

OMG I have that one!

What is that?

Ooooh very swanky

♥ the latest blog

What? now you're flogging printers? Jeez thot this was bout SEN ffs 😒 👺 #disappointed

DO YOU HATE UR KID OR SUMMAT

How dare you promote a machine that so profligately promotes the use of plastic? #cancelSpecialMum

These are not just from the Blog2Book website. I have now set up my feed so that every post automatically generates on Twitter and Instagram. This was on the suggestion of the McConnells, aka they of the chicken blog, who have proved a font of social media knowledge. We first started chatting when I forwarded them their misaddressed messages. They're called Don and Brenda and they've been in the poultry PR biz for ten years. They also have a son with ADHD and were very enthusiastic about The Special Mum.

"He's a 35-year-old programmer now, but Davey had his moments growing up!" Brenda had written, adding that she could relate to a lot of what I was going through.

They advised me on how to set up The Special Mum's social media accounts securely, as well as giving me tips along the way about hashtags, scheduling posts and what they called SMetiquette, i.e., social media etiquette.

I see a message pop up from Tepid Mess.

YAY!!! You won't regret it. XMAS Prep is a go.

Tepid Mess has been equally generous with advice. It was she who convinced me the laminator was a vital purchase and not an added luxury. Not that it was a hard sell.

Anyway, the way Tepid sees it, Christmas is, to a special needs household, Armageddon and must be prepped for accordingly. Now, I think she might be exaggerating ever so slightly. But there again, I dare not question the word of Tepid.

Prepping For Christmas: A Doomsday Plan

1. Make all plans as clear as possible: I have made (and shall laminate) a visual calendar of every day of the Christmas holidays. This to to be hung up in the living room. This includes a menu and a list of everyone who will be at Christmas lunch, complete with corresponding photos of food, people.

2. Maintain a routine of sorts: Wake up, eat, screen time, eat, screen time, eat, sleep. Bosh.
3. No expectations: Liam will not be forced to sit at Christmas lunch and can decamp to the quiet space whenever he wants (see point 4).
4. Designate a quiet space: We'll be at the in-laws, so I've picked their spare room.
5. Ensure that everyone involved in Christmas is aware of your requirements: Which entails telling Delia and Archie. Which is Jake's assigned role. Because all managers must learn to delegate.
6. Have an exit strategy: Which basically means have an excuse ready in case Liam wants to leave. I wanted a secret phrase like "the canary is restless", but Jake vetoed. So, if we need to leave, we're just going to claim someone has a headache.

Jake doesn't think it'll be a problem. I have just finished showing him all of my Christmas materials. I felt a bit like one of those old-timey gameshow girls pointing at a washing machine or a car to *oohs* and *ahs* from the studio audience. Or I might have done if Jake hadn't been making you've-gone-overboard faces at me the whole time.

'It'll be fine,' he says breezily. Then spots Liam's latest pile of pebbles on the coffee table and leans in to take a closer look.

Jake looks genuinely fascinated. He reaches in and pulls out what looks like a coin. A one penny piece to be precise. He examines it, turning it this way and that.

'What are you doing?' I ask warily as he uses his phone light to get a better look. As though he's a pawnbroker assessing goods.

'Do you know what this is?' he asks eventually.

'Do *you*?'

'This is a 1971 penny.' I await further explanation. It arrives in the form of, 'Very rare. See how it says "new"?'

I look at this husband of mine. This husband I am supposed to know inside and out. And wonder when the hell he became sodding Lovejoy.

'Why do you know that?' I ask, not wanting to know the answer.

'Oh, I went through a numismatic phase in primary school,' he explains far too casually. Then adds, 'You know, this could be worth something.'

I press my lips together to prevent suggesting that it might be worth 1p. Not that Jake would notice. He's looking at his find with an intensity that usually precedes an utterance of "my precious". He goes with, 'I'm going to check eBay.' Which is basically the same thing.

Thursday, 13 December

Why? Why are they doing this? Tomorrow is the last day of term. I'm busy planning our End of Days Christmas. Why do we need today to be Christmas jumper day at school?

'That looks like a reindeer, right?' I ask Charlie as I present him with a DIY Christmas t-shirt.

'Why is it sad?'

'It's not sad.' I insist, turning the previously plain top to look at my attempt at Rudolph. Actually, he does look like the morose drunk at the end of the office Christmas do. 'He'll cheer up,' I promise.

I decide not to draw any more depressive Christmas characters and just write "Merry Christmas" on Liam's t-shirt.

The penny was worth £5 by the way.

Friday, 14 December

Last day of term. Spent it behaving like it was my last one on Earth. Ate all the cookies. Feel sick. No regrets. Well, maybe some.

Monday, 17 December

There are many things I thought I would never do as a mum. An uncodified but incontrovertible list I compiled as a starry-eyed parent-to-be. Every prospective parent has one. It is, I am convinced, an evolutionary imperative. One without which the propagation of the species would be a non-starter. It is nature's way of ensuring mums- and dads-to-be don't take one look at the future that awaits them and run screaming into the night.

It is a cruel trick of the mind this list. We convince ourselves that the only reason that horrible child we see in the supermarket/aeroplane/restaurant is so naughty/whiny/ugly is because their parents didn't set boundaries. Or didn't play with them enough. Or let them have too much screen time. I may have harboured some of these notions on my own list. Today it serves only as something at which to laugh hysterically.

And then there are the things not on the list. The things you wouldn't even imagine yourself doing so as to add them in the first place. The it-goes-without-saying list. Today is a prime example of such an entry.

'I'm sorry, Dave,' I say pointedly to the 23-year-old elf clutching his clipboard possessively. 'But what was the point of me booking a time slot to see Santa if there are no time slots?'

'The time slots were for guidance,' Dave replies. Then really sticks the landing by adding, 'Madam.'

I look at the mob laughingly posing as a queue and back at my nemesis. This achieves nothing. Except that Dave's ears are changing colour to match his red bobbly hat.

'Mummy it is 9:55,' Liam says, impatience leaking out of him like oil from a tanker.

That's it. I'm pulling out the big gun.

'Look,' I begin. Dave does not, but I continue. 'My son is on the spectrum. He expects to see Santa at 10 A M. I laminated as much on a flow chart. A flow chart, Dave. Your company said he could see him at 10am. So that's what needs to happen.'

'We do have a special autism friendly hour,' Dave says. As though this is my first day on Earth.

'That was from 9 to 10 am during the week. In term time,' I say through gritted teeth. 'There wasn't one for the holidays.'

Dave the elf shrugs. I resist the urge to request to speak to the manager. If anything because surely that would be Santa.

'Mummy it's time for Santa. You said ten o'clock. It's ten oh one.'

It is. *Think dammit. Stay and wait? Or go?* I plummet into a crouching position and look my son in the eyes.

'Santa's running a bit late,' I tell Liam. 'We'll have to queue in that line over there to see him. Do you want to wait?'

'But you said 10am.'

'I know. And I don't know why this has happened. So now we have to choose. We can wait in the line or go home.'

Liam considers this with grim intensity. And I hold my breath. Because if he wants to go, we will. Which means explaining as much to Charlie, who I know would happily wait. This is unfair. And wrong. I know this. But I also know that staying if Liam doesn't want to will end badly for everyone. But especially Dave.

Both Dave and I are saved though as, with a sober sigh, Liam decrees, 'We will wait.'

He speaks with a calm and composure I haven't seen before. Then waits in the queue for the full thirty minutes, asking me the time at one minute intervals, but showing no sign of giving up.

As we near the grotto door, I heap praise on both boys, telling them just how proud I am of their patience. I can feel a tear threatening to escape at this display of maturity and emotional growth. I am already thinking of how I will relay this Christmas miracle to Jake.

'Daddy will be really proud,' I tell them.

'That's okay mummy,' Liam murmurs. 'I had to speak to Santa.'

'Look boys, it's Santa,' I beam. And indeed it is. A smiley, fluffy bauble of a man, with a pair of happy elves. It's magical.

'How dare you.'

These are Liam's first words to Old Saint Nick, delivered with the understated menace of Batman swearing revenge for his slain parents. The elves are agog. One drops a candy cane. But Santa is a professional.

'Ho, Ho, Ho,' he booms. 'Hello young man.'

'You were late. And I am not a man. I am a boy.'

'Well, you know, Santa is very busy this time of ye-'

'Mummy said 10 o'clock. It is 10:33.'

'I-'

'And you were late and we had to wait in the smelly line. All of the people are smelly.'

'Liam,' I say, employing my own take on forced jollity. 'The nice people will hear you and get sad. Why don't you tell Santa what you'd like for Christmas?' I suggest.

But he is having none of it. Having said his piece, my son spins on his heel and storms out.

I don't think I have ever been as proud.

This is the point at which Charlie decides to pipe in.

'He's not wrong, mummy. They did smell. Hi Santa. I want an Inspector Gadget toy.'

Wednesday, 19 December

Christmas meltdown number one began as follows:

'When do I get my presents?'

'In six days.'

'*Six days*? But that's ages.'

'That's Christmas.'

Thursday, 20 December

'How many days until Christmas?'

'Only five sleeps.'

'*Five sleeps*? But that's ages. I can't wait that long.'

'Should we just give him one present?' I whisper to Jake, as Liam rampages through the house.

'No. That'll teach him he gets what he wants through bad behaviour.'

Friday, 21 December

'But if I give you your presents now, you won't have any on Christmas.'

'Don't care.'

Saturday, 22 December

'Maybe we should give him one present,' murmurs Jake.

'No,' say I. 'He'll get them all on Christmas just like everyone else.'

Sunday, 23 December

'Just one present,' I tell Liam.

He proceeds to rip open the Nintendo game my parents bought for him. Which means explaining to my mum why there is no magical shot of Liam's eyes lighting up on Christmas morn.

Monday, 24 December

'Surprise!' Gabby exclaims from my doorstep.

That's one word for it, I think, as I take in her, the twins and their three suitcases.

'We've come to visit.'

'From down the road?' I quiz.

'That's what *I* said,' grumbles Mila, as she trudges past me, her sister in tow.

'Yes,' Gabby declares with extravagant joy. 'In you go girls. Find your cousins.'

Her smile is about as genuine as a Prada bag in a flea market. And, just like such a bag, it promptly falls apart.

'It was the life coach,' she fumes. 'He was shagging the sodding life coach.'

And in she storms.

I am left pondering the possibility of running screaming into the day. But with a sigh, I acknowledge the pointlessness of this idea. They'd find me. My eyes travel to the suitcases.

'I'll just bring these in then, shall I?' I call after my sister.

Three hours later, I have performed a Rubik's cube of room allocation, made more beds than a hotel and conducted several staccato conversations with my husband and sister.

Jake: But why has she come to stay *here*?
Me: I don't know. What's a life coach?
Jake: I don't know.
Me: I guess she didn't want to be alone at Christmas.
Jake: But she lives five minutes away in a sodding mansion.
Me: Just help me put this sheet on.
Then:
Gabby: Look at this.
Me: I need to- Jesus, what the fuck is that?
Gabby: Clit pic.
Me: Why are you showing it to *me*?
Gabby: Forwarded it from Hugh's phone. *She* sent it to him.
Me: I looks like a stretched nipple.
Gabby: It does a bit.
Me: Yes. Now help me put this duvet cover on.

By some strange alchemy, Liam is coping beautifully with the sudden influx of people. Having been in a crappy mood for days, he is happily chattering to his cousins and hasn't bothered me once. Maybe this is what he needed. Maybe he didn't need social stories and laminated flow charts.

'Mummy,' he says as I try to make enough food for everyone.
'Hm?'
'Why is auntie Gabby here? Is not on the plan.'
'She decided to visit.'
'But is not on the plan.'
'I know. It's a surprise.'
This is met with silence. Then, 'Okay.' Moments later, he asks, 'Is it still Christmas tomorrow?'
'Yes.'
'Okay.'

Three guests is not an onerous undertaking, but it does rather curb the opportunity for a private chat.
'Fuck it's cold,' Gabby breathes.

'Open the door.'

'I'm doing it.'

The lights on my sister's Range Rover flash as it unlocks and, with two dull *thunks*, we are inside. The shelter of the vehicle has cut off the bite of the wind and we both take a moment to recover. I sip my tea, savouring the heat.

'What the fuck is that?' Gabby asks, peering into my mug.

'What?' I ask, pulling my mug towards me. 'We said we'd bring drinks.'

'Yes,' she exhales tersely, pulling a bottle of Pinot Grigio from inside her coat and holding it aloft. 'Drinks.'

'Did you bring that from home?'

'You never have wine at yours.'

We stare ahead, not at the road outside, but at the ice on the windscreen obscuring it. Which is apropos. Like one of those frosted conference room windows. Privacy, after all, is the whole reason we are sitting in our pyjamas in Gabby's car. It was the only place we could guarantee the absence of small ears listening in. Well, I suppose we could have met in my car. But that's *just* a car. A tool to convey its contents from A to B. *This* is at least 30 percent boutique hotel and 20 percent tank. Its seats are more comfortable than our sofa.

'I'm okay,' Gabby says eventually. Then takes a swig of her wine like she's Captain Jack Sparrow from *Pirates of the Caribbean*.

Questions hang in the air between us, but there's no need to ask them. We are both aware of their presence. Plus the wine. So I say only, 'Okay.'

'I gave him a couple of days to get his shit and get out.' She shifts to face me. 'I should have stayed, shouldn't I. Fuck. I should have made him leave. I just...'

'Did you storm out?'

'Yeah.'

'You were always the best at that.'

'Really?'

'God, yeah. Nobody can slam a door like you.'

'People think it's about volume, but it's all in the timing.'

We burst out laughing. Then reminisce about some of Gabby's most heroic teen dramatics. Like the furious argument she had with mum when she forbid her from dyeing her hair pink. And the time she accused me of calling her fat because I asked her to pass the sugar.

She confesses she's terrified that her girls will worry about their weight like she did.

'More Mila really. Allegra is level-headed enough for the both of them,' she muses. 'Like you.'

We share a smile, before her expression becomes pensive.

'I'm not sure how much they know,' she admits. 'I mean, they obviously know *something's* up.' Gabby thrust her head back into the headrest. 'Shit. What if this fucks them up? Like, I know it will. But what if it *really* does?'

I want to say it won't. I want to promise her that everything will be okay. But with both options unavailable, I opt for what's left. I take her hand and promise we'll figure it out together.

Tuesday, 25 December

Christmas Day. Everyone is awake by 5am. The boys are acting like I gave them rocket fuel for breakfast. The presents are open by 6. By the time we leave for Archie and Delia's I feel like I have lived fourteen Christmases.

My in-laws are delighted with the additional guests. We arrive to find Matt and Kelly already there. As are Jake's mad uncle Fred and his wife, Jane. The house is filled with noise and people. But at least it's not *my* house. Huzzah.

Kelly's bump is more bump-like. She and Gabby greet each other with the overfriendliness that can only come from deep suspicion.

'Who are you with?' Gabby asks her.

I would have no answer to this question. I wouldn't even know what it meant. But Kelly and Gabby are both fluent in unspeakably affluent and thus my sister-in-law replies with ease.

'Mr Gordon.'

'At the Portland?'

'Kensington Wing.'

'Oh. I was at the Portland.'

I've seen this episode of *Our Planet*. It's the one where the moose lock horns.

At the table, I find myself sandwiched between Liam and Uncle Fred. Fred's favourite phrase is "that's what they want you to think," which he says roughly every thirty seconds as he explains why the Earth must be flat and the Moon landing was a hoax and how vaccines are full of mind-controlling mercury.

With nowhere to run, I decide to embrace the madness and ask him his views on Bigfoot. He looks upon me with abject pity.

'Don't be silly, Maya. The evidence just isn't there.'

At 5pm, Liam begins getting angry. At everything.

He wants to leave, but he doesn't want to stop playing on grandma's iPad. No, he doesn't care that we have iPads at home. Grandma's is better. Even though it's not. Delia says she doesn't mind if Liam borrows her iPad. Charlie whines that that wouldn't be fair. When we finally leave, sans iPad, Liam demands absolute silence in the car. Except for him talking that is. No talking. No music. And Charlie's breathing is annoying him. We are twenty minutes into our forty-minute drive home when things turn existential.

Liam asks why Christmas is ending. And what is there to look forward to now? And is there any point to anything ever.

Wednesday, 26 December

I love having Gabby and the girls living with us. I wonder if I could convince Jake to make it permanent. We all went for a walk in the local nature reserve and it was all so wholesome and Christmassy and Insta-perfect. We even managed a group selfie. All of us gazing into the camera. Then Gabby and I made lunch and we all chatted and laughed.

Is this what it's like to do the thing with the village raising the children? Because I get it now. We could be that village. Or like those polygamist families in Utah. But without the polygamy.

Thursday, 27 December

'Mummy, I need the toilet.'

'So go.'

Where are the spoons? And the mugs? They can't all be in the sink.

They are. All of them. In the sodding sink.

'But they're *all* busy.'

'They're not,' I say, confident in the knowledge that all three of our toilets can't possibly be occupied at once.

But they are. Mila and Allegra are in the kids' bathroom, Jake is in ours and Liam is in the downstairs cloakroom.

'Maya, what's up with your Wi-Fi?'

'Mum, I can't find any of my clothes!'

Our "village" has become the kind with torches and pitchforks.

Thursday, 28 December

Gabby and the girls left this morning. The door had barely closed behind them when Charlie declared, 'Thank Thor for that.'

January

Friday, 4 January

I don't get people who say the best day of their lives is their wedding day. Or their child's birth. It's like saying you prefer the plane ride to the holiday. I love being married. I love my kids. But the days those things became part of my life were uncomfortable, unpleasant, involved way too much small talk and are, quite frankly, a messy blur. All of which to say, it has arrived.

This. This is the best day of my life to date. Tis a day of hope. This. Is my Independence Day.

Liam has started three quarter days at school. I will not be collecting him at midday. Nay, not even 1pm. We are bypassing the entire lunchtime period my friends. I have until 2pm before I am due to re-mother.

No need to send gifts.

I am, at this current moment, living my best life. I am listening to murder podcasts and tidying the house. Not cleaning. Tidying. I have organised the Lego. The Lego for fuck's sake. It's pure decadence.

I might post to Pinterest.

No. Sorry, I'm overreaching.

I am not Pinterest ready. But I am ready to follow some Pinterest ideas, which is a step up from the put-the-lotion-in-the-basket pit in which I have dwelled for too long.

I am now folding underwear. It is glorious.

My pocket buzzes. I would normally ignore it, but today is different. Today is a good day. Nothing bad can touch me today. Oh, there's a tornado-earthquake-volcano? Don't care. The Lego is sorted into shape types. Which is, according to the pin by Brick Architect, far superior to sorting by colour. I'm listening to a tale of multi-murders and police incompetence. I am happy. I am entertained. I am –

Fucked.

Fri 04/01 09:01

From: Liza Merriweather
To: Liza Merriweather
BCC: Maya Harris
Subject: Kell's Baby Shower!!

Hi everyone! I know we're all super excited to celebrate baby Harris's imminent arrival. Not to mention the beautiful, gorgeous, amazing Kell joining club mummy! It's a big one so we decided to make it a full weekender.

All deets below. Please pay by end of next week.

Ciao Bellas!

Liza

'Did you know about this?' I demand of Jake when the first of his feet makes the mistake of crossing the threshold that evening.

Jake thinks it's funny.

'It's not funny,' I insist. 'I have to pay to spend a weekend with Kelly's friends?'

That gets him.

'Pay? How much?'

I point to the amount. 'By the end of next week.'

He's definitely not laughing now.

Monday, 7 January

11:34am

Always check caller ID. And I mean for every single call. To quote Bon Jovi, ALL-w-ays. This is not optional. This isn't a forget-once-in-a-while situation. Not even a just-this-once oversight. Oh no. Because that's when they get you.

If you are lucky, it'll be a cold calling robot. Or personal injury lawyers.

Or one of those scams where you get charged for them calling you. I, on the other hand, get...

'Mrs Harris?'

'Yes?'

'This is Mrs Keen, the school secretary. Miss Flowers has asked that you come to collect Liam. He's unsettled.'

We have had this conversation already. I didn't like it that much the first time. But I'm a good sport so I play along.

'Unsettled?'

'Unsettled.'

It's bloody Groundhog Day.

Mon 07/01 21:04

From: Applegate Primary
To: Maya Harris
Subject: Liam Today

Dear Mrs Harris

I am writing about an incident with Liam today. He did not want to take part in guided reading and punched Mrs Gripp in the face. She had a red mark for the rest of the day. He also threw several items around the room, resulting in the class having to be evacuated. One of the items he threw was the class iPad, which is now broken.

In light of this, I think it is best that we revert to the midday stop time. Please talk this through with Liam.

Yours Sincerely

21:05

Jake: At least they haven't excluded him again.

Me: I know.

Me, after a pensive pause: What does it say about us that we're just grateful our four-year-old hasn't been expelled yet?

Jake: You really want to open that can of worms?

Me: Good point.

Tuesday, 8 January

What with all the holidays, bastard cheating brothers-in-law, school shenanigans and whatnot, I have barely checked social media. Look at me. I'm growing. But I decide that I should check. I need to. Just to know what's happening with the world. Anything else would be irresponsible. One cannot live in a vacuum. Weighing up my options, I decide that the best place to get a real and balanced view of the global status quo is Instagram.

The good news is, the status is as quo as it has ever been. Cats are still watching their owners cook, celebrities are still hocking tat and Ingrid is still dominating my feed.

Bloody hell. She's been busy.

Photo after photo of her family over the festive season. There they are with Santa. And cutting down a Christmas tree. And putting up the Christmas tree. There are her girls all hugging Dante. And there's Orwell hugging Dante. And Dante looking in awe at their enormous Christmas tree wrapped in an anonymous embrace. And there he is on Ingrid's lap as she opens a present for him.

Why are they always hugging? Even when they're putting up the ornaments. Don't they need their hands for that? And how does she get them all to look at the camera? And to do it at the same time?

Dante features in every shot. He really is very sweet. He isn't smiling in any of the images, but he seems perfectly content. Even when he's pictured in the bustling maelstrom of London's Regent Street.

I cannot imagine taking Liam to Regent Street. At Christmas. No, that's not true. I can imagine it all too well. Every detail. From my overly stimulated son deciding to play chicken with the number 13 bus to the frantic calls to emergency services as I restrained him from running into one of the busiest roads in Northern Europe, right down to the words yelled at me over the megaphone from the police helicopter. I am not ready for that.

Of course, I cannot have these thoughts without the obligatory guilt and doubt. Maybe I should be taking Liam to Regent Street. And Hyde Park's Winter Wonderland. Times Square in New York. And all the noisiest, busiest places on the planet. Maybe by not doing so I'm not exposing him to the world.

All thoughts of days out in urban hellscapes are banished from my mind however as I see Ingrid's latest post. Now I'm thinking, hey, I know that blonde pixie cut.

And I do, as confirmed by the caption underneath:

Meet Roisin, Dante's new ABA tutor! So excited to start on this journey. Dante loving it so far. Look out for updates as we go. #ABAUK #Specialneedsmummy #specialparentingmethod

My eyelid twitches. Then does so periodically for the rest of the day, a stenographer punctuating my thoughts.

Maybe we made a mistake. *Twitch.*

Maybe we should have stuck with ABA. *Twitch.*

Dante's responding well. *Twitch, twitch.*

To my credit, I keep my thoughts to myself. That is, until I can contain them no longer. I reach this point at 8:32 pm.

'Did we do the right thing stopping ABA?' I ask Jake.

My husband freezes mid-fridge-rummage. Head still hovering by the cheese, he asks, 'Did you really just say that?'

'I know…' I fret. 'It's just that Ingrid is doing it now and her son is really responding to it.'

He is upright now. 'Do you not remember? How they were properly mad?'

'I suppose.'

'You compared it to waterboarding.'

'Did I?'

'Yes. You really have to get off social media.'

I shuffle away.

Wednesday, 9 January

'But mummy, it's recycle your Christmas cards day.'

'I don't know what to tell you. I already did it.'

'So what will I bring to school?'

Cue me considering faking a load of Christmas cards specifically so they can be recycled.

In other - and I use the word loosely - news, Ingrid's children have been to the hairdresser.

HAIRCUT DAY REVEAL VIDEO!!! ✂

FOURISMORE ✅ • 1 HOUR AGO

Ingrid: Hey everyone. Big day here at casa Four Is More, isn't it, Dante? No, no, no, you know we don't grab hair. Can you look at the camera, precious? Haha, he's shy. Dante, let them see your haircut.

Orwell: I got a haircut too.

Ingrid: Yes you did sweetie, but we're talking about Dante. Dante was super brave. Don't you want to show everyone your haircut? And how handsome you look? Who's mummy's handsome little man? Ow Remember, Dante. We don't grab hair.

Thursday, 10 January

Fenella Gordon-Bley phones.
 Her: We've got the money.
 Me: I'm sorry, what?
 Her: The EHCP. The council approved Liam's EHCP.
 Me: No.
 Her: Yes.
 Me: No.
 Her: Yes.
 Me: But I thought they always rejected the first one and made you go to appeal. To put people off.
 Her: Apparently, this was such a severe, clear-cut, extreme case not even the council thought they could try it on. They said they've never seen such violence so young. Even they couldn't claim that Liam doesn't need support. Isn't it wonderful?'
 Me: Wonderful.
 After having much the same conversation with Jake, I decide to share the news on the blog. Only there is something is wrong with my Blog2Book account. I'm not sure what it is, but it looks different. I squint at the screen, mentally retracing my steps. I had logged in, as normal, ready to write my blog entry. Actually that's it. All the steps. So just one step.
 And now my dashboard looks different.
 It's definitely my account. But the page looks busier.
 Aha. I spot an anomaly. That's definitely not right. According to this, my ranking on the Blog2Book site is….
 I refresh the page.
 Then I log out and in again.
 Then I switch off the computer, reset the Wi-Fi and log back on and–
 It's still there. The thing that cannot be true.
 Yesterday I was number 203 in the chart. Today, it has me at number 5. The Special Mum is right there between For the Love of Dog at 4 and number 6, Sex for Beginners.
 How?

I can no longer feel my toes. My heart is performing a convincing rendition of the beat to The Killers' *Mr Brightside*.

I check my messages. And now my fingers are also numb.

Hundreds. There are hundreds of them.

You Have 202 messages.

How?

'Mummy!'

'One minute!'

I do not get one minute.

'I'm hungry!'

It's no use. I can try to delay, but he knows and I know that I will go down there. I may as well get on with it.

I don't manage to get back to my computer. Not before Charlie gets home, at which point I must be on constant watch. I must, at any given time, be able to eyeball each of my children when they are both in the house. Otherwise neither of them is safe. Nobody is.

When Jake gets home, I tell him I need to do some filing. I then rush up to the study where I repeat the same exercise I've been doing for weeks just to allow myself time to check on the blog. It's my version of "filing". Which means shoving everything into my desk drawer. I have done this for long enough now that said drawer is ever so slightly full.

Yes, I coax silently as I attempt to jam yet more paper into a space that is no such thing. *That's it.* Into the drawer you go, letters and random post. Sit in the lovely, lovely drawer with your fellow paperwork until I have time to put you all away. I'll just... shove... it... in there. That's it. It's closed. Oops. Slightly crammed. Just... Need... To....

Hah.

There.

It's like nothing ever happened.

Although the drawer is looking a bit bulgy.

It'll be fine.

I have a mystery to solve.

It takes some extreme lateral internet sleuthing, including venturing into the bewildering free-for-all that is Reddit, but I discover the source of my newly acquired Blog2Book votes. It was a chirp.

Hilarious blog alert. The Special Mum writes about the trials of being a mommy to a kid with additional needs. Coffee just flew out of my nose and across the room was laughing so hard.

High praise indeed. And whose nose did I make coffee shoot out of? None other than Farrah Fjord. As in, the CEO of the website BabyBaby.com. Only one of the most popular parenting websites in the American northwest. And she chirped it to her 635,432 followers along with a link to my blog.

My hands are shaking with excitement as I scroll through the comments.

Love it!

This is EVERYTHING! 😊 🤣

I just shat myself 🤣

So many cry-laughing emojis.

I become the cry-laughing emoji. Then I think, I can't wait to tell Jake. Because that's always my first thought when something good/bad/unimportant happens. That's my first thought about everything.

But I can't do that. Jake doesn't know. And there's a very good reason he doesn't know. Because he would hate the idea of any sort of internet notoriety. In fact, telling him my blog is now making the rounds on Chirper is only likely to make things worse, not better.

My eyes flick back to the drawer. It's like a physical manifestation of my lie by omission. Like in Edgar Allen Poe's *The Tell-Tale Heart*. Where a murderer's guilt makes him think his victim's heart is beating at him from under the floorboards. Only my guilt is silently judging me from a drawer.

Oh god. I should tell Jake. I will. As soon as this all dies down. Yes. Because this will all die down. It's a flash in the pan. One chirp. Nobody will even remember it tomorrow. Although I hope it doesn't completely die down. I quite like being number 5 in the chart. But Chirper will forget and I can show Jake how it's totally harmless.

With that settled, I send a photo of the chirp to the LUNCH WhatsApp group and receive a series of overexcited messages by way of return.

Nisha:

FUUUUUUUUUUU

CCCCKKKKKKK

Gabby

OMFG WTAF

They too indulge in many, many emojis.
Then Nisha ruins it.

> **Nisha:**
> So you've told Jake?

I explain to Nisha my plan of telling Jake once everything has calmed down a bit. Nisha informs me I am an idiot.

Friday, 11 January

The hashtag #thespecialmum is trending on Chirper.

Jake asks if I filed the latest tax bill because he can't find it. Then if I'm okay because my eyes are a bit "bulgy". So then I laugh a deranged high-pitched laugh and say things like "Yeah. No. Yeah, why wouldn't I be?"

I swear I hear the filing drawer beating. Or rustling.

Saturday, 12 January

It's out of control. Chirper is out of control. Last night, someone made a comment about how it's not right to make light of special needs parenting. A furore ensued. There are sides. And calls to action. And people asking why The Special Mum hasn't commented. And yet others saying she shouldn't have to justify herself.

Now Mummyweb has a thread about it, the tone of which is entirely reasonable. It is entitled "AIBU: The Special Mum is a selfish cow".

I had to look up AIBU. It stands for "Am I Being Unreasonable?"

Apparently, we are supposed to disregard the fact that posting on Mummyweb automatically qualifies for a positive answer to that question. As for how The Special Mum - AKA yours truly - is fairing in the thread, the jury is out. Or Missing In Action. Presumed dead.

Sample posts on the selfish cow thread

> She all me me me. How SHE feels about her sons disability. How SHE cant work. UR SON IS THE 1 WITH DISBILTY!!!

> YES

> WTAF. What's wrong with you? What's wrong with her saying how she feels?

> Ignurunt. Tantrums not the same as meltdouns.

100% selfish. Her kid shdn't be in mainstream. What about other kids in class? He should be in special school. That's y school standards so low. We pandering to selfish parents

This is wots wrong with th world. Snowflakes. Wah wah wah.

More like the shit mum

As for messages sent directly to my Blog2Book account, these range from declarations of undying love and fealty to diatribes about the depth and breadth of my ineptitude. And then there is a death threat. I'm pretty sure it's a death threat. It is from an account with the username "somebody" and reads:

I will kill you. I know where you live.

This presents a conundrum. If it's a death threat, I should definitely tell Jake. But is it really? I mean, obviously it's a death threat. But it doesn't exactly sound serious, does it? I've said a portion of those exact words to some of the people I love most in the world and not come even close to meaning them. Although not those exact words. In that order. And not anonymously on the Internet. I can see how this might be different.

Argh. I have to tell Jake, right?

Yes. I will tell him. And I will do so in a clear and sanguine manner befitting a grownup mother of two.

'So I've started a blog and now someone *might* want to kill me.'

We are in the office, the children safely in the hands of Nintendo.

Shockingly, or not shockingly at all, Jake is less than thrilled. At first he's just confused. Can't blame him for that. I have sprung this on him apropos of a nothing so obscenely nothingful it is practically something.

I then proceed to ramble, at length and at a speed that should only be attempted under professional supervision by Aaron Sorkin characters, telling him everything.

Eventually I stop. And we sit there in silence until finally, he speaks.

'That was a lot,' he says. 'And I'm not entirely sure I got all of it.' His elbows are on his knees. His eyes are unfocused in what may be contemplation or exhaustion or shock or all of the above. He is a browser with too many open tabs. Finally, he says, 'Show me the message.'

Which I do. I will do anything right now. Anger is coming off him in waves and I will do anything to make this better. Including asking if he'd like a coffee.

'No thanks.' His tone is Denmark flat. He then just stares at the screen, emitting disappointment and resentment and stress. And I stand behind him. This goes on for an interminable amount of time until he leans back and sighs.

'We won't call the police. Not yet. Keep an eye and tell me if you get anything else like it.'

'Okay.'

'I'm going to watch TV.'

'Okay. Can I get you anything?'

'No thanks.'

I do not check my phone for the entire afternoon. I exile the bloody thing to the office so it can think about what I've done. I then devote myself entirely to one cause: keeping the children away from Jake. It is my act of contrition. My mea culpa. My Cersei Lannister walk of shame, complete, at one point, with the throwing of vegetables at my person.

Jake emerges at 6:15 and we perform The Nightmare Before Bedtime. Except I'm falling over myself to do everything and he keeps telling me it's "fine" in a tone that's anything but.

So thorny is the atmosphere that it punctures the oblivious bubbles that usually encase our boys. Both accede to every request and step before climbing into their beds without so much as a single request for a drink or complaint about a pain in their pinkie finger or question about the meaning of life, the universe and/or everything. This is unprecedented.

The boys in their rooms, Jake doesn't go downstairs for dinner as normal. He trudges up to our room. And I, unsure what to do, follow gingerly.

'You okay?' I venture.

I receive only a vague, distracted "uh huh".

Google Translate does not, to my knowledge, include the international language of "cold shoulder". It should. It would provide much needed clarity in these situations.

If I had to guess, which funnily enough I do, I'd say that Jake's utterance could roughly be interpreted as "kindly fuck all the way off". But there's always the chance it doesn't. That's the genius of the cold shoulder. The inbuilt uncertainty. Jake might be furious. Or tired. Or possessed by a sloth. Or, alternatively, he might be fine.

Of course he's none of those more palatable alternatives. No. Jake is pissed off. Which means I am faced with a choice between three options, none even remotely appealing.

OPTIONS WHEN ON THE RECEIVING END OF THE COLD SHOULDER

1. Do the time. The cold shoulder is a finite sentence. Some speculate that this is because of the exorbitant energy required to power that much

passive aggression. Eventually, it runs out. That's the good news. But before you settle in, be aware that this is an indeterminate, but inevitably lengthy process. Which is why I subscribe to the notion that it ends when nobody can remember why it started.

2. Face Off. Not in a John Travolta/Nick Cage sense. Nothing positive ever came of that. I speak of the straightforward approach. Also known as the elephant-in-room gambit. The one where you cut the bullshit, say, "I know you're pissed off with me. Let's sort this out" and brace for impact. This is the quickest way to resolve matters. It is also the riskiest. Nobody wants to startle an elephant.

I go for option 3.

3. Denial. Pretend everything is totally fine in the hope that eventually, it will be. Also known as fake it 'til you make it.

'Charlie got a PE certificate today,' I jabber. 'For gymnastics. I was thinking of seeing if there was a club he could go to or something.'

'Yep.' Daleks have more intonation to their voices than Jake's. But, like the stupidest fly at the picnic I overlook this verbal swatting.

'He seems to really like gymnastics. I loved it when I was his age. I think I did some sort of awards scheme. I might have the certificates somewhere. I used to be able to do the…'

As I babble on about how I can no longer do the splits, I overlook a critical flaw in option 3. There is a risk that it unintentionally leads to option 2. In that you annoy the cold-shoulder-giver so much that they can no longer maintain their icy calm. This is what happens now.

'Oh my god, will you just stop?' Jake erupts. 'Don't act like nothing is wrong. You've been lying for, what, weeks? And posting private facts about our lives online without telling me. And yes, I know it was anonymous. But you're hardly the master of digital disguise and people get doxed all the time. What if that happened? What if everyone found out and then Liam's name was out there? His face? Your face. It would be a nightmare.'

He stops and I think he might be finished when he asks, 'You know what?' His tone has lost its edge ever so slightly. But he still won't look at me as he climbs into bed. 'I probably wouldn't have wanted you to do it. I think it's a monumentally bad idea. But I also would have tried to help. Because I know how much writing a book means to you. And now I don't want to talk anymore and I'm going to sleep.'

With that, he switches off his light and rolls onto his side, his back to me. This allows me uninterrupted silence in which I can reflect that Mummyweb is right. I *am* a selfish cow. I have put my own family, my children at risk. I have lied to my best friend. And for what? In the hope of winning some stupid competition? What is wrong with me? Instantly, I know what I must do. Tomorrow, I will close down The Special Mum. I will end all of this. And I will do what it takes to make it right.

Sunday, 13 January

'Wait. You're shutting down your blog?' Jake asks.

'Yes.'

'Why?'

This is not how I was expecting this to go. I thought I'd tell Jake I was shutting down the blog, we'd hug and put it behind us and get on with our lives. Instead, he looks annoyed. Almost as annoyed as he had been when I told him about the blog.

'I... I'm sorry. What's happening? I thought you wanted me to stop the blog.'

'I didn't say that. I-'

'I want WATER.' This furious demand is yelled from two floors down.

'One minute,' we reply simultaneously.

'I was annoyed that you've been hiding all this, but-'

'I'm THIRSTY.'

Again, we respond as one with, 'One second.'

'MumMAY!'

With a sigh I descend two flights of stairs, during which time Liam continues to yell "mummy" at ever higher volume.

'Is that how we ask for things?' I ask.

To which he grumps, 'Water please.'

This is nowhere near acceptable, especially as his tone is more rude than repentant. Plus, there's the whole don't-shout-up-come-find-me issue. These are matters that I would usually iron out before any dispensing of goods and/or services. However I have an incomprehensible conversation to get back to, so I hand over the water and dash back up.

Back in our room, and things are no clearer.

'Ah jus wih oo tol' meh,' Jake burbles through a mouthful of toothpaste.

'What?'

'Hoe on.' He disappears into the bathroom, from whence emerge the sounds of a single spit followed by that of running water and, finally, Jake.

'I said I just wish you'd told me,' he clarifies. 'It's like you think I'm some sort of controlling monster who would have forbidden you from doing it. And now you're telling me you're stopping it and it feels like you're doing that because of me too. And none of this says good things about how you see me or us.'

'I see that,' I say lamely. 'And it wasn't that. It's that I didn't want to be talked out of it, I think. Something like that.'

'Yeah. That I might have tried to do,' he admits.

'And then I wouldn't have done it.'

'I *am* very persuasive.'

'Shut up.'

We're both smiling now. And the weight that lifts off me is heavier than I'd thought I'd been shouldering. I shuffle towards Jake and he envelopes me in a hug. We stand there for a moment, in relieved silence.

This is quickly broken by Charlie's voice one floor beneath us.

'Where *is* everyone?'

Tuesday, 15 January

It's been a relatively quiet couple of days. We've had one Lego-related meltdown and Charlie lost a shoe. So basically normal. No death threats, ambiguous or otherwise have been issued. In fact the blog has gone unmentioned in our house. I have interpreted this as Jake pretending it's not happening. Which is fine. Especially as I've been doing the same. I have convinced myself that my sudden stint at the top of the rankings will be short-lived. That The Special Mum will soon slip back down into the obscurity in which it belongs. Just as soon as everyone moves on to a new Chirper fracas. Not feeling the urge to watch this happen in real time, I've stayed off social media and Blog2Book.

Nevertheless, in the long run, it is for the best. It's not like I could have won. And this way I don't have to worry about being trolled or doxed or murdered. I have chosen to see this as a good thing. Which is why it is somewhat perturbing when Jake brings it up tonight. We've just finished dinner and are at the point in the night where he's supposed to browse Netflix for something passable to pass the next hour. Instead he produces his laptop.

'So, I've been thinking about your blog.'

'Why?' Such is my surprise that this springs from my mouth much as a razor does from a switch blade. Jake doesn't seem to notice though, busy as he is booting up.

'I think you could win this.' He turns his screen to face me. 'And I made something to help.'

There is a spreadsheet. Slowly it comes into focus, and I see that it's data about my blog. Reader numbers and message frequency. Jake has made a spreadsheet for The Special Mum. For me. To help me win.

Either that or he just wanted to make a spreadsheet. It's been a while.

'You haven't even read it yet,' I hear myself murmur.

'Er, yeah. I have. And while I don't love having our life out there for everyone to read, we're in this now. And you're doing brilliantly. Almost in the top three. You'd be mad not to at least try.'

'This is amazing,' I breathe, scanning the detailed columns. 'But there's no point.' I explain my theory about the recent success being a flash in the pan. 'It'll be down to number 400 or something by now.'

'It's at number four,' Jake says.

'No. It was at five on Saturday.'

'Yeah, and it was at four the last I checked about an hour ago.' He leans towards his laptop and taps on the keys. 'Look.'

There, before my actual eyes, I see he's right. The Special Mum has replaced For the Love of Dog, taking the fourth spot. Above it are just three entries:

The12

Ol' McConnells

F*ck Picnics

'You can do this,' Jake insists, surprising me with the strength of his confidence.

And now I can no longer see any names because my vision's gone blurry.

'Are you crying?'

'No,' I sniff.

'Okay,' he soothes. He places his arm around my shoulder and pats it.

'It's just so nice,' I bawl.

'I know.'

Wednesday, 16 January

I think I might be on the PTA. The Christmas event WhatsApp group was my gateway. It sucked me in. So maybe not a gateway. A wormhole? A Stargate? Doesn't matter. The point is, the name of the WhatsApp group changed last night from PTA XMAS Event to PTA Easter Event. And everyone was summoned to a meeting for the next day. And now I'm here in the school hall. At a PTA meeting.

Ingrid and Queen B are looking very important conferring over a clipboard while the other mummies, Wunder Mummies to a woman, chat. I play Candy Crush.

'Can I sit here?' A woman is gesturing to the empty seat beside me.

'Oh, yeah,' I say, faffing to exit Candy Crush before the Wunder Mummy can see.

'Hi, I'm Jo,' says the new arrival Wunder Mummy. In a not very Wunder Mummyish way. That is to say in a way that conveys warmth rather than a declaration of superiority.

'Maya,' I smile back, noting that Jo doesn't dress like any Wunder Mummy species with which I am familiar. No activewear, no Boden. Instead, she wears baggy jeans and a t-shirt that says... Does it really say that? It does. "SUMMERDALE HIGH. CLASS OF '99"

'It's Buffy,' Jo says, noticing me looking. In other words, noticing me staring at her tits. How long was I staring at her tits? 'The vampire slayer,' she adds awkwardly. To me. AKA the woman STILL STARING AT HER TITS. I force my eyes upwards. Jo's smile is one I can only describe as genuine. Maybe slightly bemused.

'I love Buffy,' I blurt, possibly a bit too effusively. Especially to a stranger I have only just finished ogling, albeit unintentionally.

'Alright everyone,' Ingrid decrees. 'Welcome to this planning mee-'

'Thank you Ingrid,' interjects Queen B, every syllable emerging for her lips a shard of glass. 'I'll take it from here.'

The two women exchange smiles so frozen they could claim Disney royalties. And I'm hooked, instantly riveted by the power struggle being played out on stage.

It's Queen B versus Ingrid. Veteran versus newcomer. Winner takes all. So far, Queen B has managed to maintain her dominance, but it's come at a cost. She looks flustered, an impression only confirmed as she attempts to retain control.

'The first item on the agenda is deciding on our main fundraiser I know we all agree on the traditional Easter egg hunt so let's vote.'

What might have been two, even three sentences are denied any semblance of punctuation. So it becomes one interminable sentence. A multi-car pile-up of verbiage.

'But of course,' drawls Ingrid, her tempo glacial by comparison. 'I'll be hosting an Easter egg hunt just before the holidays. And I don't think we want two of them now, do we?'

The flush in Queen B's cheeks makes a bid for the rest of her face as a nervous murmur shudders through the Wunder Mummies.

'Excellent news though,' Ingrid continues, silencing the din. 'I have the solution. I was chatting with Colleen just yesterday as we were getting our makeup done for *Loose Women* and we thought a retro bingo night would be just fab. Susannah even said she might be able to get it featured on her show. So let's take a vote. All in favour of having two Easter hunts?'

Exactly zero hands rise into the air, a fact that doesn't stop Ingrid from making a show of counting them.

'And all for the fabulous bingo night?' she chirps.

Ingrid counts the manicured hands. Slowly and deliberately. So that I wonder if Queen B might spontaneously combust.

Although, can she even be called that anymore?

I take in what's just transpired, both impressed and chilled by what I realise has been a masterstroke. This was no a vote on the issue of excessive egg hunting. It was a plebiscite on the future leadership of this PTA. And the mummies aligned with Ingrid.

What just happened here was the quietest of coups. A magnificent one.

Queen B is dead. Long live Queen B.

Of course, the fast-paced, high stakes world of school fundraising leaves no time to honour its casualties. No sooner has power been siezed than it's back to business.

'What will the money will be spent on?' asks one mummy near the front. 'Because year 3 really needs a new teaching assistant. The one we have spends all her time on one kid.'

'The PTA can't raise money for things like that,' snaps the Alison formerly known as Queen B. 'We've had this discussion, Emma. We're not allowed to-'

'That's because she's not a TA,' interrupts another mummy. 'She's that kid's one-on-one help.'

'What? A whole TA for one child?' the Emma-mummy guffaws. 'Are you kidding me? Are you actually joking?'

'It's special needs apparently,' scoffs the other mummy.

'If a kid needs their own whole adult to look after them, why are they in a normal school? I pay taxes so *those* children can go to special schools. They're stopping all the other kids from learning.'

'Why does reception class get two TAs and the other classes don't? Apparently the new one taught all of the kids to read. Even the thick ones.'

There is a quiver of indignant agreement around the room.

Hold on. Did she say reception? Reception class doesn't have two TAs. They have one TA and one...

'Yes, we're very lucky to have Cheryl,' Ingrid says. 'And, as the mum of a child with extra needs, I know that it's completely unnecessary for one child to take up so many resources. I've suggested to Mr Davies that he invite the parents of these children to one of my No Stress Special Parenting Method classes, but he's dragging his feet. But now that I'm becoming special needs governor, you can be sure that things are going to change.'

There is so much wrong with what Ingrid has just said. Too much. And it's overwhelming my ability to sift through it all. There's a special needs governor? What do they do? And why haven't I heard about it? And what do they mean about Cheryl? There must be a mix up.

I can practically hear the main fuse in my brain blow. And now I have only my emergency brain power. Just enough to allow my body to function.

Oh look, the nice mum next to me is standing up.

'Excuse me,' she says. Her voice is somehow both quiet and powerful, compelling salon-perfect heads to turn her way. 'Hi, I'm Jo. My daughter's in year 4 and I just wanted to clarify something. If a child has one-to-one support, it's because they have an agreement with the council called an EHCP that pays for it. So they're not taking resources from the other kids. If anything, schools have a nasty habit of using the money allocated for one-to-one support to fund teaching assistant roles. So it's the special needs child who doesn't get enough support.'

Wow.

Ha, take that Wunder Mummies.

'That's all well and good,' snaps the Emma Wunder Mummy, 'But why are these children in a school they can't handle? I mean, I'm all for inclusion and I do want my Poppy to see difference and seek tolerance. But it doesn't seem fair to these children who are somewhere they don't belong. And what about the other children's right to learn?'

'Yeah, not being funny,' squawks another disembodied voice. 'But every kid with a behaviour problem gets a label that lets the parents off the hook. They're all ADD or ADHD. Just say it like it is. Some kids are just naughty and some parents can't control their own children. So the rest of us suffer.'

'Can we get back to business please?' commands Ingrid, earning instant silence. She uses this to begin delegating roles.

'Where's Maya?' Her eyes search the room. 'Ah there you are. What with your experience, you're best placed to run the hook-a-duck.'

For duck's sake. Why did I come? All I want to do is leave but can't face the inevitable tutting. So I slump in my chair and count the minutes as Ingrid and Alison tussle for dominance. This involves each one of them trying to have the last word in every interaction. And the first word. And all the words. In the end, the total number of minutes I will never get back reaches 48. It would have been 40, except Ingrid and Alison wouldn't stop thanking everyone for coming. Each time it looked like one of them had finished, the other began.

I am so keen to escape when it's over, I almost don't notice that the nice mum – Jo? – is asking me a question.

'You alright?' Her smile hints at mischief.

'Oh, yeah,' I assure her. 'Fine.'

'Is it always that... lively?' she asks.

'Oh, I don't usually come to these things,' I mumble as we amble to the doors. 'I was on the WhatsApp group and... I have no idea why I'm here.'

'But they need you,' she declares, her instant solemnity catching me off guard. 'I understand you're the foremost hook-a-duck expert.'

'Ha. Oh, well, yes. I suppose I do have a responsibility.'

'I need to know,' Jo prompts. 'What sort of qualification are we talking here? Degree level?'

'Oh, I'm working towards my duck-torate.'

Jo lets out a joyous cackle, earning her several craned-neck glares from clusters of Wunder Mummies dotted on the school's front lawn. Which she either doesn't notice or ignores. Water off a duck's back, if you will.

'That's bloody awful,' she chides.

'I'm here all week.' I redden. 'Really interesting what you said by the way,' I offer, pressing the security button to open the school gate. 'About special needs and TA's. Sounds like you know your stuff.'

'Yeah, well, I've had to learn. It was the only way to get my kid the help she needs.'

I remember her saying her daughter was in year four.

'So, your daughter has a special need?'

'ADHD,' she replies. Her ease with the subject matter is fascinating. It's also emboldening. So that when she immediately reciprocates with 'Yours?' I hardly even hesitate.

'Oh, yeah. My son. Autism. It's all quite new. Actually, you're the only other special needs mum I've met at Applegate. Or anywhere.'

'What? Seriously?'

'Yeah. I've only just realised that.'

'Well I can tell you there are loads of others at the school.' She checks her watch. 'Listen, I've got a work thing at twelve, but do you fancy a coffee?'

'So Jo's daughter was refusing to go to school and they threatened her with jail.'

'The kid?' Jake is askance.

'No, Jo. Anyway, after that she decided to train in education law and that's what she's doing now. Part-time while she holds down a job. Isn't that amazing? Oh, and Jo says there are loads of parents of special needs kids at the school. She's thinking of setting up a WhatsApp group. Why are you smiling like that?'

'Like what?'

'Like you do at Sir Francis when he acts like he's people.'

'I've just never seen you like this. You've got a little friend-crush.'

'What? No. Shut up. Fine. I'll stop talking.'

'No. Oh, come on. I want to hear more.'

'Nope.'

I maintain my silence. It is excruciating. Like the words are clambering to get out. After what might be an hour but is more likely a minute, I decide Jake has been sufficiently punished.

'So Jo was shocked when I told her about Liam being excluded.'

'*No*,' he gasps, adopting the tell-me-more pose of Pink Ladies at a sleepover. This means exaggeratedly placing his elbows on the table and resting his face on his hands.

'She thinks it was illegal.'

Jake's expression morphs into a more thoughtful one.

'Really? That's interesting.'

'Right?'

'Well, it'd certainly be worth looking into if they try to do it again.'

'So you admit it then.'

'What?'

'That Jo is interesting.'

'I only ask that when you inevitably leave me for her you take the children and the cat.'

'No deal. Oh, did I tell you what Jo said about the school using Cheryl as a teaching assistant rather than as Liam's one-to-one?'

Something happens over the coming hours. And, later, in the light of day, I will trace it back to this question. You see, every couple has its individual dynamic. Ours is based on a fine balance. I am the ranting, raving lunatic who, left unchecked, would burn everything to the ground on a bi-weekly basis. Jake is the check. He is level-headed, he is diplomatic, and the world doesn't know what gratitude it owes him for his service. However, every now and then, our positions flip. It is a curious and extraordinary phenomenon. Some have linked it to the phases of the moon. I call it the Freaky Friday Effect.

The Freaky Friday Effect

1. In the film *Freaky Friday*, mother and daughter switch bodies. Shenanigans and hilarity ensue.
2. The Freak Friday Effect (FFE) is basically the same thing. Except Jake and I swap temperaments. There is no hilarity and rarely a shenanigan. Instead, Jake becomes the ranting, raving lunatic and I remain calm.
3. FFE is rare, but it is also relatively harmless. As long as each party performs the other's duties responsibly, the result remains the same. The problem arises where there is a unilateral FFE. That is, when only one party experiences the effect. This is perilous. It is unpredictable. It is what happens tonight.

As I tell Jake about the PTA meeting, he becomes ever more incensed. Incensed at how the other mums see kids with special needs, incensed at the idea that funds intended to help Liam are being circumvented and, finally, just incensed. Essentially a human ball of fire.

My role here is to act as a cooling agent. I must nod, I must commiserate, but I must not under any circumstances participate. I cannot emphasise this enough. The one thing I must not do is get swept up in Jake's ire. And so it is unfortunate that I do exactly that.

'You know what really pisses me off?' Jake seethes. 'That those mums have the nerve to say that our child doesn't belong in a class with theirs.'

'They're witches,' I boil right back. 'Proper bloody monsters. And I bet this happens everywhere. You know what?'

'What?'

'I should write about this. For the blog. I mean, the Special Mum has, like, a voice. And people need to know.'

'Yes.'

Our eyes lock in silent understanding. Before we bolt up the stairs to the office.

Thursday, 17 January

LUNCH

(You, Gabby, Nisha)

Nisha

Anyone got a squirrel costume I can borrow for Aran? Sodding red squirek

appreciate day on Mon

You

Red. Squirrel. Day... ?! For the whole school?

Nisha

Nah year 2. Mrs Maize. Loves sodding squirrels.

Gabby

Yuck. Rats with good PR.

You

Feather duster tail. Red t-shirt. Bosh.

Friday, 18 January

Jo knows. She knows I'm The Special Mum. I can't believe this. She knows my secret identity. This does not bode well for my skills in the art of discretion. Even Superman managed to keep shtum, and his only disguise was a pair of glasses. That's the same tactic used in 90's movies to pretend beautiful women were hideous. I have the anonymity of the internet and I get made in under three months. And that's not even the whole story.

It happened like this: I was walking to my car after drop off when I saw her. I said, 'Oh, hi Jo.'

And she dragged me into some shrubbery like she was an alligator getting a takeaway.

I did think this a bit strange. But I am out of practice making new friends. And was open to the possibility that this was a normal occurrence. Maybe this was how things were done now. Like how people say "bae".

Wrapped up in these considerations, I almost didn't catch her gleeful whisper of, 'You're the Special Mum.'

This raised some immediate questions. So. Many Questions. Should I deny it? Should I admit it? Should I obfuscate? Do the politician thing where you answer a completely different question than the one asked? Although she hadn't *asked* if I was the Special Mum. It had been a statement. I briefly wondered if this was a she-knows-too-much sort of situation. As these thoughts rammed into one another like commuters on a rush hour tube carriage, I just stood there. Gawping.

'It's okay.' She'd whispered, her eyes glittering sheer excitement. 'You don't have to worry. I swear. I won't tell anyone.' Then she breathed, 'Maya, I'm Tepid Mess.'

And my reaction?

'Well fuck me sideways.'

Like I was Crocodile Dundee.

That was half an hour ago and I have only just barely recovered my power of speech. The cup of tea Jo made me is helping though.

'It was this week's blog that made me realise,' Jo marvels. 'It was really good by the way. But I recognised details in it. Like how it was the first time you'd met another special mum. It just clicked.'

'Shit. Was it really obvious?'

'Mm, don't think so. It was only 'coz you had literally told me the day before you hadn't met another Sen mum before.'

I make a mental note to be more careful. Then I remember the blog post that almost was. The one I – or rather Jake and I - had written. My cursor had been hovering over the "submit" button when Jake had stopped me.

'We should sleep on it,' He had said. 'If we're still okay with it tomorrow we'll put it up.'

Rereading it the next morning, Jake had breathed a sigh of unencumbered relief. 'What were we thinking?'

I'd thought it was fine. If anything, it was far tamer than I'd remembered. It compared parents bickering about scant school resources to toddlers learning to share. A sort of skit/rant hybrid. I couldn't see how it could be even remotely controversial to any reasonable human.

'It's just too easy to twist what you're saying,' had been Jake's argument.

'How?'

'They'll say you hate any non-special mums. Or that you think your kid is more special than other kids. Or special mum says kids are cash cows. Or they'll just call you a communist.'

My eyebrows made a bid to soar to the skies.

'Bloody hell. Easy there Rupert Murdoch. It doesn't say any of those things.'

'It doesn't have to. All it has to do is piss off someone with a half-decent Chirper following and they can say it says whatever they like. And this could do that.'

All it has to say is... to do... Something about Chirper. Nope, couldn't parse that last bit.

In the end, I'd decided it was easiest just to write a new article.

Friday, 26 January

It is Annual Penguin Day. The kids have the option of wearing something special in honour of penguins. Jemimah B is bedecked in a magnificent, bespoke penguin costume, so authentic she'd blend in at the zoo. Orwell has made his own costume, complete with papier-mâché beak. Ingrid posted a video of him doing so. And my boys? Black jeans, white t-shirts and a bow tie I cobbled out of some black fabric, glue and elastic. They look like the groomsmen after an open-bar wedding.

FEBRUARY

Friday, 2 February

'Happy birthday mummy!'

This is yelled directly into my left ear canal by my firstborn. The right ear canal has escaped by virtue of it being on my pillow. So now I have tinnitus in one ear while the other one insensitively carries on as normal.

'Thank you, poppet.'

'Charlie, I said to wait for mummy downstairs.' Jake's voice.

I roll out of bed. I'm going to put on makeup today.

'Can we have cake?'

'Cake for breakfast?' Liam chimes in.

'No cake for breakfast.'

There is an almighty groan at this.

'But you said.'

'Nobody said anything.'

Sensing rebellion afoot, I turn a 180 from my position at the bathroom door. They are all there, my boys. Even Sir Francis, as evidenced by a peek of fluff just visible from under our bed.

'We'll have cake after school,' I promise.

Liam looks like he wants to protest and I prepare to cave in. It is my birthday after all. Good parenting be damned. But, to my eternal surprise, he doesn't.

'It is your birthday,' he decrees, much as a medieval monarch would pardon a wretch. 'It is okay.'

Tis a birthday miracle.

The boys have made me cards and I receive confirmation that I am in fact not dead inside because my heart melts at their earnest scrawls. Charlie has drawn a picture which he says is of me but looks like an octopus. He wrote inside that I am the "best mumee in the world".

'No picture,' my younger son warns me warily as he hands me his creation.

It is a folded piece of white card. As has already been represented to me, it is devoid of imagery. In fact, all that's on it is his name. Or at least "Lian". Which is close enough.

Both items are masterpieces. Definitive evidence that mine are the most caring, talented boys in the known universe. I tell both boys as much, thus ensuring I ruin them for all future partners.

Jake gets me a box of my favourite cupcakes and a couple of items on my subtly named "STUFF I WANT" Amazon wish list.

Nisha and Gabby take me for a birthday coffee.

I take a luxuriant sip of my latte, savouring its foamy comfortness. Then my sister attempts to choke me to death by delivering massive news with absolutely no warning.

'I'm seeing someone.'

Foam goes up my nose and down my windpipe, which I had always assumed were mutually exclusive events. I start hack-coughing.

'Oh my god, who?' asks Nisha, while absently patting my back.

'Her name is Clara. She's a yoga teacher. Actually, that's how we met. She was teaching me yoga.'

This is torture. I want to say "yeah she was" à la Joey from *Friends*. But I can't.

'Yeah,' I manage to croak, before coughing once again overtakes me. I make the sound Sir Francis does when evicting a lodged hairball.

I also have many, many questions. Do the girls know? Does Hugh know? Does mum know? How long has this been going on? No. That's a song.

'What's she like?' Nisha asks.

'She's lovely.' Gabby is glowing. And buzzing. And floating on air. All of which makes her sound like a firefly. Gabby is being a firefly. And it's bloody adorable. I don't think I've ever seen her this happy.

'What's it like with a woman?' Nisha asks. Then, as if she needs to, she whispers, 'The sex.'

'Fuck off,' Gabby laughs. Then, 'Although it is pretty awesome.' Then she performs yet another handbrake turn of a non-sequitur, presumably to switch the subject as quickly as possible, asking Nisha how things are going.

'Yeah, good.'

We stare at her.

'Is that it?' asks Gabby. 'Yeah, good?'

'What?'

'Would you want your gravestone to say that? Nisha Bakshi. Yeah, good.'

Nisha glares at my sister, but Gabby's not done.

'It's like the opposite of TMI. No information.'

'NI?' Nisha asks flatly. 'National insurance?'

'We can workshop it,' Gabby dismisses. 'Anyway, tell us something that's going on in your life.'

'What do you want me to say? There's nothing going on. I wake up alone, look after my kids alone, go to work...' She considers. 'Actually, there are quite a lot of people there. Then it's back to look after my kids alone. I can't remember what my husband looks like and I talk more with his mother than I do with him. Oh, and someone stole my sodding blue bin this morning.'

Now that she's begun sharing, Nisha is on a roll. She explains how Rishi's hospital is understaffed and how he's working even more insane hours than his previously insane hours.

'Have you had a chance to talk to him about it?' I rasp.

'And say what? Stop doing your job?'

We agree that this would not be ideal.

'But there must be a way for him to ease off a bit,' Gabby tries. 'And he needs to know how it's affecting you. Plus, you are not alone. You have us. *Use* us. You know I'll happily take your kids for a night here and there. Give you a break. Then the two of you can talk. I really think it would help.'

'I don't know...'

'It's settled. I'll send you some dates and you can tell me which are good.' Gabby takes a decisive and decidedly pleased sip of her Chai latte. But as she lowers her cup, her face furrows in considered confusion. 'Maya.'

'Yeah?'

'Is it possible I have never had your kids to stay over?'

This is entirely possible. I'd go as far as saying that it is a fact. Nobody has ever had our kids stay overnight.

'Never?' Gabby is appalled. 'So how do you, say, go away for the weekend?'

'A weekend?' I guffaw. 'We don't go out for an evening.'

'But what about your babysitter?'

'Gabs...' I begin, only for Nisha to take the wheel.

'Gabriella,' she scolds. 'She's never had a babysitter. Have you ever properly read your sister's blog?'

'Yes. Of course I have. It's great.'

'You haven't, have you?'

Gabby attempts to maintain her composure, but like a bad Western film set, it collapses, revealing only truculent exasperation.

'No, okay? I haven't read your blog. Can we stick to the point please?'

'What's that then?'

'That... Okay. When you say you've never had a babysitter, you don't really mean...'

'Never?' I offer, receiving a nod in return. 'Yeah. Pretty much never. We did try once, but we never got past the front door. There was an, um, incident.'

I hate to admit it, but it's gratifying watching the reality of my life dawn on my sister's face. It is vindicating to see how restrictions I now take for granted, like not being able to hire a babysitter for a night, are such pure anathema to her that her features are unable to settle on a single expression.

'But when was that? The babysitter thing?'

'About a year ago.'

'And you haven't tried since?'

'The agency banned us.'

'There are *other agencies*, Mai. Look, I'm only saying this because I love you and I can't stand the thought that you're stuck at home forever just because you're too scared to try. I mean, you get one crappy babysitter and decide you're never going out again? It makes no sense. I know Liam can be difficult, okay? But he is also four. I think a qualified childcare professional would manage. You might be building this all up in your head.'

I sincerely hope the floor of this establishment is regularly cleaned, what with the fact that my lower jaw is now resting on it. Even if only figuratively.

'Like how you talk about him hitting or running away from you,' Gabby continues. 'As if it's some major thing, it sounds a bit...'

Gabby does not pause for long. Possibly just a second. But everything slows down as I wait for her to finish her sentence.

'Much.'

'Oh fuck,' I hear Nisha breath.

'A bit much.' I repeat. *That's good, stay calm. Stay sane.*

'Yes, a bit much. You're saying you've never let anyone else look after your children so you and Jake can pop out to eat. I love you, but yes I think that's a bit much. I mean, look at Nish.'

'Don't you dare,' Nisha laughs, but Gabby's on a roll.

'She just told us how she looks after both her kids basically by herself most of the time. And they're hardly a walk in the park.'

'And you dared,' Nisha sighs resignedly.

'Oh.' Gabby's eyes widen as she raises her palms skywards. 'The park. You won't even take your own two children to the park on your own. What's that about?'

'Gabby.' I am surprised by the strength in my voice. Evidently, so is my sister as she abruptly stops talking and clamps her lips together. Unfortunately, I can't seem to form a sentence worthy of this excellent start. This is not because I have nothing to say. Far fucking from it. There is too much to say. I feel better equipped to squeeze a hippopotamus through my nostril than to get the many words inside my head out of my mouth. In the end, I go with, 'You're wrong.'

There is a moment where none of us move. All of us are certain I have more to say. When this proves incorrect, Gabby asks, 'What about me? Are you seriously saying you don't think I can look after your boys for one evening?'

'I am saying that nobody can,' I squeeze out with more than a touch of desperation.

At this, my sister does a convincing impression of Daenerys from *Game of Thrones* addressing her army.

'I am their aunt,' she quavers. 'I am a mother. And I can look after them for one sodding evening.'

Which, I think you would agree, is basically the same as "I am Daenerys Stormborn, of House Targaryen, of the blood of Old Valyria – I am the Dragon's Daughter. And I swear to you, that those who would harm you will die screaming."

'If I was to trust anyone else, it would be you, okay?'

'So you'll do it?'

'No.'

Mum calls. She asks after the boys then proceeds to tell me about her new bridge club. In detail. What she doesn't do is wish me a happy birthday. I consider pointing this out, but it seems churlish.

I order a giant double cheese pizza for myself for dinner. I rarely do this because nobody else in my house likes melted cheese and I never feel right ordering just for me. Then Jake and I settle in front of the TV. *Ahhhh*. Bliss.

Saturday, 3 February

'It was your birthday yesterday.'

'Hi, mum. Yes. It was.'

'Why didn't you tell me?'

She is not so much wishing me a happy birthday as accusing me of having one.

'I'm... Sorry?' I do not ask her how she can forget the day that she pushed a human being out of her body.

'I had to hear it from your sister. She's not getting fat, is she? She sounded echoey.'

'What? No. That doesn't even make sense.'

'Because she'll need to look presentable if she's going to find someone else and you know how she stress-eats. Had to put locks on the cupboards when she was in secondary. Still, at least she's got that lovely face.' There is a pause. 'Everything okay with you and Jake?'

'Yes mum.'

'Good. Because if it's hard for Gabby to find someone, you can imagine what it would be like for you.'

'Love you too mum.'

'Don't make a fuss, darling.'

Monday, 5 February

Something's happening on Facebook. Oooh, the SEN For Help Group has a post with 205 comments. Now 207. *Some-one's in trou-ble.* The post itself is a link to an article, but the headline is conveniently visible without the need to click.

> MUM BLOGGER: BE GRATEFUL SPECIAL NEEDS KIDS ARE IN MAINSTREAM SCHOOLS.

The secondary headline declares, "Special needs mum claims violence in classrooms is a price worth paying for inclusion."

Wow. That's a bit extreme. Violence is a price worth paying? That makes it sound like people should expect special needs children to be violent. Whoever this blogger is, she's not exactly doing the rest of us a favour, a sentiment expressed by many of the comments underneath.

> Why make it us versus them? I have 1 ADHD child, 2 non-ADHD and I wouldn't accept violence in classroom

making excuses for her kidz behaviour

makes us all look bad

THIS IS WHAT HAPPENS WHEN NOT ENOUGH FUNDING FOR SEN EDUCATION

Great. Now every1 will think we all like that

Who is this mum blogger? I click on the link, hoping to find out more. The article is by someone called John Sweeting. He writes:

> I think most of us agree that children deserve to be safe at school. That violence in the classroom is unacceptable. And yet one special needs activist claims it's a price worth paying as long as her son can attend mainstream school.
>
> The Special Mum, whose son's violent outbursts frequently require his classmates to be evacuated for their own safety, thinks...

Hold on. My eyes flick back to the beginning of the sentence. It really does say that. The Special Mum. But it can't be me. I mean, I know it's not me, because...

Oh shit. It's me, isn't it.

'This is war,' I declare darkly. 'If that online hack thinks he can misrepresent me and get away with it, he has another thing coming. I will not stand by and have everyone angry at me about stuff I never even said. Like – and I quote - "parents who don't have special needs kids have it easy". Or that kids with special needs should take priority because their funding subsidises everyone else. We will fight on social media. We will complain to his editor. We will see him in court.'

Jake, whose silence thus far I have interpreted as him being rapt by my stirring soliloquy, blinks. Then sighs.

'Do you fancy a takeaway?'

'What the - Okay first of all yes, Chinese – but also what the frack? Why aren't you angry about this?'

'I *am* angry about it,' he says, sounding about as irate as a Care Bear on muscle relaxants. 'It's wrong. But there's nothing we can do. Plus-'

'I just listed a load of things we can do.' This comes out in the high-pitched rush of a recently burst balloon flying around the room.

'All of which are either impossible or would make things much, much worse.' He considers, then adds, 'Or both. You can't engage. Nobody cares what you wrote. It only matters what someone louder *says* you wrote.'

'But we have to do *something*.'

'No. We don't. Do you want seaweed?'

'Yes,' I mutter, making sure to express it grumpily.

'You want to know what I think?' he says.

'No.'

'I think this won't change a thing.'

'Is he mad?' Jo splutters.

'Exactly. Thank you.' And I also silently thank any listening deity for friends who are not my unreasonably reasonable husband.

'The internet doesn't work out in anyone's *favour*,' she continues. 'Everyone loses. That's the whole point.'

This is, admittedly, slightly less gratifying.

Tuesday, 6 February

Great. Now Mummyweb is involved.

AIBU: VIEWS ON SPECIAL MUM?? (4444 COMMENTS)

So this special mum think we shld be thanking special needs kids for being in normal schools!!!! WTAF? They r the 1s who cause problems in the 1st place!!! There's a boy in DD class who pushes hits and school has done NOTHING. All cos didums has a SPECIAL NEED. I don't even think it's true. Half these kids should be in borstal.

Yeh who does she think she is? Cancel this waist of spaice. 💀

And that name. Special Mum? What makes her so special?

Have any of you actually read the blog? I have She doesn't say amy of that. All she says is that the school used her son's funding for a teaching assistant.

Oh, great. An apologist 🙄

I pay taxes so my kids get n education. Not so this 😡 says she pays for our kids?!?! MY TAXES PAY FOR YOUR KIDS

F&*^k taxes

OMG did she really say that?

Oooh is this a new show? Need something new to binge.

Wednesday, 7 February

'I think it is such a shame that this Special Mum blogger chooses to pit herself against other mums. To tear down rather than build up. I also think it's, like, really unfair she's putting her child in that position. You know? Putting him in a school where he clearly doesn't belong. Or at least not teaching him enough so he can survive in that school. That's what I'm doing with Dante. It's like I tell my followers. It's only as hard as you let it be.'

Ingrid is on Colleen's morning show, with her face and her teeth and her No Stress Special Parenting Method™. Colleen asked her what she thought of the Special Mum's "controversial blog" and is now sympathetically and emphatically nodding at her answer.

She doesn't need sympathy, Colleen, I silently direct at the TV presenter. *She's fine.*

I, on the other hand, am not fine. Not even remotely. I have spent the past day and a half being lambasted on social media and now on TV. I think I might be cancelled. Unsure. Do you get an email informing you when that happens?

> *Dear The Special Mum, we are sorry to inform you that you have been voted off the island. Yours sincerely, the Internet.*

AIBU: VIEWS ON SPECIAL MUM?? (5214 COMMENTS)

Did you see Ingrid's take on this on Rise and Shine? She is so right.

Her dress is from ASOS

She s amazing

Where is Ingrid's dress from? I want it.

Do blogs still exist?

SHE's Not SPECIAL

More like shit mum!

Saturday, 10 February

The SEN For Help group has 3,000 comments. The Mummyweb post has 10,000. And The Special Mum still maintains the same spot on the competition rankings. Nothing has changed.

Jake is smug. Although he denies it.

'There's no downvoting on the system,' he says.

'What system?'

'The Blog2Book system doesn't give the option to downvote. So all the negative people couldn't really do anything. The only thing that could have happened is that new people discovered the blog.'

'They could have voted for the other entries so they would do better than me.'

'True, but that would require a coordinated effort. Or some sort of hack. I couldn't see that happening. And it didn't.'

Bastard.

Tuesday, 12 February

I have kept Charlie off school today because he's got a really bad cold. I would like it noted that this was entirely voluntary on my part, what with him not having a temperature and not even asking to stay home. He just looked so tired and snuffly that I couldn't stand the thought of him struggling through a whole day at school like that.

I thus congratulated myself on being a lovely mummy who sacrificed human adult time for her child. My burst of self-esteem lasts a whole thirty minutes, until it's time for Jake to take Liam to school.

As I help him with his shoes, he comments, 'I feel fine now mummy.'

'Okay. That's good.' It takes a moment for my beleaguered brain to realise and inform me that something is wrong.

'Wait,' I say, just before they leave. 'You said you feel fine now. Why now? Did you not feel fine before?'

He looks at me like I'm an idiot. 'No. Before everything hurt.'

'When?' I ask, just as Jake asks, 'What hurt?'

Eventually we establish that several parts of Liam's body - including but not limited to his head or maybe parts of his head - hurt for a period of more than one day at some point in the past fortnight. We believe the throat was involved, but Liam insisted it was his neck.

'I thought I was going to die,' he informs us conversationally.

Confused and harried, we extracted promises from Liam that he will tell us the next time things hurt.

'Every time?'

'Every time.'

Then we took his temperature, which was fine, and they were off.

And now I am replaying the last few days and chastising myself for being such a horrible mummy and not realising that my son was ill. And feeling even worse every time I see Charlie whose illness I did spot. What signs did I miss in Liam? But I can't think of anything. God. I can't even remember him being grumpy or sad or moping. If anything, he's been remarkably happy.

Naturally, I turn to the internet for answers. And, of course, I soon wish I hadn't. Because now I am more confused than ever.

THINGS THE INTERNET TAUGHT ME ABOUT AUTISM AND ILLNESS:

1. People with autism can be relatively insensitive (hyposensitive) to pain. Or they can be averagely sensitive to pain.
2. People with autism can be highly sensitive (hypersensitive) to pain from things that wouldn't bother non-autistic people. For example, the sound of a vacuum cleaner.
3. Whatever they might be feeling, they are likely to communicate it in different ways or struggle to communicate it at all.
4. There's something called The Fever Effect, in which mothers of autistic children reported an improvement in their children's autism-related symptoms whenever they had a fever. This led me down a rabbit hole which involved neurological deficiencies in mice, but the short version is that it is believed to be linked to a fever-induced immune molecule.

More research needs to be done.

Saturday, 16 February

Whole day ruined by one email.

Sat 16/02 09:12

From: Liza Merriweather
To: Liza Merriweather
BCC: Maya Harris
Subject: RE: Kell's Baby Shower!!

One week to go lovely laydeez!!!

REMEMBER to bring baby photos and a change of clothes. You'll get your tshirts on the day. And no I won't tell you what yours sez b4hand you cheeky minxes!!

Kells asked that nobody wear strong perfume and no bright colours not found in nature.

Gina and Maya I still don't have your fave photos of Kell. PLEASE EMAIL THEM TO ME.
Ciao Bellas!
Liza

I have one photo of Kelly. From Christmas last year. Or rather of about a third of Kelly. Side on. You have to squint really hard to recognise that it's her and not a finger over one side of the lens. She just happened to be in view in the photo I was trying to take of Liam and Charlie not eating their lunch. Charlie is mid-sneeze and Liam is mid-scream. Ah, memories.

But I am a beggar not a chooser. I send the photo.

Thursday, 21 February

Parents' Evening. I remember being excited about parents' evenings as a child. For my mum to go and see all the work I'd done and learn what a good, good girl I had been. God I was a swat. Jake remembers the experience differently. For him it was the one time in the year when his parents had an insight into his abject delinquency.

Our boys are unaware it's even happening until I am by the front door.

'Where is mummy going?' Charlie asks suspiciously, earning an earful from Liam telling him to stop making noise. 'Where are you going mummy?'

When I explain, Charlie looks perplexed, then worried.

'Who will make dinner?'

Right then.

Jemimah B is at the school entrance, acting as a docent or traffic cop, directing parents into the hall. It seems unnecessary. I don't think she was allocated this role. There is, after all, a sign that does much the same thing.

Gone are the days when parents used to queue for teachers. Now it's all prebooked slots, which Nisha got for me because the sign up sheets were only out at pickup time. Why not drop off as well? Who knows? Tis one of the many mysteries of school admin logic.

'You must wait in the hall and the teacher will come and get you,' directs Jemimah. She frowns. 'Why haven't you brought your children?'

'I didn't know I should,' I explain. Then hate myself.

She is 7 years-old for Christ's sake. I cannot be intimidated by something younger than the contents of my knicker drawer.

I am then faced with Jemimah B's mummy. Literally faced, head on. The Alison Formerly Known As Queen B is selling coffee and cakes from a table set directly opposite the door. Presumably so she can catch the eye of each entering parent before they realise what's happening.

'Coffee and cake?' she asks, like a spider toying with the fly struggling in its web.

'I don't have cash,' I apologise.

'We have a card reader.'

'Great.' Since bloody when?

'Five pounds please.'

One day, I think, as I tap my debit card, I will tot up all the money I have paid to this school. It's probably the equivalent of private school fees.

Her former majesty makes a big show of looking behind me.

'Where are your boys?'

'Oh, I didn't realise people were bringing their kids. And Jake was able to get home in time.'

'Oh how lovely,' she drips. 'George's hours at the firm are just monstrous. But then they can't do without him. How fortunate that your husband can just come home like that. And you with the evening to yourself, you lucky thing.'

The evening to myself? Is she high?

'I can see why you wouldn't want to volunteer for the coffee stand.'

There is steel in her eyes.

'Oh, I would have,' I say. 'I didn't know about it.'

'Mrs Harris?' It is Mrs Rochester. Charlie's teacher. Hallowed be the fruit. I am saved.

'I wasn't expecting you to be here tonight,' says Mrs Rochester as we wind through the labyrinthine mess of classrooms. 'Very good of you to make it.'

'Oh, yes, well. Parents' evening. I wouldn't miss it.' Weird. But there again most people think *I'm* the weird one. So that might have been perfectly normal.

'So, Charlie.'

We sit on tiny chairs at tiny desks.

'Such a bright boy. Really knows his history.'

I glow internally. He is bright. So, so bright. And lovely.

'And what a character. Always makes us laugh. We're always saying he's an old soul.'

This is quite fun. I'd been expecting lots of "could do better if he stopped talking for even one second". And instead I'm getting compliments. Or Charlie is. But that's the same thing, right? I made him after all.

'Maybe next term, once things have calmed down, he can settle into doing his work more regularly.'

Hold on.

'Excuse me?'

'Once you're back home and don't have quite such a long journey in.'

'Long journey… in,' I repeat.

'From Bournemouth.'

I've never been to Bournemouth. Or maybe I have. No. No, that was Brighton. Christ. I don't even know the difference between Bournemouth and Brighton.

'I'm *Charlie's* mum,' I say. Because maybe she has me confused with another mum. One who lives in Brighton. Bournemouth. Shit. 'Charlie H?'

'Yes. I know Mrs Harris.'

Maybe she doesn't mean to say Bournemouth. Oh, maybe she's suffering from aphasia. Like in that episode of *House*, where that man kept saying "investment" when he meant "head". What had the diagnosis been in that episode? Not lupus. It was never lupus.

But Mrs Rochester is not suffering from aphasia. She explains that she has been under the impression that our house had been besieged by squirrels and that, while we were having them removed, we were living with my parents. In Bournemouth.

'And that's why he hasn't been able to concentrate as well on his work,' she finishes.

With each revelation, my head sinks lower and lower until it is in my hands.

If she didn't hate me before - which she totally did - she does now.

I return to the hall to await my next appointment. At least that's with Miss Flowers. But it is not for another twenty minutes. And Ingrid is in the hall.

Ingrid and her library of children, sitting in a neat row in order of height. And no doubt the Dewey Decimal System.

'Maya, such a surprise to see you here. Where are your lovely boys?'

Why is everyone asking me that? So I repeat that they are at home with Jake and she says how lovely it is that he can just leave work and isn't so important he can't be spared.

'How are things with Liam?' asks she. 'You know, Orwell was reading me a chapter in *The Magic Faraway Tree* last night and he mentioned Liam's not reading yet. I hope you're not worrying too much. It's like I said to Holly Willoughby. You just take it one day at a time. And they all learn at their own pace. Of course, we're working with a specialist reading professional with Dante. Just to give him that extra boost. It's a shame you didn't know about Liam earlier, isn't it.'

Her eyes bore into mine expectantly. Am I supposed to say something? If I open my mouth, the only thing liable to emerge isn't suitable for young ears. So I smile and nod.

'I just wanted you to know that if you ever need any advice.'

Oh. She is now gripping my arm.

'I am here for you. And you're always welcome on one of my Special Needs Parenting Courses. Unfortunately, I can't do mates' rates. It wouldn't be fair to the other mums. But I'd love to have you there.'

How does she do that? How does she make it sound like I begged for a discount on a course I never even asked about? And why is there nothing I can say that doesn't sound like I'm disappointed I don't get said mates rates?

'Mrs Harris?' The voice behind me is ice cold. It is definitely not that of Miss Flowers.

Mrs Gripp stands before me, a resigned look giving her face the drooping quality of a Dali clock.

'Miss Flowers is unwell. I am doing the appointments,' she says flatly, anticipating my next question.

At home, I ask Charlie why he told his teacher we were living in Bournemouth. He doesn't know. I check that he understands that lying is wrong and that he mustn't do it. He does.

'Why Bournemouth?' I ask. It is not the most pertinent question. But I have to know. I get only another shrug and a 'dunno'.

Saturday, 23 February

'Sniff it and guess.'

Surely the English language has ne'er found a less appealing combination of words than this. I am willing to accept that there are equally unfavourable sentences and phrases out there. Maybe "burns when peeing" or "we need to talk". But this...

Not only have these words just been squawked at me, but they have been issued as a command by a maniacally smiley woman called Liza. She of the emails. Liza is holding a nappy inches from my face and hers. We look like we're about to recreate the spaghetti scene from *Lady and the Tramp*, only with a nappy.

I am in a spa hotel in deepest darkest Berkshire, surrounded by smiley women smiling expectantly.

'Go on,' giggles a horsey-faced woman I think is called Janine. Janet? Janine.

I consider saying I have a cold. Or pretending to pass out. But Liza would only shove smelling salts up my nostrils and ask me to guess what they were.

'Um, Marmite?'

The nappy is snatched away.

'Write that down, Janet,' Liza instructs.

Ah, it is Janet. It's not easy remembering the names of twenty women I only met today. Especially when they all look so similar with their spiderweb eyelashes and prominent eyebrows and glossy lips all signalling they have far too much time to be mothers. Either that or they all have nannies. Most wear matching t-shirts that read "Kell's Baby Squad".

My t-shirt, along with a handful of others, is different. It reads "I can't keep calm. I'm going to be an auntie." Apparently, this is mine to keep; one of the items purchased with my payment. Delia and Kelly's mums bear tops that read, "Glam-Ma". Liza's says "Honorary Auntie" and Kelly's "Best Mum To Bee" with a picture of a bee.

The nappy sniffing is the latest in an excruciatingly long line of baby shower games that we have played thus far. Is it the worst one? Unsure. Is smelling a nappy worse than being asked to use a piece of string to estimate the size of Kelly's bump? How long *is* a piece of string? I can tell you that mine was barely the length of my own finger in that game lest I unintentionally implied anything *at all* about my sister-in-law's physical appearance. Then there was the guess-which-baby-photo-is-which-guest game. Where I brought in a photo of Jake because all my baby pictures are in storage. And everyone thought it was me.

And the worst part of today isn't even having to endure the terrifying boredom of it all. Not even when they played a montage of all the photos of Kelly everyone had brought in, set to Billy Joel's *Uptown Girl*. As soon as my contribution appeared, all laughter and cheering ceased with scandalised abruptness. The way Kelly's mum had gasped I might have done better with Hugh's clit pic.

The point is, I can handle all of that. That is *fine*. It is the loss of precious child-free time that I truly mourn. Just think of all the things I could have cleaned today. Or laminated. Or organised. I can think of a million things I'd rather be doing than this.

Things I Would Rather Do Today

1. Undergo root canal surgery under the care of the dentist from *Little Shop of Horrors*.
2. Sit in a meeting that should have been an email.
3. Soft play.

'And the winner is....' Liza pauses for what passes for dramatic effect. 'Maya!'

Oh, dear god.

Next, there is a gift opening segment and a litany of items so impractical, Kelly would be better off with Gold, Frankincense and, yes, even Myrrh. Take, for example, the onesies announcing baby's "arrival" in various guises. Chances are, baby will either be too big or too small for them, and thus either won't get to wear them at all or be wearing "welcome to the world" when they are six months old. But that's fine. Especially when compared to some of the other gifts.

The cloth nappy kit with its beautiful patterns in bold colours seems like a torture device that will only remind a future Kelly that she is only dealing with one colour – brown.

I actually snort when she opens a post-pregnancy pampering kit. The exact one that I still have unopened at home. Then have to pretend to cough.

I am so relieved to finally get home that at first I don't notice it. The total silence. No screaming or banging. At the very least my re-entry should have triggered an automatic request for a snack. Instant, freezing panic courses through my veins. There can be but one explanation. The kids have been taken. Jake is dead. Oh god. Where is Sir Francis?

Then Jake emerges from the living room and delivers a louche, 'Hey. Um. Did you agree with Gabby that she'd take the kids?'

'No,' I say, my tone so horrified I need not add, what the fuck would make you think that?

'Oh. She said you had.'

'And you *believed* her?'

'She said it was a surprise for me,' he says peevishly, as I yank my phone out of my bag. 'Plus you know I find your sister scary.'

I ignore this and press play on a voice note I find from Gabby.

'Don't be annoyed at Jake. I've taken the boys to mine. Everyone is fine and happy and you two can have a night to yourselves. See you tomorrow.'

'What are you doing?' Jake asks, as I stab at the screen and put the phone back to my ear.

'I'm calling her.'

'Why?'

'Because.' Then, when I can't think of a reason, 'Shh, it's ringing.'

'The way I see it, this is win-win,' Jake says, as I bite my fingernail for the first time since I was ten. 'Either everything will be fine and we have a new babysitter,' he continues. 'Or she'll get a wakeup call about just how different your life is. But more than that, if you go taking him home now, she'll see it as you not trusting her.'

My eyes treacherously slide to where my husband is looking at me, a cheeky smile dancing on his lips.

'Fine,' I huff, rolling my eyes by way of relenting. 'But when she calls because it's all gone to shit, you're collecting them.'

Which he does. At gone 9pm.

'He got really upset by the bedsheets,' Gabby rushes to explain as Jake is disappearing through the front door.

'Were they pink?'

'How did you know?'

'Yeah, he sees that as you saying he's a girl,' I explain. 'Massive insult. We're working on it.' I do not add that it's not looking good.

'He's going to hate me,' she whines.

I dismiss this with a quick 'No, he won't,' before asking the pertinent question. 'What did he do?'

'It doesn't matter. It's fine now.'

That's when something clicks. I can't hear any screaming or crying.

'How did you calm him down?' My voice is an elastic band stretched to breaking point. Not because I think that she might have gagged Liam or put him in a cupboard, but because I am sure – 100 percent certain – that

Gabby will be better at this than me. That she has effortlessly stopped Liam's meltdown. Which means she'll have to move in with us. Forever.

'Not me,' she scoffs. 'Charlie. Babe, he was incredible. Made a joke about the sheets sneaking themselves into the room. We were all in fits by the end.'

My first thought is that he *already* lives with us. Before I am filled with pride at Charlie stepping in to help. This is quickly replaced by guilt that he's probably traumatised and that he's one of those kids who's had to grow up too fast. He'll learn that it's his role to make everyone happy and won't ever be happy himself and-

But then Jake comes home with Liam and reminds me that yesterday he made Charlie laugh so hard that he fell off his chair and kept laughing. And that Charlie was having a great time and decided to stay.

'Plus, when I asked him if he was okay after what happened he had no idea what I was talking about and asked if I was there to sleep over too.'

Sunday, 24 February

BONUS EPISODE!!! No Stress Special Parenting Method: The ABC of D-escalation

FourIsMore ✅ • 2 HOURS AGO

'Okay, so a big part of the No Stress Special Parenting Method is how to de-escalate when your precious angel has a meltdown. I get lots of questions about this and now I'm going to demonstrate for you the super easy ABC of D-escalation. It's the ideal moment because Dante is having a massive meltdown right now. Can you see? You see how Dante is crying and running around and hitting things. He does this all the time. Seriously, like all the time. It's exhausting. So I'm going to demonstrate the A. The A is for acknowledgement.

'I can see you Dante. Yes. I can see you crying. And hitting.'

'The B is for breathe. Take a deep breath and release. And do this so your special angel can see. And eventually, they will tune into your breathing. Just like they did in the womb. So do that for a while until your breathing syncs. This might take a few minutes.

'Welcome back and well done. You are now breathing with your precious angel. So we can move onto C. C is for come to an end. This is where we hug it out and carry on with our day. Lovely, lovely cuddles.'

COMMENTS

I LOVE YOU INGRID

This didn't work for me. How long should I try the breathe sync bit? I tried for an hour.

You're doing great! Keep trying!! Ingrid XXX

Comment removed

Comment removed

What a previous baby he is. You are AMAZING XXX

Comment removed

Comment removed

Where can I get that dress?

I'll tell you what c is for…

Comment removed

Monday, 25 February

'Mummy can I take my scooter?'
　'Scooter! Scooooter. Yes, yes, yes.'
　'No scooters.'
　'Pleeeease.'
　'No. We will walk, but no scooters.'
　It is Walk to School Week. In theory, this is a well-meaning national campaign to encourage healthy living and environmental consciousness. But I know what it really is: a passive aggressive message directly aimed at me. Or at least at mums like me. Who drive the 2 centimetres to school.
　'They can't have it both ways,' I had ranted to Jake last night. 'They can't expect me to get them to school *and* make me do it on foot.'
　Of course, this is the one time Jake had to go into work early and so isn't here to help. And now we are by the front door, ready to start our trek, everyone wearing their shoe-
　'Charlie, where is your left shoe?'
　I receive a shrug. Then another request to take the scooters.
　'We're already late,' I say, tearing through the downstairs in search of

one shoe. 'You don't have a shoe, and.' The shoe peeks out at me from Sir Francis's cat cocoon. 'Here,' I say, handing over the footwear. 'Let's go.'

'So, no scooter?'

I know what he's doing, my clever, clever boy. He knows that if he mentions it enough, Liam will take on the battle cry as well. And, right on cue, Liam collapses onto the floor and belts out a sort of Whitney Houston *I Will Always Love You* long note except with 'I want scooter'.

I shoot Charlie a look that says, *I know what you did.* And he shoots me one of pure innocence.

I want to remonstrate with my mini Machiavellian mastermind, but there's no time. We need to get to school.

What do I do? The fact is, I can't give in on this. Oh, I want to. But I have no sodding clue where the scooters are. There's a chance they're in the shed. Or the car boot. Or I might have sold them on eBay. I cannot let on, however. Even though they never express any interest in them. Even though this is the first time Charlie has wanted to ride the bloody thing in about a year. And even though both of them will lose interest in the things just in time for me to have to carry both monstrosities up the hill. Why can't I do that? Mostly because they wouldn't believe me. They are suspicious souls my children, always convinced the truth is out there and that Jake and I are making sure they don't find it.

There's nothing for it. I stand my ground.

'Either we walk, or we drive.'

'But we get special badges for scooting,' Charlie whines.

Cocking crap. Really? Why? It's supposed to be *walk* to school week. Why did they have to bring scooters into it?

'So, tell them you scooted. I'll back you up.'

'That's lying, mummy.'

I can see no possible way of getting my children to school at this moment in time. Charlie, sure. But not Liam. He's moved on from his power ballad and has started slamming doors. It's the beginning of a meltdown. If we were in rural Kansas, this would be the point where we'd dive into our storm shelter and await the inevitable tornado. And none of us are going anywhere until it's over.

Or…

I remember Ingrid's ABC De-escalation. I'd thought it looked like utter tripe. But it's not like I have a better idea. Fuck it.

Okay, so the A was for…

'I see you Liam,' I croon in my attempt at acknowledgement. Liam does not reciprocate, focused as he is on his assault on the door between kitchen and lounge.

The next one is breathing, right? I need to breath, so he sees me and copies. It's the seeing me bit that's tricky. He's preoccupied what with the house decimation and all. I skirt around the area where my son is thrusting the door to and fro, trying to find the ideal location. There isn't one. Getting anywhere near Liam puts me in door-whacking range.

This conundrum is solved for me however when Liam notices me, releases the beleaguered door and starts pushing and kicking me instead. I take my chance. I crouch down.

'Okay Liam. I'm going to breathe and you copy, okay? Ow! Fuc-dgesticks, bollards, argh.'

So. Mostly good news. The boys are at school. Both consented to being driven and we were only four minutes late. And – *and* - in a rare display of humanity, Mrs Keen even agreed to sign them in on their class registers. Thus, the late book was denied my patronage. Huzzah.

I have to hand it to Ingrid. Her technique worked. When I tried to get Liam to do the breathing, he punched me in the eye. Then was so shocked by my response – yelp-screaming, toppling backwards, and clutching my face - he snapped out of his meltdown. I'd call that a success. Even if I do have a slight, not-so-slight black eye for my trouble.

March

Friday, 1 March

Something of an achievement today. Liam and I collected Charlie from Nisha's house.

If this seems unremarkable, that's because it is. By any reasonable standards it is insignificant, mundane, boring. But mine are not reasonable standards. They are, at best, very *un*reasonable. More likely, they are no standards at all. Nevertheless, this was an accomplishment.

One short walk for most, one giant accomplishment for Liam.

For this was not just a walk. It was a series of acts that meant riding roughshod over some of my son's most sacrosanct post-school imperatives.

THE SACROSANCT POST-SCHOOL IMPERATIVES OF LIAM

1. Thou shalt not leave the house on the same day thou hast returned to it.
2. Thou shalt not cast thine eyes away from a screen.
3. Guard the living room TV remote at all costs. This does not apply to dropping it. That's fine. Do that with abandon. This is more of an if-I-can't-have-it-no one-can situation.

Normally, Nisha drops Charlie off on her way back from school. Thus enabling me to enable my son. And yet, today, I convinced Liam to abandon it all. It was impromptu. It was unexpected. And it was entirely thanks to Cheryl. It went something like this:

Me: 'Shall we go and collect Charlie from Nisha's?'
Liam: 'No.'

Me: 'But don't you think it's bit unfair that Nisha always has to drop him off?'
Liam: 'No.'
Me, already resigned: 'Okay. I just thought it was a nice day for a walk.'
Liam, dropping the remote without further prompt: 'Walk?'
Me, watching Liam stride to the front door: 'Yes.'
Liam: 'Cheryl said walking more means I will not die for longer.'

So I got to spend an entire hour chatting to Nisha. With tea. And biscuits. Chocolate ones that we hid under the table any time a child walked in. And she told me that she and Rishi were leaving the kids with his parents for a night and staying in a hotel.

'Nothing special,' she said. 'I told him how hard I'd been finding everything and he said he wasn't sure how to make it better but that maybe we should do small things every now and then just to remember who the other one is.'

Which we both agreed was a good first step. Before we disagreed about something else, namely whether or not I should attend the awards ceremony for the Blog2Book competition. I had received an email informing me that these would be taking place on the 30th of March. Which meant there was less than a month to go.

As I relayed as much to Nisha and marvelled at how quickly the time had passed, she checked her phone.

'Yep. Nothing in the diary that night. I'll be there.'
'For what?'
'What do you think? The ceremony. Not a chance I'm missing this.'
'You know *I* won't be there, right?'
'I know you *said* that.'
'And I meant it.'
'But... what if you win?' she splutters.
'I won't.'
'But what if you *do*? Seriously, you've done so well and you deserve to bask in it a bit.'
'If I win, I'll be happy that I won. That's enough. I can't risk being found out. The only reason I feel okay doing this is the anonymity. I'm writing about *my kid*, Nish. Nobody can find out it's me.'

In that moment, Nish's expression bore the same unique mix of disbelief and belligerence as it had at age 12, when her parents had forbidden her from playing Mortal Kombat.

'This sucks,' she grumbled, just as she had back then.

'Noted.'

Tuesday, 5 March

11am:

'Mrs Harris? It's Mrs Keen here. The school secretary.'

Oh, Mrs Keen. Must we really go through the same rigmarole every time, I think.

How can she possibly think I don't know who it is? Even without caller ID, I would know her voice. I possess Siri-like familiarity with every intonation. It probably unlocks my bloody phone. I reckon, I could identify her without her uttering a single word. Solely by her initial intake of breath.

We have had this conversation before. So can we please skip to "Liam's unsettled" and be done with it?

'Mr Davies has asked that you come in.'

Eh? That is not how that was supposed to go. What's changed? *Why has it changed?*

She's supposed to tell me Liam is unsettled. Then I ask "Unsettled?" And she says, "Unsettled".

'Mrs Harris?'

'On my way.'

I reach the school gate in under two minutes, during which I manage to compose a whole imaginary conversation with Mrs Keen. Me pleading that I'll never take her for granted again and that she can do the usual intro any time she likes. She can call me at 3am on Christmas morning to tell me "It's Mrs Keen, the school secretary." I will welcome it. Just as long as she *sticks to the script*. Because, as horrible as that devil is, to quote Elaine Paige, "I know him so well." I have a general idea of what happens after that call. And now I don't.

But I don't say any of it when Mrs Keen opens the main door. I'm far too winded to speak. I may have run the whole way here.

'You can go right in.' There is sympathy in her voice. And her face. Oh fuck. This really is bad. Has something happened to one of my boys?

But almost as soon as I think it, I see them. Both of them. Charlie and Liam are sitting in Mr Davies's office. They are glum, but unharmed. At least from a cursory visual inspection.

'Ah, Mrs Harris,' says the headmaster. I barely notice him. I'm focused on my boys. My tiny baby boys. Charlie notices me first.

'Mummy,' he cries and slams into my legs, wrapping his arms around them in a tight squeeze. Liam follows suit.

'What happened?' I ask, not entirely certain who I'm addressing.

'It wasn't our fault, mummy,' Charlie begins. But he is cut off.

'Why don't we take a seat.' Mr Davies indicates a chair and I shuffle towards it, both children still hanging on to me. Even once seated, Charlie huddles in and Liam climbs onto my lap.

'I'm afraid there was a very serious incident at break time today. Your boys assaulted another child-'

'Mummy.'

I shush Charlie.

'And he was badly hurt,' Mr Davies continues. 'This is the first time Charlie has done anything like this so I'm minded to let him off with removal of lunch privileges. But I'm afraid I have no choice but to temporarily exclude Liam.'

'Mummy,' Charlie says urgently.

'Hold on,' I murmur.

'And, in accordance with our school behaviour policy, I must warn you that if this sort of behaviour continues, we will have no choice but to permanently exclude him.'

It's a punch in the gut. Worse than the time Felicity Cornwell, head of games, accidentally hit a rounders ball only for it to travel directly into my solar plexus. It did not pass Go. It did not collect £200. It just rammed the air right out of my lungs.

'Mummy.' It's Charlie again. He's fixed me with solemn eyes that break my heart. I cannot speak. No air. Which he takes as his cue. 'It wasn't Liam's fault. He was defending my honour.'

I smile. I can't help it. And make a mental note to tell Jake of Charlie's funny turn of phrase.

Oh god. Jake. He'll be devastated.

But I don't have time to dwell on this as Charlie continues.

'The new kid, Marco. He's in reception. I was playing football with Dominic and Saffron. Myca played too for a bit, but he got bored. Myca always gets bored. Saffron says we shouldn't play with him because of it but I think he'll grow out of it.'

'We don't need-' Mr Davies attempts to interject. I shush him.

'Then Freddie joined in and then he left because he had a guitar lesson so it was me and Dominic and Saffron and we were using the year one class ball. We're in year one. I know it was the year one class ball because it is blue and he came up to me and snatched it and said it was the reception class ball but it wasn't mummy it was year one. Reception's balls are red. So I tried to snatch back and he thumped me and Liam saw and ran up and said "that's my brother" or something and thumped *him*.'

Bless him. My boy is trying to stand up for his brother. But he must have it wrong. I can't believe the school would call me in and exclude Liam without there being more to it.

'What did the playground supervisor say?' I ask Mr Davies. He looks grumpy. His face is all squished into a sullen frown. But as soon as it's his turn to speak, he reverts to his usual supercilious self.

'We conducted interviews with all the witnesses to the incident and I can say with confidence that your boys attacked the other child without provocation.'

'There wasn't a teacher, mummy.'

'Charlie, you mustn't interrupt,' Mr Davies warns, but I am no longer listening to him.

'No teacher?' I direct this to my five-year-old, who answers with a fierce shake of his head. 'So who else saw what happened?'

'Let's see now,' Charlie starts counting on his fingers. 'There was Orwell and Felix and Dominic and Saffron.'

Of course Orwell was there. Why wouldn't he be? Ingrid will have a field day with this.

'And Jemimah B,' Mr Davies hurries to add.

Oh that's just perfect. Five other children all with a completely different account to Charlie's. And two of them with parents on the board of school governors. Fan-fucking-tastic.

Charlie is talking again and I force myself to tune in.

'What was that, Charlie?'

'Dominic and Saffron saw it too.'

'Saw what?'

'They saw the same as me. They said so.'

'I'm sorry,' Mr Davies says. 'But Charlie is a very popular boy who other children want to follow and given his recent propensity to...' I can see him choose his words. He settles on, 'Dabble in alternative facts, we had to go with the more reliable accounts.'

Hold on. Hold the fuck on. He can't be saying what I think he is.

'Let me get this straight,' I begin, my voice shaking. 'There was no teacher to see what happened.' I raise my hand to forestall Mr Davies from interrupting, which he seems keen to do. 'No teacher and two of the kids who were there have given the same story as Charlie. But because Charlie lied once about something and because the other two have parents on the board, you're taking their word for it over his and two others?'

Mr Davies is not looking me in the eye when he mumbles, 'There is also a history of violence...'

'You'll have to speak up,' I say through gritted teeth. But he does not repeat his last sentiment.

He chickens out and goes with, 'I'm afraid the evidence is overwhelming.'

Something inside me snaps. And for once it's not a neck muscle. I am engulfed by fury. It is pure, it is visceral and it is white hot.

'No.'

'What?'

'No.' It comes out much louder this time. My heart is racing, my whole body is trembling and I feel dizzy. But this isn't fear. This is adrenaline. And confidence.

I look Mr Davies straight in his spectacles 'You will not be excluding Liam. Or taking any of Charlie's privileges away. Not without a proper review of what happened. And, given that two of the children have parent governors, I think it appropriate that it be conducted by an external party, don't you?'

I don't wait for a response. 'Because you wouldn't want to open up the school to possible accusations of unfairness. You wouldn't want, say, your special needs practices to come under scrutiny.'

He squirms. I push my advantage.

'I'm sure everything is being done above board,' I continue. 'But who knows what might be seized upon. You know the kind of thing. Are special needs children receiving sufficient support, compliance with discrimination laws.'

I swear I see his eyelid twitch.

'You do, after all, have a responsibility to the *whole* school.'

What is happening? Who am I? I seem to have tapped into the same font of power frequented by the likes of Angela Merkel, Beyonce, Boudica and Elle Woods.

'Don't you agree?' I ask.

Mr Davies surveys me with the furious certainty of one who has met his match. Then he clears his throat.

'You know, I think, given the uncertainty surrounding the circumstances, that we can give the boys the benefit of the doubt.'

'Oh how lovely,' I gush. 'Also, as I'm sure you're aware, Liam will be turning 5 over the Easter holidays. So I presume everything's in place for him to attend full time.' I turn my attention to Liam and Charlie.

'Okay boys, All sorted. Off you go to your lessons.'

It takes some effort to peel Liam off me, but I manage that and then open the office door. There we are met by Mrs Keen. Has she been listening? She has. Her cheeks are all red.

'I'll take them to their classes,' she mumbles sheepishly, ushering away my boys. And, as she does, it's like she's taking with her all my adrenaline.

As my children are led away and I am left alone with Mr Davies, reality seeps back in. I believe what I just did may just qualify as making a fuss. A colossal fucking fuss. Possibly even a scene. It's time to leave.

But even through my awfully British awkwardness, I am aware of a new sensation. A little warm light, dim, but definite, is glowing inside me. I struggle to identify the emotion. It's something I haven't felt in a long time.

I think I feel powerful. In control.

Still. That doesn't change the fact that this is bloody uncomfortable. Must get out.

'Thanks so much for seeing me,' I call, practically hurling myself out the door.

7:15pm

Jake is thrilled by the story of Liam versus new boy. Makes me tell it three times.

'He stood up for his brother,' he marvels. Then, 'God, that kid really didn't know who he was messing with,' he chuckles.

'Fuck's sake, Jake. It's a child.'

'You said he was fine.'

FFS.

Wednesday, 6 March

At school, I am busy avoiding eye contact with Mr Davies who is simultaneously avoiding eye contact with me when Charlie interrupts.

'That's him, mummy,' he declares, projecting like he's live on stage at The Apollo.

'Don't point, Charlie,' I mutter. 'It's not polite.'

'But that's the boy Liam thumped. That's Marco. The new kid Liam thumped.'

Throughout this performance I am making shushing noises through a clenched smile. Charlie cannot hear me though over the megaphone that is his own voice. It is all anyone can hear. And now Liam's joined in. So all and sundry are all looking at us, which only makes me shush louder. I sound like a gas leak.

'Okay,' I coo, now laughing with exaggerated joviality. 'Mummy heard you.

In my desperate attempt to look anywhere but at the people staring at us, I accidentally catch the eye of Mr Davies. Both of us do that thing where we quickly look away. And I finally eyeball the boy in question.

'Hold on.' I place a hand on Charlie's arm. '*That* boy?'
'Yes mummy.'
'But you said he was in reception.'
'Yes.'
'That boy is almost as tall as me.'
'You are only a small grownup, mummy.'
'True.'
'Why are you smiling mummy?'
'I'm not.'
'You are. Is it because daddy said the kid didn't know who he was messing with?'
'Shhhhh.'

Friday, 8 March

This afternoon, I attempted to recreate the collecting-Charlie-from-Nisha's-house scenario. I thought it could become part of our routine. That, on a Friday, we could meet up at Nisha's. And it was working brilliantly. We got there, the kids had fun. All was well. And that, it transpired, was the trouble. Because Liam didn't want to leave. Conversely, Nisha *had* to leave. Her kids had a dentist appointment. And then they were off to Birmingham for the weekend.

To slash a long story to tiny shreds then grind those shreds into a fine powder, things escalated. Fast.

There was crying, then growling, then growling and crying. And then we were off. Quite literally. Running. Liam bolted down Nisha's road and I followed. This might have been useful had Liam run towards our house. He did not.

What followed was a chase scene straight out of Benny Hill. But without the nurses in short skirts, randy pensioners and jolly music. This involved Liam jumping kamikaze-style into the road, being caught by me then wriggling free, repeated on loop, all to the soundtrack of maniacal giggling.

I did eventually manage to trap my son in a bear hug. About half-a-mile from Nisha's. And that's where I am now. Clutching a writhing, thrashing Liam as tightly as possible and thinking, what now?

I briefly wonder if I can carry him home. That's what I used to do in these situations. When he was more "portable". I even developed a specific underarm lift for such occasions. I found that carrying him sideways like a surfboard meant maximum stability with minimal risk of injury to us both. Then I would have Charlie on my other si-

Charlie. Holy shit. I left Charlie in Nisha's driveway. What if she didn't see? What if he's alone?

Before I can properly hyperventilate, a black Ford 4x4 I recognise as Nisha's slows to a stop beside us. And... I can breathe. Charlie is in the back seat, chatting nine to the dozen with - or perhaps more accurately at – Saira and Aran.

'Hello,' Nisha says brightly out of her open window. 'Everything okay?'

'Oh, you know,' I say, as nonchalantly as I can. 'Just out for a constitutional.'

'Lovely,' she breezes. 'Okay if Charlie tags along with us? I'll bring him back to yours.'

I mouth a frazzled "thank you" and she departs.

And now it's just me and Liam. Stuck outside number... 43 Fallows Road. We're less than a mile from home. But I cannot conceive of a way of getting from here to there. Not without Liam's assent.

Okay, think. But all I can think is that I need to think. What about Ingrid's ABC? But I can't remember any of it. And Liam's close to breaking free again.

I try to recall everything I've ever read about meltdowns. Or anything. Anything will do.

There is always a reason for a meltdown. True, but doesn't help.

He's anxious, needs reassurance. I try this, offering calming words in a soothing tone. He kicks me.

I try bribery, i.e., 'Liam, walk home with me now and you can watch *Blaze*. Wouldn't that be nice?'

Nope.

Then discipline, as in, 'Liam if you don't come home with me now there will be no treat after tea.'

Nothing works. If anything, he seems to have found a second wind. Whereas my arms are getting tired.

There's nothing else for it. I need help.

'Liam, mummy is just getting her phone to call Auntie Gabby,' I trill. I release one of my hands and rummage in my coat pocket, relieved to find my phone there. But that's short-lived when I get my sister's answerphone.

I can't think of anyone else close enough and who knows Liam well enough to actually help. So I call Jake. Even though he's at work. And at least an hour away by tube.

Jake answers but is tetchy when I explain the situation.

'I was in a client meeting,' he mutters. 'And I'm not sure what I can do from here.'

So now I am tetchy.

'Okay,' I respond, injecting enough ice into my tone to transform hell into a ski resort. 'But what do you suggest I do?'

There's a pause.

'Try making him laugh. Be silly.'

Holy overreach, Batman. I close my eyes, trying to summon the energy for a performance.

'Hey Liam,' I venture. 'Are you ready to go home? To our house?'

Only I don't say "home" and "house". I replace them with "gnome" and "mouse". It's the classic word switcheroo and I've seen it slay whenever Jake does it.

Liam lets out a primal scream.

'You didn't sell it,' laments my treacherous backseat driver of a husband. 'Word switching is all about conviction.'

'Are you seriously giving me notes?' I demand coolly as Liam twitches in my arms.

'Let me talk to him.'

So I do.

'Hey little man,' Jake calls out cheerily over speakerphone. For a second, Liam stills. I hold my breath. Is it worki-

Liam jerks and I emit what in my mind is a slow motion '*Noooooo*' as the phone slips from my grasp and crashes to the pavement.

Jake, unaware of his newly grounded status, is still giving it his all. I think I hear him doing his Daddy Monkey™ character. Or maybe he's being a minion. Hard to differentiate at this distance.

But then I feel Liam relax in my arms.

'Mummy.'

'Yes poppet?' I say, not daring to move.

'Is your screen smashed?'

'Maybe.'

'Oh dear.' Then, 'Can we go home please?'
'Yep.'
Later, Jake asks me the single question I despise over all other questions.
'What set him off?'
I hate this question. I hate it so much. Jake hates it too, but we seem incapable of *not* asking it. Had he come home with the same story, I would have been the twat who'd asked it.

REASONS I HATE THE "WHAT SET HIM OFF" QUESTION:

1. It is usually unanswerable. Except to say that I don't sodding know.
2. Even when I do know, as in this instance, it serves no purpose and yields no benefit. As demonstrated by the exchange that follows.

'He didn't want to leave Nisha's.'
'Oh, right.'

Saturday, 9 March

Ingrid's Easter Egg-Stravaganza was today. Both boys insisted on going and so I insisted that Jake come too. And so he insisted on behaving like a stroppy teenager. Lots of huffing and eye rolling.

The event was flawless. There was a map, a maize maze, and a bouncy castle. There have been royal weddings less elaborately planned than today. And with fewer cameras. An entire crew was there to film every moment. It was disconcerting. And inconvenient. I couldn't play Candy Crush or check my messages for fear that I would look up to find a camera lens peering at me like a curious ostrich.

Keeping Liam on an even keel was a non-starter. He lost it somewhere in the maze, but with Jake there we were able to manoeuvre him out together like workmen carrying a window. Albeit an angry, thrashing window.

'Did you notice?' Jake asks once we're home. 'They didn't have the little one there.'
'Dante?'
'Yep. They probably thought it would be too much for him.'
'Doubt it,' I guffaw, trying to remember if I saw him. 'Ingrid's taken that kid to much crazier places. He was there. We just didn't see him.'
'Well, if he was, then he was with one of the nannies.'
'Ingrid doesn't have nannies.'

'O-ho yes she does. I counted three.'
'How did you know they were nannies?'
'They were a bunch of random women who ran after Ingrid's kids.'
To which I say again that Ingrid doesn't have nannies. To which he replies that I'm too quick to believe Ingrid's propaganda.

Sunday, 10 March

'Mummy, why does d'lady look car sick?' asks Liam.

He's talking about Kelly. Kelly, his aunt, whose name he is still yet to learn. Kelly, who, to be fair to my son, does look like she's been off-roading in a Reliant Robin with shot suspension. She has the pale complexion, the sweaty sheen and heavy breathing. All classic signs. Or they would be if Kelly wasn't very nearly nine months pregnant. Even then, she might have been travel sick if she was actually travelling.

Only Kelly is not travelling. She is with us, sitting at Delia and Archie's dining table.

I may not be Doctor Gregory House. I may, in fact, be no doctor at all. Who knows? But I would wager my entire future supply of Hobnobs that I can diagnose this one.

I am, however, forbidden from doing so. All of us are. Kelly has made it very clear that she is *fine*. She is definitely not in labour. And could everyone please stop making such a fuss?

So we all sit there, pretending to eat our chicken soup, the dulcet sounds of Kelly's panting acting as our soundtrack.

'Auntie Kelly sounds like a train,' Charlie announces.

'Kelly, why don't you go and have a lie down?' Delia suggests.

'No,' pant, pant, 'Thank you. I'm,' pant pant, 'Enjoying this soup. Do I taste,' pant, 'Ginger?'

'Yes actually,' says Delia.

'Kel,' Matt begins.

'What?' she snaps.

'Maybe it is possibly...'

'I told you... It's Braxton Hicks,' she gulps. 'The baby is due on the 20th. Today is not the 20th. The birthing pool is arriving in two days. Why would I be in labour?' She lifts another spoon of soup. It hangs in mid-air, suspended like all of our breathing. 'I'm going to stretch my legs,' she announces, standing up.

'Oh dear,' Liam laments. 'The lady had an accident.'

Kelly lets rip some rather impressive expletives.
'What's a fucking hell, mummy?' asks Charlie.
Oh, fucking hell.
There follows a brief debate on how to get to the hospital. There are questions over whether this qualifies as enough of an emergency to warrant an ambulance. Then a rumination on parking difficulties at the hospital and questions as to the fixtures list for Watford FC.
'The stadium is right next to the hospital you know.'
Finally, Delia steps in and volunteers Archie to drive Matt and Kelly.
'Yes, yes, of course,' says Archie. I note his eyes flit to the wet patch from Kelly's waters breaking. Despite the fact that it had carpet cleaner foaming atop it within seconds and is probably as clean as one of Dexter's crime scenes. Archie, clearly imagining his car being similarly defiled, proves himself a quick thinker. 'Car's on the blink though,' he chunters. 'We'll take yours,' he tells his son.
It is Matt's turn to look sick as he realises his beloved Jag will never be the same again.
'Good luck,' I say to Kelly, smiling in a way that I hope is encouraging. And I am about to go and find my children when my arm is gripped in an iron vice. Actually, it's Kelly's hand, but it may as well be iron. Bloody hell she's strong.
'Do not leave me with them,' she gasps. Her eyes are wild, wide and unblinking. 'They don't know what they're doing.' Her eyes dart in the direction of Archie and Matt, who are arguing over which route to take, before returning to me.
'With-' I am about to clarify who she's referring to, but Kelly yanks me down so our faces are inches apart.
'There was a plan. *My* plan. And it's shot to ever loving shit. And if anyone knows how to wing it, it's you. You never plan. And somehow you muddle through.' She giggles. It is terrifying.
'I-'
'You must come with me.'
Absolutely not. No.
'Maya is coming too,' Kelly yells.
And that's how I find myself in the back seat of Matt's Jaguar, breathing along with Kelly and getting birthing flashbacks. My hand barely survives the fifteen-minute journey, what with Kelly having clutched it the entire time.
When we get to the labour suite, I hang back. Surely I can't be allowed in there.

'Maya!' Kelly bellows from beyond the threshold.

'Um,' I say nervously, only my head peeking into the room. 'I think there's a limit to the number of people allowed in the room.'

'Oh, that's alright love,' breezes a midwife I hadn't noticed. 'We allow two birthing partners.'

'Yay.'

Fortunately, Kelly is enthusiastic with the gas and air. And within the hour she is acting like the hippiest hippy to ever hip at Woodstock. There is much hand gesturing and dreamy gazing. And face touching. Kelly insists on touching everyone's face.

'I think you can go,' Matt murmurs to me after Kelly is done squeezing my cheeks like an overzealous great aunt. 'Thanks for coming. I think it really helped.'

And I am so touched by his words, I almost offer to stay. Almost.

Monday, 11 March

It's a boy! Kelly and Matt have had a boy. He is called Barnabus. All are healthy and well. Or as well as one can be when one is named Barnabus.

'Everyone will call him Barney,' Jake muses.

Telling the boys they have a cousin yields varying responses. Liam is suspicious until I promise him that the baby will not come to live with us. Then he is unconcerned to the point of boredom.

Charlie frowns, tells me he'll have to think about it and keeps eating his cereal. To be fair, he does so while looking thoughtful.

Tuesday, 12 March

5:01am:

I dream that my phone is ringing. And that I am answering it.

'Hello Mrs Keen,' I mumble. 'I'll be there in five.'

'The poo is the wrong colour.'

This unexpected response, flung at me by way of greeting through my phone's speaker, brings me to the realisation that I am very much awake. Then whoever it is proceeds to burst into tears. Checking my caller ID does not offer any clues as to who this might be.

I must stop answering my phone. Nothing constructive ever comes of it.

'It's *green*,' the caller continues through sobs. 'It's supposed to be yellow and-' There's a pause and muffled talking on the other end. 'Shut up Matthew it is not the light making it look like that, it's gr-' More muffled agitation then a remarkably calmer voice I recognise as Kelly's says, 'Oh. Yeah. It's yellow. It's fine. Thanks Maya.'

'What was that about?' grumbles Jake.

'Kelly just phoned me about poo.'

'Oh.' He rolls over, presumably back to sleep.

8:15am:

'Maya? Are you there? Am I supposed to sterilise my nipples?'

10am:

'People keep calling him Barney.' Then, screamed away from the speaker, 'It's *Barnabus*. Twat.'

Wednesday, 13 March

Kelly has phoned five times today. The latest was an hour ago, at the height of bedtime shenanigans, to inform me of the arrival of the birthing pool. She oscillated between abject desolation at thought of the orderly birth that might have been and abject fury that the birthing pool company had not managed to stop the package in transit. I remained mute, not wanting to fall into the hidden, bottomless crevasse of Kelly's ire should I utter the wrong word. Or the right word in the wrong way. Which was fine from the Kelly perspective, but did mean I had to perform all bath and bedtime duties communicating solely by semaphore.

All of which to say that when my phone rings just as I am about to get into bed, I mentally prepare myself for round six. But it's not my newly and unexpectedly dependent sister of the in-law variety. It's the other one.

'Hey Ga-'

'Shut up. Have you seen?'

Another voice chimes in.

'Has she seen?'

'Nisha?' I ask, already knowing it's her, but surprised to be on a three-way call. It's something I haven't done since school. Very retro.

'Maya.' Gabby's voice is a coiled spring. 'Have you seen YouTube?'

'No. Why?'

'Just look.'

'Okay, I'll call you back.'

But I have to stay on the line apparently. They are both very insistent on this. That means going downstairs to the computer. To the first floor.

'No,' I say, scandalised at the very thought. 'I'll wake the kids.'

'Just. Go.'

'Fine,' I grumble. 'But if they wake up, you're sorting it. What do I search for?'

'Nothing. Just get onto YouTube.'

I enter radio silence as I descend the stairs. Then I endure the excruciating experience of logging onto a computer while other people wait.

'Are you on?'

'Wait.'

'How long does it take?'

'That won't make it happen faster,' I hiss whisper.

Finally, my screen displays the grid of sensory overload that is the YouTube homepage. Dr PimpleSimple, a dubious dermatologist whose spot popping videos I find disgustingly watchable, has a new video. There's a cat watching an omelette get made and...

'What the fuck.'

The rest of the page is dominated by Ingrid's face. She's crying. Why is she crying? One of the clip titles catches my eye:

> Influencer Mum UNADOPTS Son

'Are you watching?' Nisha blurts, earning a shush from Gabby.

'I think she's watching.'

And now I am. I am watching Ingrid and Fergus sitting at their dining table clasping each other's hands and looking anywhere but at the camera. Fergus is puce. Ingrid is crying.

An Announcement
FourIsMore ✓ • 40 minutes ago

'It is with great sadness... that we announce that, after so much heart searching, we are unadopting our precious Dante. We love Dante and he will always be in our hearts and part of us, but we understand he belongs with another family. And we have found him a lovely home. It was the toughest decision of our lives, but one we had to make for him. We thank you in advance for respecting our privacy at this difficult time. Thanks guys. We love you. Subscribe for updates.'

'Well?' Nisha's voice wrenches me from my stupor. I'd forgotten she was there. That Gabby was there. This is despite the fact that my phone is so tightly pressed against my face, it's going to leave a mark.

Huh. I think I'm shaking. Yep. Look at that. My hand is all movey. *Shake, shake, shake.*

'Maya. Maya?'

'Uh huh?'

'You okay?'

'I, um.' I search for something that might convey the maelstrom playing out in my brain at this moment. 'What, um. What the actual fuck?'

The Actual Fuck: Facts Known So Far

1. The video was posted under an hour ago. Since then, the Internet has been working hard to ascertain facts, real or fake, to answer my very question. This has involved forensic inspection of every post, video and photo Ingrid has ever made and not made and might have made. Ingrid and Dante's names and #unadopted are trending on every social media site as people speculate on what's happened or is happening.

2. And the answer that screams resoundingly from all corners of the web is that nobody knows, but that they are very, very angry. The anger is a fractured affair, spreading, like an untreated crack in a windscreen, in disparate, jagged fissures.

However, by far the most virulent debate, the biggest, widest crack that spells doom for the entire windscreen, is that relating to the definition of the word "unadopted". There are several schools of thought.

Linguists have cited the dictionary definition of the word, meaning "(of a child) not having been adopted". The consensus amongst this group, as expressed by Chirper user @AmancalledJeremy and liked 10,442 times so far is that:

> This is an adjective and not a verb as incorrectly employed in the video. Further clarification is required.

There are outliers within this community. Those who might fairly be called semantic bastards. The Instagram account of @Imeanthisliterally epitomised this group when he posted a picture of a road, with the caption "(of a road) not taken over for maintenance by a local authority."

And then there are those, possibly pragmatists, who have assumed it means that Ingrid's family are giving up Dante to be adopted by someone else. Gabby, Nisha and I fall within this camp. However, even if we're right, we still don't have the answer to the one crucial question: Why?

Thursday, 14 March

Ingrid is not at the school gate this morning. Which meant that the gang of burly men wielding cameras looked bored and disappointed as mums dragged their curious children past them. With the exception of the small gaggle cornered by Jemimah B. They looked increasingly scared and desperate as she fired questions at them.

As I watched, thinking that even paparazzi didn't deserve such brutal treatment, Charlie asked me for "lots of pounds". It was only after I had fruitlessly searched my bag for coins that I discovered he intended to give them to the "homeless men".

My explanation that they were not homeless, but photographers was greeted with haughty scepticism and the sonorous declaration, 'Of course they're homeless. They stink.'

By the time Mr Davies came outside to ask them to leave, the few that were left looked grateful for the escape.

At home, I sit at my screen wondering what the hell I can write for The Special Mum. I know I'm not going to comment on Ingrid or Dante. But do I say that I'm not? Will people expect me to say something?

Then I get a grip and realise that, were my shoulder-dwelling angel to make an appearance now, she would be severely unimpressed.

'Exactly how far up your arse is your head?' she would ask. 'Can you see any light at all? Because you know the right thing to do and that's to say nothing.'

'Cock off,' I imagine my devil would scoff. 'What's wrong with saying that we're not going to comment on the story? The audience will expect her to say something. It's everywhere. It'll look weird if she doesn't.'

'How big is your ego that you think people will give a shit what we think? It's none of our business. Leave it that way.'

'She announced it on YouTube. It's hardly private.'

'There's a child involved, you monster.'

'Virtue signaller.'

'Sociopath.'

I decide to leave well alone and write about something – anything – else.

Saturday, 16 March

Overheard at a birthday party:

Wunder Mummy 1: Nanny's still bringing the kids to school. Nobody's seen her since the announcement.

Wunder Mummy 2: I never trusted her. I told Mark. I said, nobody that slim makes so many cakes.

Wunder Mummy 1: She never mentioned she had a nanny. Not once. I wonder what agency she used.

Wunder Mummy 2: I feel like such a fool. I followed her carrot and courgette recipe. Tasted like chalk. Christ. How is it conga line time already?

Sunday, 17 March

It is a day of firsts. For the first time in years, we do not go to Delia and Archie's for lunch. Instead, like pilgrims paying homage, we make a long and arduous journey through hell and high water – Central London and crossing the Thames – to visit Matt and Kelly in Clapham.

What's more, we leave both our boys in the care of someone else.

'Did Gabby look nervous to you?' I ask, as Jake drives onto the A41.

'She was shitting herself.'

'Don't laugh,' I chide, trying and failing to suppress a smile. 'She's still traumatised from last time.'

The journey takes an hour and a half through concrete jungles, roadworks, being stuck in single-lane diversions, honking horns, rancid air, and angry drivers. It is bliss. Jake and I talk, then listen to music and, crucially, do not need to provide moment by moment updates on expected arrival times.

We arrive to find that Clapham is still unnervingly trendy, that Matt and Kelly's flat is still up three flights of stairs but that Matt and Kelly are no longer Matt and Kelly. At least not as we knew them. Both look like they've had their souls sucked out by one of the Dementors from *Harry Potter*.

'Coffee?' the husk that once contained Matt asks in a monotone.

'*Shh*,' Kelly interjects. 'He's sleeping. For once.'

'They said noise doesn't bother them this early,' Matt whisper whines.

'You want to find out?'

He does not.

And so we sit, coffeeless, whispering pleasantries, with us asking how they are and how they're coping. They make jokes about how little sleep they've had which are clearly not jokes at all. This awkwardness is occasionally interrupted by one of Matt or Kelly stiffening like nervous meercats. Then whispering something along the lines of "is that…" or "did he make a noise?" We then all hold our collective breath until it has been confirmed that the answer is no. Until it isn't. This is when we meet Barnabus.

Fortunately, Kelly is of the outsiders-are-germ-mongers persuasion and so I am saved the trauma of holding him. I can think of nothing more terrifying than being handed someone else's newborn.

'Does it make you broody?' Matt asks, his haunted expression briefly becoming one of pride.

I follow his gaze down to this small and snuffly and sweet new member of the human race. And I am filled with relief. Only relief. Thank God we don't have a baby anymore. I will take our potty trained, talking, walking catastrophe factories over the uncertainties of new motherhood every day of the week. Of course, I don't say that.

Kelly, now free to talk at standard volume, does so at length. It as if she's in a confessional box. She tells me every last detail of the past week, stopping now and again to gage my opinion.

After the fourth such consult, I point out that there are far better mums out there to ask such things.

'I think you do okay,' she murmurs. 'Especially with the challenges you face.'

My eyes are on stalks that have their own stalks. Did she really just say that? I look over at Jake to see if he heard. Dammit. He's talking to Matt. Can I make her say it again? But Kelly's moved on.

'How much tummy time is too much tummy time?' she asks.

Wednesday, 20 March

Alison B is back. Back to being Queen B. Now that Ingrid has gone into hiding, Jemimah B's mummy has reasserted her iron grip on the PTA throne.

'She's really got the gleam back in her eyes,' Jo observes dreamily as Alison barks out orders with imperious zeal. Around her, Wunder Mummies buzz obsequiously, setting up for Bingo Night.

'It's like everything's right with the world again,' muse I.

'Who printed these cards?' Queen B demands of the room at large. 'They're not properly aligned.'

'We'll sort it,' someone assures.

'Shit,' Jo mutters, abruptly fussing with a tablecloth. 'She's seen us. Look busy.' And so I make a show of examining Jo's work. Then we pretend to discuss the tablecloth until we're sure Queen B's attention has shifted elsewhere.

Guests begin arriving at 7pm, which can only mean one thing. I find my coat and call to Jo.

'It's hook-a-duck time.'

'You're not serious,' she scoffs.

'Yeah. Why wouldn't I be?'

'Er...' I follow her gaze and her finger, which is pointing to the field outside. There, the inflatable pond is valiantly resisting being winched away by gale-force winds. In fact, if it wasn't for the extra weight of the water from the torrential downpour still in progress, it would probably be halfway to Oz by now.

All of which changes nothing.

'We either face that,' I point my own finger at the maelstrom. 'Or Alison.'

As if on cue, the voice of the Queen B herself rings out.

'It's only checking some coats, Monica,' she scolds into her phone. 'Not running the bloody London Marathon. How far apart are the contractions?'

Jo's eyes meet mine.

'I have a hood. It'll be fine.'

'Ada girl.'

But just as we are about to embrace the prospect of death by duck pond, I hear my name. Then, 'What are you *doing*?'

Jo and I freeze as the Queen B bears down on us.

'Ducks,' I blurt.

The Queen rolls her eyes. 'Oh nobody cares about that. We need you on coats.'

And so, we replace hooks for hangers and a downpour for a deluge of outerwear. I cannot claim to remember everything that happens next. I know that we are beset by a flood of people, wet coats thrust at us like microphones under the nose of a disgraced politician. There are tickets and umbrellas and then, they're gone, disappearing as abruptly as they'd arrived.

'Are you okay?' Gabby asks, as we finally join our table in the hall. 'You look like—'

'Maya,' Nisha all but shouts, bouncing in her seat. 'Maya look. It's Clara. Clara. Gabby brought Clara. And she's nice.'

'Dear god,' Gabby mutters, giving a convincing impression of the facepalm emoji.

'Hi,' I direct at the woman smiling sheepishly in between Gabby and Nisha. 'I'm Maya. I'm sorry, I didn't catch your name. You are...'

Clara doesn't miss a beat. She proceeds to enunciate her name with loud and deliberate exaggeration before offering to spell it for me. Yet more introductions are made, including some year two mums also on our table. Thus we are all far too engrossed to notice the newcomer approaching our table.

'This looks fun.'

'Fuck me,' bursts Nisha. Then develops a sudden and overwhelming fascination with her bingo card.

'Ingrid,' I manage.

Thoughts. Many many thoughts. Too many. They cram up against one another like commuters on a rush hour train. Why is she here? Why wouldn't she be here? What if she wasn't here?

'Could everyone take their seats,' instructs Queen B. Her tone is sharp enough to pierce a slab of lead encased in yet more lead.

'It's okay if I sit here, isn't it,' Ingrid sighs, midway through casually plopping into the seat next to mine. 'There was a mix-up with my table. Maya, how are you.'

I note that there's no head tilt. Not even a little one. Her head is completely upright. I find this both baffling and fascinating. I don't notice that my head tilts. This might be a natural response to confusion or it may be that I am incapable of viewing Ingrid without a 45 degree angle. And then I just sit there, silently gaping at Ingrid, my head in the aforementioned tilt, for far longer than is comfortable or polite or, as regards my neck, advisable. When I finally remember her question, I respond in a garbled rush. As if I can offset my delay in doing so by upping my overall average speed.

'All good. Good, good, good. Yes. Brilliant. Love bingo. Numbers are great. How are you?'

'I'm moving to the States,' she declares. Then adds, 'The United ones.'

'Okay.' This is more than my recently tilted brain can process. Which is perhaps why it chooses to focus on the more esoteric side of the conversation. 'Is there anywhere else that's known as The States?'

'The Federated States of Micronesia,' cries Clara, with the triumphant urgency of a pub quiz contestant mid-lightning round.

At which point, the first bingo number is called. This is excellent. Not because I love bingo. Contrary to previous assertions, I have no feelings towards it either way. At least I didn't until now. Now it is the most welcome, necessary, and wondrous of all things: a distraction. And judging by the intense concentration allotted to it by everyone on our table, we all feel the same.

All, that is, except Ingrid.

As Alison calls 'Three. Cup of tea, three,' Ingrid informs us that she's been offered a "network deal".

'They say I'm going to be the next Oprah. Or Nancy Grace.'

As Gabby and Nisha bicker about the one number they each need to win, Ingrid talks blithely about her new swimming pool and the evils of chlorine.

Two other mums call bingo at the same time and Nisha and Gabby groan like they've lost the cup final. Meanwhile, I am treated to Ingrid's thoughts on Californian schooling options. The same two mums almost come to blows over which of them was first to call bingo. Which coincides quite neatly with Ingrid saying something about the stand your ground law.

Eventually, it transpires that neither of the two mums have won, instead having completely misunderstood the rules. Several other participants realise that they too have been playing by different rules. Thus effectively not playing at all. A frustrated hum rises. People threaten to stop not playing. There is a sense of unrest, possibly a rebellion afoot. But like any military strategist worth their low-sodium salt, Queen B reacts with swift brutality. The Romans salted the Carthaginian earth. William the Conqueror harried The North. Queen B reminds all assembled that she oversees seat allocation for the Christmas show.

And through it all, Ingrid has been talking. I'd zoned out for a bit, what with trying to fathom how anyone could misinterpret the rules of bingo. This is fine given that I am well-versed in the art of feigning attention. Years of enduring campaigns of verbal siege from my mother have equipped me well for the task. I have developed an uncanny sixth sense as to when to throw out an "mhm" and when a "you're so right" is more appropriate.

'It's just such a relief, you know,' she muses now. 'To get back to normal.'
'Mhm.'
'Eighty-five, staying alive,' chants Alison, as Ingrid gabbles on.
'Fuck's sake. I need eighty-four,' mutters Nisha.
'I mean, *you* understand.'
I think I throw out a "You're kidding." Possibly a "That's so interesting." Either way, Ingrid's stony silence alerts me that something has gone awry. That, and the laser beam glare burning a hole in the side of my head.
'Sorry,' I hedge. 'I think I misheard. What were you saying?'
'I said that you understand how hard it is to look after those sorts of kids.'
'Those sorts of kids …' I repeat uncertainly.
'Special needs kids,' She huffs behind finger air quotes. 'I mean, look what it's done to *you*. You're a complete wreck. Totally ruined. Obviously *you* don't have a choice. Plus it's different if you give birth to them. It's your genes after all so some of it is you.'

She's definitely talking about Dante. About the unadoption. I think.

But she hasn't said his name once. I dazedly observe as Ingrid attempts to refil her glass.

'I think that's empty,' I offer numbly, referring the wine bottle. She holds the green glass an inch from her face in consternation, before thudding it down. Then strides to the nearest table and returns with one of their bottles, ignoring the protests in her wake.

'The point is,' she says, pouring roughly as much wine around her glass as in it. '*My life* shouldn't be ruined just because I tried to do something good. But that's the curse of being an empath. I care too much.'

Oh Christ. This is the epistemological equivalent of being punched in the face. And the hits just keep coming.

'The thing is, everyone's blaming *me* without knowing the facts,' she sniffs. 'Because let me tell you, *nobody* could have coped with what I put up with. Fact is, they never should've given him to us. To anyone. So irresponsible.' She shakes her head. 'I'm thinking about the children of course.' She seems to consider something, then adds, 'And Dante. I mean, it's not exactly fair on him. Being made to live with normal kids when he's like that. At the day of the end kids like that can't be placed with normal families.'

I assure myself that I'm hearing this wrong. I must have taken one too many verbal blows to the head and now I can hear only in eugenics.

'If you think about it, I'm the only one that's being kind. Children like that should be... Like, they should have their own special homes.'

Nope. No. I heard it that time for sure.

'Ingrid-'

'Nice homes,' she clarifies thoughtfully. 'Obviously. With specialists and lots of space to run around. But... away.'

I think about little Dante. About the confusion and turmoil of having his life uprooted. Of the trust implicit in looking after a child. Every child. And I think of Liam and how much he just wants to be loved.

Anger suffuses me in the form of adrenaline. I'm shaking. This makes talking tricky, but needs must.

'Ingrid.'

'Mm?'

'Shut the fuck up.'

Jake and I once watched as an ostrich pecked another ostrich on the bottom. The peckee seemed completely unaware of the fact and several minutes elapsed before it raised its head, looked to its posterior and admonished the pecker. I am reminded of this now as I watch Ingrid's reaction. She seems onfused. Then perturbed. Then incandescent. Her bloated lips part to reveal those enormous teeth, no longer shiny, but stained red from the wine.

'Excuse me?' she demands, a human sack of haughty indignation and hyperbolic disbelief. Basically a Chirper spat made flesh. And she'd be terrifying, had she not pronounced it "ecsusmee".

'You've obviously gone through some shit,' I say, with great effort. The shaking has now spread to my teeth, which are attempting to chatter. 'And I'm guessing you're about fifty percent alcohol right now so I'm going to give you the benefit of the doubt. But, and you need to hear this.' I pause, attempting to conjure another way of saying it. Not finding one, or at least not without a decent PowerPoint presentation and several hours, I keep it simple. 'You *really must* shut the fuck all the way up.'

Remorse tackles me as I await a reaction. I worry I may have gone too far. What if she cries? *Please don't cry*, I beg silently.

The good news is, she does nothing of the sort. But nor does she heed my advice vis a vis shutting up.

'You're jealous,' she sneers. Actually sneers. I didn't think people did that unless they were in black and white, silently tying a damsel to some tracks. 'Jealous coz I got to give mine back and you're stuck with yours.'

The sound of chairs scraping back is my first clue that we have an audience. Nisha, Gabby, and Clara are on their feet. Ditto the year two mums.

'Leave,' Nisha growls.

Instead of backing down, Ingrid doubles down.

'Oh please. All of you are jealous. I'm rich and famous and beauf... Beauf... Pretty. And what do you have? Nothing. Your lives are pathetic and small.'

'Hey. Ingrid.'

This pronouncement originates beyond our table, all the members of which swivel in its direction. Queen B stands in superhero stance, legs apart, one hand on hip, the other holding her phone aloft like a vampire slayer might a crucifix. Several Wunder Mummies are staggered behind her in a loose yet definite battle formation.

'I got that whole thing on my camera,' sayeth the Queen. 'So why don't you get out before I post it to Insta.'

It might be fear that flashes across Ingrid's face. Or maybe nausea. Unsure. It is far too fleeting to reliably identify, replaced by staunch defiance and a grumbled 'Whatever.' Struggling to her feet, she makes a show of grabbing the nearest wine bottle before stalking out of the hall.

The air is infused with stunned silence. And something else. Relief?

Solidarity? I think both. Smiles are exchanged, nervously at first, then more freely. Then everyone is laughing and talking once more.

Thursday, 21 March

RECEPTION CLASS CHAT
TODAY

Ingrid has left the group

PTA EASTER EVENTS
TODAY

Ingrid has left the group

Friday, 22 March

I deliver one last decisive tap on my keyboard and lean back to survey the screen.

YOUR LATEST POST IS LIVE!

Wow. That's it. My final blog post.
I'm just going to take a moment. A moment to consider how far I've come. All the things-
Downstairs, there is a thud, a scream and a yell.
Fuck.
'Nobody move,' I call as I launch out of my chair.

Saturday, 30 March

'I shouldn't go,' I say to Jake for the gazillionth time.
Tonight is the night of the Blog2Book awards ceremony. The one we had decided I would not be attending. But then The Special Mum earned a place in the top three blogs. And Jake, Nisha, and Gabby insisted that I go. What's more I must do so alone, Jake being required to stay home with the kids. Well, I'm not doing it and nobody can make me.
'You're going,' he says, firmly but calmly.

'But it's not fair on you, having to do bedtime without me again.'
'Nice try,' he laughs. 'It's fine. Mum's coming again. And you're not missing this. For god's sake, you're one of the finalists. You have to be there.'
'But nobody will even know who I am.'
Oh yes. That's the other thing. Even if I do win, it's not like I could take to the stage. Not while maintaining anonymity. So I'd just be in the room, watching as one of the competition organisers accepts on my behalf.
The usual next station this conversation stops at is for me to say that I won't win anyway. But I don't get the chance. Because the doorbell ring announces Delia's arrival. With Jake in the midst of a monster snack preparation run, I go to answer, swinging the door open to find-
'Jo, hi.'
'Hello,' she twinkles. 'Big night.'
'Don't remind me.'
'Can I come in?'
Only then do I notice she is holding bags. Lots of bags. Some in her hands and one on her back. She looks like an overladen camel. A fancy one in a black dress, pink hair in a loose updo.
'You look great,' I tell her. 'Where are you going?'
'I'm coming with you.'
I just stand, mouth open, instantly aware that this means she must have spent a fortune on a ticket.
'You shouldn't have done that,' I say. 'I'll pay you back.'
'You will not,' she guffaws. 'But you will help me with these bags.'
I obey, only thinking to ask the obvious as she leads me upstairs.
'What is all this?'
'You, Cinderella, are going to the ball,' she replies. 'And I am here to get you ready.'
'Does that make you my fairy godmother?'
'Whatever works.'
For over an hour, Jo fusses with my hair and makeup. I can't remember the last time I took more than ten minutes on those. Total. It brings back memories of dressing up for clubbing nights. Those times when me and my friends would turn the music up just high enough to be heard above the hairdryer and spend ages singing and dancing and drinking as we got ready.
'Okay, time for your dress,' Jo instructs.
I walk to my wardrobe, where I pull out my trusty blue dress. It's my only formal dress and I have had it for decades. It too has been on many a

clubbing night. And weddings and bar mitzvahs and funerals. And I have never found one to replace it; never found anything that is both as timeless and as comfortable.
'Not that one,' Jo says.
'Oh, you wildly overestimate my options.'
'No I don't. Check again.'
'I promise you there's nothing else.'
'Just check,' she whines.
'Fine, but unless you think I'd be better off going in a maternity jeans skirt, I-'
Oh.
Hanging there, along with my jeans, is a dress I've never seen before; a black knee-length shift with a halter neck. Anyone else would think it plain. But I see it for what it is. It's my trusty dress, but all grown up.
'Jake wanted you to have something new.' she says. 'Sadly we couldn't go too over the top, what with you being incognito, but-'
'I love it.'
Jake's eyes light up as I enter the kitchen.
'Thank you for the dress,' I say.
'You look beautiful.' He steps forward to give me a hug, only to find a hand barring him.
'If you move so much as a hair on her head, I will have to murder you,' Jo says sweetly.
Jake stills. Then extends one arm and, under the watchful eye of Jo, gingerly pats my arm.
'Be good for daddy and grandma, okay boys?' I call.
'Mummy, why does your face look funny?' asks Charlie.
'That's not mummy,' Liam scoffs.

🐌

The venue is a small theatre just off Shaftesbury Avenue. And, as we enter, I spot familiar faces. Don and Brenda McConnell are by the stairs laughing with a man holding a teddy bear. He must be behind F*ck Picnics. At the bar, I spot a couple of the students from The12 blog. Kayla and Megan. Oh, and that's their housemate Jin.

I wish I could go and introduce myself, but it's just not a good idea. It wouldn't be very "anonymous". And anyway, I'd explained as much on the blog messageboards and everyone had been overwhelmingly supportive.

'Come on,' Jo says. 'Let's find our seats.'

We are the first to arrive at our table and I take the opportunity to take stock. I can't believe I'm here. At an awards ceremony. I did something. Achieved something. I did this.

A tall brunette in an a-line black dress takes a seat further down the table. We smile at each other politely. We are soon joined by a Japanese woman, also in a black dress. Then a statuesque woman with glorious curls. Huh. A black dress. Black must be the new black.

'God, this is embarrassing, eh?' I joke to Jo through the side of my mouth. 'We're all in basically the same dress.'

She snorts, keeping her eyes straight ahead.

Another woman sits down. God. She looks exactly like Clara. Which is funny because Clara is hard to miss, what with her tattoos and partially shaved head and…

Yep. Yep. That's definitely Clara. In a black dress.

'Hello ladies.' Nisha. Bloody Nisha sits to my right. My addled brain does all sorts of mental gymnastics trying to figure out why my friend is here. Does she also have a blog? Is she here by accident? And is she really in a sodding black dress? 'Eyes straight ahead soldier,' she instructs. 'Wouldn't want to blow your cover.'

This is incredibly frustrating, but I try to do as I'm bid. Only for a voice on my right to distract me.

'Alright?'

Almost as soon as I've peered to confirm the speaker, I snap my head back to its forward and upright position.

I should have seen this coming.

'Gabs,' I say, my casual tone infused with a quaver. What in the actual fuck. 'Can somebody please explain why we look like the congregants at a feminist funeral?' I aim for neutral, but my voice betrays me with a crack at the end.

'If you win,' Gabby begins. 'We wanted you to be able to go up on stage to get your award. It was all Jo's idea.'

'Everyone helped though,' Jo says. 'Even the organisers. They gave us loads of free tickets.'

"Helped with what," I want to scream. None of this explains anything. Not to me anyway. I'm sure somebody else, someone who has not accidentally stumbled into a questionable remake of a Robert Palmer video, would get it. But in my current state, frozen in nonchalant confusion, I am none the wiser.

'If you win, we all go up,' Nisha summarises. 'So you can go and nobody will know which one is you.'

My mind can't wrap itself around this. Around all these people coming together just for me. Just so I could maybe, perhaps, collect an award that surely nobody else really cares about. Speaking of which...

'Who are all the other people?'

'Fans of the blog,' Jo provides. 'That's MoodyMummy over there.' She shifts only her eyes to the statuesque woman with the curls. Then to a full-figured blond she identifies as FMLauren. 'Next to her is GinnyFizzy. The bloke with the fab legs is Dad of Dan and over there at the far end is NotTigerMum. They all jumped at the chance to do this.'

'Why?' The word escapes my lips without me willing it to.

'Free bar,' Nisha quips, before Jo interjects.

'Because your blog means something to us,' she says. 'You created a community for mums who felt like they didn't belong.'

Did I? I mean, I'd hoped I would, but–

'Ow,' I emit, far too loudly at a sharp pain in my arm. I glare at my sister. 'Did you just pinch me?'

'You were about to cry,' she says, unrepentant. 'And we wouldn't want a big crybaby giving the game away now would we?'

I rub my arm. Fuck.

'Did you have to do it so hard?'

'Yes.'

'Ladies and gentlemen,' booms a woman's voice over the speakers. 'Welcome to the Blog2Book awards. And now for your host, Marcus Everhouse.'

'Oh, I like him,' Nisha murmurs. 'He's funny.'

Marcus Everhouse is a skinny 30-something comedian. You know the sort. Adorably messy mop of hair and a permanent 5 O'Clock shadow. He's also a mainstay on various panel shows. I can't help but be impressed that he's the one hosting.

He gets the crowd laughing straight away with a set about his own blog and a post he'd written about conspiracy theories.

'I'm not sure how much more meta you can get than when your post deriding conspiracies then spawns a load of other conspiracies,' he declares, to raucous laughter.

By the time he gets around to announcing the first award, I think most of us have forgotten why we're there.

'And the award for best travel blogs goes to... F*ck Picnics!'

Huge cheers go up around the room for Milo, Dan and Ted. Milo is wiping away a tear as Dan accepts the trophy from Marcus.

The12 accept the Best Reality Blog award, stumbling onto the stage in a happy, slightly (very) sozzled mass. And Jo and I hoot and holler when Don and Brenda go up, having won the Best Lifestyle category.

'And now, for the final award of the night. The big cheese. Although obviously all cheese is good. Gouda. Sorry.' Marcus clears his throat. 'Best Blog. The winner of this award got the highest number of votes overall and gets a publishing deal and ten thousand pounds.' He pauses, presumably in pursuit of evoking suspense, but it feels suspiciously like torture. 'And the award goes to...'

I don't hear who won. There is too much screaming. All around me. And then I'm pulled to my feet.

'Hey.' It's Gabby in my ear. 'Snap out of it. Just walk.'

She squeezes my hand as she tugs me along in the sea of black dresses. Shivers tingle all over my body. I've lost circulation in my hands and I have no idea how the hell I'm walking, but I am. We're among the last on the stage, which is basically a sardine can of eveningwear.

'Bloody hell,' Marcus exclaims. 'Where's Wally's gone up a notch.'

A titter glitters around the room.

'Do you all write the one blog then?'

I had lost track of Jo, but I see her now at the podium.

'No, no. Just one of us. The rest of us are fans.'

'But you're not telling who?'

'Nope.'

'Ah. So this is an "I am Spartacus" situation.'

'I suppose?'

'Alright, I-suppose-I'm-Spartacus,' he declares. 'Take the wheel.'

'Hi everyone.' Her voice is clear over the sound system. 'Everyone here on stage tonight is the parent or carer of a child with additional needs. And it's The Special Mum blog that brought us all together. Behind me is a mass of experiences and diagnoses and stories and families. And I doubt any single one is the same. Nobody's is. But ours... all of ours, are more different. More other. We don't share the experiences of the other mums in the playground or the school gate. Many of us feel alone in our challenges because they're not reflected in the media or in society. And this blog, this funny, insane diary of a mother coming to terms with that otherness... it made it into something else. Something to laugh about instead of crying.' I hear a hitch in Jo's voice and the next words are said on a sob. 'It reflected... the things... I face.' A tear trickles down my cheek, and I quickly reach to wipe it away.

There's a sniff alongside me. FFS. Nisha's crying too. And Gabby. Everyone. Everyone is crying.

'It showed me I wasn't alone. And it gave me a place to belong. A support system. A... a...' There is an extended squeak followed by a sniff.'

Marcus leans into the mic.

'I believe that last word was "family",' he clarifies. 'Family. Can I have a massive round of applause for The Special Mum!'

The room erupts once more.

April

Tuesday, 15 April

It's the first day of the summer term. Everyone is dressed, everyone is in the car, and we are all on the way to the school from which nobody has yet been permanently barred. It doesn't matter what it took to get us here. We will not mention the horror show that was inset day. We shall not relive the convincing *Hunger Games* meets *Gulliver's Island* mashup that Nish and I oversaw. All that matters is that we have reached this point. This is what passes for succe-

'Mumeee,' Charlie moos from the back seat.

'Yes.'

'Mummy.'

'Yes.'

'What is your favourite thing about grandma and grandpa's house?'

Dear god. Don't make me think. I am not equipped for this.

'Um. Maybe the garden?'

'Oh.' There is a distinct pause. 'Mine is grandma and grandpa.'

'My favourite is a poo,' contributes Liam, giggling uncontrollably at his wit.

You know what? I think his diction has improved slightly. I could really hear the "p" in poo. As I park, I add this observation to the tenuous list of even more tenuous evidence that Liam is ready to attend school full time.

Because that is happening. Today.

Yes, Liam will turn 5 this term. Which means he is now officially of compulsory school age. Not only is he *entitled* to attend full-time. It is required. By law.

And thus, on this the 15th day of April, I shall be collecting Charlie and Liam at 3:15pm. 15:15 by military time. Probably. Possibly. That's the theory anyway.

Naturally, I am unable to enjoy the wonder of this moment without the requisite guilt and anxiety. Like the fact that I'm still not sure if Liam can cope with such long hours. For this reason and others, I am girding my loins and, once I have secured the boys behind school bars, make my way to the office.

As I do, I find myself scanning for Ingrid in the mummy milieu. Then remember she won't be there. They moved last week, as gleaned from Gabby's sighting of removal vans outside their house.

In the past, an event as significant as a relocation, let alone an international one, would have been extensively documented on *Four Is More*. However, as of about a fortnight ago, *Four is More is* no more. The account has been deleted on all its platforms.

Ingrid had initially persevered, continuing to post and do interviews. But then she lost her sponsors. First all the parenting-related ones and then everything else.

But even with her self-imposed social media silence, Ingrid's story continues to spur debate. It's been featured on everything from YouTube to Newsnight. There is talk of a podcast. It even made an appearance on Prime Minister's Questions:

'Following the case of a social media personality returning her adopted son, would the Prime Minister please assure the house that there will be a review of the process of adoption from foreign states?'

A series of women claiming to have worked as nannies for the Dannings have sold their stories to media outlets. If true, they paint a very different picture of Ingrid's home life than the glossy one she showed the world.

As for Dante, several reports were filed with police in the aftermath of the so-called "unadoption," leading to an investigation of his whereabouts. They have since released a statement confirming he is safe and happy in his new home. More than anything else, I hope this is true. That little boy deserves all the love and happiness in the world.

Reaching the school reception area, I find Mrs Keen, ready and underwhelmed to see me. Her lips are taut, her eyes are dead. That is, until I ask for an appointment with Fenella Gordon-Bley. Now there is a twitch. A subtle but definite widening of the eyes. A purse of the lips. Then an 'Oh.'

I am frozen in place by this departure from protocol. I watch, hypnotised, as Mrs Keen glances around furtively, then leans forward and whisper-shouts, 'She's gone.'

'Gone?' I ask. I am envisioning some form of spontaneous combustion.

Perhaps a dramatic poof leaving nothing but a plume of smoke and a charred fur coat.

'Gone,' confirms Mrs Keen. 'Couldn't hack it. Went back to banking. It's for the best,' sighs she. 'Working in a school is not for everyone.' She concludes this, the longest string of words I have ever heard emanate from her lips, with a solemn nod. As though she is committing Fenella Gordon-Bley to the earth. And then makes me an appointment with the new SENCO, Sally Perkins.

On my way out, I pass the Queen B and several of her swarm. Ever since the bingo night, I have wondered if the events that transpired would lead to some version of unification of the mummies of Applegate Primary. That is yet to be seen, but there has certainly been a warming of relations.

'Don't forget,' she coos in my direction. 'PTA meeting on Thursday.'

I already know this from the WhatsApp Group. Because I am still on the sodding WhatsApp group. Now renamed "PTA Summer Fayre," it is forevermore a permanent part of my being.

So, I smile and nod and exchange pleasantries. And depart having completely chickened out of telling her I can't go. Which I genuinely cannot. For a real and proper reason.

I, Maya Harris, have a meeting.

It is with my publisher, Ostrich Books. To talk about my book deal.

I have a book deal and a publisher and a meeting. It's all moving very fast. Dizzyingly so. The people at Ostrich do not hang about.

Apparently, they want the book out as soon as possible in order to capitalise on the publicity from the awards. This included clips from the ceremony going viral before it was even over. Jo's speech was shared by millions, after which Ostrich had her doing interviews with outlets around the world for days.

Incidentally, I have learned several ostrich facts since the awards ceremony.

Ostrich facts I now know

1. Ostriches are both the wrong shape and too heavy to fly. They make up for this with land speed, in which they are unmatched by any other bird.
2. They can sprint at speeds of up to 43 miles per hour and run continuously at up to 37 miles per hour.
3. They can cover 10 feet in a single stride.

But hey, what's in a name.

Unlike most authors, my anonymous status means I won't be setting off on tour. Not physically anyway. But I am doing virtual interviews and blog tours. I am also the newest regular contributor to Mummyweb. I have a weekly column as The Special Mum. In it, I talk about different aspects of neurodiverse parenting, but especially therapies. As a result, Liam now has regular sessions of occupational therapy and speech and language therapy, all paid as expenses.

When this had first been proposed, I was thrilled. This was, of course, almost immediately replaced by guilt.

'How can I write about being a normal special needs mum when my son gets private therapy that most people can't afford?'

'Weren't you the one who told me The Special Mum has a voice?' Jake had replied. 'Use it.'

And that's what I'm trying to do. Next week, I am working with a specialist thinktank to lobby the government on special needs therapies. The aim is to make them both more easily available on the NHS and more affordable outside of it. Part of me wants to run away from all of this. It seems far too big and far too important for me to have any impact. But what if I do? What if I change something for the better? What if I help mums like me? Because someone has to. Right?

HELLO!

Thanks so much for reading Odd Mum Out.

Writing this has been so much fun and has meant so much to me.

I hope you enjoyed it and that you might consider leaving a review in the places reviews live; Amazon, Goodreads, Amazon. Not only do I really want to hear your thoughts, but every review helps the book's success.

If you'd like to stay up to date with my work, follow me on Amazon or on Goodreads.

Printed in Great Britain
by Amazon